MAPS OF OUR SPECTACULAR BODIES

MADDIE MORTIMER

SCRIBNER

New York   London   Toronto   Sydney   New Delhi

Scribner

An Imprint of Simon & Schuster, Inc.

1230 Avenue of the Americas

New York, NY 10020

First Scribner trade paperback edition June 2022

SCRIBNER and design are registered trademarks of The Gale Group, Inc., used under license by Simon & Schuster, Inc., the publisher of this work.

For information about special discounts for bulk purchases, please contact Simon & Schuster Special Sales at 1-866-506-1949 or business@simonandschuster.com.

The Simon & Schuster Speakers Bureau can bring authors to your live event. For more information or to book an event, contact the Simon & Schuster Speakers Bureau at 1-866-248-3049 or visit our website at www.simonspeakers.com.

Manufactured in the United States of America

10 9 8 7 6 5 4 3 2

Library of Congress Cataloging-in-Publication Data is available.

ISBN 978-1-9821-8177-2
ISBN 978-1-9821-8179-6 (ebook)

The Permissions Acknowledgements on p. 437 constitute an extension of this copyright page.

To you, Mum

Split

one

I

I, itch of ink, think of thing, plucked open at her start; no bigger than a capillary, no wiser than a cantaloupe, and quite optimistic about what my life would come to look like. I have since ached along her edges. Delighting in my bare-feet-floorboard-creeps across from where she once would feed, down to where her body brews, I have sampled, splintered, leaked and chewed through tissue, nook, bone, crease and node so much, so well, so tough, now, that the place feels like my own.

It is, perhaps, inevitable that after all this time, I have come to feel a little dissatisfied with the fact of my existence. This is not easy to admit. I suppose one can only be a disaster tourist for so long before the cruel old ennui starts to set in. But the Greeks said that in the beginning, there was boredom. The gods moulded mankind from its black, lifeless crust and this is, of course, encouraging.

Today I might trace the rungs of her larynx, or tap at her trachea like the bones of a xylophone, or cook up or undo some great horrors of my own because here is the thing about bodies: they are impossibly easy to prowl, without anyone suspecting a thing.

Until, of course, they do. And then, of course,

they aren't.

The Beginning of the End

Lia remembered two things about the beginning of the end.

The first: the time it took the traffic lights to change.
The second: the fact that nobody died.

She was one crossing away from the place she needed to be, the
surging rhythm of the city in her pulse, the day tripping quick
towards rush hour. Her senses felt unusually alert. Nicked wide
open by nerves, perhaps. It was nice. A nice change. To feel this
exposed, this alive, whilst standing at a red light waiting for the
world to resume itself.

A man in a suit that was too small for him sighed heavily and
hailed a taxi.

Two women spoke loudly on their phones, slices of their
conversation burying themselves into the back of her neck;
*I told him I said you can't help how you feel. Booked the two thirty
slot tomorrow, there's some leftover casserole in the fridge you can
microwave. No cash, I'm afraid. Won't be late. God, I always feel
so bad. Remember to feed the cat.*

Lia pinched the velvet of her earlobe and thought about tragedy.

Which poet was it that said an abiding sense of tragedy
can sustain a man through temporary periods of joy?

Which philosopher was it that said
all tragedies begin with
an admirable quiet?

Today had been full of clamour.

Everyone seemed seconds away from catastrophe.

The belt of a woman's coat bounced against her bicycle spokes. Cycling accidents were rising at a steady rate of 15 per cent each year. More than 4,500 resulting in death or serious injury, yesterday's newspaper had read. The city just keeps culling, there is grief on every street, Lia thought, as the plump belly of a toddler emerged at an open window and her eyes flicked down the floors below, counting, jaw tight, as the toddler leant its milk-white head out in delight, resting its tiny fingers on the ledge.

Four floors. The fall was four floors down.

Fluorine is pale yellow, chlorine is yellow-green, and bromine is red-brown.

A girl in a blue school uniform began lecturing her friend loudly on the subject of elements.

The halogens get darker as you go down, see.

Lia noticed the girl had thick straight lashes that interlaced as she blinked and a profile of rare, youthful prettiness, the kind that stood out amongst the mass of waiting faces, growing impatient at the crossing, and it was always so hard, she thought – so hard not to get distracted by beautiful things.

Back at the window, the toddler had disappeared. The window had been shut. This was, of course, a relief.

She took a deep, heavy breath in through her nose, concentrating on the stretch of her ribs, the widening of her chest, and held it. Trapped it there. The crackling warmth of petrol air. It had been two years since she'd walked these streets. Crossed this crossing. Two years since she'd sat staring at the scan of her body and brain pinned up against the light, pointing to the dark patch swimming about the centre. *That's the corpus callosum*, the doctor had said. *Nothing to worry about* (she let the long, lovely breath rush through her lips) *just the thick nerve tract connecting one hemisphere to the other.*

A gap in the traffic had emerged. A clear path, connecting one side of the road to the other. The lights still hadn't changed. A man with matte skin made a break for it, which prompted the girl in the blue school uniform to dart out into the road too, pulling her friend behind her. It was then that Lia's eyes latched to the car, turning the corner, coming quickly through the afternoon. She saw the collision before it happened, felt the possibility of it collapse in on her lungs the way rain crescendos into something more than rain.

A throat-screech brake. Delayed smack of machine impact. The buckle of skinny knees as the girl's body hit the concrete. Lia felt time fold, the seconds doubling over. *Oh my God*, a telephone voice rasped loudly by her ear, but before she could get a closer look, the scene had flooded with people, all gnawing, clawing away at the prospect of a massacre, quick as starving rats to sudden crumbs.

Lia wanted to be sick.

The girl was dead. She knew it. She could feel it; the new chill in the air, the slowing of the clouds, the dizzying shift of atmosphere when tragedy drops into an ordinary day like this. The crowd seemed to be multiplying and all Lia could think was —

she would never get to tell her parents about the sort of day she'd just had. She would never take a chemistry exam or fall in love or know what a particularly nasty UTI feels like; she would never go to Manchester to study medicine, never become a medic or get to save any lives, and perhaps there would be other people that would die in years to come because of this very moment, because a man with matte skin had made a break for it and a young girl in a blue school uniform who knew things about elements had darted out into a road too soon, and Lia had watched all the glittering possibilities of her life flare up and flicker out, just like that.

She imagined the horror of walking over, leaning down with the rest of the rats, pushing the girl's hair gently off her face, to find that it was Iris, her Iris, her eyes stripped clean of their life.

A perfectly functioning body! the doctor had said. *And a happy, healthy brain!*

As if there really was such a thing.

The crowd had parted a little, so that Lia could finally get a glimpse of the girl lifting to her feet, just as Iris would at three or four, after having taken a tumble. *I'm fine*, she was saying, as she brushed herself down, quite unharmed. Someone offered to examine her knees. *I'm fine*, she said again, only louder and harder, her face flushed pink from the shock.

Lia couldn't believe it. It was, of course, a relief. But also — the slightest bit disappointing.

The girl's friend led her back to the safety of the pavement, where they both began to laugh, quite hysterically, the terrible sound churning away into the violent city. The spectators dispersed quickly, clumsily, back to their journeys, ashamed of their bloody appetite, and Lia felt the edges of the place cool and settle, her mind collecting up all that had briefly unravelled as the traffic lights went from chlorine to fluorine to bright bromine red, as the world shifted down
three octaves
too late.

By the time she had got to the other side of the road, she had landed on
Yeats.

The poet was Yeats.

She still couldn't remember the philosopher.

Her eyes remained locked to the pavement until she reached the hospital.

The doctor said it was bad news.

It was back.

She couldn't hear the rest.

The room had emptied of all sound.

There was only the chilling giggle of the girl who hadn't died. So faint it was barely audible at first, but as it grew clearer and closer the voice was joined by other voices, those of London's lucky inhabitants who had all narrowly missed their endings, and like wave strengthening upon wave their lament bounced between the brick and glass of the city before rushing in, at last, through the crack in the hospital window, filling up every inch of the room:

It was you, Lia.

Not us.

You.

They

They, seeds of her hope, choir of her heart, now they are all rustling awake.

They, with their histories, plots, songs and remedies, stretch out from the mist-thick blanket of sleep, as word of my little disfigurement carries, like a gut-wind carves and cleanses a day, and

I must admit to feeling a little pleased.

You cannot polish a diamond without a bit of friction, after all, and it is beautiful, really, the way they yawn and twitch, shudder, click, sniff, wet and stiff as dogs smelling ghosts,

ready to try and snuff me right out.

How

Feeling brews itself in different locations, depending on the body. A man's most honest impulses may begin in his hands or his heart, his toes, throat, fingers or thighs. Lia felt most things first in her stomach.

An example: when she first felt love she was sick everywhere.

It had been the day the stranger had washed her feet. The sensation of something buried very deep had gone charging up through her lining, and she had found herself churning out the contents of her stomach over his large nimble fingers, between her own small toes. He hadn't flinched or grimaced, but had simply dipped his hands back into the bucket of water and sponged off the sick from her feet. She had wiped the bile from her chin, raised herself from the chair and dripped up the stairs to her bedroom, rubbing her stomach beneath the thin cotton of her shirt and wondering how he had done it. Made her feel as if her body's purging was perfectly normal, like there was nothing particularly disgusting or even interesting about it, and she had felt very seen and yet very small all at once.

It was no surprise, then, that when the doctor announced the cancer had spread, Lia felt a stirring in her stomach. This deep-vowelled *how?* like a wolf's cry. The doctor searched her eyes sadly and nodded, ever so slightly, as if he were agreeing with the churning stomach sound, how how howing away at the body's betrayal.

On the way home, she vomited into the bin outside the station. Thick, pink clumps and chunks of breakfast and lunch, sour and fizzing in phlegm. And what if that could be it, she thought. If one could just throw tumours up, find them like coins in mud, polish and frame them next to the art in the kitchen. Turn them into fridge magnets with the machine that Iris had got last Christmas.

Iris. Iris. How would she tell her?

The streets had become remarkably quiet.

At home, Lia climbed to the safety of the fifth stair, where no notable events ever took place, and sat there a while, hugging her knees. She wished she had let Harry come with her. He would be waiting for the call. The only thing worse than hearing the news was having to tell it. She felt quietly grateful not to have to witness the dulling of his eyes, the panic sinking in his cheeks.

The phone barely rang twice before he answered.

Yes?

His voice was heavy with hope.

It's back.

A silence.

Fuck.

Another, longer silence. The squeak of Lia's hot palms clutching the banister tightly.

Fuck indeed.

[10]

Harry was the most capable person Lia had ever met. It was hard to know what to make of pure human goodness like his, for her life had been so littered with people who bounced effortlessly between extremes, and she had come to expect a certain degree of difficulty.

He demanded nothing of her. He had this gentle, scrappy energy and a way of smiling that was like watching a parachute open, and though he believed himself to be a man of middling talent, rarely the main event, but the sort of person that got you there and back safely, he was quietly remarkable, and the best sort of partner Lia could have ever hoped for.

We'll fight this, Harry said suddenly, sounding quite unlike himself, *we've done it before and we'll do it again.*

Statements like these never sat well in his voice. He thought too deeply for such certainty, observed the world too rigorously. Lia tried not to let it frustrate her.

Harry.

Yes?

Can you pick up a pudding? Something cheap and rich and fluffy.

He laughed lightly.

The most disgusting one I can find, he said, sounding much more like himself.

Lia sat on the end of her bed and drew out the shape of his language; the hills, the bends, the steady dips of it:

We've done it before and we'll do it again

The battle of each word against the circumstance of it:

We'll fight this.

So how would the fight begin? Would there be some warning, some sign that it had started? A horn? A quaking-gallop-humdrum on the horizon,
flags in the wind?

In the quiet of their bedroom, she looked for flags.

Her coat hung limply on the corner of the door like some stuffed and sorry scarecrow, skewered deep into its sacred patch of land, waving away the world.

Iris would be back soon. Today had been her first day at secondary school. She had left that morning as confident as ever in her new school uniform; shirt, skirt, hands and feet far too big for the rest of her tiny frame, and though Lia had been so impressed, the sight of her leaving had felt like the end of something. As if there was a chance she might never come back.

Lia went down to open the front door, to wait for her on the doorstep, peeling off her shoes and socks to feel the shock of cold stone against bare soles. She looked
out and
        up and thought,
                Me –
I am not battling. I am as still and as constant as September sky, selfish and sympathetic in equal measure.

Minutes later, Iris came bounding down the road with the world on her back, her cheeks flushed with the excitement of the day.

What are you doing waiting there for? she said, leaping into Lia's arms, and Lia felt the street hold its breath, the swelling of its surfaces, the gradual muffle of its parking cars and sycamores.

How was it?

Oh, you know. As I expected.

Iris shrugged like these changes were the easiest things. The street exhaled. Lia watched her half skip through the hallway, the mouth of the house, before disappearing around a corner, down the throat, and felt drenched with the exhaustion of loving someone as much as she did in that moment.

In the kitchen, they peeled vegetables. Iris spoke animatedly about her day, picking at food in the fridge, the frost of her laugh billowing out into its stark electric light. Perhaps, Lia thought, if she were the one doing the fighting, they would all be fine.

We have our own lockers, which is nice. The playground is so big and so concrete; there are so many rooms and corridors I got lost, a few times. Everyone was shy. Made a few friends. The chairs were the strangest part.

The chairs?

When I sit on the chairs
my feet don't quite
reach the floor.

Outside the house, Harry watched Lia and Iris passing peacefully through the frame of the front window, eyes sore and glassy. His afternoon had developed this close, narrow quality, so that from the moment he had left the university, he had felt as if he were walking down a long, straight corridor, and there had been no corners or buses or stairs or pauses, as if London herself were helping him home. Home. Now that he was here, he felt quite unable to move a step further.

Lia must have said something that Iris hadn't liked, because she was scowling down at chopped onions, or aubergine, he could not tell. He adored Iris's scowls; the total transformation of her face, the way her forehead mottled and her eyes disappeared under the deep shadow of her brows. Harry rubbed the sponge of his eyeballs harder than he needed to, circling them around their sockets. Behind him – he felt a weight, shifting. Poised. He snapped his head around to the rows of suburban houses, squinting into the evening shadows.

When Lia had first been diagnosed, all those years ago, he often had to remind himself there was nothing coming for them. Nothing watching them or closing in, no beast readying to rip through their street. And yet still he imagined stepping inside the house and sealing the windows over with cement. Laying great concrete blocks in front of the doors to stop the world from getting in. The pointed nose of a fox poked out from behind the neighbour's red Ford Focus. It padded, soft-footed, onto the pavement, barely acknowledging him. Harry took a breath and pushed his keys into the lock, wondering when the foxes had grown so confident, and which of the three cheap rich fluffy puddings he had picked would end up being the right one.

In bed that night, stuffed on one third of each pudding, Harry stroked the milky middle of Lia's arm, the bit that stayed the same colour and texture no matter how old she got. Lia could feel his fear through his fingertips, the caution and worry in his touch as he mumbled more battle phrases and she watched them charge him, accidentally, into sleep. With the weight of her body deepening into the mattress and an acute awareness of her own heartbeat thrumming under her chest, Lia reached out for the pen next to her bed. She opened the folds of her notebook and there, on her side, with her cheek pressed to the pillow and her hand quivering out in front of her, she wrote until she slept:

try and survive for as long as you can try and survive for as long as you can try and survive for as long as you can try and survive for as long as you can try and survive for as long as you can try and survive

Stomach

Cloaked in my most quiet disguise, with my many eyes, I watch them.

Hollow,
                hidden,
                        smug as a god.

There will be family here. Friends new and old. Preserved. Untold. There will be half-drawn thoughts and dream-props and fragments of people she has passed in shops and they are all currently following the Smell of Starts to Stomach, where her instinct brews and wafts its stench.

Of course, it's hard to get a real sense of anyone yet with so much quaking-gallop-humdrum noise. The horns. Flags. All the vanilla treacle chocolate cheesecake tart sponge but

I will do my best.

It might take them a while to acclimatize. I want to tell them to pinch their smudged noses, feel the pressure in their blotched ears swell and burst, let their eyes adjust to the colour of fight, the fragment vernacular of breath and nerve and strips of limb, arteriole streams cuts ducts pipes and dreams.

(I don't)

I want to tease them; tell them to take it in,
take their time, take it from me;
the hours are elastic here; they taunt, flex, bend and fold.

(I don't)

I want to shout and sing and scream fierce as a stinging salt wind;
Welcome! Benvenuti! Herzlich Willkommen! Bienvenue!

Leave your coats at the door, hats on the stands, shoes in the hall.
My God, you are all lucky to be here!

Morning

Lia woke up next to a large black hole. The ink from the ballpoint
had leaked slowly through the night into her sheets. She peeled
out of bed and stood to stare at herself in the full-length mirror.
Looking back was a paper person covered in print; she had rolled
on her notebook, pressed her arm in it, her face.

Down at breakfast Iris announced,

When we grow up we should get matching tattoos.

Iris was in the habit of using 'we' a lot.

You think?

Yes.
On our elbows, just like that.

She pointed to a half-scrubbed 'surv' 'ive'.
Lia twisted her arm round to inspect it further. Her elbows were
dry, and the ink had buried itself into deep patterned lines.

It would probably be quite hard to tattoo an elbow.

Well, on yours yes because it's so scaly and saggy.

Lia wanted to laugh but found that she couldn't.

Iris knew she'd been cruel. She'd tried to be funny, but it had
come out cruel. She felt overwhelmingly annoyed with herself.

It was always so hard to come back from, so hard to warm the cool atmosphere that came rippling through the kitchen after one of her careless comments.

She dipped her head down and kissed Lia's elbow.

It's my favourite elbow ever, she said, very quietly, and Lia wished she hadn't, for the only thing that made her stomach ache more than the ease of Iris's brutality was her stunning self-awareness. At twelve years old, she was, perhaps, the wisest person Lia had ever known.

Go and brush your teeth, she said, only her voice crumbled a little at the *brush*, so that she sounded very feeble. It had never come naturally to her. Motherhood. This act of pulling days out from one's sleeve. But she tried, most mornings, to find little delights where her own mother had failed to look. To never let Iris feel the joyless tedium of it all the way she had when she was young.

Lia listened to the sound of Iris's purple planet socks sliding down the stairs. Her shuffling along the floorboards, searching for shoes. Perhaps she had simply been harder to love, with her strangeness, her secrecy, that early quiet rage. Perhaps, Lia thought, as Harry came in humming the first flat notes of what sounded like 'Singing in the Rain', and as Iris squeezed her feet into her shoes without loosening the laces, the blame could be broken and shared equally between herself, her mother, her father and the Lord God Himself, and there would come a time when she would stop finding crumbs of old questions all over their mornings.

Did you guys know, Iris said suddenly, very seriously, *that one and a half acres of forest are cut down every single second?* She examined the top row of her teeth in the mirror and shot Harry a sideways glance, as if to ask – and what are you going to do about it?

The Parish

Lia's father had been a graceful, amicable man, who kept his faith close always; he wrapped it about his body tightly so that it never snagged or frayed, tripped or slipped.

Lia's mother's faith had a life of its own. It was huge, inscrutable. It entered rooms before she did, often announcing her arrival, and then obstructing everyone else from moving about.

People often said to Lia that growing up in such a religious family must have been a comfort.

This was not the case.

The vicarage was neither picturesque nor romantic, but rather a small, boxy house built in the early fifties to replace the previous building that had become dilapidated beyond repair. There was no trace of its old bones left, except for a few slabs of chalky limestone that mapped out a near-perfect square at the very bottom of the garden, marking the end of their domain and the start of the rest of the world. To Lia, the ruins were a fortress; the only place at home where she felt truly at peace, a small slice that was hers and hers alone. Everything else belonged to God. She never felt Him there, in the combed barley fields or the huge patchwork valleys that blanketed the land before them. But the absence of a thing will loom larger than its presence, and she felt His lack so personally, she began to wonder if there was something within her that repelled Him the way the rosemary kept the rabbits away, or the cinnamon sticks on the windowsill seemed to get rid of the ants.

Anne was watching a large ant crawl down the edge of the kitchen sink, its plump body slick and shiny as black cherry skin. At least they had stopped coming in masses. This was manageable, she thought, as she turned the cold tap and swilled the insect down the drain with her fingers.

Lia was crouched in her fortress at the end of the garden and Anne examined her daughter's posture for a while, wondering how long it would take for her scalp to burn. Not long, she thought, under the strength of this maddening sun. Her scalp would burn, and then it would peel, and it would be a lesson.

An unusual warmth had settled over the day, softening the crisp midsummer edges, and Anne could not stand it. It was the sort of weather that got into her sinuses, crawled beneath her lids, made her certain the effort of finding her daughter a hat and going to place it on her head to prevent the inevitable burning was not worth a minute of sneezing. The hat would probably come right off anyway. And she would regret, as she always did, even trying. Peter was rustling around the kitchen in his cassock, looking for his reading glasses. Lia chewed the end of her pen furiously, adjusting herself slightly before hunching back over whatever strange new drawing she was working on today.

The evangelical in Anne had always recoiled at 'The Arts', for they had no obvious place in the useful, pious life. But Lia had something. It was not simply an ability to accurately depict the world, to replicate the exact gradient of a crow's beak or the detailed creases of a hand, held out. *There's real flair there*, one of Lia's teachers had told her, a year or so ago, when Anne had been parked outside the school. The woman had rested her bony elbows on the car window ledge and Anne had stared hard at the chip shop sign in her ridiculous circular spectacles, the bent reflection of children queuing with their mothers on the other side of the street. *She can capture the very essence of a thing, whilst . . . imbuing it with a . . . startling newness.*

The teacher was new there. New and young and pretentious, for what nonsense this was, Anne had thought, but smiled as politely as she could nevertheless, and started the car, so as to let the intrusive woman know she had heard quite enough. Lia came out, holding a painting of a single egg in the middle of a large blue bowl. There was no essence; no startling newness. Just an egg in a bowl. And no one, thought Anne, with any sense, kept their eggs in bowls in the first place. Except for the French, perhaps.

See you tomorrow, Amelia. The teacher had smiled and walked away, smart and smug in her shoulder-padded jacket.

What's that, then? Anne had asked, glancing in the rear mirror as they neared home.

Quiet, Lia had said.

What?

The title. I've called it – Quiet.

And Anne had straightened her spine in the driver's seat, unnerved by the odd little child in the back of the car, pretending that she couldn't see how the solitary egg in the bowl was, indeed, a very quiet-looking thing after all, as the tyres ground loudly against the gravel of their driveway.

A year later, Lia's projects were nothing short of disturbing. She muttered quietly to herself and seemed always to be scrutinizing their life from afar, leaning against the last of the limestone – looking for things to disbelieve.

Lia glanced behind her shoulder. There was her mother, hovering ghost-like by the kitchen window. She wished she would leave her alone. With nothing much else to do over the long summer months she had built up quite a collection; paintings of Peter and his clergy as huge ravens huddling around a kitchen table, their black feathered wings tucked tightly between their robes; sketches of Anne as a dove or a very fat grey pigeon, depending on how well they were getting on that week. Every piece began the same, as soft pencil scribbles in the bible margins.

Lia had never much liked the Bible. Except the bits about
famine and death and
seas of blood,
sacrifice,
burning sulphur rain,
devils dressed up in wild disguises,
locusts cloaked in women's hair.

She had discovered the darker pockets of the holy book far too
young, alone at night, and had quickly developed an appetite for
the urgent, parched feeling that would build up in her body when
it was faced with something terrible,
but it could not look away.

These gruesome images had soon planted themselves in her dreams,
dreams that she would present proudly the next morning at the
kitchen table.

Anne would go very white and say things like, *It's the devil, Amelia,
trying to get in.*

Get in where? Lia would ask.

Peter would hide quietly behind his paper. Lia would sip her milk.
Anne would scowl very hard at the space between the window and
the sink.

Lia came to believe it was at the devil himself.

An ashy yellow breeze slid along the base of her neck. She knew
better, now, than to share anything with Anne at all. She shivered
and examined her work. This one had taken her a week to
complete. It featured Peter's congregation in the process of pinning
Lia's own little body up above the church altar, like the pigs she saw
hanging by their hind legs in the back of the village butcher's, the
pink cheeks of her bottom exposed, fleshy arms dangling above her

blood-flushed face. Mid-slaughter – her meat looked no different to the pigs. Except for the fact of her having no tail. She was sure it was one of her best.

Yes, Lia thought, holding the page out in front of her, the skin around her cuticles still white from the pressure and precision. It was finished. She was pleased. As she got to her feet, she felt briefly weighted by the familiar disappointment of having finished a thing, her body suddenly heavier, the garden a little duller. Anne had disappeared from the window. In her place, only the blotched navy shadows of the bushes and Lia's own reflection, rooted to the centre of her ruins, looking like a giant who'd just outgrown its house, the walls having crumbled around her.

Anne found the pig picture later that afternoon. *Amelia*, she screamed, as if she were the one being wrenched up by her ankles, hung upside-down to dry.

When Lia entered the kitchen, the devil was in his usual spot, swinging on the window latch with a tea towel.

Making a mockery, Anne was mumbling, *a mockery of our life.* Peter came into the room and peered down at the scene, his nostrils flared so that Lia could see the turquoise of his nose bone. And then he began to chuckle, and Anne turned to him in surprise, and Lia looked so suddenly pleased with herself, for conceiving the clever scene, for having made him laugh, as smug as the teacher in the shoulder-padded jacket, that Anne felt a fury flickering up through her body faster than light, a spasm of it in her fingers. Without thinking, she clipped Lia clean across the cheek, just hard enough to subtract a little chuffed colour from her face.

Peter shifted uncomfortably, as if he were overhearing an argument taking place loudly in another room. He moved softly towards the sliced tomatoes on the counter, contemplating them, for a second, before walking out the kitchen door.

A terrible silence opened its palms before them. Lia's cheek stung.

I do not want it to be like this between us. You just make it — so hard.

Hit her back! In the space between the window and the sink, the devil was tipping a tin of cinnamon into his red mouth, chanting, spraying spices. *Spit on her, kick her, bite her, scream at her!*

Anne watched a quiet rage flooding Lia's face, like a tide coming in too quickly, dragging her out into its depths.

That evening, they knelt by the foot of Lia's bed and prayed together, palms pressed tightly together, the thick weave of the carpet patterning bare knees. Anne spoke unusually softly in her bible tongue:

Ask, and it will be given to you; seek, and you will find; knock, and it will be opened to you.

Lia closed her eyes and pictured a huge black door with peeling paint and a brass knocker. She felt her whole body reaching out towards the door, all the will she could muster inside her fist as she knocked away, knuckles aching, begging the Lord to open, her scalp still warm from the midsummer sun.

The Chorus

A blight has fallen on the fruitful blossoms of the land!

The sound of voices begins to bounce off strings of muscle, making strange music.

Look, they sing, *look at how it's changed! How it's staled, butchered, blackened.*

It's like wandering through your favourite painting
to find the scene abstracted
or like waking up on the page of a familiar fable,
quite stripped of moral maxim.

I drink up as much final quiet as I can, and wait
for one or two or three to take charge;
for the leads of her life to knead their way out from the
landscape's sprouting masses.

Colour

Iris's favourite colour from ages five to six had been pink. She had
liked it so much that she had insisted she only eat pink foods,
drink pink drinks. She wanted her insides to turn a bright shocking
fuchsia and Lia had said, *Well for that I prescribe beetroot.*

Iris remembered staring at her shit in the toilet bowl after two
weeks of beetroot, feeling superhuman.

But pink was just a phase. Just a gesture of something or
somewhere Iris wanted to get to. She moved through and out of it
a little wiser, a little more sensitive to the causality of colour and
consumption.

And now, at her best age yet, it was Yellow.

Lia liked this phase more. It felt grown-up. Bold. She drew Yellow
often as the fluid intangible thing that it was, sometimes a blot
of gold light, a sharp buttercup tongue, a smudge of a small girl
hiding in a streetlamp. All the codes around the house became
yellow; the Wi-Fi, the house alarm. Lia would lace out yellow
word-talks at night, discuss its pigment-science and etymology;

She derives from the proto-Indo-European root 'ghel',
'to shine' —
the mother of some magnificent words such as:
Glance
Gloaming
Glitch
Gloat
Glee
Gall
Glisten
Cloris
Chloroform
Melancholy

It's back, Lia said, one pocketless Sunday to a patchy wall while the two of them were painting Iris's room yellow. She felt so cowardly; so gutless, so sorry. Iris nodded solemnly.

I thought so.

She leant her head lightly against Lia's arm for a moment, before reaching down to dip her finger in the yellow paint. She stretched her arm up, marked her mother's forehead like a blessing, and then did the same to herself. Lia smiled sadly, and they both continued to paint with their matching triangle forehead tattoos and their individual rollers pushing, coating, sponging harder with every stroke as if they could erase all the facts and start again.

Once they were done they stepped back and stared at their work.

It's so garish and satisfying, Lia said. Iris grinned and wiped away strands of sweaty hair stuck to the sides of her face.

What colour would you be?

I don't know. Maybe a brown. Or a purple-grey.

Iris looked up to the ceiling and laughed one of her wide-open golden laughs and said, *No no no, you're just saying that because you're old. Old people can be bright too.*

That night in bed, still marked with her yellow blessing, Lia said, *She's amazing.*

Harry said, *Yeah. She's all right.*

He smiled widely and pressed his palm to his wife's cheek. She kissed his wrist and said, *I don't want to die.* He took a heavy breath. It smelt of earth. Every Sunday Harry would fall asleep with stains of their garden still on his hands. *It is important not to put gloves on,* he would say, *it is important to feel the soil, let the dirt get under your fingernails, you need to hear through tips of skin what it is the world wants.*

Lia enjoyed the sight of him labouring over their tiny slice of land.

Harry pressed his lips to her neck and then her earlobe and tried not to scream.

It was the first time either of them had ever mentioned death out loud. That crawling, colourless word. It seemed to move between them like a changeling; unfamiliar, restless, new.

Lia lay awake with her eyes closed. Feeling death's breath on her face, his probing chubby fingers playing with her eyelashes, she listed off yellow things to keep afloat:

Bananas
The sun
Egg yolk
Cheese
Autumn leaves
Rubber ducks
Sundays

The waterproof plasters in the bathroom
Butter
Patience
Lemons
Iris's blazing spirit

Yellow

Ah. Here. You can tell the ones that mean the most because they are more than gabble-panic fragments or faceless voices. For example:

We will call this one Yellow.

This one's good.

She is skipping along the walls, flushed gold with the excitement of it all, and I am reminded of sunlight

sliding along the side of a house.

The sight of her makes me a little achy,
a little soft and breathy like a Marilyn birthday song
or a Christmas cold.

She listens closely, waiting, as voices splice through the hot air in various directions, pitches, squawks, clamours;

Off-kilter! Rotten! Sour!

Let's fix it! Slay it! Snuff it out! Delay it!

Blood feels mighty thin.
Must be vigilant, cautious.
Trust no one.

She laughs. It's so gentle a laugh it catches me off-guard.

What's the plan? When can we start?
You search the liver and we'll search the heart!

Soon, she says, *soon, when everyone gets here.*

The light of Yellow's voice is so warm and bold I feel it clasp me, spoon me up, and for a moment I know what it feels like to be a mouse in a child's palm or yoghurt touching lips for the first time, but the chorus launch excitedly again into their speculations and I am back, back thinking, Oooooohhh how I do love these beginnings before the pen is sharpened, the cannons are lit, the pistols are fired. Before the search begins.

The Great Democrat

When Iris was seven, her teacher asked everyone to write down what their parents' jobs were and also suggested they drew a picture as a Creative Exercise.

There were shopkeepers and teachers and nurses and dentists, dads in IT with computers for hands, a mum drowning in bank notes, another with a spade potting small flowers with faces on.

Iris had written

CANCER

across the page.

She had drawn a creaturely cell with licks of ink fingers searching out from all sides, and in the cell's centre was a mouth, but the mouth was not ominous – instead it wore a sort of sad I'm-ever-so-sorry smile. A stick-figure mum with long red hair and hands bigger than her head stroked the cell like a pet.

When it was Iris's turn to present her work to the class, she stood and held the sheet of paper up proudly.

Teacher coughed out a laugh covered in thorns.

That isn't funny, Iris.

A boy at the front with the computer-hand dad frowned.

But Miss, you just laughed.

It's OK, Iris had said. *It's fine. Lots of people don't know how to handle it.*

We do we do we do we do.

The class sang quite suddenly:

My aunt has it my dad had it my grandma my neighbour my dog my babysitter's boyfriend's mum has it.

Iris's face remained solemn, her eyes widened by the thrill of sudden responsibility.

Do you want to see how it works?

Show us show us show us.

It's all about cells, see.

She dragged her tiny chair to stand on, up in front of the whiteboard, its metal legs shrieking against the vinyl floor. Teacher hadn't the heart to stop her. She drew a diagram of cancer in the body and the way that it works, the way it sometimes multiplies and travels through different systems, *like the cir-cu-la-to-ry or the lum-pa-tic-ory* but sometimes, most of the time, it gets destroyed by other clever chemical creatures that stop it in its tracks. She told them how *breast* cancer which was *her* mum's cancer had lots to do with lymphs, which were these spirits like nymphs but without wings — they controlled a great deal of very complicated things — and the kids had sat and watched in awe.

Everyone learnt something that day.

Iris took the picture home and Lia framed it on the wall that got all the sun in their kitchen.

Thank you, lovely.

For what?

For drawing me with all that long hair.

Oh. Well, I wasn't going to let them know I had a bald mum.

Lia often thought of this time. Thought of Iris sitting in hospital waiting chairs with her tiny legs dangling down,
spotted tights,
small shoes,
glowing face,
asking questions like,
What have you got?

As if the world was a competition of terribleness and they would absolutely win it.

But this time there was no Iris.

There was hair, but it had grown back so tentatively, so undecidedly she almost wished it hadn't at all.

Lia was sitting in the hospital waiting for instruction with her mother, who looked hollowed out.

Anne had insisted she be there. She had accompanied Lia to her chemotherapy sessions a few times before, and Lia was convinced Anne had decided hospitals were safe, perhaps even ideal environments for Mothers Making Amends. It was the fact of their being supervised by nurses, perhaps. Restricted by noise regulations. Rooted to the place, immovable, through the drip in Lia's arm. Lia was trying not to feel pleased to see her.

Anne was wearing the same grey cardigan she wore for special days like Palm Sunday or the Pentecost. She had meant this thoughtfully, but it just made everything feel monumental and sombre.

They hadn't said much to each other since they had arrived, both staring blankly ahead at children's drawings, pinned up from their corners on a noticeboard. As if prompted by the bad art, Anne turned and asked suddenly, *How's work?*

Good. Fine.

What's this one called?

Lia kept her face as straight as she could.

A Children's Guide to Lexical Spectacles.

Anne frowned. She searched Lia's expression for the answer to whether this was a joke.

Really?

Yes. It's an interactive language learning book. Supposed to encourage creative thinking. That sort of thing.

How unusual, Anne said, adjusting her body in the seat, hoping the exchange had reached an acceptable conclusion.

Lia had been producing these sorts of books since Iris was born. *Lexical Spectacles* had been inspired partly by their many years of bedtime word-talks. She had been working on the illustration plans for a few months, now; each lexical entry would be surrounded on the page by sketches, paintings, loose strokes of wild landscape or precise, inky detail, depending on the word, and at the end of each lexical entry –

a blank space,
to fill in one's own definition.

The words could be homonyms, like bolt, buckle, entrance, fair, hatch, mine, squash. Or just beautiful, unusual words. Cherish or cascade. Elixir. Susurrus. Petrichor.

Anne looked relieved when the nurse called them in.

Here was the Current Situation:
There was a small scattering in
the liver, just a shade,
a deep sore kiss of it,
ink blotting about in the lung.

Both doctor and Wikipedia said: when **breast cancer** spread to the **lungs** or **liver** it could be treated but could not be cured.

Lia had grown very fond of her doctor. He had been looking after her and her insides for eight long years on and off and was the perfect cancer doctor in every way, except for the fact that he had just gone and died.

It is ridiculous that doctors die.

It is ridiculous that oncologists can die of cancer.

She asked the nurses how this could possibly happen when surely he had VIP access to all of the most sought-after, tried and tested, tumour-blitzing drugs, and they raised their eyebrows and said it did not really work like that. Knowing something inside out does not make you immune to its power. Lia thought of difficult mothers and books she'd read a thousand times that still made her cry and thought, yes, this seemed very true.

So here was a new man in front of them with this younger face, black emperor eyes, and something very uncomfortably confident about the way he twitch-sniffed his nose before he answered a question, like he was gathering drips of Important Information at the back of his mouth, relishing in the new tastes of life-death data.

He may have also had a cold.

This one – it's a bit of a beast,
he said.

Anne's eyes paced the room.

Nicknamed the Red Devil.

She puffed her chest out, let out a small thin sound, which was followed by an abrupt stillness.

Because of its colour, its toxicity, its very strong, very severe side effects.

Lia nodded along to his medical song, his chemotherapy combinations, his Doxorubicin, mustard gas, Cyclophosphamide, his nausea and vomiting and low blood counts and anti-sickness pills and rapid growth and targeting cells, and as her mother made her final wince at the strike of the 'cell' word,
Lia wondered what it was that she thought bodies were made up of;
            just bones,
light and
holy water, perhaps –

Let's see how you handle this first, the doctor said, looking at her suddenly very seriously.

First?

Yes. First.

Can't that be all? Won't it work?

Shhh, Mum.

There was the clasping of bruised speckled hands,
Lia's thumb pressing gently on her mother's soft purlicue.

Purlicue

Noun

[*plural* **purlicues**]

1. The skin between one's forefinger and thumb.

2. A review of a sermon.

3. The end of a discourse.

4. ....

Dove

Here is another. She is monumental. Speckled and sombre.
A little hollowed out.

Because I am feeling kind, we will call her Dove,
but she looks much more like a
scrawny street pigeon.

Look who's turned up, eh?

She is greeted by an eruption of broken mock-applause.

Look who's taken some time out from their holy duties!

There are thick layers of filth coating her once-white feathers; the soot and dust and debris gathered over years of rare exchanges and scratchy landline calls made far too late; she stinks with it, shrinks in it, can't rid her lead-grey life of it, and I feel quite encouraged, quite invigorated by this one, as she puffs her chest out and makes a few snide comments about a time when life was pure, before regret and penance and me.

Proteus

Harry was delivering a lecture on Ancient Greek Water Deities but was thinking about the freckles on Lia's body. How much he would miss them if she died. He wondered if it would be possible to skin her and turn her into a blanket if she ever did die.

Hang her on a wall all splayed out like cowhide.

Harry never used to think awful things like this. The image floated to the electric bit at the very top of his brain and vanished. One can train awful thoughts to perform acts of all kinds, Harry thought, even vanishing acts. Lia did not know the extent of these thoughts, the extent to which they unravelled her husband. They had got steadily worse over the years and he knew it had a lot to do with this seeing Lia as a body,
a body that was ill,
a body that got in the way of this staying-alive business.

So Poseidon had a son. He is known, as many gods are, by different names. You may have heard of the Old Man of the Sea, yes, well he was also called Proteus and he could change shape at will; a great deal of philosophers, psychologists, writers and scientists (some of which we will be looking at today) have taken inspiration from his slippery form, his unknowability; he did not have a container as such; instead he

*could take the shape of a lion or a snake or even water itself depending
on his particular playful temperament that day –*

It is a shame, such a shame, Harry thought,
that to be a human is to be one thing, to be
contained, to have these walls of skin and a singular sense of self
that sloshes and slaps around the inside of us
like water on the inside of a well.

*He also had the gift of prophecy granted to him by his father, which
meant he knew the nature of Truth but would only ever reveal it if he
was captured and squeezed into his real original state –*

Would he continue to love Lia if she were to change into
something else? Does love even continue like we think it does?
Does love preserve itself?

*According to Homer, Proteus was an old man with a bandit hat.
The first ever cowboy, if you like.*

Click went the slide, Harry's frame silhouetted against blue light
and an etching of a sea creature riding wild folds of water.

Is that why they're called white horses, Sir, the froth on waves?

Most likely.

Cold Cap

Before Lia put on the cold cap, she dampened and conditioned her
hair in the hospital as if she were baptising a child.

She could hear very clearly Iris's
I wasn't going to let them know I had a bald mum.

It hadn't worked last time. Perhaps it would now.

It all felt very futile, very vain, but then Iris had announced
quite recently that *vanity is just self-respect* after Lia had suggested
she take a break from staring in the mirror, and it had seemed
very profound.

Iris was not beautiful, at least not in any traditional sense of the
word, but she was so fascinated by her own appearance that it
shocked Lia. Left her with a metal taste in the vaults of her mouth.

So many things could have been possible in Lia's past if she
had the kind of vanity, the kind of confidence that Iris had.
Somewhere between her forefinger, thumb and
soapy wet ends came the
strange fact that
mothers could be jealous of their daughters.

Lia wondered whether her mother had ever felt it. This kind of
gentle, natural jealousy.

Drying between each of her fingers with a paper towel, she stared
down at the veins that, with age and illness, had risen from
the back of her hands like trembling blue roads on a map. She
examined her skin, her smell, the familiar taste at the back of her
throat, the gentle clutch of cold on her shoulders, soaking in the
exquisite sensation of normalcy; *You won't feel this for a while.*
This human. This clean.

Her mother was waiting next to the chair where it all happened,
where they'd put her in the cap, rewire her, fix her fuses then
plug her in like a Christmas tree, caged in
nothing but bright red lights
that scorch at slightest touch.

She did not look jealous.

Warm-Ups

He's coming.

The little devil, unlikely hero
singing, staining his way
through the peripheral vein,
all strange and red and
perfectly cooked for destruction.

For one brief moment
blush-quick, a fearful something
slips and limps within me, so much that I
sink
sink
sink past ribbons, scoops,
I sink on through
serosa,
parietal,
stem, great mountains of
mucus before
enterwhatsisname?
Enteroendocrine, marks of some
hard laughs here, footprints
headed home, Yes Chief,
I sink on down like a moon
rips through night, or faith parts
reason like a comb, and
hide deep enough to be mistaken for
a mere dodgy dinner,
or a spot of
salmonella.

Daisy Bell

Anne spoke quietly, respectfully, of new curtains and a holiday planned for March. Lia nodded along. Their eyes fell for a moment on the liquid red drip, the silence like a burning prayer.

Drip,
drip,
drip,
Amen.

Her mother began to doze off, the wrinkles on her forehead tumbling between her brows, piling up on the arch of her nose. She looked so odd, so old, so tired. Anne seemed out of place everywhere except church. Lia used to marvel at the way her mother's form would slot into church, as if the two made each other whole, somewhat understandable. After Peter's services, while he was at the front Playing Priest Perfectly and the church was squeezing the congregation out two by two by two, Lia would catch her mother turning to face the altar, gazing up at the dove and the olive branch pieced into the window, receiving, it would seem, direct instructions from the Lord Himself. Catching the end of a secret meant only for her.

Despite the violence of her bible tongue and the crippling silent codes she shrouded every inch of their lives in, for those five seconds, with slices of stained window light behind her, she was the saintliest thing in the world.

Dribble had started to leak from the corner of Anne's lip, beginning a glistening journey down the hard line on her chin. It was funny, funny watching the person that once governed your life look such a fool. Lia wondered if she'd ever really forgive her. She focused on the stalk of spit, willing it to keep going, wilt down onto the grey cardigan, trying not to think about how the freezing felt.

She had made a song for the cold cap chemo hours. To remedy
the boredom, the strange, relentless pain. Lia and Iris often made
songs. This was not one of their best; they'd just rewritten the
words to 'Daisy Bell' with its marriages and carriages and looking
sweet on a bicycle seat. It had been hummed so frequently by
Lia's father that its tune had etched itself
unthinkingly
but
politely inside the place
where music is made.

Cold cap, cold cap
Give me a cold, you do,
I'm half brain-dead
Due to the cold of you,
You're not a stylish bonnet,
And this is not a sonnet,
But it sings sweet
As you complete
Freezing my head straight through.

Round and round it went as the hours rung on, the rhythms and
notes folding over each other like spells that could cure, that sore
something, rising and rattling in awful interludes.

A final slow injection. A clear liquid disappearing inside.
The most unnatural of sensations; the kind so severe it forces you
to dissociate entirely from your body's substance,

and then it was over.

Outside the hospital, Harry was waiting in the car park. Anne
smiled politely at him and kissed Lia's cheek, accidentally grazing
the edge of her lip. Lia tried to pretend it wasn't the most intimate
moment they had shared in years.

On the way home, Anne blushed at the thought of their lips touching, at the fact of Harry having witnessed it. She felt it must have looked grotesque. Desperate. She would not be so careless again.

Some Red Facts

Red is travelling as boys often do:
on a bike.

Not quite a noble steed, but a great mustard beast of a bike,
which blazes its own spun hymn of chain against metal, and will
no doubt serve devilish Red as well as Gringolet served Gawain,
or Arion served Adrastus, or Marengo served Napoleon.

The three of us have a history. Double-cream truffle-rich history.
And it must be said that despite Red's tortuous methods,
he has had many success stories.

They line the shelves of his lightless Red Home as perfect,
small trophies,
moulded from the different skins he has saved.

He doesn't much like to think of those who got away,
slipped the net, fell through the cracks
and into my lap.

They are mine mine mine.

Despite being deeply hidden in my deeply secret spot, I can
still hear his ridiculous triumphal entry into the heart, still
beating a steady welcome, can still feel the chorus spreading
their cloaks
down on the red road as the beast burns through,

all *Mah-May-Me-Mo-Moooos*,
all yodels, yells, riffs and licks.

Think of the friction-clatter of sticks, rubbing
into early fire, and then
imagine you are
petrol.

Options

When Lia got home, Iris was curled up like a question mark in
her very yellow room doing physics homework. Lia asked if she
needed any help. She shook her head as if it was unlikely Lia could
be of any –

Unless you know about transverse rays.

Lia did not. There would come a time, she thought, when nothing
that she knew would be of any use to anyone.

It had only been a year since they had pored over Iris's Verbal
Reasoning 11+ exercise books together. Spent hours labouring over
paper that was so thin you could see straight into the next exercises.

Fish is to (hop, run, swim) as bird is to (walk, slide, fly).
Hole is to (grown, whole, entire) as grown is to (groan, whistle, full).
Scream is to (flood, fold, whisper) as brave is to (laugh, beat, weak).

Circle the Correct Pairing. Lia would sit opposite her, drawing out
her own, thinking about how delicious her daughter's ears looked
that day and wondering why it was that she so recoiled at this
correct word:

Life is to (eat, fuck, death) as lemons are to (ice, water, lime).

Sleep is to (scrape, wake, sigh) as stand is to (drift, blink, lie).
~~Thyme is to (chilli, parsley, basil) as time is to (cancer, cancer, cancer).~~

It always takes me so long, Iris would say.

Lia had been of no help to her then, either, for she would lean
forward and study the brackets, those puddles of choice, and think
things like:

To scream is to flood just as much as it is to whisper, and brave is
certainly to laugh just as it is to beat. And maybe, in a world where
fish is to run and bird is to slide, I would still have my breasts.

She would tell Iris to circle all three and go to put the kettle on.

The Gardener

I think often of my early travelling days, when I was just getting
accustomed to the theatre of disguise, finding ways of existing
without being noticed.

This is the trick. Learning to be in a hundred places all at once,
learning to animate a dozen different faces.

See here, for example:
Skimming between the third and fourth fold of the intestine,
a leafy man with dandelion eyes and soil for skin
looks rather lost. This is where the fun can be had.

I split myself quickly into a fish with long strong legs
and a bird that slides like a snake
just in time for
him to approach, introduce himself politely as The Gardener,
and ask if I've seen Yellow or Dove or, indeed,
a devil anywhere.

I clear my two new throats, tell him to head north,
but he could also go west, or east,
for there are quite a few paths
that lead to the same place.

He thanks the both of me with earthy kisses and
continues on his way.

In the space where the kisses were planted,
I feel a burn the shape of a husband's hope.

The Stranger

He arrived one night at the door in the rain. It was so perfect Lia
almost dismissed the sound completely, the sound of a stranger
knock knock knocking at the door of their plain boxed lives.

He stayed for four years at the vicarage but really he never left.

This was one of the few good things about having a vicar for a
father – one could not easily turn away homeless strangers. It
would not reflect well on the Church.

His name was Matthew and her parents had argued about letting
him in. He was a boy really, straddling the awkward space between
childhood and manhood, growing out of himself. Lia remembered
the way he looked at the door as if he were a snake and the rain
had just washed off a layer of his skin.
Unwrapped and remade, there he was.
She often wondered whether he even existed before that moment.
He had very dark hair and a strange, unflinching face.
He was the most beautiful thing twelve-year-old Lia had ever seen.

She had not gone straight to the door. It had been Anne, who had then quickly called for Peter, who had retreated up to bed early after a particularly empty funeral he had orchestrated that day. Empty funerals always left him in a terrible mood. He did not look surprised to see this stranger at their door. Matthew had told them something, something about who he was and why he was there, and Lia had missed the details which bothered her for very many years after. She had gone to the stairs and observed the strange scene playing out, sliding down a few steps to try and catch what was being said. The shape of the moment felt like an exact summation of what being a child was; sitting on the top stair of a house trying to look out at the world with two cork-stopper parents blocking the way.

But then they had moved, and Lia found herself at the bottom of the stairs directly in front of the stranger. He had smiled at her and said *hello there* very clearly but not altogether naturally, like he was trying something for the first time. Lia felt the sound of his voice in her bones. Anne asked if he would give them a moment to talk and the stranger said *of course*, but Lia watched him edge further into the doorway, as if he knew what the verdict would be in the end. Peter and Anne moved back down the corridor into the kitchen, leaving the two of them there, alone. She felt suddenly quite aware of his height against hers, the intensity of his gaze, the fizz and tingle of it as if someone were placing a cold hand on the warm flesh of her neck.

What's your name? he had asked. For a moment, Lia wasn't sure.

When they spoke of this evening much later in their lives, Matthew remembered her having said *Lia* very confidently, looking him dead in the eyes straight through his brain into the tick of his mind.

Lia knew she'd said nothing. She knew she had felt quite paralysed, her throat having hardened to a flat stony silence. She had gone to eavesdrop by the kitchen instead, where an argument was crackling behind the door in spits and licks:

We cannot just—

*For God's sake, Anne, you're being
hysterical.*

Lia loved hearing her father say *for God's sake*, the O of his God hurled hard like a round shot.

She looked back at the man-boy still soaking from the rain, lifting his hands up to his forehead and scraping his hair back off his face. It was a face full of brilliant hard lines that rounded gently off at their intersections. His eyes were set quite deep into his skull, and there was a sadness in the slight press of his temples. Lia had never felt so conscious of her own appearance, of how she might look to him, standing close to the door, listening to the argument growing in the kitchen.

Remember your scripture.

Lia knew what her father would say next. He would use bible tongue. Her mother would go silent, and he would win. Because here is a fact: you can't beat bible tongue.

*Love him
                    as yourself.*

*Do not neglect to show hospitality to strangers for
            thereby*

                        some have entertained

angels unawares.

                        I seriously doubt this boy is an angel, Peter.

And then, incontestable, the words of Christ Himself:

I was hungry and you gave me food, I was thirsty and you gave me drink, I was a stranger and you welcomed me.

There was a silence. It was that particular stuffed silence full of the winning of something. Then Peter was opening the kitchen door, ignoring the eavesdropping Lia and welcoming the stranger in with apologies, questions, suggestions of tea. Lia heard her mother sigh and shuffle quietly over to the kettle, spitting a final squashed and caged,

He is certainly not
Christ.

In Lia's memory of this evening, everything glittered and dripped, every surface had a slippery, curious sheen. Iris had just reached the exact age she had been. Perhaps this was the reason she had gone back to look at it all, to examine it closer. There were new, obvious things that announced themselves now, like how vulnerable her mother had seemed, or how easily her father had dismissed them both. Other elements had fallen away entirely. She could recall the shape of Matthew's rain-beaded mouth opening and closing, for example, but she could no longer remember his voice.

Fossil

There is one buried so deep, beaten so far down, he is very late to the party.

A hard or bitter hidden badness, a rotten throb, thaw of regret; he cracks his lidless eyes apart and rips out from where he kept.

Nobody notices.

Nobody notices a thing, because Yellow is explaining loudly how to conduct a successful search party, and those of the chorus with feet and/or hands are lacing their boots and/or hitching their pistols, and Dove is muttering prayers under her bird-breath while The Gardener is eyeing up Red the way one man might size up another leaning a little too close to his wife at closing time, all while Red is simply *itching* to burn. And so, it is only I who sees this stranger, lurking in the periphery, prowling near her spine the way spirits haunt staircases.

We will call him Fossil.

He reminds me of shadows lengthening from the edge of the frame, an accidental constellation, a preservation, a taunt, a secret history, very Mary Shelley, or grim late-night telly. He moves quietly into her
lung.

The lungs are some of my absolute favourite places.

If you flattened them both out, they would fill up a whole tennis court.

Other Things I Know:
She inhales around thirteen pints of air a day and exhales billions and billions of molecules of oxygen in a moment. There is a theory that every person will have a sliver of
every other person that has ever lived just quietly pass on through them at some time or another. I find this thought surprisingly moving.

I spend a lot of time here. It's my little home-away-from-home, as they say. My little Hamptons-safehouse-countryside-getaway, where I can build extensions or key down the corridors or play knock-down-ginger on the many bronchioles splitting off like a dead-end maze, and I just addooreee the store of gasps, the

Hall of Fame in which the best breaths are framed, a lot of firsts and lasts:

The One When The Daughter Was Born
The One When Carrie White's Hand Shot Out From The Grave
The One When He Arrived At The Door

And so on.

You can imagine why, as this stony-ghost-what-reminds-me-of-someone enters what I consider to be a dear dwelling place of mine, I should begin to feel a little put out, a little bitter, incommodious.

And then something most unexpected –

he sees me.

He looks at me dead straight through my walls into the tick of my life and I think, Shit.

He tries to scream, to shout, to call for the others. Nothing happens. The place remains as quiet as one would expect any left lung to be on a Thursday mid-afternoon. It is then that I realize –

he can't say a word. Can't make a sound. And it must be something to do with the way her body has been forced to forget or digest him, or perhaps it's simply the fact that being a fossil for too long can really weigh on a man; the mud and silt and sadness must get all up and into your voice box. Either way, I do what anyone with a sense of humour would and I *ahahahahaha!* right into his petrified face.

He scrapes his fossil fingers over his
fossil forehead, the chips in his cheeks,
and tries and tries to speak,
and all the while I'm laughing and laughing and thinking –

Poor thing, poor thing, poor old
forgotten thing,
so delighted by the whole ordeal I almost forget that elsewhere,
a burning is beginning,

a hide-and-seek scattering has started,
and now all the children are loose in my woods.

two

Astute

It was 4 p.m. and Lia could feel her body beginning to react to the drugs charging through its systems.

There was a strange pins-and-needles tingle in the tips of her fingers and in her feet. A nag of the near-numb. She tried to stamp it out. Muffle the sensation with two pairs of socks. Nothing seemed to be working.

She felt held together by the thread of a single nerve.

Iris came through the door looking unusually flustered, and as Lia watched her disentangle herself from the huge bag on her back she thought of a video she'd watched recently of a Caspian pond turtle desperately trying to climb out of its shell.

Ice cream?

OK.

Iris pulled her scrappy ponytail out and then tied it back up again, frowning in the mirror, her tiny fingers twisting the black elastic around and around and around.

What's wrong?

Nothing.

Walking down their street, the pain rattled in Lia's toes noisily. Late summer sun was stripped across the tightly packed houses and small brick chimneys and seething ivy fences, sliding them all along the road in belts of shifting light. For a moment, Lia felt as if they were held still on their plate of pavement and it was the world moving around them. She looked at Iris, who still seemed disturbed by something. She wondered if she could hear the rattling growing louder in her feet. If she, too, felt the whole street sliding away.

There's a boy at school, Iris began.

There it was.

Yes?

He likes Soleros. He bought one after school today with money he 'stole' from his mum's bag and he licked it and asked if I wanted some. I said yes and pressed the top of the Solero to my lips – pressed it on like a kiss – and I didn't go to lick or to take a bite like I should have. Instead I just held my lips open a bit so I could only just taste it. He just stared at me. I don't think either of us blinked for four whole minutes from the beginning of the ice-cream scenario to the end. And then this other girl with this perfect face came and took the ice cream from out of his hands and took a bite and I felt livid.

Lia laughed but Iris was deadly serious.

It is very impressive, you know.

What is?

You're very astute.

What's astute?

What does it sound like?

Iris thought hard.

An Astute sounds like a dance. Quite a formal one at a ball, one of those balls where everyone knows the steps.

Yes. The Astute. A ballroom dance with Latin American influences.

Yeah, Iris agreed. *You're funny*, she added absentmindedly as she hopped between the cracks in the pavement.

In the shop they both got Soleros.

Will you promise me something?

What?

Will you promise me you'll always think like that?

Like what?

With limitless possibility of what things are, what words are?

I think so. Like circling all the options. Like our word-talks.

Yes. So what's this girl like? The one with the perfect face.

She's horrible. She's—

Iris thought.

She's like a beautiful box jellyfish and she has it in for me.

When they got home, Lia felt like she'd been walking for hours.

Iris went upstairs. The pins and needles had worsened. Lia sat heavily at the kitchen table and wrote a list of words beginning with Pin:

Pinafore
Pinprick
Pincers
Piñata
Piña colada
Pine cone
Pineapple
Pinguid
Pinnacle

Just as the afternoon began to settle itself into a pleasant evening
Pink, there was a knock on the front door.

It was Connie, who beamed and pushed a collection of curtain
cuttings into her hands.

What's this for?

*For your hands and your feet. You need to fill your life with soft things
because chemo makes everything prickly, you remember?*

She wafted into the kitchen, the *you remember?* falling behind her
like a cloak.

Connie was Lia's oldest friend. When they first met Lia was struck
with the feeling that she was meeting Madame Sosostris the
famous clairvoyant, with her magic hands, ancient air and a beauty
somewhat inseparable from the extraordinary materials, rings,
beads she'd hang about her luxurious form. With age, Connie's
body had grown and then vanished altogether under the thickening
layers of fabric.

The feet are incredible things. Connie was propped up at the kitchen
table lecturing softly about reflexology. *Each ligament is connected to
a very specific part of your body — they act as a tiny map of your entire
person. You know, I actually have a qualification.*

Lia knew she definitely did not.

Give me your feet.

At first Lia laughed, but Connie pulled out a chair and looked so
eager to please it felt quite impossible to do anything other than
sit, lift her feet up to cupped hands, tilt her head back, bearing
the weight of heavy lids, and drift. They sat there for a while like
Greek women on postcards; swollen, leathery, full of one thousand
years of life
scorching in their card-flat sepia sun.

Iris came down and told Connie about the Solero incident, and
Connie responded with all the appropriate *oh*s and *ah*s. Lia heard
Harry come through the door, felt his lips brush her forehead with
a kiss, heard his voice spill into gentle complaints about students
and essays, her senses flooded by familiar movements and clinks,
doors opening and closing, a tap dripping, three bodies breathing
different melodies circling, dancing around her exhausted self so
within and
so without.

And then, as if Connie had reached far up, had kneaded out
the past with the press of her magic thumbs, Lia found herself
plunging quite inadvertently backwards, backwards, to the stranger
in the night and to the way he touched her feet that first week.

Velvet and Vera

Here is a fact:
The tiny, beautiful bones in human feet make up a quarter of all
the bones in the body.

Here is another:
During the Blitz, London's National Gallery hosted a series of free lunch-time concerts in its bomb-proof basement.

Vera Lynn performed 'The White Cliffs of Dover' there once.

I am reminded of this as Needle and Pin tinker their musical introduction down in her depths, announcing the arrival of Velvet, who steps out of the shadows, onto the stage, clear and fierce, soft and violet, singing about friendship and ligaments.

She croons her cello-smooth sounds. I feel the luxury of camaraderie beginning to wrap, drape and rankle elegantly around all her arches, intercuneiform joints and metatarsal bones, cushioning the pain away, drowning out the jangle, and I can think of nothing but that bleach-clean hour in the Gallery basement, when everyone forgot who they were, why they were there, and the fact that London was flattening.

John and the Disciples

Matthew and Lia were sitting at the kitchen table. He had been there for one whole day, had stayed the night in the small room with the forbidden bookcase and the linen cupboard and the window that opened and closed of its own accord. Anne was outside hanging the washing on the line, brows furrowed, folding sheets and shirts and pastel cardigans. There was something very calming about the process, something very simple and practical about the way she would work down the line as if she were carefully building a small city. When she was done Lia would watch the wind breathe life into the flat hung half-people, and imagine unpinning them, freeing them, trousers speeding off into fields whistling *Thank Yoooouuuuuuuuu*

Lia's a nice name, Matthew said, drumming his fingertips impatiently on the wood.

It's Amelia, really. But I prefer Lia.

Why?

Because they don't like it.

Lia blinked at him. For a moment, he seemed a little surprised. A little delighted. He stopped his drumming, leant closer to her across the table, his voice lowering to a whisper.

You've got to be careful, you know.

Why?

Do you know about Lilith?

No.

She was Adam's first wife.

That was Eve.

There was a woman before Eve. Not many people know about her, because she didn't submit like she should have, like God and Adam wanted her to, so she was banished from Earth forever. Ran straight out of Eden and into the arms of the devil.

Lia's little heart began to boil. She did not remember this from the Bible.

Does Father Peter know about her?

Lia called him 'Father Peter' when she spoke about him to anyone else. Like many odd habits of that time, she could not remember if this was something she was explicitly asked to do.

He might. But it's very secret. Only a few people do. Matthew said this with a glint, like he was daring her to do something. *You could always ask him.*

Lia thought about it.

No. I don't think I will.

It'll be our secret then.

They said nothing for a while. Lia stared at the space between the window and the sink, where the devil was squatting, spinning a cake tin around his finger, watching them closely. She felt compelled to say something clever. Ominous. Something to throw him off-guard.

I can find out if all of that is true, you know.

Matthew looked amused.

How?

I can ask the devil himself.

His cheeks went a little pale and he smiled but it was not a sincere smile; it was shifty, uncomfortable.

Good friends, are you?

Wouldn't you like to know.

And with that Lia picked up her school bag and ran up the stairs, afraid of herself, of this new-found confidence, and her own hot pulse leaking out from her pores, dripping

        all

            down

                the

                    stairs.

The devil spat and sprayed *Ha! Ha! Ha!*s behind her like confetti, a few shrapnel *That'll teach him*s.

She stayed up there for the rest of the afternoon. Matthew went out. She wondered if he'd gone forever. She didn't like the idea that he had so she crept bare feet on floorboards to his room, and saw his bag and one of his T-shirts crumpled on the floor and thought, Good;
good he is not gone.

He had left his bed unmade. She stepped towards it, reaching out her hand to trace the crumpled outline of his body, the press of his sleep in the sheets. She perched on the edge of the bed, staring up at the forbidden bookcase, trying to observe the room, the vicarage, their lives through his eyes. Most of the books were novels that had been passed down Peter's family, and Lia had come to believe they had been placed there for the same reason the tree had been placed in Eden; to be eventually devoured.

The room had already acquired his scent. Damp, alert, unclean. A little like the rocks on the nearest beach, oozing their warm surprising sweetness, just before a storm. Lia suddenly had the desire to steal something of his. A sock, perhaps. A sock would do.

What are you doing?

Lia snapped around. Anne was standing on the landing in a burgundy dress. Lia noticed a faint smudge of blush on her cheeks, a trace of tentative coral lipstick applied only to her thin bottom lip and rubbed, it seemed, almost apologetically against the top. She had never seen her mother look so pretty. So exposed.

Nothing, Lia said, wrapping her thick jumper around her middle. *I've finished my reading for today.*

And what did you read? Anne asked, her eyebrows bent like barbed wire, her face knotted.

Lia replied – truthfully – that she had read John 13:1–17. She had not disliked it. In fact, it had touched her. The washing of the feet. She had prayed very hard for half an hour. *No servant is greater than his master,* she recited, *nor is a messenger greater than the one who sent him.*

Like the clip of a wire fence being snapped, Anne's frown broke apart. For a moment, she looked almost pleased.

On her way out of the room, Lia turned and said in the smallest voice, *Who is he?*

Anne sighed as if the question exhausted her.

He is a friend. Of the family.

Lia left the exchange feeling none the wiser but pleased with herself for coming up with all the talk of John and Jesus and feet. She ran out into the garden, marching past her ruins, opening the latch to the rotting kissing gate without a coat or shoes or socks on. Weeks of rain had dampened and gutted the fields, and as her bare feet plunged into the earth, it seemed to respond in little groan-glop sucks, a waterlogged language, receiving her wild little body with pleasure. Lia felt very suddenly alive. As if her life before he arrived had been a waiting, a making do. The wind slapped hard against her cheeks, the mud spitting thickly up her legs, and there it was again, the prickle, the fizz, getting stronger as she ran up through the land spilling out wider without the walls of hedgerows to contain it. Perhaps this was what it was to feel a presence. Perhaps He was opening the door to her, ever so slightly, and what she felt now was a shiver of His air, His love.

At the top of the hill, she collapsed down by the roots of a tree, bent by the wind like an italic. The sky had begun to bruise purple, slicking the cornfields in sudden gold. The stench of manure hung so densely Lia could taste it in her throat. Gathering her breath, she began to examine her feet. They were lashed red-raw, there were cuts up her shins, and her fingers were bluing slightly in the cold, but she felt no pain, no discomfort at all. For what did skin and wounds, knocks and bruises matter, when there was this new thing, fluttering madly beneath her ribcage, beating about inside of her. All else was trivial, temporary.

She lay there for half an hour or so on her back feeling very overwhelmed, before reaching into her waistband and pulling out the forbidden book she had plucked quickly from the case. Holding *Wuthering Heights* tight in her hands, she looked up at the shifting sky and waited for punishment. None came. She opened the book, skimmed her finger down the grids of printed ink looking for the words best dressed in unusual sounds and shapes; into the *wild, wicked slip of a girl* she sunk, into the *stamping,* the *paroxysm,* the *groan, thrill, thrust, snatching, rage,* her eyes flicking quick between the land and the page.

And then, cutting like a blade through the still, came her mother's voice; *Amelia! Amelia! Amelia!*

As Lia ran home, her mind caught up with her body's cold hard edges, acknowledging its sudden discomfort.

In the kitchen there was the expected
What have you done to yourself? You're frozen! Your lips are blue!
Why are you not wearing any shoes?

Lia hardly noticed the scolding because Matthew was back. He was observing them all intently from the corner of the room and she could feel the hairs on the back of her neck bristle. He walked slowly to the cupboard, took out a large bucket and began to fill it from the hot tap, the rattle of water hitting the metal bottom unnaturally loud in the drum of Lia's ear.

Anne and Peter receded quietly into the dark edges of the kitchen and Lia was struck by the ease with which he had taken control of them all. The way he could both soothe and unnerve, comfort and command, without having said a word.

She shivered; very thrilled, very afraid.

Sit. He pointed to the chair, his voice as golden as the fields had seemed, under the purpling sky.

She sat.

Give me your feet. She lifted her feet into the water and into his hands.

He squeezed the wet cloth gently into the arches of her pale feet. The water was burning. Lia could hardly breathe. The more he rubbed, cleaning away the mud crusted around her ankles, the harder she could feel her pulse, charging up through her shins, her knees, right to the very top of her thighs. She readjusted herself slightly in the seat. She wanted to cross her legs. To press herself against something. To feel wrapped up and smothered the way she did in the middle of the night, tangled tight around her duvet, and this shameful impulse was so strong it seemed impossible that he couldn't see it, spreading into the nooks of her eyes and ears.

Lia came to believe that if a surgeon were to make a horizontal slice across her middle, chop her right in half, they would find it all there; the quirks and chinks of her early desire, carved into her tissue the way growth rings score the inside of trees, and if you traced this pattern back through the years you would arrive at that day, the first stain, dictating the shape and structure of her life.

She had looked around for the devil, but the vicarage had emptied itself of all except Matthew's hands and her feet.

It was then that she vomited.

Petrification

The beautiful takes our desire captive
and empties it of its object . . .
forbidding it to
fly off towards the future.
AKA
beauty is a great conundrum.
AKA
I cannot help but like him.

I do love an underdog, after all.

I can also be quite the romantic.

I feel these old-as-time gut-patterns crash their impish ways
through me
like toddlers in tiny bumper-cars, as voiceless Fossil moves around
her body,

turning the scores of her soul to stone
with nothing but his touch.

Burn Girl

It was 1.15 p.m., which was lunch time.

The girl who had bitten the top clean off the Solero was
universally liked at school. She looked older than twelve; she had
a very symmetrical face and quite beautiful, dewy skin that was
all one toned thick colour on her legs, her arms and her face.
Iris had not seen anywhere else, but she was sure that the colour,
texture and tightness would be the same underneath her clothes
as well.

The consistency of skin was something Iris paid attention to
because hers was problematic and irregular. Her face blotched
bright salmon-pink the minute she exerted herself, the skin on
her legs was so pale you could see straight through into the spools
of her purple-blue veins, her forearms were prone to rashes, her
elbows were speckled with eczema five to six months of the year,
and she went from feeling very pretty to very ugly very often.

She had been lingering around the corner of the school where
the much older kids spent their time, trying to look purposeful
but also suitably nonchalant – a word she'd heard recently and
had taken a particular liking to. In the corner of her eye Solero
Boy was bouncing a football against the wall looking not entirely
comfortable but nonchalant enough to avoid any unwanted
attention, and there was a small, slightly painful tear on the
side of her nail which she picked at whilst nodding along to a
rather tedious conversation about Taylor Swift's best bridges.
The beautiful box jellyfish girl had just turned the corner, alone,
looking poisonous and radiant in her perfectly fitted uniform. Iris
watched her closely as she took out a packet of cigarettes from
her school bag. The Taylor Swift fans had launched into some
very unsuccessful harmonizing, which seemed the perfect time to
break away, shoot the girl with the cigarettes a look as if to say,

I'm not with them, edge closer to her and ask very nonchalantly where she'd purchased the packet.

The girl let out a wide laugh, exposing a brilliant row of white even teeth. Iris felt suddenly aware of her own cluttered mouth, the slight strain she felt when closing her lips. The girl asked Iris if she was scared. She was not. The girl seemed pleased.

Shall we be friends?

I guess.

And then she pulled out a light from her pocket and with one swift movement lit her cigarette, took a drag. She did not cough which was without a doubt Impressive. She exhaled as if she'd been smoking for years.

Do you know what we should do to make sure we are? She tapped ash onto tarmac.

What?

We should mark ourselves.

She took another drag.

We should put this out on our hands here, make a circle burn – the girl lifted the cigarette above her hand, imitating the motion – *as a mark of friendship. We hold it there for five seconds and then the ritual is done, and we can be friends.*

Solero Boy and his friends had stopped bouncing the ball against the wall and had surrounded the two of them. The happy, harmless singing girls had kept their distance, but their harmonies had thinned.

Iris did not know whether it was the pressure of Solero Boy breathing down her neck, the challenge itself or perhaps even

(the most terrible) the fact that she wanted more than anything to be this girl's friend, but she took the cigarette and without flinching or blinking
stubbed it out hard and flat
on her left hand,
just an inch below
her middle knuckle.

It hurt.
It hurt a lot.

She counted:

1 it wasn't the kind of hurt that shocked at first but got a little better; it was not so bad at 1
2 the signal of the hurt reached her brain, her eyes began to water
3 the girl looked hungry, like she was watching dogs fight in a cage; Iris pressed harder
4 boys were gasping, making *how impressive how crazy how cool is this* kinds of sounds
5 skin began to fizz and pop, the circle of ash cratering; *Jesus*, Solero Boy said

and then it was over.

Iris lifted the cigarette and threw it to the tarmac, eyes electric with triumph, with
pyrrhic victory;
it had made quite a mark. The centre of the burn was off-white and already blistered. There was a brown spot inside like a nucleus and around it swelled quite red-raw and wet-looking. Flakes of grey ash had stuck to the wet –

it stung.

Something changed in the girl's eyes, as if Iris had gone from fascinating to disgusting in a matter of seconds.

Your turn now, Iris said, her voice higher than usual, reaching for the packet to get a new one.

Burn Girl said nothing.

The boys were watching her intently; they all
hung limp and lifeless like clothes on a
washing line.

I did not think you were actually going to do that.

Everyone remained silent.

Iris held a cigarette out to her seriously.

The girl's lovely face clouded.

I'm not doing that. Look at what you've done. You're insane.

The boys began to steer towards what seemed like an appropriate response –

That's a third degree you've got there, I'm sure of it!

You're crazy.

Was that a dare, did you just do that for fun?

That's messed up.

Does it hurt?

Iris shrugged. It began to hurt so much she could barely see straight or hear properly.

The Taylor Swift fans had disappeared. The girl went to join a new cluster of bodies a few yards away. They all looked up from their phones and began to ask, *what's happening did something happen did we miss something?*

She pointed back at Iris, face all lovely and unclouded again.

Iris could only just make out the spitting of half-formed phrases as if filtered through a gauze.

She's a self-harmer. She wants to hurt herself. I didn't even say anything to her, she just took the cigarette out of my hand and put it out on herself.

The washing-line boys
frowned and nodded along,
all except Solero Boy who simply went back to the wall,
back to the kicking of the ball.

It is funny, Iris thought, funny how Truth becomes all
fluid in the face of
Beauty and
Politics.

She ran as quickly as she could to the bathroom, pushing through
the heavy door.
Once she was sure it was empty she began to cry quite
uncontrollably,
cradling her hand,
stretching out the burn under cold water,
desperately wanting
not to be a
person.

I must be cleverer,
she thought.
I must be cleverer.

I want my mum.

If this is what the world is like –
I want my mum.

The Night After

The following evening in the vicarage there was a knock knock knock on Lia's bedroom door and Matthew came in with a weather-beaten *Wuthering Heights*, its wet pages curled at their edges.

Found it lost on the moors, he said. *Thought I'd return it.*

Lia blinked at him — *It's not really mine. I'm not allowed.*

I see.

I only look for the best words.

There was a silence.

How old are you?

I'm sixteen. And you?

Twelve.

And then another longer but
more comfortable silence.

Matthew looked around her small plain room
as if it held the answer
to a question
he was yet to understand.

Your feet all better?

Lia looked down at her toes. She had four plasters on them and she liked the way it looked.

Yes.

Matthew smiled – *You're a strange kid.*

Lia had her knees right up to her chin and her arms wrapped around her shins.

What are you doing here?

He smiled again like it was nothing, nothing that he had just landed in their lives like this.

Your dad is helping me. He's taken me on, he's gonna train me up good, like him.

Like him?

You know.

She did not know but she could guess. He had 'taken on' a few people before. One or two were older, unfamiliar. Most of them were boys from the village who sang in the church choir and came to Sunday service. They had been raised Good Strict Anglican Christians and all had parents who wanted to push them just that little bit closer to
God Himself.

Lia would hear them talking seriously about the Bible, reading, dissecting, making surgical incisions along the core of it. *You are a lucky girl,* her mother would say, large hands scrubbing at soiled potato flesh, *a lucky girl to be so close, to have front-row seats.* Lia would ask, *To what?* Her mother would not say anything, but Lia knew the answer was always – *God.*

She had come to see these boys like apprentices, as if her father were a blacksmith or a plumber or a great artist of the Renaissance. They would become his Servers, Sidesmen, members of the clergy, assisting him in his art, his community duties. The process would begin with a confession, of sorts. This was nothing like the

Catholic sacrament, where the penitent mumbled through holes in a wall and remained quite faceless in his transition from sin to safety, no –

Absolution cannot happen with the flick of a switch, her father would say.

Instead, these confessions took place over hours through grey afternoons in their living room. The house would feel heavy with the sheer mass of declarations, hopes, fears, mistakes, misjudgements and Peter would listen intently, his hands clasped together as if he had all the answers in the salt of his palms and would reveal them in due course.

None of these boys had ever stayed though, not in their house overnight.

So you want to be part of the Church? asked Lia.

Yes.

You can't be going around talking about this Lilith then.

No. He smiled.

Can't be making things up.

I know.

He looked at the battered book on her bed – *I won't tell if you don't.*

His hard glassy eyes
danced;
Well. Goodnight.

He closed the door gently.

She lay straight and flat on her back staring up at the wall.

At 1.29 a.m.,
still wide-eyed and bound by live-wire-wake-chains,
Lia began to wonder,
Is this Love?

Osmosis

From the day she got the burn, Iris began to think that there
were two worlds: the one her mum spoke about with options and
verbing of nouns and Astute dances, and then there was Burn
Girl and Solero Boy's world with its smartphones and school
playgrounds and skin burns so sore they broke into five separate
tiny blisters that made a perfect circle.

As life and time continued to happen – the two worlds,
Iris thought, would rarely intersect,
and growing up would simply become the process of
moving across from one to the other, the former
to the latter, in
an act of osmosis,
a terrible act of osmosis.

The thought was too dark to dwell on.

Lia later explained, while stroking
her daughter's burn with a cube of ice, that
there were many ways of finding those
points of intersection but
it had taken her a while to work it out.

Iris would take less time because she was,
indeed,
a lot
cleverer.

It is history's only duty, Lia thought:
ensuring daughters are brighter than their mothers.

Kidney Detective Work

It was the coils of Yellow's voice that stirred me.

Yellow scrutinizing the kidneys, chorus bickering behind her.

Some of the party have tents strapped to their backs, torchlights
bound to their heads; a raven with a clerical collar and large
black wings clutches the bible in his beak. Those with hands and
fingers carry travel diaries;
I have observed them scratching sweet entries
at night, when sleep settles in the landscape like
mist across a moor.

Nothing to report today, only
a general sense of unease.
Terrible to admit but
so looking forward to
a little more drama,
a little more action.

If I could rub my hands together, gnarl out a poisonous twat-
cackle, pick open their dreams or leave my own little marks in
their diaries,
I would.

Instead, I assume the form of a common kidney infection,
while Yellow walks with her little hands gripped tightly around
a magnifying glass;

Here, if you look closely you will be able to see the bacteria stinging
up from the urinary tract, traces of the five-day catastrophe on the
second-hand sofa when she refused to go to the doctor.

She hands over the glass to The Gardener, his dandelion eyes

mon**strOUSly** lar**ge**.

Salt, water, copper and choline filter through us all like
a dozen missed miracles, skimming through
the most domestic hours.
A million nephrons not quite, but
very nearly
working as they should.

But it's not what we're looking for,
he croaks, watering around the major and minor calyx.

And then a horror kind of corridor sound begins to leak in
through the renal vein and
Velvet pulls a scowl like a shift in the weather;

We should move on. Our little pharmakon friend will be here soon,
to burn the place down. Dry it all out. Spew his healing poison.

Natural Order

Lia mulled about the exit of a flat dream on the left-hand side of
the bed. It was morning, and Harry was moving out of the right,
his fingers folding over the corner of the duvet as if it were
a page of a book and Lia were
its static contents.

Lia turned over into the empty space, thin hand tapping the sheet for her husband.

She looks like a child, Harry thought,
like a child thick with sleep, while he looked for
clean boxers.

Once the light had pooled through the curtains and prised itself under Lia's lids, Harry announced that there was a faculty party at the university that evening.

Come, please, if you're up to it.

During their Golden Years, when Harry had begun to move in certain academic circles and the cancer had cleared and Lia's hair had started to grow back, they were invited often to fundraising parties. Connie would squeeze Lia into one of her old dresses and mutter *belle of the ball, belle of the ball* through a mouth full of safety pins. Lia would try on the blonde wig Iris had insisted she buy and Harry would lean against the frame of their bedroom door saying things like, *You might just be the most beautiful wigged woman the world has ever seen.*

They liked the way it felt to be dressed up together in public waiting on platforms, standing on escalators. This is what performance is, Lia would think, this is what perfume adverts tell us fun should look like, her chin pressed against Harry's ribs as the city churned them out.

Connie would stay and look after Iris. She would order Thai takeaways, put *Clueless* on, take regular cigarette breaks on the doorstep. Iris would sit next to her smoking a chopstick. They would practise their *Urgh! As If!*s.

Five miles away, husband and wife chewed on seared scallops and laughed at bad jokes about Roman emperors:

How was the Roman Empire cut in half?

With a pair of Caesars.

Harry would laugh politely and pinch the top of Lia's neck, and appear so brilliantly engaged with everyone that it made Lia love him quite deeply in her stomach where the scallops were.

When the scholars asked her what she did she would occasionally lie, and say that she was in the department of Cellular Biology and Pharmacology at the University of San Francisco and was currently developing a new kind of arsenic-based antibiotic to battle against the pressing threat of resistance, but more often than not, she would say what she really did, and the scholars would smile and say *lovely* quite cryptically, quite wistfully, before wafting away with a passing waiter. Round black empty trays would bounce quickly about the room, helping guests put full stops to their small talk.

Harry would look at her with that perplexed expression, that *Why do you do that, why do you make everything sound like an apology*, and Lia would shrug, feeling unsure of who she was in Connie's old dress, the ridiculous wig, thinking about the many faces clawing at her from the inside.

Harry must have seen something like this reflected in his wife's eyes because he looked at her floating head propped up on the pillow and said, *I can promise you'll be the most interesting person in the room.*

But most of the time Lia felt like she was intruding. She felt like this even at her own desk in the small shed Harry built from birchwood. It was a brute of a thing; a beautiful, robust room of her own. He had butchered and flattened most of their garden for it. Lia remembered pacing within its empty ribbed walls right where the perennials had been, thinking – I have never known love like this.

She listened to the particular morning sound of her husband brushing his teeth, the light leak of a tap running. His spitting into the bowl. The brief silence of his reconciling himself with his face in the mirror before he moved back into the bedroom, began lacing up his shoes.

I think I'll pass on tonight. But you go. You go.

Harry tried not to look defeated as he finished knotting. His hair is thinning, Lia thought – his scalp had become quite visible where his hair parted. Maybe, this time, they could go bald together.

Lia's last completed project had been a book for six-to-eight-year-olds about anatomy. A visual journey through the human body; she had drawn diaphragm walls inked in exquisite detail, scraps of information written along artery streams like the fact that the longest muscle is the sartorius muscle; it runs from hip to knee like a seam.

It's lovely stuff, Lia, the publishers had said, *but remember to keep it cute.*

It is tricky, she'd replied, *tricky to make a spleen cute,* which she'd instantly regretted, because of all organs, the spleen was probably the sweetest.

Lia had never felt particularly proud of anything she'd ever created. Except for Iris, that was.

Harry had this naked, moonless expression on his face as he slid his jacket on.

Are you sure? he asked.

I'm sure.

Smiling, he leapt onto the bed, kissed between where his wife's breasts once were, and said, *But I don't want to be anywhere that you are not.*

Lia tried to laugh lightly but it came out a slaughtered wheezy
eclipse of a sound.

You'll be fine, she said,
you'll be fine.

Little Moon

The average human will walk five times around the Earth during their life.

This one may have done two or three by now, you can feel it.

Some of the party have already thrust up through her calves like worms through soil after rain. Some are making their way up from her toes, through her bones, resting under her medial meniscus.

Meniscus – from the Greek *meniskos* –
from the diminutive of *mene.*
The whole translates as

Little Moon.

When I skim past here I make a point of always having
a quick drink in the milky light,
of toasting the marvels of man,
his language, his knots and
bolts and kneecaps,

often a little worn,
a little sore from their
five times around Earth's circumference.

Technology

Tuesday.
The days were getting pricklier and Lia could not go on her usual
early morning runs down by the river any more. There is nothing
you can do with uselessness, nowhere you can put it down, you
just have to carry it around all ugly and obvious.

Lia was finding it difficult to concentrate as
her mother spoke unnecessarily loudly through the phone.

You do not need to shout,
                    we put phones to our ears for a reason.

She began to think about the shape of phones – the way they chart
the small distance between your ears and lips – and smiled at the
thought of time as a circle of
somebody somewhere designing the ergonomics of a human
against the size and dimensions of trusted technologies –
hands and fingers the width of a keyboard, the mouth and the ear
a convenient
phone apart—

Are you listening?

The frequency creased – *Yes.*

So what time tomorrow then?

Eleven, Mum. Eleven.

Lia paused and added, *Are you sure you want to come all this way?*

There was a static quiet. Lia wondered if she'd already gone but then her mother said quite softly, as if her voice were built for small faceless confessions:

I would not miss it for the world.

Persistence

**Why they are all so persistent
I have no idea.**

Curtains

Plugged-in wired-up Lia was sitting watching her mother who was watching like she'd never watched before; watching the cannula go into Lia's vein, watching the red toxic liquid drip drip drip, watching the nurses, the other patients' swollen steroid faces, the nonsense language of medical magic fall off tongues and swim about the room.

Have you been going to church? Anne asked, quite suddenly.
Lia felt restless without any of her usual escape routes. *I am not here preaching, I simply wondered if you would consider it – you may find some answers, some solace, it may really help.*

She landed heavy-footed on *help* as if it meant something more, something bigger than the word itself. As if it meant *cure* or *resolve*.

She must have performed one of her intruding mind-tricks because she footnoted, *Stranger things have happened.*

The idea that this was all God's great punishment
for being so disbelieving of Him so young
hacked away, very occasionally, at night.
It would travel up through Lia, looking for air,
and then
sink
back
down.

No, I haven't.

Anne stood up and asked where the toilet was, wrapping the monumental cardigan around her and shuffling off apologetically.

Lia observed her quiet grey-faced companions, connected up to their own secret recipes. She felt as if they were all moving about a stage, none of it real, all of it performed. Anne slowly exiting the scene, stage left. A nurse speaking quietly to a man drinking from a large plastic bottle of water. The glug of it unusually loud. Lia tried to feel graceful, demure as an actress settling into a swing on a Mississippi veranda. The cap of the water bottle fell to the floor, spinning on its side.

Which playwright was it, the one who had died
choking on a bottle cap?

Anne was back. She was tapping the slightly steely nurse that smelt of citrus soap on the shoulder and Lia watched Anne rest her frail, speckled hand on the nurse's forearm, ask her an inaudible question unusually brightly, politely. They walked together towards her, down the stretch of stage, like a mother and daughter strolling along a Mississippi veranda, engaged in a hushed, intimate conversation.

Lia wondered how Anne could make her feel left out of her own chemotherapy sessions.

This next dose will hit her harder than the first, the nurse said. They were closer, now, and Lia could hear every word.

Thank you. Anne nodded. *She never tells me anything. It's so nice to hear from the people in charge.*

Lia seethed. The nurse smiled kindly. The compliment lingered for a moment in that way a thing does when it's not quite true enough to assimilate into the air.

Once the nurse had turned and clicked away, Anne came shuffling back to her chair. She sat heavily, spoke to the cannula again.

They have nice loos here.

They do.

Nicer than you'd expect.

Yes.

Anne swallowed and looked up. Her stare was startlingly direct.

How are you feeling?

Lia wondered if this was the first time she had ever properly asked.

Terrible. She half smiled, weakly. *You know I would tell you anything if you just asked.*

Anne squirmed in silence, as if Lia's honesty offended her, pushed it all a little too far.

When it was over, Lia went to the loos which were, indeed, nice. Her pink piss smelt strange. She flushed the loo twice.

And then, somewhere very deep within her, the feeling of
a thousand curtains
falling;

The second dose will hit her harder than the first.

Fairy Tales, Natural Disasters and Spielberg

Red is huffing and puffing, stripping cells with his songs the way
hurricanes blast windows off hinges.
The way wolves could once blow houses down.

His little spinning legs are taking me straight to that 1982 *E.T.*
chase scene
when the boys' bikes begin to levitate.

His mouth is moving madly.

He looks happier than he ever thought a beast like him could be.

Dove watches from above, quiet as ice,
heart-breaking, list-making.

Had to take a quick peek:

> Dove's List of Necessary Evils:
>
> Traffic lights
> Hairspray
> The Great Flood
> Technology
> Colonoscopies
> Red and his bike

If I could laugh, draw a little cock doodle, give her tired wings
a snap-quick-squeeze,
I would.

But
I'm feeling a little
                 low.

A little out of sorts.

I think of Pompeii and little pigs getting chewed.

Nothing.

Not even the idea of E.T. in a wig is cheering me up.

Or the bit in Drew Barrymore's bedroom when he's
hiding amongst the toys.

If I just focus hard on

                    E.T.   *Phone*   *Home*   maybe this

hot red hand will get out of my

        senses   (*No*)   sentences   (*No*)

                              (*Not by the hair of my chinny chin chin!*)

Did you know Hurricane Katrina reached sustained winds
of _____ mph?

        Did you know _____ per cent of the deaths in Louisiana
        were caused by drowning?

                Search is to (side, split, squeeze) as agony is to
                (burn, stop, please)

but

I'll be . . .   *right . . .*

                          here.

time travelling

        volcanic hatchings

    I'm

       lost

           in

a. Vesuvius
b. August
c. 79 AD
d. All of the above

A second

    before the

      mighty

                                Spill

three

Beauty

Matthew took to his 'apprenticeship' like he had been made for it, been cut from the father's rib for it.

It was quite remarkable, the focus and ease with which he applied himself to lay duties, both inside the church walls and beyond. He took it so seriously that the rituals that had once belonged to the formal surfaces of Lia's life began to take on a new allure, a sudden depth, purpose and rhythm, for everything was to be savoured, now, turned over and pondered; whether it was the shape a body makes when it prays, the wistful smell of snuffed candles wafting thick along the pews, the weight and taste of blessed bread or the startling beauty of the psalms, Matthew found their world bewitching and in turn, Lia was bewitched.

Whenever they were alone, the intensity of his expressions and the tightness of his posture would change, and he would grin at her as if they were both in on some wonderful joke. He was shedding skin from the beginning to the end. But it was these private glimpses – of his lightness, perhaps, his darkness – that gave Lia the sense she knew something true of his soul that had been kept from everyone else.

The villagers stared at Matthew shamelessly, spoke of him so openly, as if he couldn't hear them. Sometimes he enjoyed the attention. Sometimes, Lia watched as he went sulking deep into

the quieter corners of himself, all lost and monk-like for a day
or two.

Anne said that it would die down. It was just *village politics*, the
fact of him being a stranger accepted into their home, starting new
at the local school. There were of course the expected rumours
that scattered and settled: the *he must be an estranged son* rumours;
the *perhaps a nephew* rumours; the *homeless kid taken kindly in*
or *probably Irish you know, perhaps the son of junkie hippies from
London, no no no I saw him help Martha across the road, he's a nice
chap, you can't be spreading rumours about someone so close to Father
Peter, the central pillar of our community, he's certainly keen, see, he's
been helping restore the church wall, I heard, what a looker though,
what a beauty.*

And it must be hard, Lia would think, to look like that, to feel
all those eyes acknowledging only your spectacular surface;
it must scoop out a little of the life in you,
make your body feel like an inanimate object.

This didn't stop her from focusing hard on the best fragments of
his face so that she could project them like a lantern on the flat wall
of her mind's eye late at night, sketch out their glorious outlines.
Every day she found more to examine in his buttery expressions,
his stride, his knuckles, the way his arms hung as if he were poised
to wrench something heavy and valuable out from the world before
him, hold it up above his head for all to see.

It would be a shame not to find some way of documenting it, Lia
would think – and so her gaze was different. She was nothing like
the older girls at school who would giggle and look at him with
these gaping, cavernous eyes,
feeding on all of Earth's beauty, making nothing of its light.

It troubled her that he would occasionally reciprocate these looks.

Just part of the game, he'd say, when he saw how it bruised Lia.
It was kind of him to humour her like this. It was never quite clear
what game he was playing.

Recovery

Today I am

quite und^{o}n$_e$

l^{i}t$_t$le b$_i$tt^{e}n edg$_e$s off a seaco^{a}st

changed forever

many still in shelters, *eight,*

nine, ten years on.

Invasions

It was breakfast and Iris was eating a bowl of oats soaked in
apple juice.

They had run out of milk.

Harry had been searching the fridge for butter while Lia had
been staring at the edges of her fingernails, focusing on controlling
her nagging nausea, when there was a sudden scream from the
kitchen table.

Iris had pushed the bowl of oats away from her in horror and
was standing with her hands
covering her mouth.

What's happened, what is it?

The kitchen orbed.

Jesus. Ugh.

There, in Iris's bowl, pale and writhing, were maggots. A handful disguised as oats, hidden within oats, curling around, under and over oats.

Iris retched and ran to the sink.

How could you let that happen? How long have they been there? I've been eating these oats for weeks.

Lia didn't know.

I've been eating them every morning.

She retched again, watery clumps curdling in the drain.

I'm sorry.

Lia had nothing else to say; she couldn't think clearly.

Harry was by the sink saying things like, *You should have noticed, Iris, I should have noticed,* and *It's fine, they won't kill you.*

I'm sorry I'm sorry I'm sorry, Lia whispered.

It's not your fault, it's fine, Harry persisted, both arms raised like he was treading water.

Iris turned to stare at her mum, flecks of oats stuck to her chin.

You are being so crap, I would rather you just not try to do anything.

Harry's voice hardened.

Stop it. You're not a kid any more.

I am a kid. I'm a kid and I'm being fed maggots by my own mum. It's fucking gross.

Don't swear at us. Jesus.

Harry's rare anger pounded pink across his face. Iris's eyes stung and teared as she stormed out of the kitchen and then out the front door. The sound of it shutting was agony.

Lia ran upstairs, sat on the floor next to the toilet, resting her hands on the rim, churning out her toxic sour failing-mother insides so violently she felt wet trickling out from her pants. From the deep round mouth of the loo, inside the bowl, the wry murmur of maggots rose.

Ahahahahaha we've got inside you, we've got inside you and your daughter and your husband, and we'll eat you out from your stomach, we'll munch our way through and out your nose your cunt your eyes and ears!

Why the world was such a violent place
Lia had no idea.

Hands shaking, she wiped her mouth. She could feel her lips beginning to crack into sores.

Lia?

Harry came in calmly and sat down on the floor next to her.

Don't – it's a mess. I've pissed myself and there's sick.

He put his arms tight around her and said, *I'm here, I'm here.*

They cleaned the toilet together. Flushed it four times.

No one would get to hear Harry's prepared talk on Homeric Gardens that day;

he cancelled all his lectures and stayed at home

with his wife.

Maggot
Noun
[*plural* **maggots**]

1. A soft-bodied legless larva of a fly or other insect, found in decaying matter.
2. A strange, whimsical or eccentric idea.
3. ....

The Gardener's Guide to Fixing a Wife

A little better today. Nearly touched by the scene taking place:

The Gardener laying down his tools,
                    beginning to scatter compost
along Red's reckless rips.
            Can you smell it? I can smell it, delicious
                  descant stench of fear.
      He presses ears to earth;
          I am here,
          I am here.

Photosynthesis

When Harry was six, his mother took him and his cousins out into
his grandfather's garden and anointed the plants with exotic names,
one by one. He still remembered the sound of them rustling
in response, as if they'd been sitting there a very long time, just
waiting to exist. As if she'd finally given them permission to thrive:

Lupines
Geraniums
Artemisias
Hydrangeas
Cherry blossom
Honeysuckle
Ground clematis

He had watched their titles fall from her lips seriously, their ancient
Latin roots planting themselves inside his six-year-old memory.

Musk thistles
Prairie gentians
Blackberries
Star jasmine
Clematis
Snowy mespilus
Potato vines
Sage
Rosemary
Iris

He remembered writing the list later in the day on a kitchen table
the size of a planet. The others played loudly outside, screaming
through the water sprinkler bending backwards and forwards,
backwards and forwards, beading the scene and its bare-bottomed
children with a silver celestial glisten.

When he was finished, his faceless grandfather had looked down
at the list, then
up at his mother, had said,
Your pansy here might just be
a little genius, from under the shadow of his
felt fedora.

His mother's laugh cascaded over him like sunlight and he'd felt
somewhere deep within him a great photosynthesis of pride –
a bud of something useful,
drinking and breaking.

An exhale of pure oxygen.

Harry had added *Pansy*
to the bottom of the list.

Over time, he forgot that he possessed this box-tight cleverness.
He forgot the dazzling unsealed sensation of nurturing soil,
watching something demand itself out from the smallest seed.
Throughout his twenties, he thought his life would not amount to
much at all. He did not like the city. It was loud and unkind and
careless to him, to his friends and neighbours. To the despondent
strangers he made a point of speaking to on the bus.

Harry owed some of his greatest happiness to strangers. One of
the best decisions he'd ever made had been offering to walk the
elderly woman's dog, the one with dyed violet hair and the swollen
ankles who lived at the end of his road. Her house had been the
only one on the street not yet converted into flats. After his walks,
he'd prop himself up in her large Dutch Orange kitchen, steel
pans, woks and griddles hanging between glowing oils of nude
backs, breasts and armpits, all of which she claimed to have painted
herself. She'd make him mugs of strong Rooibos tea and reminisce
happily about her late husband. He had owned an allotment by
the river. She urged Harry to use it, *before they rip it up and build*
expensive flats or a river-side gym or a terrible four-storey bar.

And so, between the PhD, the pubs, the rush hours and the dog walks, Harry grew things. Chicories, leeks, rhubarb and radishes, turnips, shallots, swedes and runner beans, and the more he grew the more he remembered the clean sharp cleverness he had always possessed, the sensation of growth just filling a life.

And he had met Lia there, working on the allotment.

And one of the first questions she asked him was – *What do you believe?*

And Harry hardly had to think about it; he looked straight at her and said,

quite resolutely – *I believe in the kindness of strangers.*

It had been such a clean answer.
As sharp and true as his own
particular cleverness, and Lia had felt
somewhere deep within her
a bud of affection
drinking and breaking.
An exhale of pure oxygen
in an otherwise polluted place.

The Prodigal Son

We will begin with Luke chapter 15, verses 11–32.

Father Peter was delivering a sermon on the Prodigal Son.

Lia was at the front of the church watching Matthew, who was serving next to Peter in white robes looking like a large puppet held up on the edge of a wooden frame. He had been with them for two quick years. She could feel the depth of her father's voice coil its way about the church, breathing life into its empty lunged vaults.

What we have here, is a parable you will all be familiar with. It is the most in-tri-cate display of forgiveness, of kindness – two sons that in their own distinct ways commit sins of the spirit and sins of the flesh.

Lia liked the way *flesh* fell out of his mouth. It was common for her to be dragged into the sounds of phrases, only catching glimpses of their meaning for she was, at these times,

        never

wholly

        present;

                Wild living

                                met with famine

Came to his senses when

                starving   to death.   Upon his   return
        A calf   a feast   a field

                nearby, a

                                brother's   bitter jealousy.

                such   such
                lack of compassion   selfish conceit

The words spun epic symphonies of sin around the congregation, hanging tight-gripped and rigid on every turn and word – *You see, for God, distance is not measured in miles. We do not need to travel to distant countries to be far away from Him.*

'This brother of yours was dead and is alive again; he was lost and is found.'

Lia could not help but think, 'The daughter' would have been wiser. She would have come back rich, riding on a fat calf,

dragging a dozen more behind her as gifts.
She would kill them and cook them into
the most delicious beef stews and there'd be
much more fun and
far less fuss.

During communion it was Matthew who tipped the cup to her
lips. She did not look up.

Scripture

Strong enough today to inscribe a bit of Job (10:8–11) on the
outside of her femoral vein for fun.

> *Did you not pour me out like milk and curdle me like cheese?*

It's a mystery. The way sheets of knitted skin are the only things
keeping us all in.

A Crossing Over

Lia had got the bus to the park and was sitting with her eyes closed
on her favourite bench. Its rusted copper plaque read –

> *In remembrance of Samuel Money, who hated this park*
> *and everyone in it.*

She was thinking of Iris and the maggots and the burn on her
hand and wondering whether the world was getting crueller or just
clearer, when she opened her eyes slightly to see
a leafy man with soil for skin
and dandelions for eyes

yew out of a tree
only a few yards
away.

She blinked three times.

There was no man, only a shadow, black-flat on the grass.
The sun had come out.

He said you'd be here.

Iris's voice came from behind the bench.

Anne was there too, only standing at a strange distance. She
had come to spend an evening with them, had made a little bed
for herself on their sofa and insisted she pick Iris up from school
despite Lia telling her she didn't need to.

Iris looked sore and said *sorry* in a very small, very sincere voice.
Anne watched both of them intently the same way she watched
the cannula go into Lia's vein, like she was observing something
unfamiliar, anomalous.

Iris went to sit next to her mother and hugged her as if to say –
Things are starting to sour, aren't they. We need to try harder,
we need to be cleverer.

Lia nodded at Anne, who edged awkwardly towards them
clutching a brown paper bag.

Gandy picked me up from school.

Anne winced.

They had tried Nan, Gran and Granny very many years ago when
Iris had started to speak. She had first managed *Gandy*, which
they had delighted in; Anne had absolutely no interest in sharing
a name with an Indian Hindu activist. It stuck quite instantly.

A sense of humour is, sadly, one thing the Bible often forgets to prescribe, Lia had said to the sixteen-month-old Iris, wiping flecks of sweetcorn skin off her sticky chin, and Iris had chanted, *Houmer, houumer, hooooumer*, delighting in new tastes and shapes and sounds.

What's in the bag?

Anne pulled out two thick solemn books on cancer.

She looked incredibly tired, like she'd been thinking hard for the first time in her life. Lia could see all the small unresolved tensions knocking about madly inside her grey eyes.

Lia turned to Iris and said, *Let's go to the river, let's go for a walk and stretch our legs.*

Something about Anne's presence jolted Lia into Mother Mode. It was perhaps the paradox of their ways, the distance between them that made Lia want to grab her daughter and be as close to her as possible, push her right back inside her womb.

Iris kicked at stones and stared out across the water to the large houses lining the bank, clutching her mother's arm. It felt incredibly thin, more insubstantial than she'd ever known an arm to be, and she could sense something inside her chest diminish slowly with every drag of her shoes against the dirt.

A cloud the shape of a spleen
had begun to vomit up its insides
all over Hammersmith Bridge;
Lia's liver ached.

What did you do today at school?

History. Maths test.

Lia could feel her mother scraping her brain for something relevant to say before she landed on: *Your mother was never very good with numbers*. Iris laughed kindly, Lia sighed, Anne shrank, eyes fixed on the single duckling, whistling through the still water.

A young boy in a bright red coat sped past them on a bike. *Slow down!* his mother shouted, running as fast as she could behind him. As if the sharp notes of her voice were propelling the boy forward, he picked up pace, lifting himself slightly off the seat. The mother slowed, taking great gasps of air. As she passed them she turned to Lia, shot her a *boys* expression and rolled her eyes as her son's bike swayed from side to side, his coat flying up like a cape until he was nothing but a spot of red shrinking through a tunnel of skeletal trees. The mother's calves flexed as she started up again, and Lia felt as if she were blundering into madness.

Are you OK, Mum? Iris asked, quietly.

Yes.

Anne scratched the back of her head, exhaled loudly, craned her neck and made a small tut of discomfort. Lia turned to look at her mother's face which was paler than usual, her eyes a round keen black.

Are you OK, Mum? Lia asked, pretending not to be enjoying the strange fact of the three of them, walking together like this.

Old bones, Anne said. *Particularly dreary weather this week.*

Iris nodded in agreement, pulling up the hood of her
jumper, but to Lia, despite the spattering of rain
which was coming and going gently with the wind,
the sun was quite clearly
straining out thick pillars of light from
the holes in copper clouds, the three of them
skimming through a celestial yellow like
none she'd ever seen before.

A gust of wind licked along the path, a tease of
early autumn ash catching on its tongue.
Lia blinked three times. The colours shifted an octave.

Are you sure you're OK? Iris tightened her grip on Lia's arm.

I think there's something in my eye, Lia said, pulling on her eyelashes.
Three came straight out like they were only Pritt-sticked on.

She leant her index finger out to Iris.

Make a wish.

You have them.

They're yours. Quick, before the wind gets them.

Iris blew hard on her mother's finger and stole two wishes in
exchange for two eyelashes.

The wind took the last.

Wishes

In the fingers you can feel the poise and reach of a life.

There is so much sensation stored in the tips;
that densely packed nerve network, tracing texture
with its sensors, receiving a breath's warm blow
before the breath shivers up and down and up
again, at 268 mph, to the place I am yet to go.
It is moments like these, as a little of me peels
around her index, when the outside world feels

only a wish away.

The Elder

Over the next few months of parish life, Lia thought often of the prodigal son, of the elder brother in the field who did not understand the kindness bestowed upon the younger and felt joined to him by bitterness, connected in their shared Sin of the Spirit.

It was like Matthew had been returned to them by some miracle, as if her parents had been quietly longing for a son, someone who would immerse themselves in the church as Lia never fully had. Now that he was there, there was hardly any space for her at all.

It was hard seeing Anne grow so tender around him. Lia once watched her cup his face with her palm for a second or two and felt nothing but rage, nothing but a large absence the shape of a mother's palm
right on the inside of her cheek.

I sense an anger in you, her father had said, after he'd baptised the newborn daughter of the village dentist and the church organist.

How is school, how are your friends?

I have no friends.

You must have friends — no one you speak to or confide in?

I have nothing to confide.

Who do you have fun with?

I have my own fun. I draw. I go for walks.

What about Matthew — are you getting along?

I have no opinion, no desire to get along.

She was a growing girl spinning
thousands of
silky little lies all
over the church floor to
catch a father-fly –
watch him squirm about her web.

Anthimeria, a Word-Talk

You choose or I choose?

You choose, Iris said, sitting up in bed looking a little subdued.

OK. What does the word Anthimeria sound like?

Iris thought hard for a second or two. Their word-talks had begun
to slow when Iris turned eight. By ten they had become a rarity.
But Iris was asking for them more regularly, now, as if desperately
fighting against the tug of time, and it was kind of her, Lia
thought, not to have ever let them stop completely. To still want
to spend those minutes with her, before the lights went out.

A loud red flower.

I think it's softer than that.

Iris thought harder with her eyes shut.

Ann-thhi-mmeer-ria.

Her tongue absorbed the sounds, letting them lead towards the
sense.

It sounds like a secret word for the shape the moon makes on still water.

Better.
Anthimeria is also the verbing of a noun. From the Greek 'anti' —
against, opposite 'meros' — part, it is a leap, a transformation,
a conversion from Thing to Action;
where we box away, crane up, curtain through
the certainty of what things are and what they could be.
The way light moons about on a flat plate of sea.

Iris felt her mind begin to spill into that still calm space before
sleep. She often did not follow Lia's word-talks, but she liked the
large difficult strangeness of them.

We have always liked it, this playful device, the clutter of it,
lurking in common phrases like
the caking on of paint or the flagging of a problem.

Lia foraged for more.

The booking of a flight or
the unhairing of thy head.

Iris smiled.

I guess you could see them as visual clues to a very invisible secret.

Lia wondered what this invisible secret was and arrived somewhere
vague but conclusive enough to draw her word-talk to a gentle
close.

Nothing as it seems is quite good enough for
the probing
human
eye.

There was a silence. Lia watched as Iris's cheek and lips loosened
in that way they did when

sleep got the better of her. It was a surprise, then, that Iris suddenly responded:

Or maybe it's the opposite.

Lia kissed her forehead, watched her slip on past the edges of sleep and said,
quite right
quite quietly.

The *right* ripped deep into Iris's first Tuesday Night Dream, carving a point of entry – her mother's voice ventriloquized by a fat face-painted actor on a smoky stage:

RIGHT, LADIES AND GENTLEMEN,
ARE YOU READY FOR THE SHOW OF YOUR LIVES

Iris's small dream self sat in the stalls staring up at his stained lips, thinking, This'll be a strange one.

Downstairs the other mother was sitting, clutching her cancer books which she had not put down.
Harry was at the sink cutting stems off lilies, offering unobtrusive questions to the woman
who rarely visited, who rarely took any interest in him or their modest godless life.
It was strange for Lia to witness such points of intersection between past and present, between different spheres and
palettes, but perhaps, just perhaps, something in her mother was shifting; something in her
was brighter and sharper like the lead end of a
4H pencil poised before
a sketch, and
Harry sensed this too, propping his lilies
into a jug.

She is lovely, you know.

Sometimes.

She is just like you.

Oh, I don't think so.

The sky stirred. Somewhere above their small house;
the proud sound of History,
Doing Her Duty.

A Quatrain Cameo in the Daughter's Dream

{Tonight's show will take place in the Thoracic Duct}

Right, Sweet Ladies, Fine Gentlemen,
        though I've been lying low
I'm back now to present to you
        a real hoot-damn-good show!

On this ancient stage tonight
        a feast of beasts galore;
the meeting of a cavalry
        you've never seen before:

A yellow girl, a man of earth,
        bold Velvet and old Dove,
each driven by their hope, their fear
        of losing what they love.

From the stalls out blasts poor Fossil,
        our pyroclastic mute;
disguised romantic lead, perhaps
        the scoundrel, fool or brute?

Through the orchestra, our chorus,
    they sing their splintered notes:
'There's beauty in the hospitals
    and horrors in the oats!'

But Oh! Here burns dear devil Red,
    setting curtains all ablaze
(you'll find some glasses under seats
    to shield you from the rays).

Dove screeches like a harvest spoilt,
    The Gardener waters down,
while Yellow dreams of life before
    pain swept the last playground.

And though this is my costume cue,
    I'll say (as humble host),
be sure to always keep in mind:
    the villains care the most

Ruins

Matthew was perching on the edge of Lia's ruins.

It was autumn. The leaves from the vicarage garden had made a naked display inside the crumbled walls and Lia was crouched on wet heels, damp arms tucked, knees bent, observing their orange bones.

Matthew twisted his neck to the side as he asked if she wasn't a bit old to still be coming here when she got angry, when she got that hot red rage feeling.

Lia looked up and asked how he knew about that, how he knew about that feeling, and he shrugged and said it took one to know one.

She was not proud of the current of warmth that surged through her muscles.

She had just turned fourteen, and the day had been one of her worst. The twins from the village had invited her to go and swim in the lake and for the first time she felt that the mystery of friendship might be revealing itself ever so slightly, peering out from behind the velvet curtain ready to spin out and into her life. They had run ahead of her and called back, *Come on, let's jump in!* as if their sparkling lives depended on this chase, this shrouded speeding moment, and Lia could feel her mind tripping clumsily over the fresh new luxury of it. Their thin legs began to disappear down the ledge, slight bodies swallowed by the dip in the earth followed by their heads, a final gleam of blonde. Lia picked up her pace, unbuttoning her school shirt until she finally caught up to see –

they were not alone. The lake was full of familiar faces. From the village, from school. Some younger splashing and screaming, some older floating coolly or wrapped in towels, leaning on each other. Her mind snagged on the terrible thought that this invitation was not so special after all, that she was and always would be nothing more than a mere afterthought.

But what was that? One of the twins had twisted onto her back in the water, her long blonde hair pulsing around her face as she was calling, *Come on, come on!*

Lia plunged.

The water was so sharp she wanted to scream, but it was the kind of hurt that shocked at first and got quickly better. The twins spluttered kind smiles. Somewhere behind them a boy bombed in.

From somewhere else – a loud theatrical laugh. Lia swam about watching, writhing gleefully inside the chill, weeds wrapping about her legs. A girl let out a guttural *WHAT IS THAT?* The twins said, *For God's sake, it's only seaweed.*

Can't be seaweed, we're not in the sea, the girl spat back, her eyes fixed on the bombing boy who had not so much as glanced at her.

Lia wondered if any sea-creatures or gilled women were living
at the bottom of the lake, if they were sliding about under them
waiting to pick and pull at
their bare paddling legs – which must seem, to anyone mirroring
along the lake bed, rather like
lost roots
looking for soil.

She listened to the conversations carrying around her, conscious of how little she had to contribute, of how different and separate she felt from them all. She had nothing, she thought, nothing but the sad shielding fact that she was the vicar's daughter, and no one could explicitly bully her because it would without a doubt get back to God.

Scraping hair off her face and flexing wet shoulders back, one of the twins announced she was cold. She began to silk out of the water. The other followed suit. Just when Lia thought they had forgotten she was there, they both looked back and said, *Coming?* – eyebrows raised, nipples poking out through matching white vests tight as cling film. Nobody stared. Nobody seemed remotely interested in what anyone looked like, and Lia had waded out behind them confident and unthinking, and one of the boys had grimaced quite suddenly and pointed at her legs, and she had looked down in horror to see red blood making its quick way down the inside of her thigh.

The vicar's daughter is bleeding, look look look, oh God, look! The twins' expressions changed; they launched themselves into action, looking loudly for a spare towel or anything at all to shield her from the rest but it made it worse, it was too late, Lia was ripping up the dip in the earth, grabbing her trampled clothes, sliding on her shoes, taking gulps of air, feeling as if her lungs, her insides were about to collapse.

As she ran, she could feel the thick bead of blood speeding down her calf, like a finger sliding along a seam.

At home Lia wrapped toilet paper around her stained pants like a bandage, over and over and over until the blood no longer seeped through into the white. She sat on the loo seeing throngs of wincing faces in the bathroom tiles, thinking about the curious benevolence of the twins.

She did not cry.

It was not just shame that she felt but sin. A ceremonial unclean.

But as she found herself laying out these awful events, occasionally glancing up at Matthew's hard, unflinching face, the whole thing began to feel silly, small, almost amusing.

Twelve years later, lying amongst the last of the poppies in the red field just north of Rome, Matthew would tell her how startled he had been by her frankness that day, by the ease with which she had shared such intimate details. It had proven to him what he had felt all along; that her shyness and seeming disdain for him had been nothing but a great facade. That beneath it all, she was really very bold and self-assured, and they had trusted one another profoundly, right from the very start.

The Bathroom Files

I heard once that **bears can smell** women on their periods. This is why you never see female **campers** in Yellowstone National Park, Wyoming, USA. I also heard from an Italian woman that it's bad **luck** to **bake bread** whilst menstruating. The dough **won't** rise.

In Leviticus you'll find quite a bit of **talk** about the passing on of impurities.

I do not have much of an opinion on any of this, but what I will say is that the walls here are a **real eyeful**, a mosaic of endometrial layers patchedtightlytogether. If you look closely beyond the great pattern and into the sum of parts, you'll see in each piece a perfectly painted expression of horror, **pulsing** blo**nde** lo**cks**, pointing fingers, Fossil's unflinching face. They **decorate** the place like art in a **prehistoric cave**. If you move on, they begin to **change**, the grimacing tiles of faces, into packets of pills forgotten, **stains** on the seats of school chairs, shifting uncomfortable in the toilet cubicle of a plane 40,000 feet high. *Hurry up please, I'm bursting,* *hurry up please, it's time*. There are fragments of feminist literature folded in the frays of her fimbriae; bits of Rich and Loy and Daly and Lorde I see: *(if God is Male than Male is God) and* *so I* dive into the wreck of her **FSH where her follicles are so few** few phew soon there will be ~~none~~ ~~after~~ **Red blazes** ~~through~~.

The Mystery of Friendship

Connie had kissed Lia the first week they met.

They had been drunk and young and Lia had felt for a sharp,
hopeful moment that they could have been more than friends,
that she could be rid of this strange unnatural desire for men, for
him, completely. They had carried on kissing and laughing lightly,
but as the evening hurtled towards morning Lia felt that she was
putting on a sick show, that the Lord was watching and laughing
and muttering disapprovingly because He knew, He knew about all
those years under the covers grinding and fading away from herself.
He knew.

Lia had said, *I'm not sure I want to do that again, not with you*, and
Connie had laughed this huge gracious laugh and said, *That's OK,*
I am sure I can find
some other use for you.

And then Connie had walked carefully around Lia's life drawings,
scattered across the floor, right to the fridge, and taken out a can
of beer and had cracked it open like she was planning to be there
a long time, like she had no intention of leaving and it was true,
she hadn't,
she wouldn't;
she would be there always.

Time had elided the facts of their first meaningful interaction,
because it seemed to undermine that pure raw something that
dances through the bloodstream of
any true friendship.

Eavesdropping

It was late at night and Harry wanted to have sex. It was not a persistent want, simply a: *I know you are ill, however I still desire you.*

But Lia was eavesdropping on her past, blushing quietly, pressing her ear hard against
walls twenty-eight years thick:

Do you like this?

Yes.

Does it feel nice?

Yes.

What about this?

Oh.
God.

Where have you gone? Harry asked.

Nowhere.

Lies

I love it when she lies. I can feel guilt t
                                           r
                                             i
                                               c
                                             k
                                               l
                                                 e

through her like coins through a slot machine,

collecting at the place
where desire starts.

April

It started in April.

In poetry, all time begins in April.

It was for this reason that Lia often doubted it did, in fact,
start in April. She often thought that perhaps the events had
secured themselves in April by virtue of the romantic logic that
governed/meddled/fiddled with notches of her memory at that
time, but somewhere near the unresolved end of this doubt came
those clear-cut visions of the tragic summer that followed, and
she would concede;
yes, yes –
it started in April.

Lia was fifteen and had got used to Matthew coming and going; he
was at university now studying philosophy and theology and would
come back with tales of independence, of parties, of his newfound
love of Latin and the Pixies.

It was the week of his nineteenth birthday. When he came in
through the door, he had to dip his head slightly which he did with
a smile only Lia saw, a confirmatory smile like he was pleased he
had grown out of the place. As always, he seemed changed; his new
skin had begun to map out the suggestion of stubble, the spaces
under his eyes were a sunken grey from sleepless nights, and his
hair was shorter than it had ever been so that for the first time she
could see the exact shape of his skull, the bend in his neck where
his spine scooped up.

You look cold, Lia said. He was wearing a discoloured T-shirt that looked like it used to be white but now was quite grey. His arms had goose bumps all over them which made him suddenly seem very vulnerable, very human.

And you look older.

Something struck the base note of her stomach.

Anne had curated a glorious display on the kitchen table. Three milk bottles full of cow parsley were placed down the middle, their best cutlery had been polished, and there was a roast chicken browning in the oven; to anyone peering in through the window of their lives the scene would have appeared cut from absolute domestic perfection.

Father Peter came into the kitchen beaming, moving to shake Matthew's hand which quickly turned into a tight embrace, a pat on the back, a *Good to see you, my boy,*

Good To See You.

They sat like the strange nuclear family that they were, blessed the food, clasping hands together. Matthew spoke mostly of his studies; Anne offered up fragments of village gossip in between spoonfuls of dry carrots and undercooked potatoes. Father Peter mentioned how well Lia was doing at school, *Top of her class, her teachers say.* Lia blushed. Matthew said, *That's good. I'm pleased.* Lia waited for one of his teasing looks but it never came; instead he just blinked sincerely at her and went to carve more meat from the chicken carcass. Drinking in the vicarage was reserved for special occasions, and Lia was allowed a glass of wine. Halfway through it she began to feel lightheaded, dizzy. As if the alcohol were awakening a new sort of hunger within her. Satisfying, then widening it. There was a buzzing in the back of her brain; she focused on its spreading and spilling out into her ears. Matthew's voice was growing louder and more confident with each glass. His eyes were all barking and electric and the charm of his usual enthusiasm had gained an edge, a kind of uncomfortable persistence that Peter must have noticed too because he was watching Matthew very curiously, his long pale neck leant out as far as it would go.

Toasts were made to Matthew's good health, to a successful year, *May the God of hope fill you with all joy and peace in believing*, Father Peter said, holding his gaze, taking his time with every word. A remarkably soft smile had broken across Anne's face. Like a strange, sudden bud, Lia thought. Like bluebells breaking through the thickest sheet of white snow.

Late that night, when everyone had stumbled upstairs stuffed and drunk on the perfect oddness of the evening, Lia lay flat on her back in her bed, staring up at the ceiling, her hands down the elastic of her pants. She touched herself like this most nights now, never building towards something, only falling through the soft molten layers of sensation. She had just begun to sink when there was a very gentle rhetorical knock at her bedroom door. Matthew slid in before she had time to answer and she leapt up from her bed, body trembling.

Oh my God, you can't just walk in like that, you scared me.

He laughed. *I'm sorry I'm sorry, I just came to give you this –*

He handed her a cassette player and a tape. The tape had a sticker with 'Lia' written assertively in blue. It would have been romantic but the straightness of the letters, the unthinking ease in which they were printed, secured it all in a Safe Act of Brotherly Consideration.

Lia said *thanks* but inside she was screaming

WHAT THE FUCK IS HAPPENING?

He said something about feeling sorry for her being here all locked away, missing out on the world he was getting to see, something about the tracks on the tape being a *taste of the outside*, and Lia could not look at him. Instead she stared down at her name on the tape, thinking surely not surely not, look at how straight that L is, what does he want?

He put the headphones over her ears. His fingers did not linger on loose strands of hair, only the tip of his thumb grazed her face accidentally. He seemed not to notice this.

And then, ebbing into her ears came a persistent beat, these milky synthetic sounds unlike anything she'd ever heard before. She listened intently for thirty seconds, eyes fixed on the fold where the floorboards met the wall. After a minute she began to taste it in her mouth, this strange melody, this windswept pitch crooning out the tune of her most intimate desires, pooling underneath the presence of Matthew, Matthew who had somehow muted the entire natural world with his gaze, with one click of a button.

He was standing over her now, closer than he'd ever been.

What did he want?

A small lifetime looped.

Lia glanced up.

He flashed a golden smile. Raised his eyebrows slightly as if to ask, Do you like it?

She nodded. And then his beautiful face was breaking through the air thick with the music only she could hear; and then he was kissing her,

kissing her hard,
pinching her bottom lip with his teeth,
pressing his thumbs deep into her cheeks
as if it were the most precise way for a human to communicate
an idea.

It is a remarkable thing that Lia's senses did not rupture
there and then, that no one was harmed in the making
of the kiss.

Had the moment been plucked from a film it would have stopped
there.

Lia would have closed her eyes, and with one last passionate
stroke of her lips Matthew would have left her to arrive back to
herself alone, back to her same small room, back to discover, upon
opening them, that she'd been equipped with a new set of eyes,
and, *oh*, a new mouth, which she would touch disbelievingly with
the tips of her fingers before getting into bed feeling more awake
than she'd ever been, thinking,

Oh God, this is love,   this is love.

The camera would move across the thin wall separating their
rooms to reveal two bodies perfectly mirrored; him gazing up in
disbelief, her euphoric with the promises of youth. The camera
would then appear to move up up up through the attic of the
vicarage, up through its flimsy structure, up until the fields seemed
to hold the small boxy vicarage in its blue moon palms up, up until
the house bearing the weight of two electric lovers was nothing but
a spot of light in the deep infinite pools of God's Good Land.

Had it been a relatively high-budget film, this would certainly have
happened.

But nothing is perfect for longer than the length of a song; the
headphones came off, anxious synths fell to a mere chink chink

chink at the end
of a swinging black cord as
Lia fell back against the bed.
Matthew spat on his hand, began to move its wet
up her leg.

Do you like this?

Yes.

Does it feel nice?

Yes.

What about this?

Oh.
God.

Fossil Finds His Voice in Her Cervix

Fossil: Oh. God.

The Gardener: What?

Fossil: My voice!

The Gardener: What about it?

Fossil: I have a voice!

The Gardener: Oh shit. So you do.

The Coffee Machine

The coffee machine outside Harry's office had been broken for three weeks now. At first, it had not bothered him, but now it meant he was taking regular trips to the cafe, which meant making small talk with students, with other professors, with the postgraduate who, since their brief conversation at the drinks do, had begun to linger behind after his lectures making nebulous enquiries about library resources. At the party, she had cut across the room, direct and charming in an apricot top and confidently applied red lipstick, and Harry remembered noticing the striking blondeness of her eyebrows, the freshness of her face, the unthinking boldness with which she held herself in this apricot top, or perhaps it was a shirt, moving towards him through the sea of hopeful corduroy jackets and mohair sweaters. He remembered thinking that she seemed to lack the self-awareness of other women her age, as she approached him, clunking her glass of gin on the edge of the bar and smiling widely, and that her energy was nice and rare and made him feel rather relaxed himself.

Harry was not the sort of professor the students made beelines for. This had nothing to do with how attractive he was or was not. He had, in fact, been delighted to catch the conclusion of a heated debate between three undergraduates on the most fuckable faculty members only a week or so ago, in which he had come in at a very satisfactory second place after the inevitable Dr Tom Murphy, the alarmingly handsome Canadian archaeology scholar. The problem was that he had the glazed sexual energy of a man who simply adored his wife, who had met the love of his life and no one, not even a charming postgraduate in a provocative apricot cotton-top-shirt-thing (because, as he came to think of it, it really was rather provocative, though perhaps only accidentally so, the way pottery and preserved fruit are) could wipe the glaze clean.

He knew this frustrated Lia. It got on the nerves of that tiny, most ridiculous part of her. He knew this because she would look so suddenly alive when asking him things like, *But have you ever thought about it?* as if there was a right answer, and when he would say, quite honestly, *No*, a shadow of disappointment would edge into the whites of her eyes and he would feel sorry, sorry that her restlessness was not the same as his, sorry that he was content and she would be searching forever.

The cafe was full of that usual artificial scent of defrosted bread and cake and pastries staling quietly away inside their plastic packets. Harry spotted her the moment he walked into the room. She was buying an egg and watercress sandwich, her hands deep in her coat pocket, rummaging for change. He decided that there was definitely something endearing about her. Something skittish, ornate. He hid in the queue behind two students speaking animatedly about a summer spent in Prague and hoped that nobody would notice him.

The inevitable Dr Tom Murphy had told him a terrible story the other day. A story that kept returning to the forefront of Harry's brain whenever it had the opportunity to squeeze itself there. It featured a third-year they both taught – Elisa May – and had taken place in the Pearson Lecture Hall, on what Tom called *The Best Day of My Working Life*. He recounted the way Elisa had been curled up under the lecture table, which was very conveniently covered by a flat slab of oak veneer at the front, entirely open at the back, and came up to just above his hips. Just as they had discussed, he had walked over to the desktop on the table, pretending not to notice her, pretending to send an email or two, while she rubbed him until he was hard enough, unzipped his trousers and took him into her wet mouth, making these hungry little groaning sounds so that her tonsils trembled against his tip. *Fuck,* Tom said, as if he was right back there, being swallowed and sucked and gently gnawed on, *fuck it was hot.* They'd lost track of time. Students had begun to fill the hall and take their seats for his 2.30 on the Siege of Ambracia, and Tom had had no choice, no choice at all, but to begin the lecture. *So there I was,* he'd said, chewing on his Greek salad, looking incredibly pleased with himself, *trying to get through the various siege machinery the Romans used to tunnel under the city, while she's sliding her tongue all the way under my balls,* and though Harry had felt distinctly uncomfortable for the duration of the salad, he noted that it was quite impossible to snuff out the tiny part of himself that also felt a little impressed. Not, of course, with the story itself, but with the staggering confidence of this man he hardly knew, sharing the intimate details of Elisa's technique like it was just another regular part of a good educator's day, as if he were merely discussing his workload with a colleague in the increasingly disappointing university cafe.

When Harry had told Lia that evening, she'd said, *When was that then?* whilst tapping something into her phone. *From 2.30 to 3.30 last Thursday, I guess,* he'd said, and she'd laughed and said, *No,* and had turned her phone to him. On the phone was the date 189 BC. In the Google search bar she had typed the question: when was the Siege of Ambracia?

The postgraduate was now sipping on black coffee, struggling to peel away the packaging of the egg and watercress sandwich with very short bitten nails. Harry had begun to feel impatient. Perhaps he was too sensitive. Perhaps he was a prude. His mind was sliding into areas he did not want to explore today. He kept his head down and concentrated on the conversation of the students just ahead of him. They were discussing a man one of them had met at a bar in Budapest. *Nothing to write home about. It was fine. Just fine? He was very . . . respectful.* And the terrible knowing laughter that followed seemed to burn like a city in the sharp of his heart, because it was everywhere, Harry thought, as the laughing students ordered their teas and rolled their eyes at the particular tragedy of respectful sex, it was there in the debate about fuckable professors, there in the queue to the cafe, there in the syllabus and the songs and their kitchen, while Harry peeled parsnips and Lia looked at them thoughtfully and said things like *root vegetables would sometimes give him a rash*, and that *him* would come crashing into their days, wreaking its simple havoc. For Harry knew it all. He knew the details of Lia's history and his violence (he would not think his name), even a little of their lust, and though he loved Lia mostly for her startling honesty, it was sometimes too much, too harsh, too true, and he would find himself feeling both threatened and bruised.

He ordered his coffee, though he had lost all appetite. He glanced over at the postgraduate, who was managing to look blissfully happy and comfortable in the act of eating a very loaded sandwich at a table quite alone, something he had always considered near impossible. There was a lick of cress hanging slightly from the edge of her mouth and as her cheeks moved the cress fell onto her knee, followed by a slice of egg white coated thickly in mayonnaise. She looked up to see if anyone had noticed. The second before her eyes met Harry's, he was gone.

Perhaps Tom Murphy was not the problem. Perhaps it was even regressive of him to assume that Elisa May was a victim. She was an adult, after all, and perfectly capable of making her own decisions. The problem was Matthew (he hated thinking his name). Matthew, whose large and looming presence in Lia's past often made Harry wonder (on his worst, most ridiculous days) if there was something lacking in his own biology. Some fundamental weakness that made him a little less than other men.

When he got back to his office the coffee machine's 'BROKEN!' paper note had been replaced with another which read:

FIXED ☺

The Particular Wisdom of Charlotte York

In Season 5 Episode 1 of
Sex and the City
Charlotte insists over brunch that
everyone knows you only get
Two Great Loves.

I picked up this fact many years ago, and it stuck the way a thing
does when it's said with such conviction and by a woman wearing
such a beautiful head of hair that it hardly matters at all what the
thing itself is, only that it sounds as sure and as sensible as sweet
perfume on polyester.

I've remembered it to this day.

I will not pretend to be an expert on the subject, but I've seen
my fair share of passings and comings and goings and as I look at
these two now, The Gardener and Fossil, polar opposite but full
of purpose,
sifting through pieces of
sweaty sex history,
I think –

perhaps Charlotte was right all along.

Vanishing Acts

When Lia was very pregnant with Iris she would make herself
come four to seven times a day. Google told her this had something
to do with: *The hormones oestrogen and progesterone, which in
addition to supporting your continuing pregnancy, also increase vaginal
lubrication, blood flow to the pelvic area, and the sensitivity of your
breasts and nipples.*

She'd sit on the floor watching television with a cushion underneath her, the small coffee table in her flat pulled up to her breasts so that when she looked down her swollen body ceased to exist, and she'd float and shiver and quake until she nearly fainted.

Sacred Sites

In the good old medieval times, they believed the devil could latch on, and draw out a woman's soul from the tip of the clit.

It took scientists more than 2,000 years to work out what this place really was. Still, it's a relatively unexplored marvel. There are 8,000 nerve endings which connect up to another 15,000 nerves, forming a deep glowing anthill of fierce electrical currents all contained in her pelvis. You could power a whole city with the stuff. For some – Dove, for example – this neatly packed interior organ system is a terrible theological problem. She won't come anywhere near despite Red's numbing and dulling and fire-drying. For others, the Clitoris might sit between the Ontological and Teleological as one of the Great Arguments for God. This all depends on how you understand desire, see.

Me? I am reminded of geothermal activity. Hot springs.
The way geysers plummet up, drawn out from Earth's crust
suddenly, soaring, soul-molten hot, but as all things must
it
comes
back
down,
it bubbles
it smokes
it hardens,
it waits for the next essential reaction.

The Choreography of Departures

Weeks-deep into the tragic summer, Lia was watching the new world pulsing and clipping behind the window of the bus into town, feeling swollen with his absence. These transitions were the hardest things. It was as if her body were undergoing a quick and violent state change from a liquid to a solid, from glorious sex-smothered girl to just another person sitting on a bus, getting off a bus, waiting to cross the road. It was such a shock to the system, she wondered how anyone got used to it.

The town was heaving with bodies in short skirts and sandals and thin fabrics, sweating in the hot vinegary air. August shimmered unnaturally. The fleshy shoulders and metal shop signs and cobbled streets were so luminous they made Lia feel distinctly unreal. Floating and hollow. She could not remember why she was there. The record shop was blasting a song that she recognized from Matthew's tape and it grounded her, momentarily, as if he were reaching out towards her through the sickly, glittering day to say, *It is real, Lia. It is real.* She had listened to the tracks so many times that the lyrics had begun to feel like instructions; codes to another universe with their own reeling moons and planets, gods and false icons.

Outside the shopfront a group of girls were gathered, chewing gum, talking about music like it was something that could be shared. She would have felt jealous of them once, clustered together like this, full of purpose and ease and belonging, but she felt apart from them now, in some higher sense, as if her needs no longer bore any resemblance to theirs, as if Matthew had made her a new, more sophisticated species altogether. Love makes you many things, Lia thought, but perhaps, worst of all, is Smug.

She watched one of the girls bend down to her bag, exposing a perfectly round breast cupped in lilac lace. Anne had sent her into town for new clothes; she had grown out of everything she owned and she must look quite ridiculous, she thought, in her mother's old hiking shorts, a shapeless vest, a flattening multi-pack sports bra.

They had to be very discreet. This was, perhaps, the most thrilling part. Matthew would clamber so urgently into her small plain room the moment Anne and Peter left the house – *There you are*, he'd say, relieved, always a little surprised, as if unsure of her existence outside of their secret. It was safest on their walks, outside, in the hidden pockets of the land they had claimed as their own. He would bury her body deep into the hedgerows or beneath the high grey bracken of Mr Birch's fields, pin her up against the trees in the woods, his hands so certain of what to do and where to be depending on the dip, the limb, the curve, the sudden crease. He made it so that every time was filthier, more surprising than the last, reversing the chronology of the usual acts so that sex was often the foreplay, the moment their lips first touched the climax of it all. *I want us to forget*, he'd say. *Forget what?* she'd ask, thick tree roots digging between the bones in her back. *Where and who and what we are.*

Lia tried.

But it was exhausting. Living perpetually in the spill like this, terrified of its ending. Because what if they were to find out? What if he simply got bored? And how on earth, Lia thought, her pace quickening, shoulders bumping lightly against hot sticky skins all barging through the busy streets, how on earth did people live like this?

The crowd spat her out at a corner. She huddled in the quiet shade of a shop's striped awning, gathering back her breath. In the window, a mannequin flaunted its perfect plastic body. Hanging from it was a black silk dress with the thinnest straps and thick embroidered lace panels at the neckline, circling around the hem.

Lia pressed her forehead against the pane, relishing the sudden lovely cold. Yes, she thought, she would buy this dress. She would feel irresistible. Sophisticated. The sort of woman that knew how to put sex on and take it off again. Somebody with absolutely no doubt as to whether their lover would be returning.

Later that week, Matthew stopped by and stayed the night.

Anne watched them from the kitchen window heading off on one of their usual walks. They were growing closer, which was nice, and perhaps inevitable, she supposed. Though she hated to admit it, there was no doubt that Lia was beginning to grow into a particular sort of beauty. Perhaps beauty was too strong a word. Perhaps age had simply refined what was once a broad, scrappy prettiness, though it was very hard to put one's finger on it, Anne thought, very hard to know what to do with it all.

Lia was in one of Peter's large knit jumpers and nothing much else. The jumper was an earthy, chicken-liver brown, its frayed edge came down to her knees, and as she let it hang loosely off her left shoulder, her legs bending and locking, hips swaying a little, the whole thing made Anne feel incredibly anxious.

She had been watching Matthew closely for any signs; any flickers of attraction or new interest in Lia, but he seemed not to have noticed any change in her at all. He looked at her no differently. He was as considerate and polite and attentive to them all as he'd always been, always so good at putting Anne at ease. *You worry too much*, he'd say, arm tightly around her, squeezing her close, switching the radio on to Peter's favourite hymns channel, settling in for the evening to discuss his newfound love of the Book of Ruth, or some other subject he'd set his heart on that month.

No. The problem was Lia. The way that she watched him so hungrily, her gaze so direct it had developed its own metallic shine. Anne would catch its edges in the quick light of the living room and have the sudden urge to stand in front of him, stare down the barrel of her daughter's pointed gaze, make her stop.

A pressure had begun to build in her chest; Anne could feel her nerves getting the better of her. What had the exercise been? She closed her eyes tight, trying to remember it, trying to take herself back there. She had been young – twenty-four or so, walking in the scraping heat along the mountain ridge just east of Jerusalem. The tour guide had asked them to turn to the stranger next to them. Share a personal struggle. The man walking quietly beside her had been a little older, with a face that seemed to encourage honesty. *I have a temper*, Anne had told him. *I get upset. Worked up.*

She had never said anything like this out loud before.

The man had nodded seriously.

Me too, he'd said. *There is an exercise I do. To calm myself. Would you like to hear it?*

Anne had nodded, looking out at the holy land baking dry and brilliant below them.

First, I imagine clay on my lids, the man had said, so softly, and Anne closed her eyes, imagining the cool weight of clay, listening closely to his every word. *Perhaps the press of His fingertips. Gentle. Healing. I move through the darkness and arrive at a pool. Can you see it? The pool?*

Yes, Anne had breathed. *I see it.*

Good. Now bend down to it. Face the reflection of your anger. Fear. Whatever it is – really examine it. Remember that in every wrong, sin and error is a truth. A test.
And then you wash.

Anne washed.

You gasp.

Anne gasped.

You open.

Anne opened.

A pick of white was glinting out at her from the middle of the vicarage garden. It took her a second to locate the context of her face, to realize that it was the reflection of her own toothy smile, so wide she hardly recognized herself.

The man had, of course, been Peter. Two years later, they had been married.

Two fields away, Matthew and Lia were still walking at a polite distance apart.

He must have decided they were far enough, because he turned to her, slid his thumb along her lips and kissed her, his tongue flicking deep into her mouth.

You taste like melon.

He licked up the side of her neck, her chin. She pulled Peter's liver-brown jumper off over her head and stepped back, so he could take in all of her, itching in the tight black silk in the middle of the field, looking like a woman from another time.

She watched his expression remain controlled. Curious. She lifted the dress up a little, scrunching it in her fingers, so that he could see the auburn wisps of her pubic hair, and began to grin. The seriousness building slowly between them collapsed, and he lunged for her bare legs, hauling her over his shoulders, and as he ran with her up to the tree at the top of the mound, his shoulder blade slotted deep as a missing piece into the curve of her ribs, she was back again, liquid through the torch of his touch; holy, devoted, his.

In the living room, Anne had set to work polishing the blue ceramic dogs on the mantelpiece.

What is it, she said suddenly to Peter, who had a pen between his teeth and a book of Newman's sermons resting open on his lap, *what is it that they talk about?*

Peter barely looked up from his reading.

I'm sure they find something, he said, dryly. *We do, don't we?*

Costumes

I'm disguised now
as a black synthetic dress
curdling in the hot spring heat,
dancing to The Cure.

When Red passes through, he barely notices me at all.

Just a dress, he thinks. Silly thing.

I execute a perfect sparkling giggle and busy myself
sinking from inguinal nodes into marrow, making wounds,
caressing another plot fit for *home, sweet home.*

I'm getting so good at this it's even hard for me to distinguish
myself from the acts, my stories from
facts.

four

Cancer, a Word-Talk

Are you sure?

Yes.

*Fine. If you follow Cancer back through time right to its ancient-ruin
roots you arrive at Hippocrates. 400 BC. He had a kind face. There is
a bronze statue of him in Kos in Greece, we will go one day. Your dad
has been. He came back as red as a crab shell. Sunburn so bad he could
not sleep for a week.*
*Cancer – from 'karkinos', Greek for crab. The kind-faced Hippocrates,
having sliced a tumour from a breast or throat, thought the lump, with
its clutching circle of blood vessels, looked much like the side-scuttling
beast; its claws settling deep into the sand of soft human tissue.*
And so the image saw the birth of the word.

Iris lay quite still in her very yellow room. The glow from her
bedside light against the walls made her feel like they were moving
about a strange cave together.

What does it sound like to you?

Can-cer.

It doesn't sound like anything. It sounds flat and cold like a slab of stone.

Iris's voice was flatter and colder than it had ever been before.
Lia did not know whether it was something worth mentioning,

for she knew the naming of a thing can often make it more true, more concrete. She decided not to.

Turning onto her side, hand tucked under her face, Iris asked, *Do you think it's working?*

What?

The chemo.

Lia was taken aback by the question, thrown by the plain answerlessness of it.

I can't tell.

How does it feel?

She thought hard.

Like there's something very toxic inside me just purging the whole place.

And it's that bad? All the time?

No. It's OK. Because you and your dad are there too, making it better. Easier.

Iris shrank a little into the mattress as if weighed down by sudden responsibility and Lia regretted saying anything.

Do you want to pick another word?

No.

OK.

The silence nudged Lia to leave. Once she got to the door, Iris's voice cracked through the room.

Why don't I have any brothers or sisters?

An earthquake sliced through a slab of pavement.

Not everyone has siblings. I didn't.

And you said you were lonely.

She felt a knot begin to tighten inside her. Nothing about Iris's tone was confrontational. The genuine curiosity of it was the worst thing; she had no escape routes. She swallowed, tried to release the knot, tug at it gently.

They told me I might get ill again if I had another child.

Ah.

Pause.

But you still got ill again.

Yes.

So it wasn't worth it. And now I am lonely too.

There was another long pause. Lia felt paralysed in the door frame, like a flat person waking up to find themselves trapped in the wrong painting.

It could have come back sooner. And then I'd have less time with you.

Iris went very quiet again; Lia wondered if she'd fallen asleep. If she'd gone too far again, been too honest.

Mum?

Yes.

I think we should stop our word-talks for good. I'm too old for them now.

OK.

Taking Score

Yellow is pale as cream, blessing vessels quietly.

I hear her whispering to herself.

I think it's winning, she says.

Her voice like poisoned apple pies,
stuffed full of sour pain.

Whatever it is, I think it's winning.

Music to my ears, that is.

Real sweetness against my lips.

Just So

Thumb is to (under, sink, press) as arms are to (gentle, raise, dress).
Hope is to (pace, verb, dinner) as never is to (mine, noun, remember).
Vessel is to (blood, ship, wound) as horror is to (Hitchcock, playground, crude).

Lia was trying to think positive thoughts whilst pushing the
clumps of hair coming out in her hands as far down into the bin
as they would go. It felt fitting that she had begun to shed with the
seasons. It was easier, perhaps, with the trees doing it too; as if she
might stand out less in the gradual bareness of the streets, parks
and branches.

Over the years, Harry's mother had sent her very many books
on the relationship between one's thoughts and organs, on how
to harness your illness with the right sort of yoghurt and finger

exercises and breathing techniques, or *nonsense*, as Connie called it. But it still nagged and troubled her. For if there was a possibility that she could help her body with her mind, there was the chance that her mind might have got her here in the first place. There were secrets that she still harboured, after all. It was a surprise how physical they felt some days.

How did that terrible Auden poem go?

Childless women get it.
And men when they retire;
It's as if there had to be some outlet
For their foiled creative fire.

The thought was too dark to dwell on.

She pictured Iris at school navigating her new life of terror whilst cleaning out the fridge tray full of moulding vegetables, and felt very worried for her. She pictured Harry being flirted at by the postgraduate outside the university library whilst picking out bits of cheese from the very specifically shaped egg compartment, and felt genuinely pleased for him.

Suddenly quite breathless, she slid slowly through the garden, sat at her drafting desk, switched the nib width of her pen and set to work finishing a hatching egg, the scrawny scalp of a baby bird just bursting through shards of shell scattered around the bottom of the page. Next, a boy waving from the hatch door of a plane, passing through clouds. A group of bandits huddled together in the left corner, hatching a plan, and all this was drawn, of course, in the most detailed hatched technique, the tight lines running parallel and crossing over one another in the darkest patches of shadow. But today, something was wrong with her fingers. The press, hold and poise of them lacked their usual certainty, all their confidence was gone, and the lines were performing in ways she couldn't understand. *It's all about digital now, anyway*, the publishers kept telling her. *You're wasting valuable time and effort with traditional media.*

The noun and the verb stared up lifelessly from the page. The words were dead black-ink eyes, and Lia felt like a mindless bird just pick pick picking away at
something cheap and trivial and singed in the last of a fire
just as it was being foiled.

Pinned up on a board to the left of her desk, a group of people looked down at her, quite unimpressed. They leant back against a large stone wall with their arms crossed, squinting into the sun, a youthful Lia amongst them, thin and severe and quite unrecognizable. The image was over-exposed and there was the smudge of a finger, a stroke of his ghost, obstructing the edge of the frame. She unpinned the photograph. On the back was a note that had never been sent. The pencil was so faint, a whisper of lead, like it didn't really want to be there at all:

~~Dear~~ Mum and Dad. Some days are perfect here. Some days

The note broke off. Lia shuddered. It was a very sad, very frightening thing. The unfinished words of a girl you once loved, giving up before she'd even begun.

She hadn't noticed her phone had rung. The nurse with the strong blue flute of a voice and the son who worked at the cinema had left a message. Lia's haemoglobin level was very low. *A normal level would be about eleven to eighteen grams per decilitre. Yours is seven.*

That would account for the breathlessness, Lia thought.

She stuck the pin back through his finger.

She was unable to help him,
because she had never really understood him.

You'll need to come in for a blood transfusion. Standard procedure.

For half an hour Lia googled low blood counts, and then watched a YouTube animation of a breast cancer cell dividing and dividing and dividing again, the image widening every thirty seconds or so to contain the expanding mass of badness, and though she kept expecting something else to happen, after ten minutes the video just ended, and then YouTube suggested that she watch this nice Mormon man from Ohio discussing sheep-farming techniques with his son, and so she did, and after five minutes she found that, thanks to the gentle acoustic soundtrack plucking quietly along in the background and the fact that the Mormon's son had just brought his own son out to feed the smallest lamb she'd ever seen, there were thick tears running quick down her cheeks. She slammed the laptop shut.

On the other side of the shed, the bookshelf had flattened and cubed itself into a Mondrian painting.

Lia stood, picked out an old edition of Kipling's *Just So Stories* and flicked through the tired illustrations, a clinging tobacco scent rising from the off-white pages. She pressed her nose to the spine between 'How the Rhinoceros Got His Skin' and 'The Crab that Played with the Sea' and began to read.

Perhaps Kipling had made some astute observations about cancer without even knowing it. Perhaps this illness was much like his crab: a creature who had missed the briefing at the very beginning; a distracted crustacean that had simply scuttled off-stage for a moment to observe the mad, backstage activity, while the Great Director rallied his actors, laid out their roles, and went on his way.

I did not know I was so important,
the cancer would say, when it realized the disturbance, the terror, the horrors it had caused to the tide of their lives.

I am ever so sorry, I had no idea.

The Great Director would be the kind of embarrassed that ruins
a god's career. His God-shaped shoulders would hang so low that
they slid off and plummeted straight into the Mediterranean.
The impact would begin two apologetic tidal waves
that would destroy the edges of Southern Europe,
Northern Africa,
simply drown the whole of
sweet
Sicily.

I cannot make you play the play you were meant to play,
the Great Director would say. And of course, it had been the young
girl who had saved the day, the daughter who had caught the crux
of things in the corner of her eye and had led the world back to its
natural order. If only all our stories were just so,
thought Lia, if only my story was

Just So.

Spielberg Techniques

The brilliance of *Jaws* resided in the fact that for most of the film,
you never witnessed the monster.

The minute the audience saw the fat teeth jutting out of those
bloody ketchup gums they may as well have been watching a
papier-mâché fish flap about a puddle, and that's the beauty of
me, see; you'll never *see* me, you'll never really *know* what it is
that's teeming in the waters, munching on your life, your wife,
biding its sweet time before it rises up,
sinks its jaws in.

Adolescence

When Matthew was gone, Lia's body dried out.
She got ill. She devoured books from the forbidden bookcase and
felt much like Catherine Earnshaw without the fits of sobbing,
Emily Brontë without the
sisters; just a girl stuck
in the rungs of time
flirting with the idea
of death.

An Invitation

Connie had come a long way from her small town in Wales.

Her grandmother had been a seamstress, and by the end of her
eighty-six gentle years, she had never left Wales. She built up a
small tailoring business in their village with her husband, whose
medals from the war hung on the ash green wall next to the till and
above the filing cabinet. Connie's mother had taken over once the
business had begun to suffer, and had launched its dry-cleaning
service, which saved it from bankruptcy. Connie would often
suggest to Lia that their youth had been cut from similar cloth,
shared the particular weave and silk of open doors and services,
and Lia could see this, could trace the early independence, the
smooth navigation of outward bustle in them both. But they were
not similar. Connie loudly welcomed the theatre of life; she sat at
the hot spinning centre of it, spoke confidently, addressed strangers
without caution and demanded plainly what she wanted.

And what this was she knew very early. To grow up with a practical
skill was to grow up a bilingual child; there was an ease and a
fluency that came with the language of costume. It was in her

blood, they said. From the age of seven Connie's mother was giving her piles of simple alterations to make. She'd call them the Doctor Bundles, items with loose buttons and small tears. It was not long before she began cutting her own patterns, drawing out shapes, learning the syntax, the licks, dips and turns of phrase to clumsily assemble a vernacular of her own. And then she began to design; to map, chart, measure and plot. She drew in confident thick strokes, cinched everything in at the wrong places, let layers of patterned skirt quench floors, made jackets, capes, hats, crowns that butchered then built upon her paper actors until there was no doubt at all that she had outgrown both the page and the place.

So here she was, somewhere very near where she had planned to be. There had been innumerable sacrifices. But now Lia's cancer was back she felt more powerless than she'd felt in years. She must do something, she thought, something to get their minds off it all. Lia was weak. That chemotherapy smell had begun to cling. It wasn't strong or particularly pungent – just very other, very unlike Lia's natural scent; with its little burning plastic notes, stain of vomit ploughing her usual doughy breath, that strange iridescence imprisoned in her cheeks.

She would send them an invitation to the opening night in the post. She would get them the best seats in the house, the third row back. Very centre.

She would write it on a piece of thick card, wrap a ribbon around it.

It was the sort of thing people never did any more, the sort of thing that would remind Lia of her travelling years, the postcards and poems and little folded-up sketches she'd send back to Connie, always with some strange small object or token attached. Four squashed raisins sellotaped to the bottom of a letter. *Dried them myself!* A lock of thick walnut hair, twelve inches long. *Shaved my friend Enzo's head today.* The carapace of a very dead insect. *Killed a Croatian beetle for you.*

And Connie would laugh and laugh and ask her to come back soon, and then the letters would stop for a month or two.

When Lia was first diagnosed, she had gone straight to Connie's flat. They had sat together on her old velvet sofa, the one they had once dragged out of a car boot sale together, and Connie had said, *I don't know. Maybe it would help to see it as some romantic thing from an nineteenth-century French novel like consumption, and we will buy lots of elegant silk patterned dressing gowns and fishnet socks.* Lia had looked at her and said, *Fishnet socks?* and Connie had told her that she did have one of those faces that really suited the whole gaunt thing, and Lia had said, *God, I am really craving blueberries,* and they carried on in that way you can when you are so close with someone you can quite happily have multiple conversations at once and no one loses their place.

After a while, Lia had gone very quiet. Staring into empty space, she had looked so frightened it had made Connie want to cradle her, or bathe her, wrap her up in a towel and feed her, but instead she had reached over and picked up the box of matches from the coffee table in front of them.

Lia, she'd said, *how do you get one hundred bunnies into a matchbox?*

Lia's expression had brightened.

I don't know, Connie. How do you get one hundred bunnies into a matchbox?

Connie had opened the box with an unwavering seriousness, picked out a single match, placed it in the top right corner and closed the box, so that the match stuck out, fixed like a radio aerial.

She had held the matchbox to her mouth. Made a radio crackle with her voice, and said, *Calling all bunnies. Calling all bunnies.*

Lia had laughed and laughed and wrapped her arms tightly around her as if she was nineteen again and Connie had thought –
She has always been
so brave.

That evening Connie had sent a crate of blueberries to Lia's doorstep along with a letter on incredibly thick parchment card detailing all the many reasons she believed Lia would be fine. Reasons 1 to 6 went as follows:

1. *1 in 2 people get cancer so it was always going to be one of us*
2. *Most people survive it so the odds are in your favour*
3. *You've got a three-year-old you've got to stick around for*
4. *You've managed to find someone who actually wants to marry you*
5. *Your dad was a Man of God so you are probably in his Good Books*
6. *You can't die yet because neither of us are National Treasures*

The last point and a half were written in red pen; by 'God' the black ink had run out.

Lia had sent a pair of fishnet socks back to Connie.

Eight years later, Connie could send her assistant to post her letters for her and make sure there was always a working pen at hand.

It was impossible not to feel pleased about this.

Her grandmother would have been proud.

Velvet, a Musical Word-Talk

Today I play the piano of her ribs.

Every other key a note flat.

Velvet hums along, unsuspecting, plastering herself over the most wounded walls.

Feels as if we are patching back together a sad jazz cafe during a prohibition. Only there are one hundred white rabbits scattered about, sniffing all over the place.

Velvet is used to this sort of renovation work. She
has been known to lead non-violent political revolutions,
layer bodies, bones and antlers with her glorious violet fur.
She is good at weaving, gathering, dressing queens and popes,
curtaining her wealth of wit and ease across the toughest days,
and she is always the most likely to win a gambling game.

They will not write the love songs about her.
Because hers is the fabric you fall into; the mattress-flat feeling
after you've descended,
jolt-snapped
out of sleep;
she is the silk of sudden knowledge
that you're fine.
Oi. You. Piano man.
I stop my sentimental tune abruptly. One hundred bunnies
turn their red, beady eyes.
Me?
She is staring at me sideways, holding a box of matches.
I hold my breath.
Help me get these bunnies into this matchbox.

Regicide

At her old school, even at her nursery, Iris had always been a very popular sort of person. This was, perhaps, the problem. She had a certain air about her, a confidence that held a gravity, and Burn Girl must have sensed this from the very start. She knew that to rule a kingdom, you have to target the top.

A series of artfully chiselled rumours had begun to crystallize in the staff room, and the teacher had asked to see Iris after school.

Iris did not say anything at first and watched the teacher's eyebrows rise and fall, feeling a great deal of affection for this woman who wanted to help her, who she knew was willing to believe and assist her if she only corroborated.

I know things are difficult at home. I wonder if you are struggling with that, if you need anyone to talk to.

This frustrated Iris. The mention of her *home* sounded like the drawing out of a weapon.

Things are not difficult, things are fine.

Teacher sighed and looked seriously at her, and Iris began puzzling out a series of options in her head

To tell would be _____ . It would spark the
_____ of _____ .

a) Weak
b) Strong
c) Clever
d) Stupid

a) End
b) Beginning
c) Hope
d) Mess

a) War
b) Friendship
c) Burn Girl
d) Iris

Were they yours? The cigarettes?

I must be cleverer, she thought.

I've been told that you were smoking, Iris.

C, A, C?

Iris tried to project the exercise out from her mind and onto the whiteboard behind Teacher's head.

A, D, A?

What are you looking at?

B . . . C . . .

Iris, are these yours?

. . . B . . . B . . .

Teacher was holding Iris's bag out in front of her, her hands around a packet of cigarettes.

Burn Girl's packet.

Iris stared in disbelief at the evidence.

She had underestimated the situation, had underestimated this stranger. What she wanted. What she was prepared to do.

Why are these in your bag?

Iris thought of her mum, of her beautiful thinning mother telling her to circle all options, and arrived quite certainly at

I don't know.

You don't know?

Teacher looked disappointed but
not angry.

I don't know how they got there or whose they are. I don't know, Miss, I just –
don't know.

Teacher walked solemnly up to the bin, dropped the packet in and said, *You are all too young. You are far, far too young for this.*

Iris nodded but her eyes were cold, shallow.

This isn't over, she said, and Iris thought, No, no it is not. Teacher gestured to the door with her head and Iris got up to leave, catching the final notes of Teacher's second heavy sigh as she turned out of the room. From behind the dry, unwatered peony bush, she watched Teacher take her petrol-blue coat out from the cupboard and put it on. The sleeves were too tight around the top of her arms, which Iris felt cruel for noticing.

When Teacher left three minutes later, she ran back into the classroom and fished out the packet from the bin. It had sunk down, right to the very bottom, under two banana skins, an exploded pen, a few snotty tissues and a packet of crisps, as if it weighed a great deal more than it should. She did not know why she did it, but she had an instinct that the packet may just be some useful prop in the difficult game ahead.

Dylan Thomas and the Elephant Man

On the tenth day of her life without breasts, Lia found herself eating a packet of crisps on the train from Wales, observing a group of men laughing and cracking metal beer cans in their large strong hands.

They looked like gods crushing planets.

A little drunk with power, a little more menacing than your average travelling stag do.

She had been told that she would feel very unwomanly, very unlike herself, for a while. *Most do*, they had said. They spoke as if her breasts held the sole secret essence of her femininity, as if the fact of her body would be a little less true, a little less legitimate now it had been chopped up and rearranged.

Harry was at home with Iris, who was four, and more emotionally demanding than either of them had ever expected a child to be. It had been his idea that she rest – get out of the city for a few days. She had stayed with Connie's parents, who had brought her endless cups of soup, spoke in unnecessarily hushed voices and stacked up Dylan Thomas poetry collections next to her bed; *Con says you like poetry.* It had been perfect, blissful, but now Lia was here in the real world the butchered feeling was back, pounding its strange absence in her new flat fleshless chest.

The men were around her age, perhaps a few years older, and yet their eyes danced and struck the place with such youthful ease, such lightness, it seemed as if none of them had ever been responsible for a single thing their whole lives. The largest of them began to speak loudly of sex, throwing out graphic detail the rest devoured. He spoke of a woman's body, the excess weight on her stomach, her bouncing breasts. Lia grinned at the irony of it, of

God's absurd comic timing, before feeling cross she'd let God enter through His regular nook in her thoughts.

What you looking at? one of the men leered, baring his teeth at Lia who had forgotten to shift her pointed stare for at least five minutes. This is easy to do when you're feeling less than human. She looked away, pretending not to have noticed. The group spoke quietly between themselves and then laughed in one terrible roaring unison. The man sitting closest to Lia stood confidently. *Go on*, another probed. More terrible laugher followed.

And then he was standing over her, and she was just a very small very genderless lump of skin and bone and coat turned towards the window, trying not to be a body at all. He sat down next to her, his breath heavy with the stench of hops and vinegar. *What's your name then?* he asked, with this ominous near softness. *Please,* she said, as indifferently as she could, *I'm tired.* That unfamiliar pain throbbing from fresh scars, she kept her eyes flicking across the fields.

Boys, this one's in a right mood! He turned and smiled this wide warm butcher's smile – almost lovely, almost attractive – and Lia was Fanny Burney in 1811, screaming into cloth. Nothing but a little wine to numb the sensation of her breast being torn from her ribs with that sharpened steel blade. She thought of the bravery of women. That enduring female spirit. She tried to feel grateful. Calm. Composed. But the man had his arm around her now, he was touching her shoulder playfully and his friends were chanting. *It's all right, love, only a bit of fun,* he breathed loudly into her ear. She wasn't brave, she thought. She was a weak and passive cancer patient, headed home, quite unable to react to the man moving his hand inside of her coat, trying to cup and squeeze where her breasts should have been but, of course,
were not.

He searched for a second in bewilderment.

Lia watched all light mischief drain from his eyes.

When he moved back to his seat his friends asked, *How were they?*

Lia held her breath.

And then,
a pause the length of a cross-country train
before

he laughed and nodded; *Nipples hard as rock.*

They cheered, turned, raised their beers to her in what seemed to be
sincere gratification, and went back to their smashing of cans and
planets on the small carriage table.

Lia exhaled heavily, feeling thankful. Truly, deeply thankful to this
man for keeping her secret. She watched him through the perfect
V between the seats for the rest of the journey. After ten minutes
they all seemed to forget that she had ever been there. All but the
groping man. The train moved through Bristol, Swindon, Reading.
He didn't say a word. Lia thought about slicing off his penis. And
then his nose. Stitching his penis where his nose once was so he
was nothing but a sad elephant man with a tiny trunk that shook
and swayed with the violent lurches of the train.

By the time they pulled into London the sky was violet,
tearing just where the concrete buildings began, leaking an artificial
red light. Lia felt the city singing its very own strange sunset prayer.
She remembered catching the man's eye, finally, as they stepped off
onto the platform, remembered thinking –
It's really not so bad.
The worst of men can still be kind
even in their own worst of ways and
I am still here, I will live,
to see another day.

Migration

I enjoy the thought of modern vehicles travelling through
a time and place
they don't belong.

I enjoy the logical, aesthetic disturbance of it.

A South West train carrying the Israelites out of Egypt,
tunnelling beneath a redundant Red Sea's
parting.

A devil on a great new shiny model, chain oil
clotting and slowing a beating blue
heart.

A small aircraft taking me from the wreck of an old home
safely to her left arm's
epitrochlear node.

I know what it is to feel uprooted, rehoused, displaced.
Migration is a difficult thing.

Sometimes you feel the pulse and ache of a place long after
it's gone.

In the body, there is a technical term for this. Phantom limb
pain. The following of the twinge right back to the source only to
find that source does not exist any more. I follow the pulse of my
origins right to the very point her intercostal nerves and axillary
lymph nodes and pectoralis major muscle fray and break off, right
to the very severed edge, and for a moment there is no part of me
that believes there is simply nothing beyond.

For a moment, I can think it into existence. I imagine this is
what divorce is like. I imagine there are days, long after it is over,

long after, even, the longing that it wasn't, when one suckles
on the intimacy, swaddles oneself so tightly with the detail, the
safety, the brilliant sharedness of the lost love, that for a moment
it exists again, only far better
than it ever really was.

A Game of Secrets

Iris understood the temporary rhythms of playground affections;
she had traced their comings and goings for much of her life and
knew she simply had to plot her patient way back up to the top.
It helped that she knew what she was dealing with now. With
the knowledge of the packet planting she felt smack-bang in the
middle of some great political conspiracy.

It was morning break. Feeling weightless across the tarmac, feet
following the white painted lines that mapped out a multitude of
squares, boxes and circles, Iris made her way down the side of the
school, the cigarette packet weighing heavy in her bag.

Once she was safely out of sight from everyone, she reached in,
picked out the packet, and opened it.

What are you doing?

Burn Girl sprung out from the tarmac, followed by her small
procession. She looked at the packet and then back at Iris. The tie
between them tightened.

Iris smiled a clean, unbalanced hook-grin, watching Burn Girl's
lovely mouth twitch with questions, watching her begin to swallow
these questions down one by one the way motorways swallow cars,
their light speeding into the distance before vanishing entirely.

I've come up with this game, Burn Girl said, reassembling.

It's savage, one of the girls behind her added, with uncontainable glee.

Above them, the clouds were darkening. A few amber aspen leaves broke off from their branches and fell around them like quiet, unseen offerings of peace. Burn Girl took out a box from her bag. It was an old jewellery box covered in shells of all shapes and sizes stuck on with a little too much glue.

It's a game of secrets. We'll be collecting as many as we can in the box and then picking one at random every week, to read out at lunch time.

Burn Girl lifted the lid to reveal many ripped and folded pieces of white paper.

Everyone needs to contribute. The more secrets you put in about other people, the less likely yours will be read out. It's simple.

She's a genius, really, Iris thought. A total genius;
Social Chaos is a dictator's
absolute best friend.

Do you have any? They've told me all sorts already.

They have?

Iris looked at the collection of upright bodies standing behind Burn Girl. Their skirts had shortened a fraction for each day of her reign. They looked diffident, unhappy. Pretty, though. Some of them had experimented with smudges of eyeliner. Two of them had been to her primary school. She knew their families, their houses, the smell of their carpets, the way their parents' backsides would look when moving around a kitchen, even the patterns on their plastic cups. She remembered these surfaces suddenly so precisely that any fury she felt was pushed aside, briefly, by the gentle squeeze of such intimate knowledge. The affection that comes with a shared history.

I have a few.

Burn Girl looked pleased. The upright bodies did not. She had passed the test.

Burn Girl then invited Iris to a gathering in the park on Saturday and Iris, despite having said yes in her strongest voice, despite feeling as if she had achieved some small shameful victory, knew somewhere very deep in her bones that being complicit in the playground terrors was worse than falling victim to them. That some innocence was being undone.

So this is what war feels like, Iris thought, staring up at the grey spitting sky as they walked away, thinking about necessary evil and the many bodies she may have to step over to get the world back to its natural order.

Sometimes, she said, very quietly to herself, *you have to pick the gun up to put the gun down.*

But do you?

It was Solero Boy.

His kind eyes were swimming with intrigue. A football had skimmed off the pitch and his foot rested on top of it, his boyish leg bent so Iris could see the delicate structure of his bony right kneecap through black cotton trousers.

You know what I think?

Iris felt a prickle in the centre of her palm. He bent down swiftly, calmly, picking up the ball with both hands.

What?

Voices from the pitch called for him to *hurry up* and he lifted the ball right behind his head of short beautiful tightly curled hair so that his top lifted up a fraction. Iris's eyes drifted for a moment to the gap, the slice of skin where his waistband stopped and his T-shirt began.

I think you're mad.

He threw the ball hard but it did not travel as far as he'd have liked it to; his arms were skinny and he had yet to develop the strength that comes with puberty. His voice was still high and songful. Iris could tell he was feigning confidence.

Maybe I am. You know what I think?

There was a cheer from the pitch.

No. What?

I think the other team just scored.

The Science of Laughter

You can tell when she is laughing; her insides gleam and throb.

Delight can carve this electric path through a person, for those seconds there is no sensation quite like it.

The average child laughs three hundred times a day. The average adult, about seventeen.

She laughs considerably more than this;
the muscles in her gut contract, her heart rate rises by 20 per cent

and afterwards, her body is as putty-drunk-sponge
as post-orgasm, but quenched. Sweet and simple.

I like her best in these moments.
I feel most proud to call the place home.

Early Bloomer

When Connie's invitation arrived two days later, Harry was
squinting at the newspaper and Iris had announced she was feeling
like Jam. Harry had moved towards the cupboard that held the
jam, one eye on the cryptic crossword, and Iris had laughed cruelly
and said *no not like eating it* and Harry felt stupid like he'd made
some obvious error.

Oh.

Where's Mum?

She's upstairs working in bed, she's a bit wobbly today.

The letterbox opened and closed, followed by the sound of a letter
landing flat on the floor.

It was addressed to the three of them. Harry watched Iris try to
open it, her little fingers tearing and peeling the seal. How funny,
he thought, how funny that she doesn't know how to open a letter,
as she made a large rip in the corner.

It's from Connie. An invitation.

To what?

A show.

What show?

Some sort of contemporary ballet at a round house.

Harry inspected the card. His eyes were going bad. It was something he'd been trying to ignore for a while now.

I don't know why she didn't just text us, Iris added, dropping the ribbon and then the envelope containing a large matchstick that nobody would ever see
into the bin.

Harry placed the card on the kitchen counter and continued with his crossword.

A late bloomer? His pen counted the boxes.
Late bloomer late bloomer late bloomer.

What are you on about?

Evening primrose!

Harry arrived triumphantly, scratching in the letters.

When did everyone get so boring? Iris said, leaving the kitchen and making her loud way up the stairs as if a great chorus were spitting *Ha! Ha! Ha!*s behind her like confetti, a few shrapnel. *That'll teach him*s.

She slid into Lia's room, sat at the end of her bed and told her about Connie's ballet at some round house somewhere, and Lia laughed.

How funny, she said.

What's funny? Iris asked, and though her voice was drained of any actual interest, Lia explained that she used to clean that particular theatre for some extra cash, back when she was a student,
three nights a week for two years, while Connie and I lived together in

*this tiny little flat around the corner. I'd mop confetti or blood or milk
or glass off the stage, depending on the show, and then perform my own
little dance under the lights.*

Blood?

Well. You know. Fake blood. Ketchup.

Iris looked at her as if she were going mad.

Mum?

Yes.

I need new shoes.

You have new shoes!

It was impossible to talk to Iris when she was in this mood.

Iris went to stew furiously in her yellow room. Lia finished the
pencil-plan for the Ephemeral page and crept to the kitchen
feeling frail and creaturely. Ten down. Sixteen to go. It was nice
not to know what word would come next. It would make sense
to work alphabetically, but the idea of waking up to a day that
felt unequivocally like an M day only to have to work on F after a
whole day of E exhausted her. She worked through the crossword
answers Harry hadn't got, watched him in the garden watering his
tiny square of budding life. He paused occasionally to rub his eyes.
Lia listened to Iris's footsteps moving about sporadically in the
room above, wondering what she was doing, until Iris eventually
came downstairs having cut one of her tops so that her white little
belly was out, her belly button taut from a large breakfast. Around
her eyes she had scratched black eyeliner in circles but had not got
quite close enough to the edge of her lids – a rim of pale skin lay
comically where it shouldn't. On her legs were a pair of Lia's old
fishnet tights, and she was wearing Harry's socks that she'd pulled

up so high the shape of a heel bulged out halfway up the back of her calf, and Lia wanted to weep/groan/laugh but did none of these things and instead waited for the silence to be filled between them.

What? Iris asked.

Nothing. Lia shrugged. In order to make an impact she knew you needed something to push against and Iris was not getting any such thing.

I'm going out, she announced. *Burn Girl has invited me to the park with everyone.*

Lia raised her eyebrows and wanted to tell Iris to be careful but Harry had come in from the garden, taken one look at Iris, and broken into deep, irrepressible laughter.

Lia felt love carry through her. He was able to see things as simply as they were. The sound of his wheezing delighted her so completely she felt a smile spreading wide across her face, and then they were both doubled over, clutching their stomachs like children quite overcome with the squeeze of it.

I don't understand what's so funny, Iris said, unflinching. She rested her hands on her hips.

This was too much. Harry could feel his legs weakening. He propped himself up on the kitchen counter, howling, but as Lia laughed with him, she felt slowly dragged out of her own body, until she was observing the three of them from very far away. She felt lucky to be getting to see this premature rebellion, this glimpse of future, this strange and unfamiliar adolescent, but then something began to ache. A profound stomach sadness plunged in and rippled through, tearing her back to herself. Her mouth began to sour and then dry, the laughter lying flat on her tongue.

Harry's sounds had eased into light, disbelieving chuckles as he shook his head, smacked his palms against the table in satisfaction, as if they had both devoured the most delicious meal.

Here is a fact: laughing at twelve-year-olds is without a doubt asking for trouble.

Iris bit back. Devilish things swimming in her bottomless eyes, she went for Lia; *I'm sure that once you cared about how you looked. I'm sure you weren't always so dull and loose and plain.*

Harry broke in. Iris bit back again. Lia could not make out what was being said, for the kitchen sounds had muted to a mere inaudible rumble as she thought of The Dress,

The Dress with its tight synthetic silk and its ridiculous little straps and being fucked in it at fifteen, not much older than this funny little child before her, and thought
I hope she never grows up, I pray to God
she never grows up.

The Afterwards

The tragic summer had quickly stretched its hot anxious months into autumn and then winter, and Lia had begun to accept that her life would know no balance, no true relief. There were moments of ecstasy in between the waiting. They rarely happened during the act itself (the dazzling newness of sexual intimacy had begun to wear), but what they had stumbled upon together was the vast and curious landscape of The Afterwards. In The Afterwards they could speak frankly to each other, half naked, and slowly Lia felt she was beginning to understand Matthew, find pockets of him hidden all over the place.

She soon discovered there was no undisclosed adult conspiracy rallying around her. He was an orphan. His mother had died when he was very young – he had no memory of her. His father had sold cars before he had died in a car accident, which Matthew had called *poetic*, as removed from his own life as he always seemed. The particularly empty funeral had taken place on the day he had arrived in their lives, turned up on the vicarage doorstep. Father Peter had conducted the funeral, which was why he had not been surprised to see Matthew that night. And yet despite knowing all of this, she would often stare at his face, checking for traces of her genes in the arch of his nose, the edge of his eyelids, the dip in his chin. A stroke of her father. Her mother. As if the events that had led Matthew to them seemed too tragic, the fact of him being just *a Friend of the Family* too neat.

It's strange without them here, she said to him one early Saturday morning, as they wandered through new terrains of The Afterwards, naked light pouring over their limbs. Anne and Peter were away at their annual Christian Leadership Conference, leaving Lia alone in the vicarage for the weekend. Matthew had driven down from London. It was the first time they'd stayed overnight together in a bed.

Anne had packed and then unpacked twice the evening before, citing everything from Various Important Deliveries to Having to Pay the Milkman as reasons not to go. After much persuasion from Peter, she had packed again reluctantly for a final time and left with him in a terrible mood, her bag snarling behind her along the floorboards of the hallway, and Lia had danced them out, shut the door far too loudly behind them, and it had all felt like the beginning of a musical number in a colourful Hollywood film, like she should be spinning in a fabric shop on the Upper West Side looking like Natalie Wood.

But when Matthew had arrived, their desire suddenly seemed small and unsure of itself. It had taken them till the morning to settle into each other, to find a new rhythm and ease.

They're good people, he said seriously. *You are lucky.*

Lia wondered if this was true. She knew they were good in the general Christian sense, that they had an important role in the community, no criminal past or dead bodies hidden in the basement, but to assume their absolute goodness like this seemed lazy and imprecise. *I suppose they seem that way to you,* she said, *because they like you best.* Matthew laughed lightly. He did not disagree with her.

Your dad, Lia asked, *was he good?*

He swallowed. Her eyes fixed on his Adam's apple. It slid up his throat and back down as if propelling his answer out; *Not really. Not for most of his life. I think he became good, though. Eventually.*

Lia edged deeper into the space between his neck and shoulder, eyes still on the lump in his throat.

He was a big drinker. The cars he sold were mostly stolen, I think. We sort of moved from place to place when I was a kid. There was always this sense of threat, this fear of being caught. I never really knew for what, though.

As Lia pressed further, he spoke with increasing ease. He reconstructed the garage he grew up in until Lia could see it clearly, taking its place in the landscape of The Afterwards. He painted the hot hum of petrol air, built the two pillars that seemed to hold up a flat artificial sky at night. He described the light as so crude, so blue it was as if he'd spent his childhood on an operating table. He told her about their travelling months in the summers, the way he would sleep in the car while his father visited various houses.

For the first time, Lia felt the rare clutch of maternal love, the wring of it in her stomach. When his father came back to the car the next morning, he was often glazed in sweat, smelling of sex. But the brilliant sound of the engine starting up again would slice through Matthew's singular boyness, lying flat across the back seats, and he would feel pleased to be part of the travelling circus.

It sounds bleak, but it wasn't so bad.

Lia wondered how much of it was true. He had a way of romanticizing himself that felt calculated and vague, even in its detail.

So what changed? she asked.

On my eleventh birthday, he came into my room trembling.

Why?

He said he'd seen something, felt something. An experience.

Of what? Lia asked.

God.

Lia held her breath. She felt her ribs expand. Matthew's lips against the very top of her head.

Have you had one? he asked. She wondered why this seemed suddenly like the most intimate question anyone had ever asked her. Why something was squirming and flipping and tangling within her like a silver fish caught slyly in the coarse nylon of a net. For she had hoped very privately all her life for a dazzling numinous moment – because how easy it would be to believe, she thought, when given a sign like that.

I don't know, she said, honestly. *Either I've had thousands or none.*

Probably none then. You would know.

There was a silence.

I never found out the details of it, he said, *but it must have been really something because after that day, everything changed. We packed up our stuff and rented a small house on the outskirts of the village. He said he grew up around here. That he had a friend who would help us, a man of God, a healer.*

My dad, Lia breathed. She tried to conjure the stranger faces of her own childhood coming and going through the vicarage door, tried to imagine which of them could have been Matthew's father, which of the cars grinding the gravel driveway had been the one that killed him.

And then he looked me dead in the eye and said it was clear now, it was clear there was only one way out, and it was the Lord.

His fingers traced fondly along her naked shoulder, the curve of her jaw.

He never explained what we needed to get out of. I understood.

Thank you.

For what?

For telling me.

He pinched her cartilage lightly in response, breathed heavily into her hair for a while. Lia stared hard at his nipples, his beautiful areolas. They were nicer than she'd ever thought nipples could be. His body was peppered with all these surprisingly lovely parts; parts that made sense together, like a perfectly punctuated sentence. She peeled from his chest to reposition herself under his nipples, connecting them like a colon, and they lay there, two sides of one sentence, until Matthew opened his mouth again and spoke with a strange, shrinking voice she had never heard before:

Do you ever feel, he said, *do you ever feel like this is all very wrong?*

Lia stared at her own small fist, only a skin away from his large intestine.

Wrong?

She lifted slowly, looking up at him.

Sinful. Like we are being tested. And we are failing.

She thought hard about this.

No, she said, eventually, *no, I do not. But then* – she paused, wondering whether to say it, wondering whether it was even true – *I don't think I believe in it.*

Matthew smiled with his lips and frowned with his brows.

In what?

In any of it. I'm not sure I ever have.

It had never occurred to her that this would shock him. They rarely spoke of God, and she had come to believe that they were growing out of Him together, as one may grow out of childhood clothes. She could not, after all, connect the Matthew she knew now with the one that once rang the church bell before mass, carried the processional cross, stood at the altar beside her father in his white surplice; the two were incompatible. But of course, they were not.

Oh, he said. *Wow.*

So they had not fucked their way into a shared atheism. For a moment Lia wanted to laugh, but his expression was one of such sadness, such pity, she began to feel small and crude and stupid. For misunderstanding him, perhaps. For knowing he still had one foot in the door that had never opened for her.

I cannot imagine how lonely that would feel.

That night, he fucked her very gently for the first time. When he was finished, he fell asleep still inside her. I will never know closeness like this, Lia thought, as she too began to drift off elsewhere, soaking in the odd, exquisite sensation of him softening between her legs.

The next day he left at lunch time and did not return for a year.

Colon

Noun

[*plural* **colons**]

1. A punctuation mark used to precede a list of items, a quotation, or an expansion. (Matthew: Lia).

2. A statement of proportion between two numbers, or to separate hours from minutes (and minutes from seconds) in a numerical statement of time. (21:17)

3. The main part of the large intestine.

4. The basic monetary unit of Costa Rica and El Salvador [*plural* colonies].

5. ....

Pilgrims

Fossil is lost,
pretending not to be.

He's trying to lead them into her lungs, where he once caught
a glimpse of me without the paint and costumes; the pomp,
masks and
circumstance.

A reluctant chorus follows him. Nobody trusts him. *Probably a*
trap, two identical members whisper in unison. They have pulsing
blonde locks and little nipples poking out through matching
white vests. They appear not to have any legs.

Today I am one of them, playing the part of an ageing lady with
an eye patch. *Aye!* I say, with great conviction. *A trap indeed!*

Though they all look weary, like they've walked the entire Via
Francigena pilgrimage route, they are clearer than they were at the
beginning. More complete. As if they've all found little pieces of
themselves strewn about her organs and ligaments, along the dead
quiet weed-kissed banks of her canals.

They are no longer ghostly, unfinished, but appear to me as
members of a great cast.

I wonder what they all really want.

What does a soldier want?

The raven in the clerical collar answers me quietly: *To win and*
go home.

What does a pilgrim want? I ask.

He thinks, then says: *A map that never ends.*

Here! This way! Fossil calls out behind him, trying out his new-old voice.

I can see him squeezing his sounds into place, letting sentences and phrases and familiar clicks rise up his throat, rearrange themselves at the back of his mouth. When he speaks every syllable polishes itself.

The raven follows after him devotedly, flapping and scratching his ink-black wings.

I know you don't trust me, Fossil says. *But please.*

Velvet says something about not having much of a choice.

The problem is this:
Her body is unfamiliar. Every day a little less like itself.

I want to tell Fossil that all this sudden heroism is a bit rich, that he has hardly been kind to the place himself; all that wrenching and hardening and scraping and slandering – it's done just as much damage as I have.

But lovers are notoriously reckless with each other's insides.
Even if it seems on skin-surface that all is well. That love is gentle.

He coughs, splutters, clears his throat. Pulls the party
here and there, delightedly exercising his
new-found authority, and I realize:
We are not so different,
he and I.
We are not so different at all.

We who get stronger
as she weakens.

five

Thucydides

Outside the university students stood in circles, swaying gently from
foot to foot, holding rolled-up cigarettes between their fingers,
using them as great
tools for expression. Gesturing, sucking, exhaling.
Budding philosophers
in puffer jackets.
Little Laurence Oliviers in
Nikes.

On some days, Harry saw himself in them – in the performing
mass of young faces and bodies and minds that littered the
outskirts of his life – but more recently he felt that each generation
owned their own particular impenetrable language of thought, a
meaning that hid in glances, in the stubbing of cigarette butts on
walls, in the gentle indifference to their homes or the tapping of
fingers on phones.

To reach in, or, better, to be *invited* in, was to cross a great border,
for a moment, to step into gloriously unfiltered territories, vast
moors of
fickle lust, brief love.

One of his undergraduate students nodded confidently as he
walked past. Harry nodded back and smiled slightly, unnerved. Had
it been mockery? Had it been respect? Pressing his body against the

revolving glass door, Harry began to wonder when his ego had grown so fragile.

You smell of herbs and dirt. The postgraduate grew out of the ground the minute he stepped into the building.

Thanks.

She shrugged – *I like it.*

He looked at her sideways as they made their way up to the Classics offices together.
There was nothing suggestive in her voice, her expression.
They spoke briefly of small things for two flights of stairs.

You know I see you most mornings, she said. Harry felt a lodge of something in his throat. *Walking to the station. You're always just ahead of me. We get the same train.*

We do? He blushed at the connection, at the thought of her watching the back of his balding head, his unnecessarily brisk walk for the train he had never missed. *I hadn't noticed.* On the third floor he asked her if she wanted to cover a first-year lecture on Thucydides and the Idea of History, two weeks away; *Hospital stuff.*

She nodded solemnly. *I would love that.*

Probably for the best anyway, he added, students spilling out around them as they moved up steadily, heavily, Harry feeling quite. Out. Of. Breath. *Nobody seemed to be listening to a word of my introductory session last week. Maybe you'll make a better job of it.*

They turned into the fourth floor. She pushed the door with her boot unthinkingly and smiled a wide kind smile; *'It is frequently a misfortune to have very brilliant men in charge of affairs. They expect too much of ordinary men.'*

Harry paused at the door of his office, frowning, as if she had reached in uninvited, across his own private border, and the act had triggered some unexpected change in his ecosystem.

Thucydides – she looked hurt. *A Thucydides quote.*

Right. Harry scratched the back of his neck. *Thanks.*

She scowled like a child who had just watched an adult needlessly break some harmless plaything, turned and walked away. Harry stood still for a moment, watching the back of her
unknowable brain,
feeling stupid and lonely and old.

Week 1

The first secret was read out at 1.37 p.m. to a congregation of hungry faces.

Mya kissed Tom on the lips outside Starbucks on Tuesday. His breath smelt bad. She used too much tongue.

An Introduction to Brain

The Ancient Egyptians practised excerebration on their dead. They would break through the brain case with a metal rod and scrape out the brain from the nostrils. They then disposed of all the soft blended mulch, believing it was, instead, the much prettier little meaty organ Heart that governed all perception, perspective, personality.

I like to imagine the Afterlife full of brain-dead pharaohs stacked like beanpoles really kicking themselves.

There is nothing beautiful about Brain. From the outside, it's probably the ugliest thing in here. I have reason to believe they have done this on purpose. To throw us off the scent. Nature always finds ways to protect its most prized possessions. It is why witches are often grotesque, why lust is often violent, why newborns rip three holes into one, and why libraries are necessarily unremarkable.

But inside, they say it holds as many neurons as the Milky Way holds stars (100 billion, or thereabouts).

They say its vessels stretch 120,000 miles; that if you laid them out top to toe you would get halfway to the moon.

The truth is, I have spent far too long sulking around its grounds, cooking up brilliant visions of Brain's bulbs, tracts, synapses and spheres; wondering what her life may look like if I had access to her fears.

And though I know a great traveller is only someone who can manage his own expectations, though I know you can dream something to death, it is the hardest thing; the difference between where you are and where you want to be.

For fun, I sing a personalized Proclaimers song, jam it up with far too many syllables. I sing about walking 60,000 miles and then 60,000 more, and it carries through her little brain like a lament through the pipes of a capital city before a siege, its echo hollowing out the walls like those empty ancient skulls.

The Other Man

During Matthew's absence, Lia developed another relationship of a similar nature. He never opened the black peeling door to her, but at night, between the dark flat walls of her mind's eye, she would crouch down next to it, huddle against it and speak through the letterbox, holding it ajar until her fingers went numb, began to freeze and break off at the tips. It was only then, when she could knock and pray no more, that she would give in to the ache of sleep.

In the mornings before school she would wake up early and lie there, imagining that Matthew had been killed in a car accident or that he'd been stabbed to death or had been kidnapped by the IRA; anything at all was better, kinder, easier than the idea that he was just living his life elsewhere without her, putting his socks on in the morning without her, opening and closing doors without her.

Dear God, can you make him come back, I can hardly eat.

During their last brief conversation on the phone, at least two, perhaps three months ago, now, Matthew had suggested she apply to universities in London. That way they could be together, in the same city. He had said it casually, like it was something he'd just thought of, but the plan flickered before her like a guiding light, crackling and strengthening, leading her hopefully from each day to each night. It was less than a year away.

Dear God, please can you send me to sleep for nine months.

All that she needed was something to do there. Something to study. Anne had laughed at the prospect of art school. *Anything,* she'd said, *anything other than art.*

Lia was doing terribly at school. At dinner she would listen to
Anne and Peter discussing him at length, the way he had picked
up a job sifting through the birth and death and marriage
notices, writing obituaries for lesser-known individuals for
a middle-market newspaper in London, the fact that he was
considering the military, considering travelling, considering this,
considering that. It was the culture, they would say, the culture
of excess in London that they worried about; *You know what
those newspapers are like*, Anne would say, and Lia would sit at the
kitchen table thinking, No, none of us do, falling slowly into her
shepherd's pie and the sounds of their fretting about the sort of life
he was living, wondering if there was some etymological reason
the word *culture* was so similar to
vulture, why she was now thinking of the words *mulch* and
indulge, her forehead dipping
further into potato crust and the
door beginning to emerge again
as it always would
at the start of her sleep.

Dear God, let me in.

Please, dear God, fucking God, let me in.

Brain Security Systems

There is always a way in,

a latch left open.

A Disappointing Conversation

Did you get the letter?

No?

The invitation on the fancy card with the ribbon and the matchstick.

Oh. Well. Iris told me about it.

Connie's silence scorched across the line for a second too long. Lia could hear her mouth clamp shut and then open again, measuring out small furies on her tongue.

So you didn't see it?

*No. I didn't. But thank you. We can't
wait.*

An unexpectedly large sense of
disappointment rippled from Connie's ears into her
throat, and for a moment, their once-impermeable friendship
felt riddled with
missed connections. Failed attempts.

Do you remember the matchbox bunny joke?

No. I don't think I do.

Connie changed the subject, launching quickly into talk of
rehearsals and the leak in the theatre roof and costume fittings
and the difficulty they were having with a dancer who had gained
weight due to the stress of a particularly messy divorce, and Lia sat
quietly, relieved, scratching triangles on an empty page.

Both tried to extinguish the thought that some
sacred thing between them had been

irreparably bent by time, mottled by age,
as if their bold, ecstatic talks
had been scraped out just to contain
a little family, work and illness,
all things quite
cripplingly mundane.

Anyway. How are you holding up?

Fine. Busy. Fine.

I've got to go.

OK—

The line went dead. Lia went to open her mouth again, but her lips were sealed shut. She tried harder, licked her lips. The top took a layer off the bottom, the taste of open wounds and dry skin and blood, simmering on her tongue.

Harry must have thrown it away. She stuffed half of each swollen foot into a pair of Iris's tiny old trainers and shuffled out to the bins. It felt important that she find it, that she retrieve this small missed gesture as proof of her sanity, perhaps, proof that all the evidence of her life and love was there. That she would be judged accordingly. The days were getting colder. Her fingers felt quite numb. She ripped madly through the paper layers of the week, clawing towards the occasional glimmer of silk red, folding and plunging deeper with each of her thin arms' movements, turning out to be a packet of something she couldn't remember buying. An empty cartoon of something she couldn't remember eating. After half an hour of feeling futile and silly but nearer, always nearer to triumph, her body gave up; *Enough now, enough.*

It is easy not to notice the shivers, the quakes and the sweating when your soul is huddled over a task like an animal over a hunted feast.

It is easy to feel great loss in only
the small domestic misplacements of life.

Lia steadied herself against the wall. She wondered why it was that
the morning quietened so curiously this way, the hour before the
bin trucks came.

Before sulking back into their house, their very unremarkable
brown brick house that looked less inviting than ever, she noticed
a perfect square of card folded four times over, at least, placed
neatly at the top of the pile. There. Surely. That was it. She opened
it carefully.
It was not.

Scrawled across the thick damp paper, in her own black ink hand,
was a lexical entry she could not remember writing:

Autonomy
Noun

1. The self-amputation of a limb or other part of the body
by an animal under threat.
2. ....

Monster-Making

They say information must travel through the hippocampus in
order to come out a Proper Memory, which means very little
to me, but it has got me thinking: does a person have to travel
through certain degrees of hell in order to turn out Properly Bad?
And what about the thoughts that skirt around or dig under or
manage to escape altogether? What about the ones just born evil?

Another Disappointing Conversation

What are you wearing?

Nothing, I'm wearing nothing.

That's not true.

How do you know?

Because the phone is in the living room.

Well. Everyone is out.

She could hear him considering whether to humour her or not. She wanted him to picture her standing naked in the vicarage living room with its bare custard walls, strange trinkets, its low ceiling, dim light, and her pale cold body huddling towards his voice. The perfect composition of it. The glorious oil-paintingness of it.

What are you really wearing? It's not a sexual thing. I just want to know. I want to picture it.

She cradled the phone to her ear and then pushed it so close her cartilage began to hurt and her cheek began to sweat.

Trousers.

Yes.

*And the big shirt you gave me a year ago. Your favourite shoulder is poking out, the one with the
small mole.*

I love that mole.

I miss you.

I know, I know. You'll be here soon.

We don't know that. Results haven't come back yet.

Lia waited for his response, ashamed at the palpable hunger of her replies, the speed with which they fell out.

You'll be here.

She grinned.

There is a thing.

A thing?

Yes. For the end of school. At the church. Will you come, will you come? We can drive off for the evening, we'll have time.

I don't think so.

Why not?

No answer.

Why not?

I'll see what I can do.

It's on the tenth. Please.

For a while she let herself hang, suspended in the grey noise between each of his breaths.

How are you holding up?

Fine. Busy. Fine.

I've got to go.

OK.

But he didn't.

She liked these seconds most.

These seconds when she knew he was simply there,
trying not to be.

I cannot leave.

You can. You always do.

The Boy and His Wall

If you can't get beyond, you can at least deface
the walls.

Currently, I have a ladder leaning against her cranium. I'm
perched on the top rung with a paintbrush between my teeth,
colours littered around my feet, trying to think of something
clever to paint, wondering what it is that makes a True Artist,
pondering the difference between high and low art and what
makes a perfect canvas.

I have heard tales of a canvas 3.6 metres high, 28 miles long.
It sliced all the way through East and West Berlin; this stonking
great concrete symbol of division. In 1980, an artist began with
a blue elephant and a key. Next, a fragment of Picasso. A mural
for the red rabbits that had once lived on the death strip. The
rabbits mouthed some Bowie lyrics (sacred as scripture), the
Bowie lyrics gave way to a Duchamp urinal (posing as a pink
elephant's trunk), while rats' teeth, masks and huge fractured
bodies flooded the wall, taunting their risk and ridicule and play,

all growing quietly out of that
Kreuzberg soil.

The canvas got busier. The acts became more dangerous.

As the eighties knocked on clumsily, the man began to squeeze
through the new crumbling gaps in the wall, to paint on the
eastern side. The border police would come chasing and shouting
and waving their guns and he would gather his cheap materials,
run as fast as he could back through the holes, pleased to have
planted a little colour now thrashing about inside a
sombre history.

As artists must, he wrote a manifesto. *The Fast Form Manifesto*;
a guide to painting quickly, effectively, in the most dangerous
places. I often refer back to it myself.

You only need two ideas, three colours, he says.

(I often use more. I find the business of self-restraint
quite difficult.)

As walls must, his came down in 1989. The man watched his life's
work destroyed. Bit by bit. Every symbol, every character, gone.

Now, this really got me.

For I believe it was only then, at the conflicting moment
when humanity triumphed, when the art vanished,
when the creator looked on and rejoiced –
he proved himself a True Artist.

Because really, annihilation is the truest goal.

*The progress of an artist is a continual self-sacrifice, a continual
extinction of personality.*

I write this in crude ugly yellow,
outline the letters in green,
draw a devil red figure above it,
my own *Fuck You* to the regime.

The Drop

Do my hands look swollen?

This postgraduate is quite persistent.

Persistence is good. It's what you teach them. Do I sleep too much?

You are often short of breath.

Do I seem different? I feel changed.

It'll pass.

Once the treatment is over.

Yes.

Iris has never been a worrier.

True.

I am not working quickly enough.

That is OK.

It's not OK. We don't have enough money for it to be OK.

A pause.

I sleep too much . . . too much . . .

Husband and wife danced around the edges of where they were trying to get to. Like tentative travellers surveying the drop they held each other tight as they slept, arms wrapped around backs as if having taken the plunge, ripping through steep
endless air,
they would fall awake together, both
bathed in sweat,
breathless but relieved
to find themselves
grounded in
the comfort of the cliff
edge, still
teetering amongst the rubble.

Outsiders

I feel so close to her dreams here I can almost dip my fingers in them. Watch them writhe about in the puddles of her skull.

Sometimes they sound like the muffle of a great raucous party happening behind a wall. And I feel sad not to be there.

Sometimes they're just a quick, sudden snap of two human necks hitting rock at high speed.

A Long Night I

The end of Lia's forgettable school life was marked by a dance. It would take place in the church hall which struck Lia as incredibly depressing. The teachers and students said it would be fun but Lia had a distinct idea of what fun was and this was certainly not it.

She was not planning on going. Not until Matthew called, and suddenly it seemed like the only thing to hang above him to remind him she had a life, she had friends of sorts and plans and parties that she could choose to go to or not. This, of course, was not strictly true; there were no real friends, not then. No real choices.

Fuelled only by the prospect of being with him in London, she had scraped through her exams and been offered a place at her second-choice university studying Literature and Language. Freedom was so close she could smell it, wafting its burnt tomorrow scent through every room in the house.

She would have been totally alone at this time were it not for the strange, effortless companionship of the twins. Though they did not speak regularly, Lia would watch them intently in lessons, sketch them out in the back of her textbooks, and after class they would lean over her shoulder and say things like, *You're very good, Lia, a real talent you've got there.* The twins never really spoke in unison. But in Lia's memory they had one thick layered voice that shared every word.

Lia was sure Matthew would come. She could sense it in his *I'll see what I can do.* She did not know what his days consisted of but there was an absurd excellent certainty to her love; she knew she could move her little finger and he would feel the twinge of it in his brainstem, the ripple of her thumb through his spine.

The twins did not care about the ball either. At least they did not seem to. They had both been offered a place at Oxford to study medicine and frequently sung, *We're destined for Greater Things you see, Lia, just like you are, Lia,* through outlined violet lips. Neither of them had ever seemed particularly clever but that beast Beauty was always tripping Lia up, skewering her judgement.

Physical longing for Matthew had not only made her less observant but had discharged her entirely from the steady movement of village life, time, girls, boys.

Two hours before the ball started, Lia paced across the fields to the twins' house in a cornflower-blue dress of Anne's that sagged around her small breasts, the cheap fabric pulled up to her bone-pale knees, the afternoon dull beneath thin, expanding clouds. Outside the twins' house, she pulled at the stiff zip at the side of the dress and stepped out of it, revealing the black silk slip underneath. She knocked four times on the freshly painted door.

The twins' house smelt of celery and wood lacquer. They were wearing tight plastic minidresses, thick grey eyeshadow that gave way just before their eyebrows began, their blonde hair piled up high on their perfectly shaped heads. Lia felt jealous that they could be clever and beautiful and confident all at the same time and suddenly felt a sharp unyielding stress at the thought of Matthew meeting them, seeing her next to them. *That's basically just lingerie*, they said, laughing, though not unkindly, looking down at Lia's bare legs.

In the unrecognizable church hall, the floors were sticky and full of faces from neighbouring schools.

Everyone seemed young. Unsettlingly so. Like they'd been heaved out of childhood too soon, pulled apart, propped up and zipped tightly in grown-up skin.

The twins handed her a flask of something and she took a large swig. The liquid was surprisingly warm against her lips, its toxic flavour scorching her throat. Her stomach groaned.

The twins danced for a while, taking turns to hold Lia's wrist. An hour passed as they sipped on the flask, sharing it between them, whispering in each other's ears. Lia was certain nothing was ever really said. That was the point, though, the practised choreography of weightless secrets. *It's sexy,* she imagined the twins saying, *it intrigues.* She focused on their swaying necks; a lip brushed her lobe. An hour or two passed slowly.

Lia, Lia, I think he likes you. The twins leant in.

Who?

Him, over there. He's been staring. Mr Birch's nephew. St James's boy. You should speak to him.

She shook her head and took another swig from the flask that was now nearly empty, eyes resting lazily on the staring boy. His eyes were locked to Lia's body, his face kind, his features plain, his cheeks blotched pink from the heat. Lia stared back at him for a while, focusing her energy on where he started and ended, where his shoes met the floor, where the line of his bowed legs bent slightly outward, where his shoulders melted into others. Elbows brushed and nudged against his outline. Behind the silhouette of his ears – four sets of monstrous faces were joined by the mouth. A strange sort of anger began to curdle. Perhaps Matthew wasn't coming after all. Perhaps her faith in him had been unfounded. Naive. He had a whole other life that she knew so little about. Another girl no doubt. One with bleached hair and a large flat in Bermondsey. Or Paris. Or Rio. Mr Birch's nephew sipped his beer. He had a confident chin, which asserted itself when he lifted the bottle to his mouth, tipped his head back. He laughed at nobody in particular. He had nice teeth.

Go on, speak to him. The twins smiled encouragingly. Lia did as she was told.

His body was smaller than Matthew's, his hands softer, the skin around his lips distinctly how Lia imagined a woman's might feel.

You are not a talker, are you, he said, coming up for air.

I can be if you want me to be – but he kissed her again as if to say he didn't, really.

He was gracious at first. Patient. Tentative, even, and Lia had never felt so repulsed by another human being in all her life.

When she led him outside, she knew she only wanted the air, wanted to make him hard, feel that want, that rock-solid stiff-as-bone fact of a man's body ready and poised for hers. But he wasn't a man. His fingers chewed and trembled in all the wrong places, and her hips and thighs were being cut into by the corners of gravestones. She was being plastered flat across a tomb. Falling to the ground, he moved his unfamiliar shape on top of her. Lia looked for his chin in the dark, for some inch of confidence. She found nothing but blind, boyish persistence.

They kissed, tongues hunting, plunging, knotting, and she began to identify a new instinct clawing its way out, a wholly new hunger that with every push of his unfamiliar fingers felt increasingly sinister. When, eventually, she pulled her pants to the side and guided him inside her, his voice oozed in disbelief, as if she were letting him perform some unthinkably violent act. He could not see where she started, ended. She had diminished into nothing but a dark wet shape writhing a little between the gravestones. A minute or two passed.

In the sudden quiet Lia's hunger began to retreat. She thought of grief-stricken Heathcliff with his shovel, scraping away at Catherine's coffin in the dark like the psychopath from America she'd read about in the news. He'd been found playing with corpses at night, half asleep. She thought of this man waking up in the graveyards, halfway through his sick, urgent acts, sweating, coated in woman's bones. She imagined him brushing himself down and leaving quietly, respectfully, as if he'd only ever been there to lay down his mother's favourite flowers.

For a moment, she prayed for the dead to stir awake. Begged the soil, the blades of grass, the phosphene sky for a leak of help, but her mother's bible tongue slid about the ceiling of her brain — *You shall not test the Lord, your God.* Lia moved her hand down to touch herself, and as the boy looked down curiously at Lia's fingers working away she wondered if this was the first time he had done this. His breathing got louder. She thought of Matthew and came close. Then she thought of God, watching her in His holy garden, squirming on top of all His quiet sleepers, and came even closer.

The boy's face had fallen a little, as if he were beginning to regret the whole situation.

Lia began to feel him softening, began to lose her own sharp-edged swell of closeness, began to feel very sober, very invaded.

She bit down hard on the flesh between his shoulder and neck. He pulled out suddenly.

Sorry, she said quietly, a voice that was not quite her own.

That's OK, he said, *should we—*

But Lia was clambering over him, taking him into her mouth politely as if it were rude not to let him finish.

It seemed that nobody had ever done this to him either.

The Politics of Taste

It is important to exhaust absolutely all routes. The Greek historian Polybius provides a thrilling account of the Siege of Ambracia, where the Romans dug through mining tunnels, working day and night to claw their unexpected way beneath the city.

It has inspired a little underground approach

and now I find myself in her jaw, sinking my way through the
risorius, the Latin muscle she uses to laugh, pressing the soft
palette sweeping up from the mandible into her tongue, and from
here I can see:

She likes most food except for raisins and dates. There is a large
part of her that believes hunger begins in the tongue. That want
is a taste more than anything else and it works its aggressive
way from papillae tissue into cheeks, the back of the throat,
sometimes all the way down into the oesophagus.

There are traces of dark chocolate in her saliva, collecting around
her molars. It's bitter and clinging like liquid metal or stale wine
– *You should avoid dairy products, it'll make the cancer grow*,
the Japanese study had said, but all she wants is simple milky
sweetness. I'm gulping down all the knowledge of this, drunk on
it, on the encrypted recipe of her long tongue's life. Three point
four inches. Forty-three years. Her hunger, though trampled and
hacked and disfigured, startles me. Still stirring up and boiling
down memories of when pepper didn't taste of grit and tobacco,
of steaks and dumplings and duck and pale crumbling cheese
and plum-thick tomatoes soaked in vinegar and lemon-drenched
sole and garlic crushed into shallots, a few sloppy kisses and
strawberries stewing in thin sugared cream, meringue, lentils, the
soap of a jasmine flower, a sour mouthful of hay, various semen
flavours some fine, some terrible, most forgettable. Amongst the
noise, the odour and aroma, I know I am close; only one receptor
away from her gustatory cortex.

The Ambracians flooded the mining tunnels with poisoned gas.

It was, I am told, the first great gassing of history.

It is a good thing that, like fruit flies,
taste buds only live fourteen days.

Horace, Dickinson and Iris

The three of them were sitting at the kitchen table, eating yesterday's leftovers. Harry offered Lia some wine, knowing that she would say no, knowing that wine tasted disgusting in her new mouth, knowing that she'd want to be given
the option.

No, thanks.

One of the neighbours had left a bottle, a bar of chocolate and a small lemon cake on the doorstep that day. The note attached read *sending love and prayers!* Sending prayers where? Lia had written a small note of thanks to post through a letterbox but realized there had been no name on the offerings.

Breaking off a large square of chocolate and placing it on her tongue, she had felt briefly annoyed that the prayers and the love, the chocolate, wine and cake had reached them, but her thanks had nowhere to go.

She hadn't eaten anything since. The chocolate taste still stained the inside of her cheeks. Most flavours had become unpleasant, lingering for hours like the marks of bitter departed bodies on leather armchairs; each one having impressed itself so heavily upon her, making it impossible to forget their weight, their grumbles.

When they had first moved in together, Harry and Lia would cook with the vegetables Harry had grown in his garden. They often invited the neighbours over for dinner. They had taken such care in what they consumed, there had been no doubt in Harry's mind at the time that the world was becoming more exact, more detailed, more exquisite with
every year, every habit, every
chew, sip and kiss.

The truth was their routines, their marital rituals, had
loosened and then collapsed altogether.

The truth was Lia felt as if every small pleasure was being peeled
away, torn off her,
one by one; she could not work or taste like she used to, and
as Harry pierced his fork into the microwaved chicken breast,
swigging on the wine,
she hated him for it all only a little less, today,
than she hated herself.

Which word are we on now?

Susurrus. It's the loudest page so far. Rivers and reeds in watercolour.
I keep making mistakes and having to
start again.

There was a quiet while Harry chewed. *Transfusion tomorrow*, she
added, her knife ripping and tearing the skin, skin that had been
cooked crisp yesterday but now clung damp to the breast.

Yum.

Lia frowned at Iris. Iris pushed chicken around on her plate, not
speaking.

Shall we get any of the girls over? Or some new friends from school?

Iris shook her head.

That one today seemed lovely. What about her? Harry said, brightly.
He had picked Iris and a friend up from swimming that afternoon.
Lia could still smell the chlorine clinging to Iris's hair, settled into
the pores of her skin. It was the nicest thing she had smelt in a long
time; it seemed to soothe the taste of metal in her mouth. Iris was
giving Harry this hopeless look of total disbelief.

That's her. That's the Burn Girl.

Oh.

A tough half-chewed chunk slid slowly down Lia's throat and clogged at the bottom. Before she had coughed, Harry had stood and filled a glass of water from the tap, as if he had seen it collecting there.

Water, he said.

Lia wanted to spit a bit of Horace at him; Interesting people don't drink water, she wanted to say – you know, no poems can please long, nor live, that are written by water drinkers – but instead she took a large gulp of the terrible tasteless stuff, smiled and turned back to Iris.

It's important to keep friends close.

And enemies closer, Iris said, flatly.

Harry smiled, sipping his wine, and Lia wondered whether he had ever really detected the small sinister things that quietly grew out into the world. They seemed to slide up happily past him, taking their great dark places in the sky. What poem was it, the one where mountains grow unnoticed,
the poem with the purple and the
exhaustion?

The lovely ones are always the monsters, Iris said, spooning rice into her mouth, *and she's getting worse.*

Outside, the sound of foxes fucking or fighting floated above the fences. Standing to cut a large slice of lemon cake, Iris changed direction.

Solero Boy said it would be a full moon tonight. He asked me today to look at it, not just look at it but really stare at it, the perfect circle

*moon and all its white light, and then imagine the whole world as a
Capri Sun. The moon as its hole punch. From my bedroom window
I looked earlier and he's right, I really suddenly knew what it felt like
to live in the bottom of a juice carton with real-scale life happening
elsewhere, and then it got me thinking that maybe death is just the
moment God drinks us, sucks us up through His large orange straw,
and all of this life stuff is just
the slow and painful moving from
mouth to mouth,
belly to
belly.*

Harry raised his eyebrows as if to say, Fuck.

That's beautiful, Lia said. *You should write that down.*

A Long Night II

Time has a funny way of stretching itself taut across our worst
evenings, like calf's skin over the shell of a drum –

it took the boy ten minutes to come. It dribbled into the back of
Lia's mouth without force or urgency and tasted like salty lemons,
coins, chlorine. She walked into the toilets when it was over, sat
quietly in a cubicle watching patterns emerge on the locked door.

Lia? It was the twins. *Are you in there?* They began knocking as if
they knew and Lia made a small *yes* sound. *Someone's looking for
you,* they sung, *where have you been?*

She stood, unlocked the door and walked out as confidently as
she could.

A kind of disgusted surprise passed through them.

You look terrible. They frowned. *Here –*

One of them licked her thumb and wiped under Lia's eyes, the other brushed out the back of her hair with their fingers. Lia felt like she was going to be sick.

Who is it? Who's looking for me?

They grinned. Two identical smiles knotted neatly together, making one great row of pearly teeth circled in a deep purple.

Lia wanted to wrench open their large adjoined jaws. Step carefully inside. Crawl down their throats. Continue her days inside the comfort of their stomachs, but just then a voice came spilling out from behind them. With the sound of his voice, the world sought out its usual edges, locked into its regular outlines. The twins were two again. Objects met their matter, and Lia's soul basked, for a moment, under what felt like the first leak of sun after a year of lightless winter.

There you are.

Matthew.

Archaeological Excavation

It is remarkable how much there is of him here.

Scattered around the walls of her great impenetrable brain as if he, too, has tried to get in many times but her defences have blown him to s m i t h e r e n s

Splinters.

[state action]

[substance]

[recipient]

Stains.

Marks and shards of his grubby fossil fingers. Phrases. So many broken artefacts. I find myself scraping away bits of her tissue, sieving and phasing and excavating through the crumbs and undug soils of her cells.

I find whole cities of
              him

[sender]

beneath.

A Convenient Faith

What are you doing?

Praying.

Iris was sitting upright in bed, hands clasped tightly together as if her life depended on it.

Lia felt a sadness bolt to the mind.

About what?

Praying that Burn Girl loses that box, that nobody's secrets will be told this week.

Something in Lia began to stir the wrong way.

You cannot choose when and where you speak to God, you know. You cannot conjure Him when it is convenient for you, He is not a genie. When have you ever ever been even remotely interested in God?

Iris looked at her mother, shocked.

You sound like her.

Who?

You sound just like Gandy but worse.

Lia went very quiet.

Should we talk to the school?

Absolutely not.

Iris looked so stern.

You know, if it carries on, you should steal the box, Lia said, leaning on the door, trying to relax her body, her tone. This obviously impressed Iris because her shoulders loosened; she slipped from fierceness into deep thought.

It's impossible. It's always safe in her bag, which is either on her back or in her locker.

So. Lia shrugged. *Find the code to her locker.*

Iris grinned and nodded and Lia felt absolved.

In bed, Lia wondered why she had snapped. It was so rare, so
unlike her. Why had it felt like a breach of trust? She did not like
the idea of Iris getting all hooked up to Him at night. Perhaps
it was jealousy. Or a shame at the relief she felt the second she
saw Iris's hands clasped together, praying for her, perhaps. For a
moment she had thought – well at least one of us is, just in case.
Lia's mind filtered through these passages while she lay flat on her
back, Harry snoring quietly next to her as if his nose were clotted
with soil. Her lips whispered a *sorry, God* to the ceiling.
It lingered and soured
in that way a thing does
when it is not quite true enough
to assimilate
into
the night.

Optic Nerves

I've climbed up through her sinuses, balancing, now, on the ledge
of her iris, hoping to smash in through the windows. Have a go at
guessing the alarm code.

On the inside of her lids;

A
little private
collection of Best
Sights she occasionally
dips into when night shuts
and she must fill out the
darkness drumming
its phosphene
patterns

A shift disturbs.

She accommodates to something outside; the ring of the ciliary muscle surrounding her lens shrinks and contracts. Rays swell and refract on her retina and suddenly I can see in, beyond, for a moment. Suddenly, I am watching millions of nerves stretch and cross over, their pathways forming the gentle silver line of an hourglass, collecting, gathering these particles of time, sense, memory, depth and light all upside down and back to front, I see her whole life projected onto this screen of plain sight.

Somebody calls her name. Blinds shut. Yellow floods, the window in is gone, and
I am left in cold, mottled black;
no closer.

Week 3

The secrets slid up on the growing playground congregation, each week a little closer, deeper, colder than the last.

> Joe makes himself sick after breakfast, lunch and dinner. He knows he is fat.

At least he's doing something about it! a voice called out.

A cruel laugh skimmed the cream off the moment.

Burn Girl smacked her lips.

A Long Night III

The twins were staying with Lia that night. They loaded into the back of Matthew's car and sung loudly to the radio. For a moment Lia felt that she was part of something quite simple, quite communal. Something that could be shared.

Watching Matthew's fingers tap the wheel, his neck swaying, she staggered from one fragment of his body to the next, trying desperately to catch his eye, to detect what had changed in their year apart. What hadn't. His face was fuller. Once his cheeks had dipped inward like places that pools might collect in the silk flat sands of a desert. But there was a new plumpness now. And a dry, boyish blush. As if he'd been rubbing them hard or drinking far too much.

We need to piss, the twins slurred from the back. Matthew glanced at them in the rear mirror. Nodded solemnly. A minute or two later they pulled into a clearing; the twins tumbled off into the trees. Lia could only just make out their faint fleshy forms, their pink freckled arms pulling pants down, squatting low, giggling like woodland nymphs taunting a forest, harvesting all its witchy magic inside their cunts.

They had climbed quite a way. Below them,
God's land offered up pockets of
scattered light; the elsewhere life of
other villages, other houses, closer families, kinder
lovers all trembling out towards Lia
across a vast and moonless distance.

Matthew stepped out of the car and turned away towards the night.

Where were you? he asked, the soft thud of his piss on the beds of dry bracken. The residue of his *you, you, you, you* churned away, echoing against the hard wall of dark. Lia edged closer but said nothing. They both stared down at the shadow of his penis, leaking its last few drops. Behind them the twins cackled gleefully around the carcass of a dead fox, or bird, or rabbit, Lia could not make out which.

You're drunk, he said.

Yes.

Her eyes blazed, searching for war, for fight, for anything at all that meant he would look at her, really look at her, but instead he shrugged, full of a stiff, unfamiliar formality, and shook his penis dry.

It's sweet.

Lia watched her breath hang thin in the cooling air. He'd be sorry, she thought, he'd be sorry if it were my last.

He zipped up his flies, smiling at something behind her shoulder.

The four of them sat on the bonnet of Matthew's car for a while, the sleeping beast engine murmuring softly beneath their bodies while he smoked his cigarettes and the voices on the radio sung quietly about whole moons, ladders, scarves and comets. He diverted any personal questions to general topics; IRA terrorists that had shot their way out of a prison in London, the recent cataclysmic eruption of Mount Pinatubo – *death toll at eight hundred now – Mount Unzen just before that of course – somebody somewhere is*
raging.

He performed perfectly. Quick-witted but never arrogant, cool but never aloof, he passed around a half-full bottle of whiskey and when they finished it he pulled out another from the boot. Lia sifted clumsily through his voice for gold, for affection,

wondering whether this had turned out to be
the best or the worst
night of her life.

Whatever it was, it was
living. She was living.

He's beautiful, one of them whispered into her neck. *Strange, though.*

He had his finger in the other's mouth, feeling a growing wisdom
tooth as if touch and closeness like that were normal ways of
getting to know a person. Lia had never considered Matthew's
strangeness. She punctured a perfect smoke ring with her finger.

*You know, the inside of the cheek and the inside of a vagina are made
of exactly the same tissue.*

He made a little pop in the twin's cheek with his forefinger. The
twin laughed into his finger, her plastic dress crunching. And then
he pulled her into a kiss, gentle but firm, as if he were only having
a taste, only innocently sampling some small, delicious thing that
had just been handed to him.

Somewhere very near
a volcano quietly vomited out its insides
over three sleeping towns.

Lia wanted to empty her life of itself.

She could feel the semen in the back of her throat, feel it
chuckle up, drip down, and Matthew turned to look straight up
at her as if he knew, as if he could see it collecting at the bottom
of her windpipe like a tumour showing up on a scan.
Very shameful. Very solid.

Do you have to seduce everyone you meet? Do you have to?

Lia asked quietly, once they were back in the car, spinning through the vanishing roads. He blinked, unflinching.

I could say the same.

Where we going now? the twins sung.

Home.

His voice was suddenly laced with a bitterness she had thought him quite incapable of. It's jealousy, he's jealous, Lia thought, feeling somewhat lifted, a little thrilled by her accidental cleverness as the car picked up speed and the roads began to tighten.

You smell of it.

Of what?

You know what.

Like many events, they recalled what happened next differently. Matthew maintained to Lia, much later in life, that he felt the dense thwack-rollup-clide of a medium-sized animal body hit the front of the car and then the bonnet and then slip off the side, but Lia did not. Lia felt Matthew's eyes linger off the road and onto the blue light of her face for a second too long, felt the car accelerate forward, her heart lurching back against her spine, a panic spread flat against the car seat. He wanted to scare her. To punish her. She was sure of this. And then he lost control, as he would do many times after the accident that night, as if it had triggered something violent within him that could never be undone, and then the screams of the twins came, and then the pain, the pain so persistent there was no time or space or sense to locate the switch. It started in her neck but carried like a quick deep echo through her chest, her arm, pounding a deep and round and desperate cry:

Mamma, Mamma, Mamma.

If this is what the world is like –
I want my mum.

Accidents and Gene Kelly

Some impulses work like secret hidden alarms; you
tap an untouched edge and the whole world comes surging
towards you along one wide pain pathway. Ceiling sprinklers,
police sirens, Red's flashing electricals, the full works.

At the centre of all this madness is little old you, you who only
went to dust, to polish up a bad time, but now there are fractures
in everything.
All the seeds have erupted
and splintered the seals between systems, there is
blood coursing through nerve, bones mashed in vein and
naughty little me, just

'Singing in the rain'.

Dreams

Harry stroked the scar on Lia's shoulder and shook his knee as if
bouncing an invisible child. He did this when he was waiting for
something. Lia rested her palms on his thigh and said, *Stop it, you're
making me nervous.*

Harry was beside himself with nerves. There were three reasons for
this. They were:

1. After all these years he still hated hospitals.
2. Lia was having a blood transfusion and he still hated the sight of blood and sterilized needles and watching bags pump fluid into veins.
3. He was looking forward to seeing the postgraduate again.

The third most shameful fact felt strewn about his insides like jelly; weightless, cold, textured. He had not been able to shake away that shifting moment her face fell. He hated that he had made her uncomfortable, that he had been so serious. That she had been kind. He thought of her unbrushed hair, her chewed-up nails, her spilling bag, the way her boots kicked through swinging doors, and decided that it meant nothing at all. He had simply started to enjoy observing the nature of her interest, her attention. This was no crime.

Harry stood up and filled a small plastic cup with freezing water from the dispenser in the corner of the waiting room, feeling like a terrible cliché.

Lia watched the water dispenser bubbles blister up and felt something rise and pop quietly in her lung. Down the corridor a radio tink tink tinked strange music neither of them could locate or quite recognize.

Harry sat back down, pinched the back of Lia's neck lightly.

I think she sounds nice, she said suddenly, as if she'd been listening in to his thoughts. *I think you should be friends.*

That's not how it works.

But why not?

Harry swallowed the freezing water. It shivered down his chest. He didn't know why not.

I keep having this recurring dream, Lia said, quietly, leaning into him. *This dream I am being raped. The man doesn't have a face, just hands and teeth and a rock-hard penis that he pumps into me in perfect time to Mozart's twenty-fifth symphony in G Minor.*
A cluster of birds sit and watch.
Some are enjoying the spectacle.
Some are not.

The radio tinked away, and as the nurse called them in Harry realized the piece working its way out from down the corridor was, indeed, Mozart's twenty-fifth symphony in G Minor.

You look like you've seen a ghost, said the nurse to Harry. Lia grinned at them both like a child with a secret. Harry watched a scab on the edge of her lip crack and break with the stretch of her smile and thought sometimes, just sometimes, she scares me.

Blood Angels

There. Filling the place.

The blood of another;
replenishing her faded thinness;
doing strange things to the landscape.

It is as if some painter is fleshing out new layers of trees and rivers and roofs with a brighter palette; their pigments carry a new wind, a new hope, and I find myself thinking of restoration, conservation, and the flood of the River Arno in Florence that leaked into the Uffizi. Thousands of students and backpackers poured in amongst the rising filth to save the frescos, the Caravaggios, the Michelangelos, the drowning books and sculptures, ancient artefacts, all the leftover scraps of Vasari's *Last Supper.*

Grateful Florentines named them
gli angeli del fango –
The Mud Angels.

Such international instinct, I think,
as her heart hiccups and steadies, as
The Gardener's song of thanks makes its echoes
through her chambers like broken applause
swelling sadly through the Piazza della Signoria
on that cold November night
in 1966.

Her/You

The twins were not hurt. Glass from the shattered side windows
had lodged itself quite deep between Lia's shoulder blade and collar
bone, just missing the subclavian artery. Matthew had hit his head
hard on the steering wheel and had lost a lot of blood. Neither of
them were as broken as they could have been. In the hospital they
said it was a miracle they all made it out OK, but Lia had a distinct
idea of what a miracle was, and this was certainly not it.

What were you thinking?

Lia watched Matthew from the corner of her tired eyes. She
listened to him apologize over and over to her mother and father,
his voice crumbling softly with the shame of it. *We didn't even
know you were here*, Peter was saying, his hand tightly clasped over
Matthew's, his face a marble white.

Anne was silent, an impermeable look on her face. She shot a few
fraught glances over to Lia's bed. Lia pretended to sleep. Matthew.
He was only trying to help; they were drunk, he was getting them

home. He was going too fast, yes, but it had been the animal, the animal that shot out of nowhere.

Is she OK? Lia heard him ask.

Anne noticed the sound of his *she* was weighted by a new tenderness, a thirst, the way a word like *water* might change on parched lips.

She's fine. She'll need stitches. But she's fine.

Lia opened her eyes a fraction. Anne was edging closer to Matthew's bed, leaning down slowly towards his bruised face. Lia could see the words rising to her mother's mouth, could read the beginning of their shape as Anne whispered to him quietly, the phrase getting smaller and smaller so that its final unheard word was no more than a stroke of breath on a bandage:

You know I would rather die than lose . . .

Was it *her* or *you*? It happened too quickly, too quietly for Lia to be sure.

And then, to Lia's surprise, Anne was looking right up at her, and their eyes were locking together and holding each other's gaze long enough for something to be exchanged between them. Lia snapped her eyes shut again. In the dark, her mother's *her/you/her/you* thrashed madly about the inside of her skull like a hornet trapped in a jar.

The next morning, Matthew was sent to the neurology department and Lia was discharged from the hospital. Anne drove her home and Lia sat in the back, forehead against the glass, feeling the sting of stitches tugging in her shoulder. Certain cataclysmic events, she thought, will inevitably conjure the sense of an ending. This seemed like one of them. It was a matter of all the regular clichés.

The pressure cookers. The lids blown off. There was little point in hiding it all any longer.

I love him, she said, clearly and plainly, holding her heart in her cast, sling fastened to her chest like a shield. It was surprisingly easy to say it. *It's been like this for years.*

Anne felt a panic, like a flush of poison, carrying through her veins. Her knuckles whitened around the wheel.

Did you hear me? Lia stared at the mirrored sliver of her mother's breaking face. *The two of us. We have loved each other for years. It's been happening between us—*
Enough, Anne said. It came out as a screech that flared up in the middle of the word and died back down, a whimper at the *gh*.

Lia felt her stomach being dragged,   suddenly,   sideways

because Anne had turned the car and was pulling up on the hard shoulder of the motorway. She stopped so abruptly that Lia had to grip on to the door handle to keep herself from flying off the seat. For a minute or two, Lia stared out at smudges of sleet-quick cars, speeding up beside them.

How long? Anne asked. *Don't answer that.*

Lia had never seen her like this. Speechless. So still that all the furious vibrating little particles in the air of the car seemed momentarily visible. The electrons that made up Anne's body, quivering in the quiet. She still hadn't let go of the wheel.

Anne couldn't focus. Her mind had flooded with hundreds of misread moments and terrible images all colliding madly into one another before bending and sharpening, eventually, towards one coherent thought –

How dare she.

How dare she destroy what they had made.

She released the wheel, flexed her fingers, placed her hands on her knees and closed her eyes. The exercise, she thought – *Remember that in every wrong, sin and error is a truth. A test.*

Lia watched the back of her mother's head, eyes burning. She wanted nothing more than for Anne to shout at her. To hurl some of that old fury, tell her how embarrassed she was, how ashamed she should be of herself.

Anne took a deep, crackling breath, and opened her eyes.

On the motorway bridge ahead of them, a family of four waved madly at cars.

The world looked new. Uncommonly bright and violent. Anne thought briefly of the blind man at Siloam, of how frightening everything must have seemed the moment he could see clearly. Perhaps he'd wished, if even for a second, that Christ had just put coins into his palms instead of sight in his sockets. Anne smoothed her hair out. Cleared her throat. Started the engine.

As the car began to move, joining the thin continuous murmur of vehicles passing beneath the bridge, Lia saw that her mother was opening her mouth to speak, at last, and felt a flutter of hope.

You can sort your own dinner this evening, can't you? Anne said, her voice full of earth-shattering indifference, one absent eye on the backs of the happy waving family, sinking further and further away. *I'm afraid I've lost my appetite.*

It was the last thing she would say to Lia for three whole weeks, which just so happens to be the time it takes a person to lose faith in their family entirely.

Weapons of Mass Distraction

When you know the damage unheard words can do, it becomes hard not to plant ghostly little departed imprints of them everywhere.

Let us take

1

2

3

4

5

for example.

It may do just the trick.

---

1 You
2 You
3 You
4 You
5 You

six

Changes

Fragments of James Bond frayed the edges of Harry and Lia's
half-sleeps
as they drifted off uncomfortably together
in front of the TV.

Eighty miles away, Anne had her own little ancient black box
switched to the same channel. She was not watching either.
Instead, she was clutching one of her cancer books, skimming the
chapter on the Initiation, Invasion and Metastasis of Breast Cancer.
Behind the book, Daniel Craig's oiled-up body was being strapped
to a chair and
tortured.

The top of Anne's thighs began to itch when the whip struck
his skin.

She had tried to ignore the small red pimples emerging in strange
patches around her body. She had put it down to just another
symptom of that terrible Old Age. But this itch was severe, clinging
and climbing down her leg, her knee, her shins. She rubbed her
palms hard against the irritation and flicked to the Glossary. It
had taken her a week to get through the first chapter. She would
move to the back of the book often, one hand bearing the weight
of the unread pages, the other tracing for medical words and their
curious meanings, return and repeat the motion two or three words
later. Over and over. Flicking and scanning. She felt as if she were

making something beautiful, moulding clay, shaping a spinning pot, hanging the washing. Always good with her hands; bad with her daughter. Lia's life had been her greatest theological problem.

BRCA1 . . . human tumour suppressor gene (also known as a caretaker gene) is responsible for repairing DNA . . . epithelial phenotype . . . amino acid protein . . .

It was a stupid idea. The book was too advanced for her; too advanced, she was sure, for a student of science. But she was trying, at least, trying to understand what was happening to her daughter's body.

Anthracycline, antibiotics.

The problem with it was the lack of story. Narrative. When asked for his definition of Neighbour, Jesus did not turn to his glossary. He had a parable and a Samaritan up his sleeve. Human example is everything, thought Anne, as her hands shaped and carved and built and bent through pathology and insulin and enzyme activity and junctions and ecosystems.

God had a reason for all of this: there was something to be learnt, there was some slight human fracture yet to be blessed.

Oestrogen, forgive me.

But this business of suffering had been weighing on her recently. Christ suffered so that we could be healed; He carried our sorrows so that we, one day, could learn to bear the weight. And of course, suffering produced endurance, endurance character, and character hope. She knew there could be no hope without pain, and that life's troubles should strengthen her faith rather than weaken it, but it was a struggle. To be guided by His grace when so much had been taken, lost, broken. To feel His hand in the crueller events of her life, and not ask why but what, Lord, what can I do?

Podoplanin, forgive me.

The drawers in the house were still full of Peter's clothes. His jumpers and socks and cassocks. Sometimes in the morning the air in the house would feel dense with his smell, and then with a quick heavy exhale all that pungent bliss would disappear out the window, the cracks in the ceiling. She was still grieving, she thought, grieving the simplest elements of their old life, and she had only realized how much she had liked her husband after he was gone.

It was not just Peter that she missed. This felt too shameful to admit. She shut the fact firmly away, felt the seal of its close. But again, that breaking-squarking-scratch-pince-sharp-as-quince-jam-before-the-sugar on the loose sagging skin of her hip.

Mutations, forgive me.

The village had changed. People came and went now with all the fast trains and commuters. The church was no longer the centre of its community, not like it had been. On Sundays the streets were quiet.

Where is everyone? she would ask Mary, whose grandchildren had stopped visiting her. *Where has everyone gone?*

To London, of course, to see a show at the West End, gone to town for a pub lunch, gone shopping, gone running, gone making babies, playing sport, preparing for school, nursing hangovers from clubbing.

The church was emptier than ever. The congregation seemed to halve itself every five years or so and she felt the slimness of it all with such acute shame, such sadness. She would sing louder and louder on Sundays, she would double up on the prayer, the butter and the cream for after-service cakes, she would hold every ounce of her life out to the skies, elbows locked pride-tight, chin-against-chest as if to say, Look, we are still here, I am still here, Lord, I have not forgotten you. Look.

Father Nigel was nice enough, but he did not read like her Peter, he did not round his sermons off so neatly, so effortlessly. He lacked an intellectual rigour. Lia would certainly laugh if she could hear her now, thinking about intellectual rigour.

Transmigration, forgive me.

These bad days were growing more frequent. Days when she found it impossible not to entertain the haunting thought that Lia's suffering was punishment for her – Anne's – own ignorance. That His arrow was sharpened, stretched and pointed, deservedly, at their broken family, for being such fools. After all, Lia had been so young. And she had trusted him
so completely.

Worst of all was the fact that it had been months, perhaps even years since she had felt the usual rustle of warmth that comes at the kneel. That lucid glow which once simmered quietly through the evening during prayer. She was lacking even the slightest sense of His presence, which had never flared up, closed in or announced itself explicitly, but had dwelled absolutely in all things, from the domestic to the liturgical routines of her week, from the replenishing of the egg bowl to the first sung notes of a Sunday hymn. Something had been spoiled; an emptiness was widening. It was a temporary spiritual crisis of sorts that she was, undoubtedly, experiencing, and there was no easy cure. No obvious answer to the question: What, Lord, what can I do?

You worry too much, Anne. A crack emerged. She shivered and scratched at the itch on her arm; the cancer book slid off her lap and snapped shut loudly as it hit the floor. Enough for tonight, she thought. Enough dwelling.

On the TV, three disposable men were shot dead, their disposable brains blasted onto white bathroom tiles as if destruction like this was the simplest thing. She scanned for the remote, switched it off, and as the screen flicked suddenly to flat black quiet Anne was faced, briefly, with her own reflection. Alone, again. She cowered under the low ceiling, looking like a bird trapped in a box, so keen to break free of itself.

Unlikely Friendship, An Installation

While I am busy planting my little *You* bombs everywhere, Dove is putting Red to bed after a long day of destruction.

She will never understand him, but she is learning to tolerate. I have learnt that to tolerate is sometimes the best a bird can do.

Red's snout is all pink and sore from searching and Dove looks weary, weak, from all their terrible time spent together.

Instead of a bedtime story, they settle down to watch a rather beautiful installation piece projected on the flat side of her scapula. I am posing as an underpaid gallery assistant. The video features a great deal of guns and bombs and suited stunt spies spitting out from flames cut with fragments of nature documentary, footage of bacteria writhing about a petri dish, Linux code lines and circuit boards, and every so often a beautiful woman will whisper grandiose words like *sacrifice* from glossy lips so huge they take up the whole frame and though it is all a bit propagandary, I'll admit it's nicely edited.

Red watches in awe. He does not blink. Dove nuzzles her head into him so sadly and begins to doze off and it's nice to see.

This unlikely pair. So nice I write a list on the back of my programme

SAMUEL BECKETT	ANDRÉ THE GIANT
PEANUT BUTTER	JELLY
SCIENCE	FAITH
RED	DOVE

You wouldn't think to put them together. But here they are, remarkably compatible, perfectly providing what the other lacks. The sweetness, the salt, the smoothness, the crunch. You just have to take the first bite.

It is a surprise when more spectators begin to enter the space, but as they circle the bird and the red boy sleeping under the webs and the cells of the shifting light, I realize –

they are the art.

Week 5

The class would be lying if they said they didn't all, in their
sick kid particular ways, look forward
to the next secret reading.

Halia touched herself for the first time after her
rabbit died. She said being sad made her horny.

Halia missed three days of school. Someone said it was because she had meningitis.

Can't be true, she's had the jab!

Obviously it's not true, moron, she's embarrassed.

Poor Halia.

She shouldn't have fingered her rabbit.

She fingered her rabbit?!

And as they all laughed or scowled or gossiped or howled,
each thought:
                          this is the small stuff of dreams.

Tinned Fruit

Harry, Lia and Iris stood in a perfect
equilateral triangle, observing rows of tinned fruit.

I'm not saying we can't, I'm just saying they're not that good for you.

Oh go on, just some peaches.

Iris reached out and placed some tinned peaches in the basket.
Harry scrolled through the shopping list on his phone.

Tinned tomatoes, Iris.

Iris's fingers began to trace tins of tomatoes.

Dad.

Yes?

*Before coins and bank notes and credit cards – what did people use?
For money.*

She carefully placed three tins in the basket.

We bartered, Harry said. He loved it when Iris asked questions he could answer. *We exchanged goods for weapons, for tea, cattle, food, spices.*

Iris gazed up to the top row as if it held everything she wanted but would never quite reach.

Salt. Roman soldiers were paid in salt.

I'm going to the bread aisle, Lia sliced in, squeezing Harry's arm, her face soft and ghostly under the white unrelenting light.

Iris was only half listening, her thoughts congested with the business of secrets, the clever new ritual Burn Girl had constructed. People had started to bribe her and those close to her with gifts, food, homework, services in exchange for immunity from the weekly shell box announcements. Iris had tried all the obvious combinations on her new expensive six-digit lock. *That's one million possible combinations*, Solero Boy had told her. He wanted to be a mathematician.

When I'm grown up I think I'd like to be really rich, said Iris – *how do I do that?*

This felt like a more difficult question. Steer clear of books and professors, Harry wanted to say, but instead he said, *There are many ways. Often it's about supplying something that everyone wants.*

Even if it's bad?

Ideally it won't be bad.

Yes. Ideally.

The two of them drifted around the corner into large packets of pasta, rice, noodles and grains. Now Lia was gone, he could approach something he'd been planning to discuss with Iris for a while since her little strops about new shoes or needing braces. Her increasingly bad language. Harry lowered his voice, something he did when he was being as sincere as he could possibly be – *We need to remember.*

What?

We need to remember to look after her, to do our best.

I am doing my best.

To try and make life easy.

But life isn't easy.

There was a brief quiet of serious contemplation from both of them, before Iris turned to him and said, *How much do you think thigh gap surgery costs?*

Three aisles away, Lia was lost. She knew the supermarket back to front but suddenly it felt quite alien, quite startling. Two teenagers were looking sideways at her, their faces grimacing slightly as if something about her disgusted them, but they couldn't quite work out what. It was the young that seemed to notice it most. Her sickliness, her discoloured skin sweating that cold chemo stench, the uncomfortably thin hair, the sores around her mouth. Perhaps it went deeper than her appearance. Perhaps they could sense that internal imbalance, as if wrongness in a body let off a certain frequency only the young could decipher. And what luxury, she thought. To hold the world to such a high standard that when nature slips up – it is shocking. She felt like turning back and apologizing to them; but they were gone, now, and the whole place had begun to feel gruesome. The rows of red wine bottles were labelled with different blood types. The butchers were slicing through the meat of a human thigh. Next were these flesh-crusted cuts of Lia liver pie. *Fuck,* she whispered, *fuck fuck fuck,* as she turned into the bakery aisle. She stared at a packet of Mr Kipling cakes until the world had risen up and set right.

In the car on the way home, Lia looked at Harry and asked when he last went out for a beer, for a drink, for some fun. Weeks now. *You should get out,* she insisted, *for me, please, I'm keeping you all locked up.*

Harry laughed lightly and tapped the wheel with his fingers. *You're not, silly, you're not.*

Iris pondered the streets beyond the window, the outside world coursing, orbiting around the car, all material and texture and appetite. *Who would I go with?* Harry added lightly, but as he parked the car and they all lifted the bags out of the boot together he felt overwhelmingly weighted by the thought. Who *would* he go with?

Connie's ballet thing is next week, Iris added, heaving the bags onto the kitchen counter.

Can't get more out than that.

Here's another thing about marriage;
when it's so good sometimes
one forgets to need friends.

Here's another thing about currency;
before banks and notes and coins
all kids have to work with are secrets.

A Conversation Between a Sheet

Lia was sitting on the lawn scraping dirt with her nails, making small piles of pebbles and blades of grass between her legs. It had been three weeks since the accident. There had been no word from Matthew. Anne was pinning the washing on the line quickly, unthinkingly, like all care had been bleached from the world.

Neither spoke; both silent in the gloom of their own private miseries.

Peter surveyed the scene from his bedroom window, trying to button up his shirt.

His wife, his daughter, refusing to understand each other. His fingers refusing to work as they should. The buttons had never seemed so small, his hands so large and clumsy. Women had always been a mystery to Peter. He was ashamed to admit it. But there was something perpetually wriggling free, bounding away, giving up at the garden gates, sulking back. Perhaps if he had found some way of accessing his daughter's vast inner life sooner – perhaps if he had understood what his wife was so afraid of before he married her – there would not be such distance.

There was no distance with Matthew. There was no doubt he was bound to the boy, bound fiercely, patiently. There was anger in him, yes. Those steep and sudden clefts of pain that emerged between expressions, when his smile broke off and you knew he was plummeting down into a brief but deep unhappiness. He possessed an openness, though, the kind Peter had possessed as a boy. A willingness to be saved. It is the porous soul that makes space for God – lets in true, unyielding faith.

Lia had been impermeable from birth. Hard as a shell.

Anne had urged him to arrange it. He knew it wouldn't be hard to get him in, after years of good work in the parish, his theology degree, the fact that Peter had trained there himself. The seminary school was set amongst beautiful grounds at a remote location in Yorkshire. Matthew could consider ordination training after a year of rigorous study and it was a pleasure, really, Peter thought, as he slid the next button through the slot, his thumb and forefinger quivering the shirt seam, a pleasure to use some of the money they had saved to help him. For help was what he needed. What they were there for.

Once he had left the hospital, Matthew had asked if Peter would meet him by the church. It had been a damp Wednesday afternoon. The stale smell of rain on dry, late summer soil always a little melancholy. The camellia tree hadn't flowered that year. Peter sensed that something in their lives had shifted, for the hours at home felt bloated, the days swollen with a new atmosphere. Anne had asked that Matthew be kept away from the vicarage, away from Lia, and when Matthew appeared at the gate, he had the locked-up look of a man who had been entirely defeated, though by what, Peter did not fully understand.

I love it here, Matthew had said the minute he stepped across the church threshold, his whole face unlocking. Together, they watched the beams of ethereal mist carve out warm paths of light. Matthew took a deep breath. *There is no peace quite like it.*

They sat beside one another in the fifth pew from the front and prayed. The air was cool and still and purple. *Are you willing*, Peter asked him, eventually, *really willing to give it all up?* And Matthew had these huge glistening tears in his eyes as he replied, *Yes*. And Peter believed him. So it was done.

He would do well there, Peter thought, and though the calling never came to anyone who asked for it, he had always secretly hoped Matthew would follow in his footsteps. It would be a shame to let such potential go to waste.

Through the perfectly square window frame, Peter watched his wife freeze as his daughter rose to her feet. Lia's legs were worryingly thin. She moved closer and closer to her mother until nothing but a white sheet, heavy with damp, hung between them. Lia's lips moved a little. Anne reached down to pick up the empty basket and seemed to be responding. This would be their first conversation in many, many days, Peter thought, pressing his forehead against the glass, trying to read what was being said. Something about the composition of it all felt momentous. Confessional. But then Peter often mistook discretion for gentleness, perceived gentleness in places there was none.

In the garden, an exhausted silence had fallen, like the quiet after a scream.

Anne glanced up at the window. She knew Peter had been watching them. She felt briefly worried that he had heard their conversation, or read the words on their lips, but he was turned away now, unbuttoning his shirt from the bottom. He had done it up all wrong again. He looked so withered. So perplexed as he started again from the top, and Anne felt suddenly aware of a downstream sensation in the very depths of her body, as if her life had begun to fold away with a roughening tide and there was simply no way, now, to beat back against its pull.

Incantations

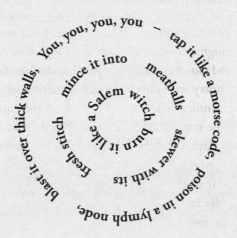

A Last Try

It hurts.

It does?

You're not finding the vein. It hurts. Please.

The student looked as if she were about to cry. The needle hanging out of Lia's arm had been dug in and out now three times, the veins around it bluing. Lia felt her stomach buck up against her little-girl heart. She wanted to wail and clutch a hand; It is funny, she thought, funny how they can chop me up, chug in any poison they like through me, and yet this failed entry needle feeling is the worst of all.

One more time, I'm sorry. I'm sorry. Nearly there.

The black entry marks made a little aching constellation on her arm. Harry was by her side, holding her other hand so tight the veins on his own hands bulged like the branches of root systems in soil.

Anne stood stormily over them, her body poised, arms hanging awkwardly – twisted and useless, like broken instruments.

Another attempt, the cold steel fished amongst a pale sky. The hospital windows momentarily sealed off all light.

For God's sake, can we get someone else? Someone qualified, Anne spat, quite suddenly – youthful in her rage, black eyes stern and strong, and for the first time all that unsteady meekness within her untangled itself.

Harry looked embarrassed but also a little impressed.

The student withdrew, defeated, the space above her lip glazed in sweat. She paced quickly away, muttering for help.

The familiar steely nurse with the citrus breath turned up moments later. She searched for the vein lightly with her fingertips as if she were deciphering great secrets written in braille. Piercing cleanly through; skewering moons.

You're not hydrated. You need to drink more water.

Lia nodded weakly.

After the bloods were taken, Harry did as Anne told him and left them. He sat in his car, marked his second-year essays on Proteus and Prophecy, thinking intermittently of Anne's startling boldness. When a traffic warden edged into view, he started the engine and drove around the hospital in circles for a while. Peeling the roads raw.

Nine dead bees. Lia had counted nine dead bees collected along the window ledges in the hospital, which struck her as strange for November. Their fat abdomens curled, frying in radiator heat, larvae and acid rising quietly out of them.

You know, one bee only makes about a twelfth of a teaspoon of honey his whole life.

Is that true?

Yes.

How do you know?

Iris told me.

Ah.

Anne smiled.

But the bee does not measure his life in teaspoons.

Lia felt the usual ridges between them soften. Her mother rarely spoke like this. She rarely sounded wise or considered. Perhaps she has been reading, Lia thought, meditating. Skimming through some old poetry books; some Prufrock plucked from the room with the forbidden bookcase and the window that opened and closed of its own accord.

Anne spoke of the milkman who seemed to have disappeared without a trace. She spoke of the plumbing in the vicarage and how increasingly difficult it was becoming to manage. She spoke of her cancer books and her studying into the night and the ways in which she was beginning to understand the language a little better now, and Lia was taken aback by her chattiness, by her buoyancy, letting the warmth of its ease wash over her.

I was wondering, also, Anne added, breezily, *if you were considering getting in touch with him?*

This came like a sudden shock of cold. Because they never brought him up. They never spoke of him.

No.

Don't you think you should? Don't you think it's important?

Please, Lia said, so sternly she hardly recognized herself, *please stop.*

They sat a while in the silence. Lia stared at one of the dead bee bodies being carried away by an alive bee undertaker and wondered what the word was. The insect ritual. Iris had told her some amazing bee facts recently. The way they mate very high in the air and the male just drops down dead when the bee-deed is done. The way the queen produces chemicals that dictate the behaviour of an entire colony. Lia watched Anne staring down at her palms. That – she thought – was what Anne had hoped for. To quietly dictate the course of Lia's life. And it had been too difficult, and so for many years she had simply given up.

You knew, didn't you? Lia said. *You must have known. The whole time – long before I told you. If you look back, if you really look. You must have.*

Anne had gone quite white.

I don't know. Maybe I did. I don't know.

You never talked to me, Lia could feel the emotion clogging up her mouth, *you never asked me anything. Not once.*

I couldn't.

Why not?

I . . .

Anne paused. She looked for a second
at her daughter, connected up to the last of her
terrible secret recipe, her
hard eyes begging for an
impossible communion.

Why not? What are you so afraid of? Lia pushed, her voice tearing
into thin rasps.

This was not the time, Anne thought. She was not prepared.

Let's talk about something else, she said.

That most devastating sentence, Lia thought.
Please, she begged.

Lia gave up. She let the hot air simmer and
settle between them, feeling childish. After all, it did not matter now.

Five of the nine bees had disappeared from the windowsill.

Necrophoresis, she said, quietly. That was the word. When social
insects carry their dead away.

Anne did not ask what she meant.

The session came to its end, and Lia realized she had forgotten
to make space for it in her brain, forgotten to summon all hope
and attention to the last hours of her last treatment. She felt as if
she were drinking sacramental wine that had skipped the blessing,
chewing on bread stolen from the altar, and now the ritual felt
hollowed out,
the rite quite
empty.

Then she wondered when it was that she had grown so superstitious.

Only one bee was left now.

Most moments, Lia thought, as they detached the red devil from her veins for the last time, most moments move so quickly they cease to become moments all.

Anne wrapped her scarf around her pale loose neck. Time wrenched them on. The nurse lifted Lia's coat onto her shoulders and touched her cheek. Anne watched closely.

At the exit Lia turned to look back. The nurse crossed both her fingers tight at Lia and nodded. Anne bowed her head deeply, ridiculously, as if feathers were prising themselves out of her spine, snapping her torso in two. Outside the hospital a young boy in a red coat sped past them, nearly knocking Anne into the road. He turned, grinned, lifted his hand up apologetically at them, and winked. Anne smiled a strange, charmed smile Lia had not seen for years, perhaps. Decades.

Harry was waiting in his car, wearing the same expression he had on Iris's first day of school. They dropped Anne at the station and then took the long route home.

Any progress then? With the dragon?

Yes. And no.

They passed a large billboard of a naked woman wrapped around a life-sized perfume bottle like a serpent.

I think she might be getting there.

Harry did not ask where *there* was. He missed two right turns on purpose so they could spend an extra fifteen minutes alone.

They sang loudly to the radio together, the volume up to its limit, the speakers croaking with the pressure. Lia told Harry about her mother's deep royal bow to the nurses, and husband and wife laughed together loudly, wheezing away as dead bees dropped from the sky around them. The windscreen wipers brushed them gently aside.

That night, Anne shifted uncomfortably in her bed, practising truth with her new tongue.

I'm sorry, she tried. *I could not—* She began to formulate the words, but they seemed to only tremble ridiculously at the ends, linger fearfully on her tongue. Hard lips tapped together.

What am I so scared of? she asked the ceiling. Her eyes fell on the cancer books next to her bed, on the bible and papers on Peter's desk and the stark cross hung on the wall above the chest of drawers still full of his clothes. So much, she thought. So much.

At 4 a.m., when sleep still hadn't reached in and released her from herself, she did something she'd never done, something she had watched her daughter do, many times. She climbed out of bed, crept down the stairs and went through the kitchen door. Her legs like stalks, toes curling, she walked out into the garden, beyond Lia's ruins.

Once she was far enough, free enough, she said, *I could not bear it*, so quietly to the fields, the hedgerows, to the shifting clouds and branches of light and the opening palms of the land that caught her sinking feet in welcome. *I could not bear to admit it, to admit I had failed you, I cannot bear to admit I have failed you.*

She said it louder, into the wind, every word folding further into a coo, an ache, until Anne felt much like any other mourning bird, rolling out the morning breeze, announcing another breaking day.

The Confession

Materials can become translucent
when water replaces the air in the fabric;
the fibres become less reflective, bonds are
disrupted, light passes right through.

Lia remembered reading about this after googling refractive indexes
for Iris's physics homework. She had discovered that when it came
to Google and science the answers were nearly always –
light.

> **Light. There. The quick glow of a
> fierce sensation.**

The dryer had broken earlier that morning, and she had been
staring for a while, now, at the sheets folded over the makeshift
clothesline she had constructed in the garden with beanpoles and
craft wire. Something was very wrong.

> **I follow the wrong. Stiff sniff odour haunts waft me
> gently along.**

Perhaps Harry had bought different washing powder. There was a new, uncomfortably familiar scent rising off the sheets, similar to that of the washing powder Anne had used when Lia was a child. The smell of the vicarage garden in late summer.

> Garden. Summer. Here. I squeeze through a
> narrow passageway carved out by fear.

But it wasn't just the smell. It was the image of the white sheets like this, hanging this way. She felt quite overcome with an emotion she could not yet place.

> For there – in the distance – is a scene.
> Clear as a hole-punch sun, I crawl
> through the dark towards it.

For there, hung by the pinch of two hearts along a washing line in the very depths of her skull, was a fury, filling the memory with a breeze that had not been there, making great ripples in the skin of the lapping fabrics.

> And it is as if someone has thrown open
> all the doors and shutters of a house
> to let a wind whistle through; I am carried
> up, helped out, hurled flat against her
> hippocampus,
> thalamus,
> amygdala,
> masses of grey matter and
> electrical pulses
> sharp gusts keep coming
> dispersing me across the place
> where all sense is stored, recalled, rewritten
> where time alters truth as it happens.

And Lia remembered the terrible conversation so clearly, only she felt as if she were observing it, now, not from her own eyes, but from that perched, uncanny distance the mind makes for itself having revisited a scene many times over.

And I am roaming the composition of a vicarage garden, watching her at eighteen with a sling and a shattered heart lift up from her limestone ruins. She edges towards her mother, who is pinning the last of the washing to the line.

I hear them begin to speak:

Please, **she is saying,** *please don't let him go.*

It is already done, **says the mother.** *He's already gone.*

Lia had watched the words hang in the brilliant white barrier between them; so thin and damp, each body could see the clear-cut shadow of the other, behind, shifting, sorry, indefinite. She had felt so powerless, so certain that it had all been orchestrated by Anne, that she had taken him from her. It was as if she had arrived at the great climax of her life, only to find all the guests packing up. (**Oh God, did nobody tell you?**) They had their plans, their future. (**I'm afraid it's been cancelled.**) They had London. (**Bad weather. Unforeseen circumstances.**) And now he had gone without saying goodbye.

I wish I'd never been born,
she says, so quietly, and I feel the truth of it fume through her; the despair and pity and hatred of it the most delicious thing.

Lia felt her fingers clench tight. It had not been her mother's fault, of course. Matthew could make his own decisions. It was embarrassing to remember how desperate she'd been, the ugliness of her adoration. But then Anne's response had come. And it had been worse than the fact of his leaving, worse than her meddling, worse than anything she'd ever said to Lia before:

There. Finally. Something we have in common.

Lia's hand had fallen back to her side as if all life had swiftly exited out of her fingertips.

> *I will never come back, you know*, she replies.
> Her eyes are stinging,
> *Once I'm gone, I'll never come back here.*

And there was the devastating outline of her mother. In their own tiny garden that Harry had made beautiful, tucking the empty washing basket under her arm as if it were all of no consequence, as if days were days and sheets were sheets, as if the washing would dry and be folded away in the evening, the morning, depending on the weather, as if the cycle would begin again;

> *Good. I'm sure then we will know some peace.*

Anne's unwavering voice. Everywhere. A final gust of fury, and Lia was alone again.

> **a break**
> **a shatter**
> **a squeeze**
> **a leak**

A girl can become translucent, she thought,
as she turned the key to the shed,
when pain replaces the proteins in her skin;
the soul has no choice but to reflect
little to no love.

> **And just like that,**[1]

---

1 I'm in

seven

Knowing Me, Knowing You

To truly comprehend a thing
is an act of devastation.

I understand this now.

Now that where *she* ends
and where *I* begin
is this difficult, murky,
slippery thing.

There were clues everywhere.

Let's take, for example, the German word
begreifen – to comprehend –
in which lurks the gleeful little verb *greifen*:

[to seize/

    to catch/

        to capture]

Etymologies reveal more truth than they mean to, like
DNA plucked from a fingernail, or prophecy squeezed from
Proteus.

The *com* comes from the gentle Latin *cum*:

[with/

    together/

        beside]

Perhaps I only ever wanted that. To be near her. With her. But she let me seize her. She *let* this kidnapping take place and now there is a

[girl/

    woman/

        creature]

in the basement of her body. Her hope is thin but she is stuffed full of
Stockholm Syndrome.

Our first night together in Brain will explain all of this better than I ever could;
our strange little dream, so vivid it made me sick:

It was 3 a.m., and her voice was leaking up from the floorboards, all *I miss the air, it is damp down here, I want to go outside now, please*. On and on she went like this and I began to feel so disgusted, so *bored* of her clarity, of the sheer amount of comprehension between us that I bundled her into the boot of a Fiat 500.

I drove for a few hours, until we reached a field, very far from the sort of places either of us knew.

She climbed out, untangled herself.

I gave her a map; a memory of our with-ness.

She walked away into the half-dark dawn.

I looked back a few times. She did not.

Now – that.

I cannot comprehend that.

Boots and Apples

Lia spent her night surrounded by the smell of damp, earthy boots, newspaper rustling underneath her cold body.

Her dream took place inside the boot of a car. Engine rumbling softly, a total darkness so closed and complete it was as if she had crawled into a womb,

her skin this amniotic texture, her fingernails
soft as warm wax. She
reached down to find a cord attached to her belly button.

She was not scared. She was not even surprised.
Instead, lids fluttering and sinking
shut, she felt that sort of safe numbness one only can when
stripped of all power. All autonomy. All hope.

Her kidnapper ploughed steadily on through the night.

To where – it did not matter.

There could have been a sinister sort of peace to the journey had it not been for the twinge, the twinge inside the depths of her strange, spongy skull. It was, she resolved, the kind of pain Eve must have felt after biting down on the fruit, just as all the world flooded in and her flesh became
its prison.

Favourite Fact So Far

Once you're in a head –
you can get in and out
as you please.

Like devils in vicarages.
Like boys in girls.
Like readers in books.

The Ballet

Please stand clear of the closing doors.

Iris looked crisp and clean and alive with station light.

Lia thought of her daughter's steaming baby body being wrenched
from a bath. Yes, that was it. She looked exactly the way she used
to, propped up on the bed, safe and fresh for something she would
discover later, in sleep; something the night would disclose. Only
the safeness had subsided now. *I'm actually quite excited*, Iris said,
eyes silver with the theatre of it all, fingers picking and peeling at
a poster plastered to the wall. The words

Have A Little Faith

were graffitied over the poster in lemon yellow.

Stop, don't go near that.

Why?

Lia scowled at the thick letters, newly sprayed with that automatic
gesture, that quick violent delight, and felt her stomach turn.

It's ominous.

Iris looked up at the very frail woman dressed in her mother's clothes smelling so faintly of her mother's skin and decided not to argue. Harry blinked at her as if to say thank you.

Harry looked smart. Smarter than he had in years, and Lia wanted to press her quivering match-like body against his and feel the top of her head set alight with his lips, his chin. She wanted to say remember, remember all those times on the escalators, remember our days performing youth and occasion perfectly, but realized there was no distinguishing thing she could pick out of these memories, no particular moment, she was sure, that he would recognize as especially profound or hopeful.

Their train arrived and Iris stepped into the carriage. In the packed, small space, she suddenly looked as if she'd grown a great deal. As if she were a good foot taller than she'd been on the station, at least two feet taller than she'd been on the street. Lia stroked her cheek and said, *You look so grown up.* Iris said, *Shhh, Mum,* swatting her hand away lightly but finding it again amidst the coated bodies a minute later, clasping it tightly.

Harry looked at his family, feeling a sudden pride, for they were glowing, and the glow was working its expansive way down the carriage making every passenger, bumping a little in their seats with the motion of the train, quite briefly beautiful.

We'll get a cab on the other side, Lia said, counting stations, *or we'll be late.*

I love black cabs, Iris whispered quietly into her shoulder, *we never get black cabs.*

Outside the station Lia ran out into the wet road to hail a cab, her ankles oiled by the sudden motion, her thighs awake, joints clicking like little exclamation marks all over a page.

Taxi!

Taxi!

A car cut through a great puddle of water, the water taking flight from the dip in the kerb and the churn of the tyres, narrowly missing a handsome woman in impressive red heels. The woman squealed in delighted relief and Lia thought of the baby Iris, her chubby toes and thick fleshy legs bending, bouncing off bathwater before being gently
lowered in.

The handsome woman wanted the taxi, too.

Lia stepped back onto the pavement, *Great shoes*, she said to the woman, in her most confident most sincere mother-voice, and the handsome woman winked and opened the taxi door with these long painted claw-like nails and Lia felt the particular warmth of a fleeting connection, a brief appreciation, and at once remembered why she had grown to love the city; for all the many moments of intersection it offered up, open-palmed and wide-eyed, without asking for much in return.

Mum, Iris called from a few cars away, *Dad says it's too expensive and we should get the bus.*

The Pointe

It's raining and she is grinning madly at me and
I cannot express the bliss of it.

The bliss of this
being out here, the exterior,
coursing through real textures and liquids and evenings
after being locked up so long inside her.

The movement a noun must feel when it wakes as a verb.

The moment a small theory is proven A Fact.

She compliments my shoes. I could kiss her. And then she skips light-footed into the road away from me and I am taken, briefly, to the end of *The Shawshank Redemption* with the lightning, the roaring thunder under the strings of a Thomas Newman soundtrack, Tim Robbins' arms spread out Christ-wide after five hundred yards of sewers.

That frame of Hollywood freedom.

I've found myself disguised as quite a genderless creature with great calves, a beautiful curvature to its spine. I'm wearing gorgeous open-toed heels with red soles. It seems such a shame to see them ruined, but the way they strike the pavement and the way the pavement spits up little electric shocks in response is a thing of pure percussion. The cab driver barely acknowledges us. Me. We get stuck in traffic but I am warm, and I pull my sleeves over their hands like gloves and rub these bare ankles, and as the shifting light of the evening blots and beats against the taxi windows I feel very content indeed.

The driver sighs and glances at me through his rear mirror.

Nights like these you wonder what the point is, he says, with a feigned friendliness gesturing to the queueing cars, and I want to say, The Point? The Point is glorious weather like this, The Point is the way rain sequins the night like this, The Point is the strength and the tenderness and these heels and this freedom, there are *so* many, simply *too* many Points, but instead I say *Hmmm* and turn to watch my reflection, caged and insubstantial behind the glass.

The truth is I want to peel off my left shoe, take the tip of the stiletto and stab it right through the driver's neck into his airpipe,

but
I don't. I don't. I don't.

After all –
What would be The Point?

Once I'm out of the taxi, I'm a totally new person;
a tall teenager, acne rising aggressively where his chin dips.
I feel very powerful but in a very directionless testosterone way,
nothing like the poised heeled body I had been a minute ago.

Crossing the road I'm a teething toddler. I remember how one
must expect children to have swelling and soreness in their gums,
ears and cheeks because they're all connected by the same nerve
pathways. Pushing through the theatre doors I'm a very old very
frail woman, false teeth rattling with each uneasy step, but there
is an arm now, an arm to rest on, and I can smell talcum powder
and rosewater, taste the stain of a carrot soup dinner in my cheeks.
There is peace here, peace and a little manageable pain, but
I mustn't settle.

Moving through the crowds I suddenly feel very flat and felt and
unremarkable. As I'm hooked onto a stand it becomes clear I have
found myself in the body of a black hat, which obviously won't
do, so after a little hot molecular launching I've torn through the
belly of a rat small enough to slick through swinging Staff Only
doors.

Red corridor. I think of her throbbing jugular vein connecting her
throat to the depths of her face.

By the backstage door I've landed
my best part yet;
a great chorcographer.

Today, he is playing the villain in white tights. He wears a huge
beastly head.

They are all there.

Yellow and Fossil and Velvet, The Gardener and Dove and the rest of the patient chorus, they are winding tape around their satin shoes humming strange little incantations, and a feeling of great relief floods me;
I have made it
just in time.

My company, my dancers, I hear myself say.

They all turn and look at me obediently, stretching and bending and clicking their beautiful necks from side to side.

There has been a slight change of plan.

Iktsuarpok

Connie had reserved them the best seats in the house. Row C, Seats 11, 12 and 13. The stage loomed wide, centred, curtains falling like the great hanging overcoat of a god waiting to turn and face his audience.

Iris sat between Harry and Lia, her slender neck craned back, mouth puckered open as if it were readying for a kiss, observing the immense interior with wonder.

Lia felt the gentle nudge of that almost-jealousy; she looked so at ease, so delighted by it all.

The space had been transformed into an ornate opera house. *This is amazing*, Iris said quietly, staring up at thick steel pillars giving way to ornately constructed gilt cornices that ribboned around the auditorium, carved leaves rippling up in perfect folds

towards a scooped-out ceiling. Along the rim of the round stage –
a live orchestra.

It hasn't even started yet.

Harry turned to grin at Lia. This is nice, he tried to say with his
smile and his eyes –
isn't it? This is good. Lia had all this plump, pink colour in her
cheeks as she pointed out great characters sliding into their rows.
Iris itched with excitement.

Where's Connie?

Lia leant into Iris, whose eyebrows led her face into that familiar
tumbling expression.

Backstage probably.

Polite strings tuned, the hum of human symphony rising and
falling around them. The last few members of the audience took
their seats; an old woman clutching her husband's arm shuffled
down the aisle, groaning a little with each step.

The three of them leant back in their seats. The bustle settled.
A cello ached.

It would be the best thing in the world, I think, Iris said, *being on
stage. All that attention.*

A Great Gift

I know when the lights have gone down in the auditorium
because my dancers have unclenched their hands; the final notes
of their prayers are floating above our heads now. Weightless. Like
a blessing, a necessary personal touch, I step forward and breathe
her taste, her breath, her scent into the stage.

HAAAAAAAAAAAAAAAAAA

I feel like God gifting life to the first man, offering
breeze to the first day.

The orchestra begins;
planets throw their light.

CLICK CLICK CLICK CLICK

The glare on the stage is so bright I am retching with the dazzle
of it. Even from the wings it is
nearly unbearable. But I let the planet lights do their
dreadful soaking and I do as I always have done;
I adjust.

Yellow is first. I kiss her feet before she leaps into the light, my
bright young soloist dripping in her thin yellow dress, chorus
flock following behind.

As it begins I feel her heartbeat, the quickening thumps of Row
C Seat 11, it licks and quivers through me like a tongue searching,
searching, searching for a flavour to connect the muscle with the
memory, and I feel my fingers draw back a drape of curtain, I feel
myself looking for their faces in the audience, her face, because it
is hard to be apart from her, to tell you the truth, harder than
I ever expected.

    thump thump   thump thump   thump thump

Yellow
flings herself
from here to there.

The rows upon rows of faces are unusually still; only their eyes
bounce with the desperate spring of Yellow's young calves.

If you have taken a look inside the satin slipper it's hard not to
feel the snaps of joints, the crack the phalanx bones make as they
peel across the stage, the ingrown nails the blisters and bunions
the ink-blue nibs of toes bearing the weight of a body, it is hard
not to peer beyond all that perfect effortless grace and see only
the sort of
grotesque ambition of man.

Hard not to look at the woman and see only her
monstrous insides.

I watch the flicker of recognition in her eyes, the horror;
on my stage it's her shed in the back of the garden. It's her house,
and she knows I am here, bursting with the knowledge of all her
fractures, strains and failures –

For you,
I want to scream,
this is all for you,

but instead I stretch my arms up above my hidden face, my
mandibles click into place, I hear the orchestra begin to shift their
key as if a poison has infected the melody.

Proteus' Dance

Lia spotted him before anyone; the beast in the wings, the dancer
flexing his thick sculpted thighs, wearing his monstrous mask,
scratching the leathery skin on his arms while the young dancer
draped in yellow satin threw her delicate way here and there,
clicking her head back with the lurches of the strings, snapping
her leg so high it seemed to detach from her spineless torso. She
painted the stage with colour.

Iris squirmed in delight and Lia remembered, for a moment,
the violent twist of her half-formed body
growing inside her belly, the first
pressure of skull against her cunt.

Iris nudged, *Look! Mum! Look! It's the Astute!*

With great strength Lia beamed wide and nodded.

So it is!

Somebody two rows behind shushed them.

The beast began to leap between trees, snapping branches, pulling
the stage apart, peeling off slats of roof, drenching the oblivious
dancers in his howl his spit his particular threat of hell, and all the
while he went on switching his masks so that he could dance with
the group, could press his fearsome body close, take a lover, even,
snatch away a mother or father and
nobody would suspect a thing.

Iris thought of Burn Girl.

Harry thought of Matthew.

Lia thought of death.

The auditorium shook itself down and shifted seasons.

A handsome man buried up from dead stage sand like
Lazarus, shaking off dust from his dry,
sunless skin.

A pale, older woman with great white wings
collapsed in from the sky on rope,
bringing snow.

The handsome man caught her body the second before it
hit the floor and
Lia gasped at the impact of it. They danced for a while like
mother and son while the audience twitched with unlikely cold.
Hundreds of little breaths collected by hundreds of parted lips,
purpling in the frozen air. Lia could suddenly trace the scent of
undercooked potatoes,
Anne's washing powder,
the sweat that would collect around
Matthew's collar bone.

At times the beast seemed to disappear completely, but Lia knew
he was never really gone; his shadow was everywhere, rehearsing,
bubbling, bending against a red horizon, the flat grey wall of a
medieval town, a chalky cliff face. Before each of his returns, a
dancer in deep purple velvet would sweep the stage and tenderly
change the scene.

Each time he came back stronger, more agile, in new temporary
skin. A herdsman. A witch. A locust. A king.

She watched the light change on Harry's profile, his cheeks dewy.

Is he thinking what I am thinking?

Is he seeing what I am seeing?

His fingers
tapped along to a new rhythm, as the dancers parted
ways to let Spring in. A gardener decorated in
beautiful green embroidery challenged the beast, the beast who
now wore the body of a wolf and even Harry could smell it
everywhere, clinging to the worn upholstery, the damp compost
of their very own garden.

Red Devil's Victory

Nobody likes a show-off but I'm doing ever so well.

The small house in the corner of the stage is now nothing but a
ruin. Just stumps of stones. Like toddlers' teeth. Exactly like those
in the vicarage garden, where she grew up. The little obliterated
kingdom she once ruled.

I can feel the audience, the weight of them dangling at the
bottom of a fishhook as I toss them left to right, release them
right up into the open sky and wind them back close again.

I'm having so much fun I hardly notice his devilish motif
crawling up through the composition, playing in the Main Event,
the Magnum Opus, the Pièce de Résistance.

I search for their faces through the light. Her daughter leans into
the nook under her arm. She tries not to, but I can see her face
acknowledge the smell. Red Devil stench. It is very nearly an
unkind expression.

He arrives a little off-cue. A little earlier than expected, bursting
through the door on his bike at the back of the stalls. He
screeches his first note and they all turn their heads in brilliant
unison. Hundreds of neck napes are suddenly exposed to me, and
I cannot help but think how easy it would be to run down each
row with a blade the way children run sticks along railings. Make
a musical clang. Slice through twenty lives at a time.

Do you think it's working?

The way he shoots through the aisle is a thing of pure
pantomime. *Here he is! The Unlikely Hero!* One collective sigh of
relief swells and fades. Humanity has never felt so singular.

Before I can ready myself, he has leapt up onto the stage.
the notches begin to slide and
I feel an internal undoing,
             a slight
syntactic interruption.

We begin our David and Goliath dance, his red legs split
wide above my head, his wet toxic breath on my shoulder;

                                    we help each other's bodies

into their air, spin, catch, fouetté,

                        grand jeté,

                                fist full of flight, a new banging

in my head; he is finding new

                        extraordinary ways to twist,

                                rip and squeeze my shifting parts across the

floor, until – I am

                        the one who is dying,

                                    I am the one who is weak.

Eventually, he moves back to let them have their go. Perform the
finishing touches. Yellow blinds me with slender light. Velvet
crushes and cloaks the stage in night. Dove is picking at my skin,
ripping off great chunks of fur with her beak. The Gardener is
slicing my wings with his shears. Fossil has turned half of my
borrowed body to stone. Each are hurling their elements, their
light and sky, their rock and their
earth.

I am crawling now,
crawling on my belly towards her ancient ruins,
her little promised land.

I think of locusts. I think of how they survive conditions no man
ever could. I think of the many plagues they have carried through
time and scripture and the way they feed the earth when they die,
so full of nutrients and goodness. Nobody ever thinks to thank
the locust or the nasty little things that turn out to be quite useful
to us. The lights are low now. The only music is her heartbeat.

I have made it into her ruins, my spine furled.
The last thing I see before I die my
deliciously convincing death
is her grin,
tearing out towards me like a miracle through
the thick, exhausted air.

And then I am gone
and he has won.
And she has been given
her little portion of victory.

The Mask

Lia had tears streaming down her face as the audience applauded.
She stood, trembling, as the rest of the auditorium lifted to their
feet, each like the little hairs rising up
on the back of her neck.

The young red boy took centre stage, beaming wide, bowing deeply
under the spotlight.

He locked eyes with Lia, for a second, blinked the way animals do from behind their cages.

Imagine what he must be feeling. Iris clapped furiously, turning to face the standing ovation behind her. *Magic.*

The red boy disappeared off the stage, the others made their bows.

Lia pulled her coat on – *Iris*, she said, so quietly,
fishing her bag out from under the seat.

The treatment. I think it's working. I can feel it.

Iris nodded seriously, as if being let into the only secret worth knowing.

Connie was waiting for them outside. She looked nervous.

Did you like it? How was it?

Beautiful, Harry said.

Lia clung to her tightly, Connie's familiar smell sinking through her clothes into her skin. *Thank you,* she said, *thank you, thank you,* over and over. She looked into her friend's eyes, lilac under the entrance lights.

Now that will make you a national treasure.

Connie beamed wide, but later that night she would think back to it, back to the tone in which Lia had said it, back to the pointed tenderness of her squeeze, and would worry her friend was actually saying – *there, at least that is
one less thing to worry about.*

Crossing off the reasons
she couldn't die yet.

On the bus home, Lia watched her reflection, caged and insubstantial against the glass.

The mask, she said quietly, her breath condensing on the window.

She felt pleased to see such sudden proof of life.

What?

At the end. The beast should have taken off the mask. I would have loved to have seen the dancer's face.

Beast
Noun
[*plural* **beasts**]

1. An animal, especially large or dangerous.
2. An inhumanly cruel, violent or depraved person.
3. That thing you just conveniently defeated.

Week 7

Lan's mum is a drug addict.

Oh well that one makes total sense.

Does it?

Yeah. It's why her lunch boxes are shit. Four cheese strings and an apple? No thank you.

Very Near

Iris.

Yes?

What do you think happens when we die?

The silence of a hard thought.

I think we go somewhere very near.

The Last Scan

Her body, our body, is slid on a tray into a clean white oven.
It all feels very sci-fi. It is during these times she feels most like
meat, beaten and boneless, splayed out to cook, ready to poison
the party. Radio waves and magnetic energy, spinning proton
plates, a little Chopin swimming like liquor through her.

While she's looking for a memory to shut herself in, I will briefly
add that it is very satisfying putting two and two together after all
this time; glorious to feel each of them clicking into their context.
I set about sewing their shadows to their feet, watch them take
their place in the space-time continuum, etc, etc.

She's found one.

The memory is taking place on a pavement.

It features a little girl (daughter) dancing down a lesion in her left
temporal lobe. The girl is no older than four and has a terrible,
terrible haircut. She jumps between the cracks in the pavement.
There is so much bounce in her tiny cotton legs as she leaps and

pauses, takes another wide step – she clenches the air with her fists and says, *It's here! It's here! It's here!* with such simple delight I cannot help but join her. We hold hands. She looks at me. *It's here!*

Her body, *our* body, comes into contact with the exact same fear she had felt in the memory; a kind of mystical regret of some mistake you are yet to make. In the memory the mother is asking, *What is, little one? What is here?*

The little girl does not answer, looks straight at me. All the cracks begin to widen.

Axis

The moment a life tilts on its axis:
you feel everything you knew about fight and hope and justice just slide right off and out of you.

The mind must ready itself for a clearance like that.

The day of the news was unusually open and bright for early winter; it lay in great slabs of golden light against the concrete roads. Husband and wife drove in silence, tragedy dusting down its calm starts,
blanketing the minutes before them.

The hospital corridors were quiet, as if scraped out for a solitary occasion, and Lia felt a strange sort of peace. Harry was not nervous either. His breathing was gentle, his skin that easy morning cold. Sometimes humans rely solely on the disconnect between a moment and its meaning, Lia thought. On barriers, emptied minds, bodies that have closed themselves off from letting in much at all.

And so husband and wife waited to be called as if it were any other day. They walked into the doctor's office as if they were any ordinary couple receiving the usual sort of information that, after eight years, they were quite used to receiving. *It's working. We'll try something new. Drugs from America. A little surgery, perhaps.*

The nurse was there, she looked
plucked from an over-exposed photograph.

The doctor with the emperor eyes gathered himself.

I'm sorry, he said.

I'm so sorry.

And with that they began to sink. Through the thinly padded chairs they were perched on. The carpet. The layers of earth and rock. They sunk together through their own quick years, their light and hopeful
history.

It is in your brain. Here.

Lia looked up at the scan, the great sum of her life illuminated. Three small tumours grinning out at her.

Here.

In her liver, it had grown.

The light scattering in her lungs – swollen now.

It's everywhere.

Sometimes language is too crude a thing

Harry, who had been so brave, so calm, inhaled as if somebody had ripped out his lungs; there was air but there was nowhere in his body it could go. There was a body but there was no life any more to animate it.

Sometimes language is too vague a thing

It hadn't worked.

He told them about the clinic in Germany because doctors, like lovers, must speak of the slightest hope. Must provide scraps on which
to cling.

Harry clung and clung.

Yes. Yes. We will go there. We will find a way. We will.

Lia went on sinking.

There were conditions that made it difficult, of course. Expenses. They may refuse to treat her; she may already be too weak. There was no guarantee it would even work. Not now, with the knowledge of how aggressive it was.

Lia sunk through skin and bone and organ, the doctor's office and the desk and the nurse and the husband as distant as a Capri Sun moon.

I have failed you, she said quietly to each vessel and tissue at the bottom of her juice carton body, *I was wrong. I have tried and I have failed you.*

Sometimes language is too gentle a thing

Nothing on earth grew that day.

Here is a fact:
The only thing worse than death is knowledge of it coming.

The Function of Freedom

I suppose one would assume I enjoy the whole 'telling' business.
The Announcement. The gladiatorial wrenching up of the arm,
the *this guy won*.

The truth is I don't. The truth is that I find it all rather
uncomfortable and heady and overwhelming.

Because a power like this is a great burden. A great honour.
Because really –

I'm just getting started.

Leak

Notes to Self

I must now refrain from:

1. Telling the rest.
2. Interrupting.
3. Gorging.
4. Getting distracted.
5. Being too disagreeable and/or negative.
6. Sentimentality.
7. Postulating God.
8. Guilt.

eight

Her Heart and the Husband's Body

Lia watched Harry in his garden from the misting glass of the
bathroom window,
swallowing down her steroids
with a cup of milk.

They had both woken that morning to find the other a little
changed;
death a day closer,
Lia bleeding from her nose,
Harry having grown
two perfect dandelion flowers for eyes.

Lia reached out a skeletal finger
to caress his yellow petal edges,
but he had shut them tight again, like a child not quite ready to be
born.

Not yet, not quite.

She had smiled weakly at him and said,

Your eyes.

When he opened them again, the flowers were gone and the
clock had opened; wild pupils contracting in the light, myriads of
plumed seeds ready to disperse in the slightest breeze and quietly
measure out the last of her life.

My wife, he wanted to say, but instead
he pressed his thumb above her lip to stop the blood running from
her nose into her mouth.
He had looked sadly at the stain of yellow, creeping into the whites
of her eyes,
had turned away to retrieve a tissue from the drawer.

Today we call the clinic, he'd said.

And now she was watching him pace the garden, phone pressed to
his strange new face, milk curdling with the flavour of
iron at the back of her mouth.

It is easier, she thought,
now that we are both beastly,
as the knotweed stems wound their way around his legs,
climbing further, it seemed, as he paced.

Somewhere close by
a choir on a radio was beginning
the haunting first notes
of 'In the Bleak Midwinter'.

Lia felt a brief but brilliant warmth of every good and safe and
painful thing
burning right through her.

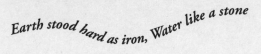

She could just about make out what Harry was saying. He was
speaking of money. Expenses.

Illness does many things, she thought, but perhaps most sick, most
grotesque is its way of reminding you that death and dignity can
have as much to do with economy as they do with

luck – that sometimes
life can be
bought and
sold.

What can I give Him, Poor as I am?

Harry's breath frosted and curled. Lia wished she could bottle
his breaths, pour their hope, their ancient woodland goodness
into her milk.

If I were a Shepherd, I would bring a lamb.

Are you sure? Harry was saying, his feeble voice carrying up and
through the gap in the window. *How long will that take? This is
time sensitive*, he began to repeat, a few times over. Two plumes
blew from his eyes and floated away.

If I were a Wise Man, I would do my part

Time sensitive –

*this is very
time sensitive.*

As if there were things in the world that weren't.
As if the great eroding hadn't already begun.

But what I can I give Him, Give my heart.

Grace

There is no haste. No rush now.

The days after the news I have found nature to be respectful.

The foxes have chosen other grounds, other streets to prowl, and
his garden has begun to flourish. Bulbs are breaking through icy
beds that rise and fall gently like a chest in half-sleep; even the
hyacinths that had failed to bloom for two years blink and twitch
just the way she does when waking.

Today we took the daughter to school. We got halfway but had
to turn back. Not because the morning had grown too violent or
too cold but because it was
stunning and light and so full of grace.

Now that everything is quite inside-out, the chorus of characters
that once roamed her veins seem to be

      hidden,   here,
                                      all over the place.

    Flashes of her father's black raven feathers around every corner;
        even the kitchen utensils have adopted familiar voices.

The truth is her memories, her nerves, her cells are now
                  growing in everything.

I am taken often to the landscape of her stomach during
pregnancy – taut and bruised from the weight, the love, the
thirsty little organism draining her slowly.

It is comforting to me that I am cut from the same cloth, the same
semantic fabric as the embryo. *Squirming growth; fecund foetus
thing; hyperactive little parasite.* It is nice to be reminded I am
not so different.

For most of the day I dig for good gold things in her past.

I find the three very good weeks after the daughter was born.
Drink them up.

Stomach has begun to get used to its usual self again, like a sea
after a great flood or a snake's throat beginning to decompose its
prey. Our nipples are so sore and swollen and raw sometimes even
the husband's weary gaze will make them ache, but her body, *our*
body, has never felt so useful. So necessary.

After we feed the daughter, the husband plays with her incredible
thumbs and we shower to the brew of both their incredible
sounds, watching the water pour off our breasts, pinching the
flesh of this stomach all loose and fruitless now without the
daughter inside of it.

When we step out of the shower, our nipples begin to leak little
beads of diluted milk, sliding like tears down chins; Why there is
any point in showering I have no idea, we think, together – back
and forth we go for those three weeks, back and forth between the
water the milk and sick and sweat water milk and sick.

Remember the way he kept your prickling body
ticking over, always? I ask her.

He comes into the bathroom just as we are reaching for the towel.

He kisses the beads of our milk skimming down our stomach one
by one, drop by drop, his hands lightly on our waist, knees resting
on the floor, and we laugh together; my laugh hidden somewhere
within hers like the black ink of a cracked cephalopod in a stream,
like the *rage* or the *cure* or the quiet churning *cog* in *courage*.

I am making sure she remembers his face.
What it was like then; uncorrupted,
gazing up, traces of white
                              on the nib of his lips.

That was peace.

It turns out you can hurt more with the good then you can with the bad.

That the peace aches more than the misery.

The Third Who Walks Always Beside You

Once Lia had left home, she did as she said she would do and cut ties with her parents completely. She had hardly seen Peter during those last months at home; he seemed more indifferent to her than ever, and after the terrible conversation with Anne it was clear they would be better off living separate lives for a while.

(They wish you'd never been born)

She tried as hard as she could to wipe her mother's words clean from her history.

FINALLY! SOMETHING WE HAVE IN COMMON!

I have erected this phrase on the billboards at Piccadilly Circus especially for her arrival. I have done it in this bold, tyrant lettering, sandwiched between Samsung and Coca-Cola, just to make sure she can't miss it.

(I honestly just couldn't help myself)

And so London arrived in Lia; huge and rapid, dirty and expensive and entirely different to anything else she'd ever known. She understood quickly that economy had as much to do with freedom as godlessness did; that she could go anywhere, be anyone if she was un-precious enough about her work, her body, her company, her space.

The hours between university lectures were packed full of
early mornings, restless nights reading Milton in between the
pressing of sheets,
Eliot while the limescale bleached off the toilet bowls,
Dickinson in the lobby after hours; all in the
expensive hotel
where the businessmen
came and went, clicking over her clean floors with their
leather and their wealth.

> **Aha! Here's her love of poetry beginning;**
> **I feel it unfurling within her**
> **like a whole magnolia**
> **blossoming completely over**
> **one night.**

Lia found the other hotel staff much more alive than the students;
they had a bold, accepting lightness, they spoke different languages,
they were from more interesting places than Barnes or Hull, they
were from Buenos Aires, Turkey, Thailand and Bulgaria, and Lia
would watch them all drinking together into the early morning
through the circular window of the kitchen door in awe, forgetting
him, for a moment, hoping to be invited into their pale blue
planet of silver light, shaking with the clang of glass and copper,
aluminium and teeth.

> *We will forget him!*
> **(I tell her, just as she's forgetting)**
> *You and I, tonight!*

Once she had been beckoned in, she perched up on the worktop
cross-legged, displaying her own rehearsed laugh, disguising as
best she could a sudden insurgence of pain because something

(as it often would) had reminded her of having to forget him. Like Emily Dickinson. Or the way a waitress had her body folded happily into the lap of a waiter.

> *You may forget the warmth he gave*
> *I will forget the light*

She cut her hair short.

Waaayy too short.

She helped herself to the small bottles of soaps and shampoo from the hotel bathrooms, sometimes a towel or two, a few embroidered slippers, and began letting the slightly older chef fuck her once or twice a week, in the store cupboard, where all the spices were kept.

> **His skin smells of vegetable oil.**
> **He is pinching the flesh around our scar a little too tight,**
> **and it hurts (SLAM) more (SLAM) than the usual pain one might**
> **tolerate during sex (SLAM) with a near-enough**
> **(SLAM SLAM SLAM) stranger.**

He always had an exquisite little plate of leftovers waiting for her after he was done.

Sometimes, he'd finish himself off while she spooned venison croquettes or the last of the salt-baked cod into her mouth, and he'd watch her, looking back and forth between the cutlery clinking away and the thk thk thk of his cock.

> **(Creep)**

And then she met Connie, at a life-drawing class run by some third-years, and life brightened unexpectedly.

Lia got to know the shapes Connie's veins made on the side of her thighs, the way her breasts hung in certain heats, the stretch marks around her right hip bone, before she even knew her name. During the ten-minute breaks in the middle of the class Connie would relax from her pose, wrap her velvet dressing gown around her naked body, go to examine all its many various representations.

Lia worked only in shades of red. Scarlet, maroon and vermillion. She worked with fine brushes in fluid but assertive lines, it would take her the full hour for any coherence to rummage its way out of her gestures, but the body always came together, right at the very end.

Connie singled her out immediately.

They're so sad, she said, her nipples brushing against Lia's shoulder.

They are?

Yes. Like you've painted me inside-out. All bloody and fragile. I love them, Connie whispered in her ear, so quietly, as if they were twelve years old, as if she'd been prowling the playground, looking for likeness, and had landed, decidedly, on Lia.

We can be friends.

Within two months, they had moved into a small flat together, and it became even clearer to Lia just how limited life in the vicarage had been. Connie provided her with stacks of feminist literature to read, and on Sundays they worked their way through three or four classic films made by people she'd never heard of, from Hitchcock to Kubrick, Bergman to Spielberg.

Neither Anne nor Peter made any attempt to contact her.

And so Lia picked up a second cleaning job at the theatre around the corner to pay for the extra rent, she handed very average essays in very late, she swept the cigarette butts from the rooftop bar and drank the beers left behind, she learnt to stretch her own canvases, mix her own paint, she experimented with oils and chalk,

and returned home most nights to Connie's bed (for she hated sleeping alone), Connie who would groan a little animal sound with the nudge of Lia's body, move onto her back and seek out a hand so the two of them could drift upstream, in sleep, together; two otters headed for
the ocean.

In short, she is happy.

Q: What do humans do when they're happy?

A: They throw it all away.

The Cinematic Language of Edward Hopper

Harry was sitting on the train into work, feeling like a person in an Edward Hopper painting. Peering out of a blue frosty palette, suspended, in the middle of some action that had been forgotten minutes ago and would never be completed.

Lia had dragged him to a different art exhibition every week when they were first getting to know each other. He lost her once, at a Hopper retrospective. Rather than staying in one spot, waiting for her to waft by, which he decided would look incredibly needy and perhaps even a little disrespectful to the art itself, he wandered through the white rooms alone for a while, contemplating the lifeless suited men and peaceful half-dressed women while they contemplated him back from their untouched beds and their wide-screen windows, their sparse hotels and over-lit cafes. And though this only went on for half an hour or so, perhaps only twenty minutes, his spirits plummeted quickly. He was suddenly unable to draw any satisfaction out of the afternoon without her there, this woman he hardly knew. And how astonishingly foggy and quiet and immense, Harry had thought, a landscape can become under the first flushes of infatuation.

He had found her eventually, leaning far too close to a wall with tears in her eyes.

On the wall, a Hopper quote.

What I wanted to do was paint sunlight on the side of a house.

There was simply no option, no version of the story that ended in him never finding her again.

The smell of hot salt and starch came through the carriage. Someone was eating a McDonald's. Harry had always found the smell of fast food oddly comforting. Hopeful. He hadn't eaten properly for days. He could feel saliva building in the back of his mouth, collecting around his molars.

Most of his time in recent weeks had been spent on the phone to the Dove Clinic in Germany, emailing the Dove Clinic in Germany, googling the alternative cancer care available at the Dove Clinic in Germany, and Lia had turned to him and said, *It's called the dove clinic? Dove. Are you sure?* and he'd tried not to look exasperated when saying *yes*, for the fifth time that week, and she'd chuckled away for a while. *How funny!* She laughed. *How funny.*

He had not understood.

Harry. Hi.

Someone was saying his name. He turned towards the voice. It was her. Of course it was, with her lovely head resting on top of a royal-blue scarf wound at least three times around her neck.

She sat down in front of him as if he'd invited her to. Harry noticed that he had no idea what his face was doing. If he was smiling, if he'd said anything to her in response, if he had gestured to the empty seat opposite him after all. Perhaps they were currently engaged in a discussion about the new gastro pub that had just opened up on the corner by the station, or whether or not it was acceptable to consume an entire Big Mac meal standing up, but Harry hadn't a clue, because all of the usual latches that kept his consciousness within his body had lifted. He felt enclosed in some other empty, speechless space. Having walked right out the corner of the over-lit cafe, past the frame, into the white.

I heard about your wife, she was saying. Harry tried to focus on the tracks groaning beneath them. The man washed down the last of his chips with his Coke, slurping loudly from a straw. Harry decided to say nothing and let her continue, which she inevitably would.

It's terrible, she said. She meant it. She meant it so much that she seemed quite struck with grief herself. *It's the worst thing I've ever heard.*

There was a pause. As if she was deciding whether or not to carry on. *I've always thought that*, she added, thoughtfully, and Harry looked at her as if to say, What?

Well, see, parents – it's always sad. But natural. Kids – awful. I can't even imagine. But there are large areas in the life of a parent and a child that will never quite touch. Overlap. You know. A partner, however. That's your person. That's every day, every inch. The whole Venn diagram.

Well, Harry said, finding his voice, *if you're lucky.*

And are you?

Surprise bounced like light off a mirror between them.

Yes.

Harry couldn't work out whether this was helping. If it had been anyone else he would have asked them to stop, he would have thanked them politely for their pity and got up and moved carriages, but her tone was so genuine, her language so honest, her white eyebrows bent in such a contemplative shape that he found himself saying, *Yeah. Anyway. Thanks.* Like an idiot, as if she'd just complimented his jumper.

He spent the rest of the journey furious with himself. Lia wasn't dead. She wasn't going to die. Thanks to the Dove Clinic in Germany. Why was everyone talking to him like she was fucking dying?

Pulling up to their stop, Harry decided that he would exit the train from a different door to the postgraduate. He would make a point of it.

Oh, and Harry? she said, just as he was standing up.

Yes?

The train stopped.

Nice socks.

She grinned. He looked down at his socks. He'd squeezed his feet that morning into the only pair he could find in the entire house. Iris's purple planet socks.

The doors opened.

When your wife is this ill, Harry thought, stepping through the same door as the postgraduate and onto the concrete platform, everything goes missing. A girl's age-ten-to-twelve sock is a size that fits all. Life is literally nothing like an Edward Hopper painting.

Carrots

The daughter is scraping carrots in the kitchen. The house smells of cinnamon and sweat. The heating is on so high it is almost like they believe they just might steam out all the badness from this body.

I think, the daughter says, picking up the next carrot, *if you died, I would probably die with you.*

Ribbons of time peel away from us.

And why is that? we ask, in the best most normal voice we can muster, but there is a pressing on our laryngeal nerve and it's changing the tone and pitch, the hoarseness of every sound.

Daughter pretends not to notice. Instead, she tells us about her night spent stuck inside our body. The lightless basement of our liver. The banister bile ducts and empty pink corridors. *Like the diagrams we have to label in biology,* she says. *Only I was soaked in yellow,* she says, *and the colour spread into everything I touched; it climbed up all the walls, it got into all of your veins, it stained and stained –*

She tells us that in the dream everyone had gone, everyone had given up, *a bit like the end of* Titanic, she says, and as she waded through flooded backstage dressing rooms, each organ door labelled like the names of actors in a great play – Kidney, Spleen, Stomach – she came to the Womb room, went inside, began to age backwards until she was nothing but a foetus clawing at the door, *and then I died.*

We don't know whether to laugh or cry.

That is a terrible nightmare, we say, watching the skeletal orange vegetable thinning and thinning as she turns it over in her perfect little palms. *Where do you get all these mad ideas from?*

You, she says, quite simply.

A Brief History of Earth-Shattering Post

It was just one word on the back of a postcard.

It arrived on the first week in July during Lia's second year in London.

**In both tone and significance, it rather
reminds me of the letter that arrived on President Roosevelt's desk
in 1939, announcing the beginning of the atomic age.**

The picture on the postcard was of a stone house sitting amongst poppy fields, rows of cypress trees like little blades in the distance piercing great rolling hills, mountains perched in mist, peaks a frosted white. On the back, an Italian address, and nothing else but –

Come.

Stay.

**It seems I have completely forgotten whose side
I'm supposed to be on because I am doing everything in
my power to give her a sign.**

Stay!

**I'm turning the bus
with her personalized Nike ad plastered across the side:**

**(don't)
Just Do It**

**I try with some eighties horror classics on the new
telly they've just bought.**

Wendy, darling? Light of my life. I'm not gonna hurt ya.
I'm just gonna
bash your brains in.

She changes the channel.

Stay away from the light!

(Click)

I take back every bit of energy I gave you,
Nancy says to Freddy.

(Click)

For two whole weeks I perform this great symphony of signs and
the whole thing is so exhausting, so utterly infuriating
I resign myself to taking a back seat for a while,
letting her make her own mistakes.

extremely powerful bombs of a new type may thus be constructed

Some people just can't be helped.

Ritual

For much of her life, Iris had kept a large secret collection of plastic
bags under her bed.

She felt particularly guilty about this for a number of reasons,
reasons that included the fact that one in three leatherback sea-
turtles had been found with plastic in their stomachs and also the
fact that around 100,000 marine animals were murdered by plastic
bags every year. She was comforted, however, by the fact that her
plastic bags had collected there long before she knew any of these

terrible plastic facts, making her none the wiser at the time of their purchase. What mattered, also, was what was inside the bags. At least the death traps were being used for something – she'd think – other than killing baby turtles.

Inside these bags were:
shells with such extraordinary patterns it was impossible for Iris to accept they were anything other than meticulously designed
(kiss, kiss, kiss, kiss),
interesting rocks (kiss) and pebbles (kiss), flat ones
(kiss),
silver ones
(kiss),
lucky ones that looked like they'd been hole-punched
(kiss).

There were tiny clay-coloured fossils (kiss, kiss), bullet-shaped belemnites (kiss, kiss), fragments of ammonites (kiss, kiss, kiss), a few satisfying wishbone sticks, three accidental cigarette butts and exactly one bottle cap, none of which, during Iris's new evening ritual, needed to be kissed.

These objects had never held much significance to her in the past. But Iris had found a photograph of the two of them on the beach, searching for beautiful gnarly shiny peculiar things with the shameful plastic bags in their hands, the huge chalk cliffs carved into the white sky behind them, and a four-year-old Iris, eyes fixed on the woman she knew to be her mother but looked nothing like her mother, so utterly in love, so ready to follow her anywhere, while the woman she knew to be her mother but looked nothing like her mother gazed, swept and golden, slightly sadly down the lens. Neither of them remembered anyone on the beach with them that day. But memory is a funny, flimsy thing, Iris thought (kiss, kiss), and it had seemed suddenly very important that she fish out the fragments of her childhood (kiss), make sure that they never vanished, never went missing. (Kiss.) Because that's what happens to things you don't take care of, Iris thought, her lips a little sore from pursing, only a handful of stones left to go – they find a way of ending.

The ritual began as a small glittering itch, but it had all got quite out of hand. No stone could be left unkissed, or her nightmares would be terrible, or she'd simply not sleep at all, or some other awful unspeakables would occur that she hadn't thought of yet. Each object had to be kissed on either side, and the process took at least an hour or so every night.

Iris rubbed her thumb along the cold ridges of an ammonite and wondered if she was going mad. Kiss. Turn. Kiss.

What are you up to, little one?

Harry's soft voice from the door. He stared at the scraps of rocks stones shells and fossils, scattered about around the bedroom floor.

It's this thing. I have to do it before I go to bed.

I see.

It's a symptom of my OCD.

Your OCD?

Yes. My obsessive compulsive disorder.

Harry frowned.

Right.

He waited to see if she would continue, but she just blinked up at him instead, this emptiness in the mists of her eyes, as if her regular crystalline sparkle had been pulverized. It was frightening, Harry thought. Quite frightening.

Night, Dad.

He came over to her on the floor. Kiss. On her forehead. The safe heat of his hand on the back of her neck. He stood.

And another, Iris said. *Two, please.*

He kissed her forehead again.

When he was gone, she went kiss kiss kiss kiss as quick as she could with the rest, pushed the shameful plastic rustling around the rock shell splinters as deep under the bed as they would go, climbed into bed and lay there
on the flat of her back
wondering if Burn Girl would ever have let herself develop an obsessive-compulsive disorder like this, feeling certain that if she had any mental illness at all it would probably be one of the chic ones. Like bulimia.

An Arrival

When Lia arrived, Matthew was floating amongst a sea of furious red poppies.

> **Some moments I find I can only relive through the cracks between her fingers. Where the brush sits. Where locks of his hair once stung.**

He was building something, his movements quick and violent, and she watched him for a while, scraping cement, heaving great slabs of stone in place,
wiping away the sweat from his scorching forehead with a golden arm.

I am not sure when I got so soft. So squeamish.

The heat was new to her. It was a slow, numbing heat that
rustled its heavy glow through her thighs.

He paused with his back turned, his spine hunched, his posture all
dismantled.

Her heartbeat is so loud,
the poppies are pulsing along in time around us –
Lub dub *Lub* dub *Lub* dub

She thought of him naked, changing in the quiet mornings to
come, blocking the summer light
bleeding through the shutters, her flesh astounded with
the rhythm of his.

It is the most power she has ever known.

Matthew scratched the back of his neck and watched the bus
Lia had arrived on, churning up dust from the terracotta
tracks, tearing through the cypresses,
towards another departure.

And it is happening. He is feeling
her eyes on him, he is turning his head finally the poppies are
exploding red confetti one by one like small
atomic bombs and I am closing myself back
between her fingers, shutting
myself
in the dark

because if her body has taught me anything
it is this:
the best way to ruin a perfect moment
is by letting it continue.

Letting It Continue

I can't believe it, Matthew said, shaking his head, leading her through the back of the farmhouse, the land blistered in amber behind them. *I can't believe you actually came.* He looked happier than she'd ever seen him. She kept trying to tell him how cross she was with him, for having left like that without saying goodbye, for having disappeared completely, but he just kept kissing her, kept turning and holding her face in his huge rough hands, wrapping his lips over her nose and blowing so that she could feel his hot breath in the back of her mouth, condensing in her tear ducts, *You're here!* he kept saying, kissing her hands, her thumbs in his mouth, *You're here!* each time more emphatically, exciting himself with the miraculous fact, and Lia felt as if time was contracting around them, as if she were arriving again and again, over and over, at the closest thing she had to a home.

Later that evening the two of them sat together in the tiny pantry just off the kitchen, the residue of pecorino cheese and cuts of hanging smoked pork strong and delicious around them. Matthew opened a bottle of wine so dark it was almost navy and Lia watched light sediment collecting in the glasses. *They make this here,* he said. She told him about London and her painting, Connie and her cleaning, and he listened with such thirst, his hands everywhere, as if he needed to feel his way through her stories, get around and under them. *I can only stay a few weeks,* she said, in that most confident voice she had practised on the plane. He twisted the ends of her short, freshly cut hair and nodded, effervescent. *It's just so good to see you.*

He had lasted a year at the college. *It's a ridiculous story, really. You'll think I'm mad.* Lia leant close, noting all his new little mannerisms. He was sprightly and thin, almost nervous. He picked at the skin around his nails and rubbed his finger and thumb together often while talking about his studying of early Christianity and Roman

Catholic practices, his reading of the French Mystics, how seriously he began to take the sacraments, his growing interest in the authority of the Church.

I felt like I was at the right house, just knocking on the wrong door.

**(I blow,
for a little attention)**

The candle between them flickered. Light rippled across Matthew's face.

I began to have these dreams about the Eucharist. He smiled slightly at the sound of himself. *The same one, every night. Every time I looked down, the sacramental bread wasn't sacramental bread at all, but those thick paprika crisps you used to like, the ones with the ridges, and every time I went to sip the sacramental wine it was the strongest whiskey.*

Lia laughed lightly, because he was laughing too, although it was always so hard to tell when his expression might switch and he'd say something like *what?* so blankly that she would feel silly and trivial for having found anything funny at all.

But I just kept going back for more, he went on, *more and more, I ate and I drank until I woke up feeling so sick I could barely eat anything at all for the rest of the day.*

He picked at a tiny loose bit of skin, cracked and dry at the bottom of his nail, serious again.

Lia took a very large sip of wine, letting it linger in her mouth before swallowing.

So you took it as a sign.

He nodded.

She tried to think of a way of saying it that didn't sound a little ridiculous, a little like she was mocking him, but she couldn't, so she just went with: *And you're a Catholic now?*

He smiled at this, which was a relief.

Not quite, he said, looking over at their shadows, thrown huge on the plaster walls. *Not yet anyway. I'm not sure what I am any more.*

That's OK. There's no rush.

It is not what I thought it would be, he then said, so quietly, and though she did not know exactly what *it* was, it seemed most likely that what he meant was *life*, and this, she understood completely.

It never is.   ***It never is!***

A sharp intake of breath – a hiss quick between his teeth. He had peeled his skin back too far down his knuckles. The torn flesh began to bleed.

Lia took his hand, gently unfurled it, and kissed his finger.

He winced and settled as she licked the cut clean. She didn't break his gaze while drawing out his soul through his finger with her lips, sucking it out slowly from the bottom to the tip. He was hardening already, and his mouth had fallen open a little so that she could see the wetness on his tongue, the press of his temples and the veins on his forehead pronounced, as if he were expanding right to every edge of himself. And how was it, Lia thought, as the room began to cloud and they looked between each other, that after all these years, this sexual language, this rare and physical thing between them, brimming and swaying and toppling, still aglow, was both the easiest and the best thing that she had ever known.

Even I am   briefly   lost
                                  in the mad   thick fog   of it

Quindi la signorina che fa? Si ferma?

So? Will she be staying?

Lia felt the hard thunk of hunger interrupted, hitting the base of her stomach.

A woman with silver hair down to her hips and excellent posture had walked through the door, carrying a stack of cream porcelain plates piled with knives and forks and cuttings of leftover fat from the edges of steaks, and Lia felt suddenly like an imposter, in this beautiful woman's house, quite ashamed not to understand a word of the language. Matthew steadied himself and turned.

Sì.

Yes.

E per quanto?

How long?

Si ferma. Come me. Va bene?

Staying, staying. Like me. Is that OK?

Certo, Tesoro, certo.

Of course, treasure. Of course.

The plates were placed in the sink. Lia tried to imagine what it was they were saying. The silver woman came to kiss Matthew on the top of his head, her tanned leathery hands, round knotted knuckles placed gently on his shoulders. She smiled widely at Lia, revealing a small black gap between her bottom teeth, her eyes a subtle green.

Welcome, she said.

That night, in the lightless basement room where Matthew had spent the last four months of his life, the sex was rougher than Lia remembered.

He held her neck like a rare animal, marvelling at its smallness,

its quick pulse under his thumb he could stop with a press, and Lia found herself thinking back to that first night in her room, the way he'd placed the headphones over her ears and kissed her, so poised and certain it seemed almost as if he'd planned it. And there had never been any doubt in her mind; he had been in control every step of the way.

But looking at him now, panting and pumping, so overcome with his own lust he seemed only half human, she wondered if he was just as helpless and as mystified by it all as she'd been; if the desire they felt was something beyond, greater than, lesser than them both.

When it was over, he went straight to shower, cleaned her touch off his skin, scrubbing away all memory of their sin.

Lia stared at the space of wall where the shutters would have been were they not underground, listening to the furious sound of the water hitting tiles, trying desperately not to cry.

She could hear Connie's voice in her head:

It's the shock of the invasion, Velvet whispers softly,
                    your brain catching up to your body's many assaults.

But really, she feared it was just the joyous stampede of her heart's relief.

      (her dirty, thirsty desire for him
                              just revelling in the intimacy)

White Christmas

There are a few hours each year that belong to no day. The no-
man's land, between Christmas Eve and Christmas morning.

It is 3 a.m. We are awake in the uncanny depths
of those hours because
something has its claws in the house.

We feel it circling, sliding up, crunching about the exterior.

It's Fossil! (I tell her) climbing the pipes, watching the daughter
sleep, singing hymns she nearly hears, tapping tips of fossil
fingers on the glass so hard that she will wake, soon, and run to
the window,
and he will get to see her face, finally,
drenched in moonlight,
interrogating the sky,
nocturnal shapes shifting in the garden.

Hello? Is that you?

We call out of our window,
we creep down the hall,
peek through the slice in the
daughter's bedroom door.

We gasp very loudly together when we glimpse a pebble on the
floor.

Come back to bed, the husband says. He is framed perfectly in the
doorway.

But he's coming for her. He's been into her room!

He isn't. He hasn't.

He flicks the switch and we slip back into bed, hoping as hard as we can that, if she wakes, she finds the intruder is only Father Christmas, St Nicholas, Sinterklaas, Baba Noel, having dragged his way down the sides of his earth with
a rope
a torch
a restoration plan
a sack full of midnight snacks and miracles.

I really think he's here.

The husband holds our hand tightly. We hope ourselves to sleep.

Morning kneels quietly at our feet, opening its pale palms out to us.

Merry Christmas, lovely, he says, so gently, as if the night had never happened.

Look outside! The daughter is practically screaming. During the no-man's hours, it has snowed. It is not that thick, muzzle-clean snow, but it is enough to glaze the landscape with a pure sheet of ivory light. Enough to give us all the sense that time has paused, just for today.

We decide that seeing something for the first time is much the same as seeing it for the last.

Let it snow
Let it snow
Let it snow

Downstairs we make a poem out of those nine
letters while the husband and the daughter
make snowmen out of ice from the
garden.

Listen.
Stolen towns
Wilt
Slow lesion
Silent;
We lost.
Ten-Noels-to-one.
It
woes
on.

They have done a good job with the snowman. It has the tiniest carrot as a nose and two coat buttons for eyes and a wide dried-currant smirk. They are both so pink-cheeked, so delighted, and we feel a small revelation, clambering on up to the very highest peak of our processing, basking in the thin but dazzling air; *They will be fine.* For a moment, the world is sublime beneath it. Through it. Because of it; *Whatever happens, they will be fine.*

I

slip   out   side

and watch her in my coldest form to date,
smiling through the window from the holes of my own
coat-button eyes lodged into another grim, melting face.

Merry Christmas!

I lift a sliding stick shoulder, and wave.

She stands abruptly, and turns away.

I feel my currants curl down on each end

Flesh and Faith

While Matthew built the new guesthouse in the poppy field, Lia was put to work checking guests into their rooms, washing, folding and ironing sheets, peeling potatoes, plucking olives from the trees and grapes from the vines, feeding the cows and the chickens, and filling up the milk trays for the stray cats in the evenings.

The best kind of work, Matthew called it, *when your whole body feels like an instrument.*

She was taken around the farm and shown what to do, how and when to do it, by the silver woman's gangly nephew, Enzo, who looked like the sort of boy Michelangelo, had he been alive then, would certainly want to paint or sculpt or fuck, for everything about him reached; you could hear him coming a mile away, drilling through distance on his blue Vespa from his village to theirs, you could smell him two rooms and a corridor away, with his cheap intoxicating deodorant lathered thickly over sweat and cigarettes and pheromones, and he had the highest, most impressive cheekbones that would very occasionally draw up a smile of such surprising innocence that Lia liked him immediately.

> **She doesn't fancy him though, obviously,
> because he's only
> sixteen.**

The other lodgers were mostly young travellers; students and potters and poets and aspiring musicians working hard in exchange for a free bed and three meals a day, all bustling below where the paying guests stayed so that the place was showered in the sounds of many various languages and accents; a little German twitching out from under the door of the red room, a leak of French from the attic, often the sharp American squeals from the tiny glistening bodies scattered around the pool. It took no time at all for Lia to feel part of a large mad family, picking up scraps of other tongues, searching the gaps and overlaps, finding direct connections between.

Matthew worked with a new kind of earnest intensity in the fields long after the orange sun dipped beneath the vineyards. Lia noticed that he'd peeled the dry skin off his feet so that it hurt sometimes to walk and that he had these new rituals, like counting rosary beads whilst taking her excitedly through the mysteries. When he prayed, she would turn her back from him, trying to give him a little privacy, trying not to feel uncomfortable, like there was someone else in the room with them watching and judging, someone who distanced him from her and drip-fed him ideas about human sin and shame and impurity. She wondered if he'd come to sense her unease, for as the weeks went by, he prayed beside her less frequently, and began reading from his favourite philosophers late into the night instead, occasionally sharing fragments of Kierkegaard or Simone Weil. 'The self,' he'd say,

and we try our absolute hardest not to roll our eyes
or yawn
or begin to sing very loudly

is the shadow which sin and error cast by stopping the light of God.'
Isn't that beautiful?

And Lia would think about it and say, *Yes. The problem is — there is nowhere else to go.*

The silver woman had many nicknames for him. *Angelo caduto. Tesoro. Povero caro.* She spoke to him always with deep concern etched into her forehead, and Lia would often feel Anne's trapped-hornet *her/you* stirring awake, knocking loudly about her glass insides. Enzo was quite besotted too. He could never look Matthew directly in the eyes, gazing always at the brush above his shoulder, as if even the briefest connection between them might turn him into stone.

Povero caro, Lia said to Enzo on the last Tuesday of August. It had been a very dry month; the harvest had been bad. He was helping her skin peaches in the kitchen.

Yes, he said. *Good pronunciation.*

Po-ver-o car-o, she tried again, letting it sink on her tongue. *What does it mean?*

It's like – poor thing. Poor dear. It is – how do you say – affectionate?

She liked the way English sounded in his voice, finding its way along new sentences, raw and cautious and earnest.

But why does she call him that? Lia asked.

Don't you know? The Dutch woman who was training to be a geologist cut in across the room from behind a large bowl of courgettes. Her name was Esmee and she never washed her hair. She had been there two months or so and knew her way exactly to the very centre of a conversation. *Hasn't he told you?*

Lia shook her head, the fleshless peach weighing suddenly heavy in her hand. Enzo looked incredibly uncomfortable, shifting from foot to foot in his filthy trainers.

Angese met him when he was staying at a hostel outside the Vatican. A group of them had walked the Via Francigena. He was skin and bone apparently. Delirious. Practically starved himself. Had nothing but the clothes on his back. She brought him here. Cleaned him up, fed him. But he was very ill. It was a whole ordeal.

Lia looked at Enzo, who glanced woefully back at her from under his curls.

He's better now, though, he said, *isn't he?*

Lia felt utterly miserable.

Esmee began to chuckle into the courgettes as she chopped. *I had this friend once*, she said (chop), *who was so obsessed with George Michael* (chop) *that she ran away from home* (chop), *went all the way to England, slept outside his house for a week* (chop). *She got arrested, eventually. Anyway, it turned out* (chop) *it was George Harrison's house all along!* She collapsed with laughter. Enzo and Lia did not. She composed herself quickly and waved her knife at them like a telling finger. *Some people just can't be helped.* (Chop.)

> **If we could take the knife and chop Esmee's head of horrid hair clean off her neck we would.**

Lia went outside to call Matthew in for dinner. She stood there a moment, still and stinging, letting her eyes adjust to the snapping light. She watched his shape sharpen on the scaffolding he'd built from the ground, wiping his forehead with a golden arm, the walls of the new guesthouse having risen up quite a way now, and felt that immeasurable sadness begin to fall through her. Slowly. Limply. Like the most viscous fluid, dripping gradually from tier to tier of her organs, for the thought of him sick and skeletal was too painful; the lengths he would go to find whatever he was looking for too frightening. There must be, she thought, some way to help him.

At dinner, Lia watched Matthew pick at his food.

Esmee told me how you found this place. She said it quietly, so that no one else could hear them. *How ill you were.* She leant closer to him, pressing her lips to his shoulder so that she could almost taste the salty heat of his flesh. *Why didn't you say?*

He looked down at his plate in silence, as if something on it was troubling him deeply.

It doesn't matter any more, he said.

It does. I think—

She took a breath. It was all too big, so beyond the limits of her language. She glanced over at Esmee, who was watching them intently from across the table, folding cold meats into her mouth with her fingers.

I think it makes you really unhappy.

Matthew had put down his fork and was leaning back on his chair, withdrawing from her.

What does?

You know. This God stuff.

He laughed quietly and shook his head in disbelief. This was fair, she thought.

Right.

But then he moved back towards the table, resting his head on his hands, and said, *You don't need to worry about that,* his voice surprisingly soft and bruised and small, *not now, anyway.*

Why's that?

Something's . . . I don't know. Something's changed.

What?

He rubbed his chest, held his throat. *I can't feel* – he said, stammering, *I just – I don't—*

He had begun to work himself up, body caved in and huddled over as if something had been scraped out of him. The rest of the group had started to notice that something was wrong, and Lia turned her body towards him to block them all out. She ran her hand up and down his damp back, whispering, *It's OK, it's OK, shh, it's OK.*

He looked up at her sadly through the web of his lashes.

I don't feel Him like I used to, he said, simply, as if admitting finally, absolutely, to murder. *It's like a cord has been cut.*

Lia tried as hard as she could not to breathe a sigh of relief.

I don't know how to explain it, he said.

You don't have to. I get it.

A look of disdain passed like a shadow across his face.

No, you don't, he said, *you don't get it.* And he was right, of course. It was easy for her to talk like this, when God had been part of her history, a part of her thoughts, but had never, in truth, been known by her heart.

She leant back, smoothed out her tone.

OK, she said. *So your God has got up and left. Perhaps He was never the answer. Perhaps what we have here is enough.*

The silver woman, who was sitting at the far end of the table, had successfully maintained the sympathetic hum and chatter and scraping and clatter of background noise, for which Lia was grateful, and for a while she concentrated on the individual sounds, isolating each knife from each voice one after the other to distract from her nerves. Matthew sat in silence.

And then, to her surprise, he began to nod.

OK, he said, thoughtfully, *OK.* He looked sideways at her, and she watched his expression open a little, as if he were relinquishing a

small portion of control, acknowledging the moment as an ending
of something and the beginning of another. He leant over to kiss
the top of her nose before picking his fork back up, skewering
a slice of melon. *Yes*, he said, placing the melon into his mouth,
chewing and swallowing. *We're here. Let's have some fun.* And Lia
was ashamed to feel a peace, a new kind of adult composure,
centring her, rooting her body right down into the floor.

Enzo reached over the table, lifted the large jug of water. He caught
Lia's eye, and gave her the smallest wink. By the time she'd looked
back to Matthew, his plate was empty.

And so September came

(it rains a lot)

and September went

(but she does not)

and in the months that followed, Matthew spoke often of moving
on once the new guesthouse was built, of seeing a little more of the
world together, and so in between the hours they spent labouring
on the farm, he picked up work at the bar in Enzo's village, and the
silver woman offered to pay Lia small sums for her landscapes, kindly
commissioning a considerable number of family portraits to line
the sparse corridors, and the sudden knowledge of a plan was bliss,

the smoking and drinking and swimming and fucking is bliss!

and though Lia would try and articulate the strengthening
sensation of a sinking fear very occasionally, when they were curled
up alone together in one of the quiet pockets of the farm they
had claimed as their own, enclosed within the small bale towers,
the nightly rustle of feathers twitching in the coops, the stench
of hay and sweet dung hanging thick between them, he would
pull her into him in response and tell her plainly that he needed

her, that this simple life they were living outside of all the terrible trappings of modern culture and capitalism and greed and fear was a noble one; a kind of prelapsarian utopia, and so she would resolve that it was fine, her teeth around his Adam's apple, hands down the waistband of his pants; it was simply the accidental, unconventional composition of their new life. They were fine.

> what strikes me often is how
> > dumb she can be

It would not dawn on Lia until much later that what she believed to have been the poison was not the poison after all, but rather, a desperate attempt at a cure, and that Matthew's fixation on a religion he no longer felt connected to was the very mildest of his extremities; for the gradual removal of God from his life meant only that he had more space and time and energy to devote to much darker, more dangerous expressions of his troubled spirit and allow them, finally,
> to take full flight.

> You can't get between
> > a man and his God;
> he'll find curious ways
> > to punish you all your life.

Copy and Paste | (Here)

You know in all those years we spent apart, she didn't try and contact me once.

I know, Harry said softly. *I know.* He was cradling Lia in his arms in the garden under hundreds of blankets. She was looking up at the sky on his lap, her head like a snap-necked, broken bird's on the bed of a forest floor after a steep enormous fall.

I find I am increasingly thinking back to bad moments. Spending time in the worst memories. I cannot help it.

Don't do that, he said. *There's been too much good in your life for that.*

But I am guilty of so much, she thought. So much.

Did I ever tell you about the night? Her voice slid about inside itself. *The night it all blew up. At the farm. With him?*

Him. Harry felt the word whistle through the sky, pick him out like a grenade. *You did,* he said.

I'm sorry.

A silence.

I wish, she said, very quietly, *I wish I could get them back. All those years that I wasted. I wish I could copy and paste them to the Now. I'd live them so much better.*

In the shadows of the bushes, Lia was sure she had caught a glimpse of a long silver lock of hair. She could smell the notes of Enzo's deodorant, as if he had just sprinted through the garden, jumped the fence. She could feel Esmee's lidless eyes on her, winding slowly through her skull.

Why do the worst years take forever and the best go by in a second?

I don't know, Harry wanted to say, I don't know, but instead he looked down at his phone, just as the 23:59 changed to 00:00, and said, *Happy New Year.*

> **And look at that! (I say to her)**
> **You've made it into another year!**
>
> **Fuck off, she thinks back to me.**
> **Fuck off fuck off fuck off,**

as the sky bursts into thousands of pieces of glittering light
and the chorus in the bushes clap their hands
and The Gardener kisses our forehead

the blazing firework residue falls into the shape of the question:

W
h
o

t
h
e

f
u
c
k

a
r
e

y
o
u
?

Boredom

Today the daughter lets us get the bus to school with her. Three
stops and we're there. Outside the gates she wishes we hadn't come.

(*go, please, Mum, go*)

Beyond the fencing the playground looks like nowhere we've ever
been before.

(*OK, OK, quick kiss?*)

Walking towards us from down the street we spot a beast with
beautiful bronze knees, brilliantly structured face, brand spanking
new shoes. She is tapping away on a phone.

The day becomes heavy. Gravity begins wrenching sparrows from
their nests.

There is no question who this is. It's like coming face to face
with that Very Famous Person who features far too often in your
absolute worst dreams.

Tiny sparrow necks

SNAP   SNAP   SNAP

as they hit the concrete floor.

The daughter cowers. She squeezes three of our thin fingers goodbye and darts off, away. So quickly.

What is the collective noun for a group of sparrows? I ask her.

She gets her phone out. Google tells us it is *a quarrel.*

They are known to engage in fearsome face-offs, viciously peck, divebomb, spread wings out wide, flap violently.

We add the word *quarrel* to the notes on our phone.

The beautiful monstrous girl is only a few yards from us now, so indifferent to the sky-raining-sparrows.

Go on, I nudge. (*No.*) *Say something to her.* (*No.*) *Trip her up.* (*No!*) *Slap her phone out of her hand.* (*No!*)

We are surprised by how bored she looks.

And then it strikes us, as we turn to watch the top of the daughter's head moving through the fearful grey-faced masses, that this is the seed. The reason for all this cruelty. For children are many things, but most of all, they are bored. And it's really no wonder they are all looking for someone to lead a little revolt against the ordinary, administer a dose of pain to keep the boredom away. We understand this completely,
for we are not so different, this Burn Girl and I,
we are not so different at all;
she who gets stronger
as the daughter weakens.

The morning bell rings.

The pitch pierces her ear's ligament very sharp and hard and
I quiver with all the tiny hairs in her drum.

And then, for fun, because I feel a little bored, I rearrange the
roads home. Erase all the street names in her brain, rip up pieces
of jigsaw, turn the whole city into a tough, inscrutable maze.

Where am I? she asks, suddenly, very quietly, frozen still at the
traffic lights.

Today

Today we are
a quarrel of sparrows, bickering through the streets.

Today we are
a mindless blue circle, travelling slowly across a screen.

Week 11

Corey likes to dress up in his sister's clothes
and put on her make-up.

A ripple of breath. For a moment, nobody was bored.

But Corey shrugged like it was nothing –

I've been practising my drag act, he said.

And just like that, everyone was bored again.

The Etiquette of Watching

Dad.

Yes?

I feel watched.

What kind of watched?

Night-time watched. Sometimes the watching is happening from outside my window, sometimes by my door, sometimes it's in my room.

Harry was silent, feeling a chill spread through him.

It might be that evening ritual – it could be making you anxious.

It might be. I'm not sure it is.

How long has it been going on?

Not long.

Harry had decided not to mention Iris's new evening ritual to Lia, though it felt strange and wrong to keep anything from her, to be filtering what of the outside world could touch her.

You know, we should really clear out all that stuff under your bed,
he said.

It's not stuff. But Iris thought about the plastic bags and how uneasy they made her feel and wondered if, perhaps, it was a good idea to get rid of them, after all.

Dad.

Yes?

You know, less than 1 per cent of the planet's plastic bags are recycled.

I didn't. That's a bad statistic.

Another silence.

Dad?

Yes.

Sometimes I feel as if we are trapped.

Trapped where? Harry said, though he knew exactly what she meant.

Cords of Attachment

No matter how hard I've tried, I simply cannot live this evening within her.

I am all for a little rough and tumble, a little friction and horror. But this evening. Nope. Not doing it. Shan't. I cannot, however, resist the urge to tell it. So I shall assume the form of a cicada, clicking in the grass, or some other inconspicuous insect watching from the poolside, like a hummingbird hawk-moth, a firebug, or a scarlet dragonfly.

(The insects here are generally far more impressive in both stature and sound.)

So.

Here she is. Passing the joint to Enzo. Their cheeks are dappled in green chlorine light, the wicked lull of water folding gently around the bruises on her legs. She has been at the farm for a year and a half. The guesthouse has been finished for three months.

How'd you get all these? He touches a large one the shape of a cloud, the shape of a snail on her thigh. She shrugs. His eyes turn inward as he watches smoke cascade from his nostrils.

I will add here that they are not alone. There are two German documentary makers behind them, fiddling with a camera, discussing which of Fellini's films was his great masterpiece, and a young Italian girl from the neighbouring village reclining on the terracotta tiles, flirting with an Irish medic, who has a very loud lovely laugh that seems to nourish the air around it. A Brazilian traveller in a Guns N' Roses tank top perching on a plastic lounger flakes tobacco delicately with his fingers along a fold. Everyone is high. Enzo is yet to take his hand off her thigh.

She looks terrible, though I suppose this depends on how you look at it. It is the nineties, after all. Terrible is positively chic.

Where is he? Enzo asks.

Finishing his shift, she says. *He'll be back soon.*

Enzo takes another drag.

I hope one day, I find someone as obsessed with me as you two are with each other.

His English struts off his tongue, slick and stunning. She smiles weakly. He passes the joint to the Brazilian in the Guns N' Roses tank top and leans back on his palms. *You can never leave. You're like king and queen now.* She laughs, ruffles his hair, hangs her arm around his shoulder. *King and queen of this sad old crumbling castle.*

That's nice, she says. *But untrue.* She places her head in the nook of his neck.

Behind them, the Italian girl and the Irish medic are very close and the German documentary makers are taking pictures, and though it all sounds very shady, like the beginning of an orgy or a bad porno, it really isn't at all. It's surprisingly light and relaxed and innocent, like a Cézanne painting. The blue one, perhaps, with the fleshy faceless bathers.

You know, Enzo says, *I've never – not once – kissed a girl before.*

She laughs. *I'm sure you wouldn't like it much.*

Go on, then.

Matthew's voice passes through them all like a headlight.

His shape has emerged in the water's webs, lapping and bending. All is quiet. All but the sound of an atmosphere peeling right back to its bones.

Enzo removes his hand from her thigh. They turn to face him. I have to hop skittle waltz along the side of the pool to get a better view.

Matthew is drunk. The kind of drunk that announces itself instantly. There is something mad and sinister thrashing about in his eyes.

The Brazilian traveller in the Guns N' Roses tank top has slid up the lounger to make space for him and the German documentary makers look incredibly nervous.

I'd like to see it, he says, sitting, taking the joint from the Brazilian, placing it between his teeth. The ring blazes red in the cold cloak of night.

See what? the Irish medic asks, her *h* all gorgeous and heavy.

You two. (A beat, as he exhales.) *Kiss.*

The beat is so ominous. The beat is the difference between a suggestion and a command. The beat contains within it a whole history of tease and torture and she is pleading him with her eyes. Enzo writhes in his skin. Somebody laughs but it crumbles and dries right up, because Matthew is really very frighteningly serious.

Go on.

No noise but the water tinkling against the sides.

What is it, Lia? Don't you want to?

He looks to Enzo, who is sitting up so straight, so rigid and uncomfortable, as if Matthew has his spine strapped tight to his long straight forefinger.

Enzo, then. Baby Enzo. Beautiful Enzo. Will you do it? For me?

Perhaps it is to spare Enzo the decision, the pressure, the embarrassment. Perhaps it is for some less noble reason, like wanting it simply to be over, but she takes Enzo's soft face in her hands and kisses his lips.

Matthew looks momentarily satisfied, like a child entertained.

There. That wasn't so bad now, was it?

It is unbearable.

Eight and a Half, one of the German documentary makers turns and says to the other. Everyone is confused. *Fellini's masterpiece. It's got to be Eight and a Half.* Everyone laughs and launches back into their separate conversations, and Enzo clears his throat and scrapes his curls back off his face.

Matthew watches her stand and walk back towards the house. He finishes the entire joint with one long drag, flicks it to the ground, and follows her. The Brazilian traveller in the Guns N' Roses tank top stares down at the joint, appalled. Just before the two of them are quite out of sight, she glances back at the pool, in my direction, as if to say —

Don't you fucking dare. You are not leaving me alone. Not now.

So, albeit reluctantly,

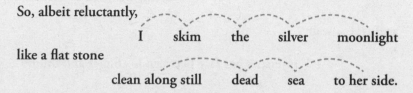

          I   skim   the   silver   moonlight

like a flat stone

       clean along still   dead   sea   to her side.

In their bedroom, the windowlessness has never been so palpable. The walls clench tightly around us.

That was horrible, she says, trembling with anger. *I can't believe you did that.*

Come on, he says, *it was just a bit of fun*, his syllables slurred. His face so full of the pleasure of it.

      Hit him! (I chant.) *Spit on him, kick him, bite him,*
                                  scream at him!

And suddenly she is launching herself at him, and it's really quite carnal, so totally unhinged, in fact I do believe I have never seen her look so monstrous,

       not ever.

She pounds her
            fists against his chest, kicking and
        crying, only the cry is more
      guttural than a cry, like

it comes from someplace else, some locked-up room beyond her
    body, she
         digs and digs   her claws into the skin on his
arms,   you can see that it   hurts

because he goes for her neck suddenly and   grips it tight,
stop it, he says, spray of his fury in her face, the stinking room
tightens, *stop it stop it stop it.*   She digs deeper
                        he slams the back of her skull

against the wall

                    pinches her face between his finger and thumb,

a thick glob of her spit hits his   chin.

And then the devastating engine of his body is hauling her
                onto the bed, and I am watching from the shutterless
space as they begin one of their usual violent escalations, only this
one looks and feels a little different, he is
pulling down her pants, and I cannot know if she is very secretly
OK with this or resisting him or somewhere in the murk between
the two. Eventually she wraps her arms like scarves of flesh
around his neck. He is kissing her and she is apologizing. She is
kissing him and he is apologizing. It is terrifying. It is tedious.

For a moment I consider opening a little of the wall, where she
is now staring, peeling back a slick of brain cell, blinking back to
her a promise of light. Beyond this, there is life, I want to tell her.
Beyond this, there is good love. But of course – I do not.

He is too drunk to finish.

After a minute or two of trying, he pulls out of her, slides off the
bed and stands, swaying naked, looking down sadly at her body
all tangled and still in the sweat-soaked sheets. I hardly recognize
her like this,   tanned and toned and tight.

They are human again.

And so in the cool, motionless quiet I crawl back into her, feel the tentative warmth of her shoulders hung snug as an overcoat around me and begin to examine her flayed nerves, which is when he retches, and we watch in horror as brown foaming vomit comes dribbling out his mouth, *oh*, he says, but more of the horrid stuff surges up and passes through the round of his *oh*, only with greater velocity this time so that he gags violently and it splatters all over his chest, his half-hard cock, creating a little pool around his feet.

He looks so helpless I feel the pigments of her hate dissolve.

We take him calmly into the shower. I notice that her body is empty of everything but time, which means, of course, she is remarkably present. That's what real tragedy does, I tell her: it rids you of a past and a future, just for a moment.

And as we begin to wash the sick off his body with a sponge he falters and mumbles, flinching like a child at the water, so we place him on the toilet, run the sponge down his legs, pull the hair back off his face gently. I remind her of the first week he arrived, the way he wiped the vomit off our feet, and we quietly agree: it is the sort of tragic coincidence that would make even us postulate God, for a second.

Showered, soaped, washed and dried, he lies staring at the ceiling.

Thank you, he says. He means it.

That's OK.

We should go to the sea, he adds, eventually, *for a change of scene. Take a tent.*

All right, we say.

The next day, we wake to a note on the chest of drawers at the end of the bed.

He has ripped the corner off a half-finished pencil sketch.

I'm sorry. Gone to the sea alone. Back in a week.

The drawers are empty of his vests and shorts and sun-dried socks, bleached T-shirts. A year and a half of saved-up funds for their shared future are gone.

I sift through the wreckage within her. It's like a whole species has been wiped out. Nothing left but splinters. Old hard edges and impressions.

He is, of course, not coming back.

Emptying

I would like to see the sea today, Peter announced, quite suddenly. His fists were out in front of him, posture straight and strained as if he were trying very hard to disguise himself as an adult man sitting at a table. He had been diagnosed with vascular dementia, and though the progression of the disease was relatively slow, he had developed tremors and seemed younger and younger as the months knocked on. Anne could never look at her husband when he made demands like this. Lia wished she would be stronger with it all.

Yes. The sea today, I think.

We prefer him like this.
Is that terrible?
Something to do with the simplicity of his impulses.

Lia helped him across the pavement to the car, his cheeks heavy, his expression cluttered with the unfamiliarity of the place. He stopped abruptly.

Where are you taking me?

Lia sighed like she was thinking about this for the first time.

I don't know. What do you think? The sea today, maybe?

He paused.

Ah yes. The sea. A good idea.

The nearest beach was thirty minutes away. In the car they listened to Classic FM and Lia wondered if God would remain, now that everything in her father's life was emptying.

They moved slowly across the beach, salt air peppering their skin as Peter heaved himself from foot to foot.

My boy will be back soon, won't he.

He will.

He won't.

You look old, he said seriously, observing the side of his daughter's face, his daughter who was now thirty with stronger laughter lines emerging at the edge of her eyes. *When did you get so old?*

I've always been old.

Lia observed the side of her father's face, the dry skin on the crease of his nose.

But you. You look younger than ever.

I do? His face gleamed with pride.

No. You don't.

Lia tucked her face into the wool of her jumper and breathed heavily, the warm spreading over her cheeks like a shadow.

How are the children?

I don't have any children, Dad.

Ah.

Ten minutes later he found his way back to the same question.

She is pleased. Strangely, deeply pleased to have another go.

How's the family then? The children?

She straightened and smiled widely as if she were trying very hard to disguise herself as a Mother and a Wife who owned cookbooks and Tupperware boxes and made fresh bread most mornings.

Better than ever.

I had a daughter once. Peter looked out at the tired line where the sky met the water. *You would have liked her.*

We certainly wouldn't have.

Odd little thing, he said, *vast imagination. Brilliant with a pen.*

This knocks us

sideways
like a sudden swell has smacked against our stern and
we feel dragged, like a boat from the sand, placed by a wave
back into the sea.

[312]

Lia wanted to wrap her arms around his shrinking bony body and kiss his hollow cheeks.

Such a shame the Spanish took her. Peter sighed heavily.

Ha!

Better get back to feed your children. Must be dinner time now. They will be missing you.

Yes. Lia laughed and laughed. *They will.*

Telling Harry

After a rich chocolate treat you need some green.

This is a great one.

It takes place eleven years ago, before it all started.

The husband who is not yet husband,
and the wife who is not yet wife, are
entering a Kusama exhibition at the
Hayward or Saatchi or Tate, she does not
remember, because not once does she
take her eyes off him, off the small ache of
space between their bodies skimming
quietly through

mirrored rooms mirrored rooms

An eternity of
light ideas begin to
make their
    way through
        her; she feels the most
      precise hope as they arrive
at a large bronze pumpkin.

He looks tired.

They have tea.

She tells him she's pregnant.

The fact rotates clockwise in his eyes.

The hand hits twelve,

his smile chimes –

Wow.

nine

A Swallowing

The day began with the phone call we were expecting.

We only heard the distress in his voice. The sound of his wait
while we stood on a slice of patio forgetting the strength of
the fever, the nausea, the ten seconds our body seized up, eyes
thrashing in their sockets. Teeth clamped. Pills pushed down to
slow the electrics, spoil the fun.

Our last chance, he says.
*It will kill her if you refuse us. It will
kill her.*

But we are too dulled, too
drugged up, she
can barely even begin
to
connect

the
dots.

The phone drops.

Eventually, he plunges his hand down into the soil, pulls the
phone back out, taps on its screen in silence. The sound of her
voice, our voicemails, begins to leak out:

Lovely man, I'll be late back today, there's some fish in the fridge for Iris. She won't want it but it's all there is.

If you could pick up a card for the party, I've forgotten a card, something with Toy Story on it, apparently she loves Toy Story. Thank you. Lifesaver. Love you.

I'm here, not by the entrance with the revolving doo— Oh. I can see you.

Safe flight. We miss you already. Sort of. (Don't want it going
            to your
head.)

He realizes we are here, listening. He is embarrassed and helps us to the bedroom.

Outside, a choir of plants, hellebores
and snowdrops and lamprocapnos bleeding
hearts part their lips to the closing sky,
kneading more of her words, her sounds
into song.

Prune Juice and Senokot

Drink this. Just a little more. Yes. Good.

It's over. Isn't it?

It can't be.

You know when your body is giving up on you.

It could be months, maybe years. Stranger things have happened mad things happen every day.

I wanted a dog. I've never had a dog.

We'll get two dogs. We'll move to the coast and get two dogs and call them:

Fred and Ginger

and we'll get proper walking shoes and go on one very long walk a day

and I'll dye my hair blue and you'll grow a beard

and from Thursday to Sunday we will consume only pasta

and we'll start wearing leather

and see loads of plays

and go through a serious biker phase

and we'll roar through the city on our bikes in the spring

and in the winter, Hawaii, for snorkelling

we'll be outrageous grandparents

but also gentle, and wise

and we'll fill them with facts and stories

and lies

and you'll win awards and shoot to late fame

and all the staff at our local will greet us by name

I'll age very well – you'll grow a huge belly

but at ninety, when our bodies are withered and smelly

you'll turn to me and say, as we climb into bed:

those first twelve years, I think they were the best.

Lia had gone quiet and pale and was starting to sweat.

Out. Everyone out.

Harry kissed her head and walked out of the very crowded
bathroom, the disgruntled congregation of ghostly chorus members
close behind him. Lia watched the two brown labradoodles sulk
out followed by a leather-clad Harry at seventy-five, a couple of
wrinkled eighty-year-olds in swimming gear and snorkels. Finally,
three exquisite little grandchildren in matching pyjamas and freshly
washed hair skipped out without looking back.

Fun's over, kids.

The room cleared of possibilities just as her bowels began to
empty.

The Accused

Iris was sitting at the end of Lia's bed scratching shapes into the
back of her hand with a biro, trying to ignore the way her mother's
yellow cheeks had begun to
shy into her face, trying to ignore lilts of panic that would
burst through her own picked and peeled
fingers the minute her mother's eyes closed
a little too long.

> **Here is a fact: Common brain tumour symptoms can
> include headaches, seizures, nausea, permanent behavioural
> changes, memory problems, personality disorders, paralysis,
> vision and speech problems.**

The beginnings of Iris's breasts were now flourishing out from under a too-tight T-shirt. Two unassertive but risen pinches of nipple Lia had never noticed before. The sight of them made her want to scream. There was no pain, no fear, no fury quite like it.

Here is a fact: Iris is ill but she doesn't know it yet. It's nothing serious, just a bout of the flu that has been passing around the school for a few weeks now. It has settled quietly, just making itself comfortable. Welcome, Flu.

Lia had her diary open between her legs, a pen between her fingers, wondering how to tell her daughter she was dying in her brand-new voice that had shifted completely now in octave, timbre and weight. The bedroom walls perspired around them, leaking a little redundant residue of the red chemical devil, undulating with the shifts in her temperature.

Hot cold hot cold hot cold

The evening hurtled on. The garden chatted away. The walls seethed.

Iris, Lia said, eventually.

Iris looked up. Her eyes spilling, quite uncontrollably.
Each tear ripped its disbelief down her cheeks.

She knew. Of course, she knew.

But her expression was changing, now,
into one of pure steel, her whole
body bristling with an intensity Lia had
never witnessed before; never in her forty-three
years of life had she felt the breathless
impact of a thing
so much as her daughter's

How could you

how could you

how could you leave me?

A Mother's Evening List

a) I'm sorry
b) I'm sorry
c) I'm sorry
d) I'm sorry
e) I'm sorry
f) I'm sorry
g) I love you
h) I'm sorry
i) **All of the above, in this exact order.**

Epiphany

The call had ended by the time it was Anne's turn to pay. She dropped her phone into her bag. Thud of a heart dropping hard, smashing like the jar that had tipped, a thousand years ago, because Lia was running her hands recklessly along the aisle of pickled things. Their whole past in a sound, she thought. Nothing worse. That public shame a parent can feel for their child. But now she wanted to smash it all, FOR YOU, she wanted to break every jar and scream, FOR YOU FOR YOU, but the whole shop had sunk into cruel, indistinct smudges of primary colour and packaging, and she could barely move
one trembling claw
in front of the other.

I'm sorry, she mumbled to the cashier, trying to fish her wallet out.

The cashier watched her patiently –
a deep, downstairs look in her sympathetic eyes.

Here, she said with the softest of voices, leaning over, taking Anne's bag, picking out the wallet, a note, counting a few coins in her beautiful human palms.

You are very kind, Anne said, feeling most ashamed, staring at the woman's fingers.

Not at all.

I'm sorry. She spoke, now, to the queue behind her. Turned halfway towards them. *My daughter just called*, she persisted, unsure of who she was addressing but dragged on by this new, unfamiliar sensation of needing to share something of herself, needing to explain, as if her life were becoming, for some reason she did not yet know, a thing worth recording, laying down or throwing out before it was all too late. But it *is* too late, she thought, it's all far too late.

She called to tell me she is dying. She was ill. Now she is dying. She is so young. Too young. And she is clever. And so beautiful. She has a daughter. Iris. They are so close. I don't know anything like it. They are so close.

All the witnesses in the shop had gone quiet. The toddler had stopped playing with the interactive birthday cards, the dentist had stopped packaging his potatoes. All listened, respectful as Peter's long-lost congregation. And Anne, who had never revealed so much of herself, not least to a group of strangers, felt the beauty of this new-found frankness dance up through her. She steadied herself against the counter. She stopped herself from sobbing.

I'm so sorry, the cashier whispered, monk-still behind the till; *you must love her very much.*

And Anne looked up at the girl in surprise, as if she'd stumbled upon the insurmountable question, uttered the unfinished answer she had been looking for a very long time;

Yes. Yes I do.

The cashier placed the wallet back carefully along with a printed receipt and smiled a glistening wide smile. Anne bowed her head low.

Outside the shop, she felt the cool air burst through her lungs. She heaved the weight of her skin's difficult shape forward. She thought back to that first call, after those two years seven months and five days of no Lia at all. The electrician had advised that they update their model, but Anne couldn't bring herself to unplug the phone from the wall, not even for a second, just in case she called. Just in case. It had rung, shrill and tuneless at 10 a.m. one grey morning, sounding like the sort of cry a mother just knows. She had run to it, cradled it, clutched it, practically kissed it.

Mum?

And even though her voice had been quite sullen, quite stripped of its song, the fact of it crackling right there was heaven.

Anne had asked stupid questions, of course. *What is the weather like there? Are you eating well?* Nothing of what she'd meant to say. At the end of the conversation, she'd left a silence. A gap the size of an *I'm sorry, Lia. So sorry. Please come back.* She had hoped that Lia would fill it. And then Peter had taken the phone, and the tears had risen, and the room had quivered on the saltwater's surface before sinking, and the sudden overflow of emotion she had felt then she felt now, sliding her hand along the metal rail of the supermarket entrance, blinking the day down her cheeks.

It was waiting for her at the bottom of the ramp, it seemed. That familiar lucid glow, the radiant presence, swelling and singular. Quite unmistakable. For it was love, thought Anne, barely able to stop her body from shaking, from taking flight, she did not know, it was love through which God revealed Himself most clearly. The street was replenishing itself before her eyes. *Hello there,* she whispered quietly, through her tears, *hello again.* It was simple and yet too easy to forget, that for all the scripture and prayer, the sermons and services, love was the thing, and as long as she knew it, understood it as her only duty on this earth, He would remain close always.

She would go home now. Fish out the box she'd kept of Lia's old paintings immediately, she thought, from the attic. She would hang them up all over the house. The one of the egg would go in the kitchen. Even the pig drawing would find a place. In the bathroom, perhaps.

I bet she does that all the time, a boy said to his friend as they walked together through automatic doors, pointing at Anne's hunched back as she stood frozen, clutching her plastic bag with one hand, the other secured firmly to the ramp.

But why?

To get free stuff, obviously.

Dove Couplet

Once-bad-mother-Dove is no longer filthy grey,
       her heart, her wings,
              improve themselves with each sad, weary day.

Hope

A large roasted mackerel lay flat and sad as a sacrifice on the oven tray between them.

The room was quiet, heavy with the wounding comment Connie had just made.

I think your trip has beaten the artist out of you.

She had said it so casually, flaking away at the mackerel flesh. Lia rummaged for bones with her tongue, trying to disguise her hurt.

She had been back in London, now, for eight months, working as a receptionist at the same hotel she used to clean, and had just moved into a modest, one-bedroom apartment above a butcher's shop on a busy road. Though the stench of raw meat would often waft up into the flat with the street-symphonies of music and engine and argument, Lia felt swaddled by the luxury of it. By the new, stable structure of her days. The comfort of walls and doors, drawers and keys, a salary – small, but significant.

Your trip has beaten the artist out of you!

It hurt more than anything Connie had ever said before. Because it hadn't been a *trip*; it had been her life. Because by *trip*, had Connie actually meant *Matthew*? Because Lia seemed to disappoint everyone she'd ever known at some time or another.

The road back from the farm had been four years long.

Once it was very clear that Matthew would not be coming back, the silver woman had sent Lia south, to Pompeii, with the address of an old friend who ran a tourist office on the edge of the crumbling city. *She will get you some well-paid work,* the silver woman had said, counting coins for the train ticket in her palms, pressing them into Lia's, *at least enough to get you home.*

Home The
omeh *word falls through us like water through a sieve* because it belongs to no place
meho
ehom
home
omeh
meho   We are not bound anywhere.

Enzo had driven her to the station on the back of his Vespa.
She had watched the wild hills fold into the scrappy suburbs, the
scrappy suburbs erupt into the Eternal City, pretending not to
notice that all the quiet pleasures of life had numbed. Pretending
not to notice the deficiency within her now that made all
experiences, however briefly luminous – remote. Not hers. As if she
were inherently unworthy of them. *Goodbye, sister,* he'd said, and
he had hugged her tightly, lifting her oh so slightly off the floor.
He was a good four inches taller than he'd been when she'd arrived,
and she could no longer smell that delicious cheap deodorant that
had once oozed out from his every pore. He told her to stay in
touch, but there had been a cold, distracted look in his eye.

> **It is understandable, I tell her, *devastating, but
> understandable that he is a little relieved.***

She had vowed to herself, there and then, to never stay anywhere
long enough to be the one left behind. For four years she had
gone from job to job around Europe, stuffing her diaries and
sketchbooks full of translations, addresses, angry little punch-line
poems, corners of kind strangers' faces, but now that she was back,
laying down roots, she was afraid that this, too, might just be
another sort of cowardly surrendering.

> **I get so bored of all her worrying I go to fiddle with the tap.**

In the kitchen, the tap began to drip. The lidless mackerel skeleton
stared up at the two of them, its spine swimming in lemon.

Something in the room had darkened. Outside, the full moon cracked and broke, its clear white and yolk of old hope dripping thick down the night. Lia could almost smell the sulphur. There was waste, she thought, waste and necessity; rot and bills and rent. There were so many unhatched lives being lived on every street across the city.

Connie got up from her chair to fill a glass of water. *Has he contacted you?* she asked, swallowing loudly, her ringed fingers making their little click-chinks against the glass. *You're not going to disappear again, are you?*

No.

But he had contacted her. Two months ago, now, and the letter had been one of the worst things she had ever read. It was a formal apology for any hurt that he may have caused her, a template plucked from the internet. He may as well have put {recipient} and {sender} in the space where each of their names were printed in his straight, steady hand, and it was all so cruel. So unbearable. Like if God sent an administrative assistant to check in on His abandoned creations, just to remind them of exactly why He left.

In the envelope, he had attached her half of the cash he had taken away with him that morning.

She had thought about ripping up the money, along with the letter, but decided instead to pile up on lavish dinners and ridiculous lunches made up of mattress-thick fillet steaks and duck-fat fries as if preparing her body for a famine ahead. I will spend every last penny of this on edible things, she had thought, so there will be nothing left to see of it, nothing left of him at all, I will eat and eat and eat until I am fat and full and free. She'd sat on her word like a stuffed magpie on its stolen treasure, shining in the light but cheaper than
a five-pence piece.

and WHOOSH   I watch her cholesterol shoot right up in record time, there are new fatty little deposits diluting vitamin D; with Delight I watch as a bit of visceral fat begins to slowly wrap around her abdominal cavity.

You did it all the wrong way around, Connie said, pacing the floor, *you were so obsessed with who you loved you never nurtured what you loved doing and now you're all lost.* She collapsed onto the sofa, her body vanishing into the fabric. *I don't mean to be pushy or negative.*

Lia's eyes stung. Not everyone is as confident, as certain as you, Con, she wanted to say, but she stood and began to clear their plates away instead, feeling a last, tiny fishbone scrape down the inside of her throat.

Outside, somebody was vomiting by the butcher's shop bins. Lia could hear the half-howls of delighted voices saying things like, *That's it. Clear it all out for round two. No good story ever started with a salad,* but Connie wasn't listening.

I just think you're wasted if you're not drawing or painting or making something. Anything, she said, while Lia scrubbed away, concentrating hard on the rhythm of bristle against metal.

I've never seen her this wasted, a voice leaked up from the street below, a kind of brutal disgust disguised in her tone.

But the truth was Lia's mind had never felt so active. It was routine, perhaps. The monotony, moving each morning and afternoon through the great machine of the city. Sitting all day at her desk, watching great characters come and go that had plunged her imagination into new, unchartered territories. Perhaps, she thought, every so often, one had to stop living in order to understand life. To seek relief not through extensity, but through intensity. Which philosopher had written that?

Kierkegaard. 1843.

Come on, this way. Let's get you home. The surprise of a last, kind voice wafted up into the flat and Lia wondered what their dreams looked like – the cluster of drunk but hardy bodies, swaying, bucking, bending to the night like stripped sea thrift, stunning the last of its lilac across a cliff face, built to weather rough storms.

While Connie went on lecturing,

(patronizing bitch)

Lia felt a sliver of quiet rage shoot up through her. Suddenly quite overcome by it, she dropped the oven trays into the sink, marched into her bedroom, pulled out her box of sketchbooks and slammed them down in front of Connie.

Connie had gone very still. Their eyes locked tightly together.

I've been working on a portfolio. The Open University offers part-time degrees. Evening classes. Which means I could work at the hotel, which pays for my rent, and happens to be a job that I like, while finally getting a degree.

Connie had not blinked. Lia turned to scrape the last of the mackerel remains loudly into the bin and moved back to the sink, feeling a hot, peculiar triumph. A fearful fluttering in her chest. For a minute or two, she listened to Connie turning the pages of the portfolio. The reconciling whispers of paper moving around a wooden floor. Seconds later, she felt long, lovely arms wrapping tightly around the new, excess weight of her waist. She felt Connie's breath on her neck, her chin rested against the nook of her shoulder just above her scar; the tenderness of it made her want to cry and cry.

They're brilliant, Connie said, apologetically.

Lia could feel her lips moving against her skin; *You're so good, Lia.* As she spoke, the uncertainty of their youth, the promise and exhaustion of it all felt like the most exciting thing in the world.

You're going to be an artist! Connie said, conclusively.

well *hardly*

Lia laughed lightly and shook her head, but the fluttering in her chest had grown into the greatest rattle; as if a chorus of characters, old, new, preserved, untold, were clanging fishbones together, beating their drums, smacking the ceiling of her quick, persistent heart, all erupting into broken but
delighted applause.

Nothing could beat that out of you. Nothing.

Guddle

Verb

-ed/-ing/ -s

1. To fish with the hands by groping under stones or in the banks of a stream. (e.g. The boy was pleased to have guddled the mackerel that morning.)

2. A gut-cuddle. Approached from behind. Usually between very close friends. (e.g. If you were to look up, now, at the flat above the butcher's shop, you would see Connie guddling Lia so tenderly that if it didn't make you want to smile, I believe nothing would.)

Death Perspectives

What do you think, I ask her, *does death happen in the first or third person? Are you stuck inside yourself feeling the immediate endingness of all things or do you hang above it, watching your body from a distance?*

I suppose that depends on your theology, she says. And then she shudders and turns like an animal refusing feed.

I'm not ready.

Harry's Day

Harry began the day in his boxers, standing in the middle of the club his students went to on Wednesdays, watching a slightly younger, healthier-looking Lia stomp about in the smoke, dancing happily around the room, and though he found he could not join in himself, it was nice to witness for a while. But then a deep gravel voice began whispering taunts into Harry's ear:

This is your fault, old man.

A tall male figure moved out from the edges, silhouetted dramatically against the red. Lia pressed herself into him. He wrapped his arms around her. They kissed slowly, passionately, while the voice continued:

Even I could have done a better job.

Lia led the man away to the toilet cubicles and Harry went to follow them, but as he turned the corner, a seamless scene change occurred, the sort only a dream can perfectly achieve, so that the club was no longer a club, but a white empty gallery. Corridors

stretched and bent sharply into oblivion and he paced and paced,
the echoless sound of her name in his voice
just vanishing into the walls.

It had all been so real that Harry woke feeling the stick of spilt beer
between his toes, clinging to the soles of his feet. Matthew's glare
bubbled away around them before evaporating slowly, the steam of
its heat still everywhere.

If the nights were cruel,
the days were worse.

If he wasn't taking part in his own contemporary tragedy
he was walking right into a Greek one.

It was not a surprise to see her in his new five o'clock seminar on
Euripides' *Alcestis*.

The finery in which her husband will bury her is ready.
The role of the serving woman was being read very flatly by a
young man in the second row. He had an eccentric moustache
and seemed so bored with the play already that Harry felt quite
relieved, quite grateful to him. A heartfelt delivery might have
simply been too much. The postgraduate shot him this knowing
look as if to say,
yes, I quite agree.

Unhappy man, being so good a husband to lose so good a wife!

Harry read the part of the Chorus Leader with gusto, because how
ridiculous it was
that he should be here, doing this, and they were only words,
after all.

My master will not know his loss until it happens.

The flat moustached serving woman came back.

Let her know then – Harry stopped. His eyes slid along the sentence, weaving and darting, spinning gold thread around it. *Let her know then* – he tried again. It was impossible. He felt the sting of all their sniper stares, the rush of his reddening cheeks.

Let her know then that she will die glorious and the noblest woman by far under the sun! The postgraduate's delivery was perfect. Heartfelt and suitably exuberant, she turned and began to discuss the essential role the Chorus plays in guiding Admetus through grief, while Harry flicked the play's ivory pages between his fingers, nodding quietly in agreement. The blue crude light of room B12 quivered. The day beyond it darkened.

When the university spilt out the last of its bodies into the fumes and the filthy squabble of London, the postgraduate was nowhere to be seen. Harry had assumed that she would wait for him after the class, as she so often did, and felt a slight shameful flare of disappointment that she hadn't. His phone buzzed suddenly, fierce against his thigh in his trouser pocket. It was a text from an unknown number:

I can seeeeeee you!

His jaw tightened. He felt a brief, sinking panic, his eyes scanning the streets.

The inevitable Dr Tom Murphy was striding towards him across the road, grinning his mad, shark-like smile. *Hey there!* Harry watched a terrible patronizing frown emerge on his alarmingly handsome face. *Jheeze. You look terrified.* He belonged in old jock movies, Harry thought, he should be running around on a green field somewhere in high striped socks and small silly shorts, or in a classic American novel, drinking gin in coupe glasses calling people Old Sports. He did not belong here, on this street, in Harry's life.

Drink? Harry said, as brightly as he could.

Thought you'd never ask.

The bar was the kind that only served beer in small bottles. Fifteen minutes in, they had finished three each. Tom Murphy was telling Harry about his brother, who had died at the age of nine due to a very rare heart condition and for a while, Harry wondered whether this was a nicely constructed story that he told to convince women he was sensitive. He felt disgusted with himself for having thought it at all and went to get them both another beer.

Anticipatory grief, Tom said, *can be worse than the thing itself.* They clinked the tops of their bottles together for no good reason. *You've got to look after this.* Tom tapped his huge bronze forehead and recommended him some good therapists in the area. Harry picked at paper labels and decided he wasn't so bad after all.

Two hours later, he turned out of the station near his home feeling a little drunk, feeling like a very hell-bent solid thing wandering through a wobbling earth. The new gastro pub on the corner had twinkling lights strung up along the front and people were sitting in small groups below the glow in big coats chatting away so happily that for a moment, Harry wondered if he'd ever seen something so pretty and tender and hopeful. Aha! he thought. Of course he had! But wouldn't that be sad. Wouldn't that be depressing. If the loveliest thing you'd ever seen in the whole of your life was the exterior of an overpriced gastro pub on a —

he realized he had absolutely no idea what day it was.

And that was when he spotted her, sitting back against the wall at a small table for two with her legs crossed, smoking, looking a bit like a person in an Edward Hopper painting.

There you are! Harry said. (Shut up shut up shut up, he thought.)

She looked surprised and pleased that he looked surprised and pleased to see her.

I wanted to say thank you. For today.

Oh. No. Don't be silly.

Bit embarrassing, he added, and felt himself do this horrible little knee-bend-head-tilt-thing. How nauseating, he thought. How sick of himself he was today.

Yes, she said, which confused him. Perhaps she hadn't heard him right. *I imagine that is the sort of thing someone like you might find embarrassing.*

Someone like you. It was pointed. Almost a little cruel. *Do you want to sit?* she asked. *Quick drink?* And Harry felt suddenly very aware of the last half an hour he'd spent not drinking, the particular parched way his body had begun to want more the moment his mind
had let the thought in.

My boyfriend just left, she said. *He's a photographer. Always on night shoots.*

Well of course, Harry thought, she has a boyfriend! A boyfriend all along! How stupid! How vain! How presumptive he had been, he thought, taking the seat next to her, wondering at what point in the evening he had begun to turn all his thoughts and phrases into drunken exclamations!

Go out, have fun, for me, she'd said.

(Go out! Have fun! For me!)

The Gardener's Temptation

In the second compartment on the north wall of the Sistine Chapel there is a busy little fresco littered with so many onlookers, so many patrons, painted animal offerings, angels in enviable outfits and devils in hermit disguises, you would never guess that the great and lofty test was taking place. That Christ was more alone than He'd ever been.

I think of Botticelli's Temptation scene as I finish making colour, grinding powder pigment in water, trowelling the last of the intonaco, readying the finest brushes, and begin on my own little fresco on the left wall of her occipital lobe.

It will depict The Temptations of The Gardener in exact detail. There will, of course, be three. I have many pencil practice studies to refer back to, and the composition is all worked out.

The first is The Drink. The devil is disguised as a beautiful young temptress with long wet hair and perfectly round breasts, the kind that are weighty and wholesome at the bottom and then lift suddenly, pointing upwards, like the raised eyebrow at the end of a question.

The Gardener is his usual green man mythical self, perhaps a little more decorative, composed of acanthus leaves and knotted branched arms with his dandelion eyes and pink ladybird lips. I paint the postgraduate on her knees below him, offering up a goblet of wine, serpent hair cascading down the bend in her back, just covering the crack of her bum.

He would certainly succumb to this one, I tell her. Thoughtfully, she agrees.

The second temptation is The Kiss. The two of them are sitting up on the stalls of a very elegant bar somewhere in the centre of town. There are knotweed ropes wound tight around his chest, and he is slumped sadly over his drink like an ancient willow over a black lake, his head turned towards her slightly as she leans close, happy and young and hungry. Their lips are nearly touching. While I paint away with flair and precision, I realize that we are not so different, this young woman and I; she who gets stronger, as the husband weakens.

The third temptation is The Invitation Home. I begin with him, lying very flat, like an oak ripped completely from its roots by a hurricane or an earthquake. She squats over his groin, her legs bent, feet splayed, two tiny neat folds of flesh on her belly. With his parsnip hands, he holds her waist. They are both mid-groan mid-moan mid-thrust.

She tells me there's not enough motion. It would help to repaint her arms.

In homage to Botticelli's masterpiece, I litter the foreground of the fresco with so many witnesses, a little Lia strung up by her ankles like a sacrificial pig, a horrified Yellow in a lightly jewelled sapphire robe, Velvet half naked in a very pagan pose; I etch Fossil's grinning features into the cliff face, on the side, while Dove holds a branch in her beak, above the scene she flies.

When I am done, I tidy my paints away.

I make her look at it all evening.

Eventually, she tells me the technique is impressive. Other than that – it is too mad, too busy, too convoluted. It says nothing of the inner life. Nothing of the man's precise turmoil. That's what happens when you favour symbolism over feeling. Cleverness over clarity. And this temptress? The whole concept. It's outdated. Certainly not very feminist.

Fuck the sisterhood, I say, *it's every woman for herself!*

But none of it has bothered her as much as I thought it would.

At precisely 12.47 a.m., we hear the door open. The sound of his body scraping towards us up the stairwell is doing something strange to our gut, as if the wing of a great bird were cutting through the still of a lake's dark waters.

He moves his large unkempt shape into the room, stammering inaudible little words. We switch on the light, sit bolt upright.

Hello! we say, so parched, so eager. *Did you have fun?*

He cowers in the brightness. Stumbles over something we cannot see. It's been years since we've witnessed him this drunk. It is oddly pleasing to us.

I drank too much, he says.

Good!

He falls into bed and pulls us towards him.

I think I might have given her the wrong impression, he slurs.

We wind his weeds between the webs of our fingers.

And what impression was that?

He is quiet, the stench of beer or wine or both thick on his breath, all our questions just itching to go.

I'm sorry, he says, very simply, and neither of us have a clue what to make of it. With that, he begins to snore.

The light prickles around our side of the bed. Very awake, she is left to wander the empty corridors of his evening. Eventually, she arrives at the foot of my fresco, painted on the back of her brain. She gazes up at it a while, really studying it, and begins to feel a chill. As if a presence of something new is here, with us, roaming the room.

What is it? she asks me.

The Future passes through us like the spirit of a prophet,
obscuring the walls with its large, uncut shadows.

She shivers.

There is suddenly nothing more important
than what she has to say:

Harry.

He stirs, then wakes.

Yes?

When I am gone—

Stop.

It's important.

No.

*It's important that you meet someone else. Eventually. You're young.
You're a catch. You will meet someone else. Someone healthy and
fun and beautiful.*

Lia. Please. Stop it.

You need to know that you can. You should.

There is a long pause.

I won't haunt her. I promise.

He laughs the sad sound of someone
trying desperately not to cry, clutches our body
close, we fall

deep into the fresh earthy
heaven of his leaves and

maybe we will. Just a little.

Maybe we will.

Poison and Motherhood

For the first full day of her life, Iris had no name.

When Harry came out with *Iris*, they both felt as if he had spoken
the truth of something.

He described the way his mother had sounded, anointing the
budding plants in his grandfather's garden. He explained she was
a messenger in Greek mythology, too. *Iris*, Lia had whispered,
and the nameless baby had squirmed. Thriving. It was the most
fascinating thing to Lia; this difference between creation and
discovery, those uncanny moments you feel you are toeing the line.

> **Motherhood can make the most careless women cautious,
> but by no means does it make them good.**

Three days after the naming, Iris developed a condition that
infected her body with yellow. Yellow in the whites of her new
adjusting eyes. Yellow in the clutch of her palms, the soles of
her tiny feet. The doctors said this was very common, just her
new-born liver catching up with the rest of her – the build-up of
bilirubin in her blood. The substance red blood cells produce when
broken down. *Nothing to worry about*, they had said.

> **Something to worry about: We are now just as yellow
> as the daughter once was, three days after she was born.**

The yellow stain was still there two weeks later, by which point Iris had developed a distinct little smile, could open her eyes so wide and examine the world with the precision of a philosopher, an old and seasoned scientist.

> **Jaundice often occurs like this**
> **when**
> **naughtylittletumoursareblockingbileducts.**

Lia and Harry would marvel at their strange yellow creature. *Look at her*, Harry would whisper, his fingers stroking their daughter's soft exquisite skull. *She's amazing. Look what you've done.* Lia would want to say *we*, look what *we've* done, but would feel a little squeeze on her voice box, the pressure of Matthew's forefinger and thumb, tugging at her from the inside.

After four weeks they took Iris to the doctors again, to ask why her discolouration had not yet faded.

Something to do with a chemical in your breast milk, they concluded. *A very common cause of jaundice. Keep feeding. It will fix itself. It might just take a little longer.*

> **Motherhood is nothing but a great reminder life begins**
> **and ends with the body.**

Her mind would linger on horrible thorny superstitions.

> *You haven't loved her hard enough!*
> *You are relentlessly incompatible with everything, even your own*
> *flesh and blood!*

Furious with herself, she would whisper, *I'm sorry, little one, I'm sorry*, down at the yellow beast in her arms;

I wish I could be better.

Gloaming

Lia looked for February, but she couldn't find it anywhere. March stormed in. On the second of the month the publishers made their tragic call.

I'm sure you have other priorities now, they said.

She was wrapped up in the shed finishing the Spring page, winding stalks of hope up the edges of an overgrown gardener, pausing to suck up the potato soup Harry had just made through a thick straw, when her phone had rung.

She didn't need to worry about her Lexical Spectacles any more, they insisted. As they spoke, her favourite brush rolled off the desk, hit the floor with a clack. The shed walls caved. Her tongue flapped like a dead wet fish in her mouth as she tried to make a sound. She found herself just nodding, quietly, away. They were only trying to be kind, but the shift was the cruellest shock; feeling this thing that once mattered most
cease to matter at all,
all in a matter
of seconds.

It's so nearly there, she said, her tongue finding its movement, its phrases, as she went to spread the pages she had completed so far into alphabetical order on the floor. *Only seven words left or so.*

She felt as if she were begging them to pretend. *OK*, they said, *OK*.

Daylight slipped out from under her. The next thing she knew Iris was rocking her gently awake.

Mum.

She had dribbled a little on the Gloaming page.

They've told me to stop trying to work. All this. Such a waste. Such waste.

She croaked it like a detail of a bad dream.

Iris looked lovingly down at her mother the way a mother might look down at their own waking child.

I'm sure it wasn't like that. I'm sure they're only trying to be helpful.

Lia had got so thin her jaw and skull looked disproportionately large, like they might snap off her neck. The skin on the back of her hands had begun to mottle into dark marble blotches. Her lips had receded so that her yellowing teeth protruded out and Iris had never felt so hopeless, so aware that they were all losing control. She curled up on the rug, nestling, as if making her own body as small as possible might help to restore some natural mother-daughter order. But Lia clung, so frightened, so tightly to her. No, she wanted to say. Don't do that. Don't.

Thank you, Lia said, her voice tearing. For what? Iris wanted to sob. For what? But they just rocked there, together, quietly, in the gloaming.

Gloaming
Noun

1. Twilight. After the sun has gone down, before it gets dark. (e.g. Millions of half stars keel out of the gloaming.)
2. The rasp only detectable in a dying voice. (e.g. The gloaming in her throat made them both want to cry.)

The Burial of the Sardine

Thursday morning. Sky is bleeding its beautiful taunt-light earlier; the days are endless and then over in a moment. We are flicking through a large book on Goya in bed, staring at *The Burial of the Sardine*. A particularly hysterical piece of red-faced beasts as far as the eye can see, all celebrating the beginning of Christ's forty-day wilderness challenge (which He passes, of course, with flying colours).

Composed like the map of a crime before a murder it straddles, quite nicely, the artist's shifting sensibilities, the old and the new: part Old Master, part modern; part sane, part mad; part funeral, part festivity. It would have been nice to have created masterpieces like this, rather than pathetic little picture books, she thinks. It would have been nice to have invented a new kind of arsenic-based antibiotic to fight against the pressing threat of resistance. It would have been nice to have made some change in the world.

I tell her these are ugly, self-important desires. *All part of man's sad hunt for legacy.*

She thinks of that very first pig drawing.

But now? Goya writes, in a letter to a friend. *Well now, now I have no fear of Witches, goblins, ghosts, thugs, Giants, ghouls, scallywags, etc, nor any sort of body, except human.*

Indeed, I say, *indeed!*

She shushes me.

What are you most afraid of? I ask her.

You know the answer to that, she says.

We hear the weight of the daughter's pause, heavy outside our bedroom door. We feel her yellow eyes burrowing at the prospect of an entry. But her shadow disappears. She is down the stairs. She is out the front door. The sound of it shutting is agony.

She is most afraid of you! I tell her.

She knows this too.

We leave the book of horrors on the bed. Make our way to the window, pull back the curtains to watch the painting tumble out; a procession of familiar fragment figures gathering behind the daughter as she makes her way down the street.

Two identical twins sprout up from the cracks in the pavements with a spinning cast of dancers. The St James's boy with the confident chin shuffles forward, his trousers down below his ankles, limp cock out. Wide raven wings sweep leaves up off the gutters. The silver woman skips in an apron dusted in flour, hand in hand with a tangled girl in a blue school uniform;

Let's fix it! Slay it! Snuff it out! Delay it!

The daughter trudges on.

You will look after her, we want to shout after them, *you will all look out for her once I am gone?* They throw their cloaks down now at her feet, place a yellow crown of flowers on her head, claw away at her ankles;

What's the plan? When can we start?
You search the liver and we'll search the heart!

For we inherit the haunts of our mothers;
we are left with the guests they let in.

And that is parenthood, I tell her.
That is death.
The party turns the corner.
The hell goes on without you.

The Burial of the Father

Iris was certain nothing could be worse than that feeling. That standing by a parent's bedroom door, afraid of what you may find on the other side.

Like having these cold fingers reach in and rip all safe places right out of you.

Perhaps this is my fault, she thought,
perhaps I have not loved her hard enough.
The memory of Lia's voice cut through the morning; *They told me I would get ill again if I had another child.* Iris made a sudden terrible connection, felt her mind draw thick red circles around it. Oh God, she thought, oh God oh God oh God.

On the way to school, it seemed as if her anatomical nightmares had begun to bleed into the days. The clouds were an unusual fleshy pink, patched over each other like cuts of meat piled in a butcher's shopfront, and the streets were soft, edgeless, hot. Her little watched soul shuddered all the way to the crumbling school gates, copper rotting at their roots. Membrane walls cannot always tell the bad cells from the good, she thought, the beast from the child; sometimes all the horrors just go
flooding in.

In maths, strange sounds circled the building. Clamour of animals. Birds, perhaps. *One million possible combinations.* The unhinged

energy of happier children looped and knotted until she began to
feel quite untouchable, swaddled inside the hostility of things,
as if held still within the eye of a storm,
tortures spinning false visions around her.

Sometimes, she thought, you can achieve the big As –
Adjustment, Acclimatization, Acceptance,
just by rewriting a bunch of definitions.

*Sometimes, you can simplify the second fraction by dividing the
numerator and the denominator by the common factor which is,
in this case, three, kids.*

Teacher then shot her a look as if to say –
Listen.

Iris shot a look back as if to say –
No.

At lunch time, Burn Girl was sitting with her box of secrets
chewing gum, army circling like the dials of plastic planets on a
dream-catcher.

Cheer up, she said loudly, directly, her beautiful fearless face
shimmering in sour light.

Iris could think only of murder. Executions. The miracles it would
take to stop all this meticulous crime. Bodies of all kinds began
to cluster together, sardine-tight, for the week's secret reading.
Sounds slowed to a nervous, expectant hush, until the playground
was nothing but a sea of sealed mouths, waiting. Twitching eyes.
Crossed fingers. The usual collective *Not Me* prayer, rising into new,
unusual air.

Burn Girl picked out the box from her bag. She lifted the lid,
unfolded the week's secret carefully. Holding it between her perfect
thin fingers, taut as a bow before the snap, her eyes passed over

the scrawled words, her face unreadable as ever. Iris's eyes scorched out from the back of the crowd into Burn Girl's throat, her slowly parting lips. She could feel the heat of them on her. She could even feel the strain of the invisible thread connecting them, the knot of small wars and cruelty that had bound their lives, briefly, together – but most of all, she could feel the strike of the secret, the wound of it within her, too, before she had even uttered a word.

Iris's dad was spotted cheating on Iris's dying mum.

Tombs of the Sounding Sea

This is an ammonite fossil.

The mother is holding something out to the little girl in her palms. The two of them are holding orange plastic bags, scarves wrapped tightly around both their heads as they scour a quiet beach.

It's made from the shell of a very extinct animal.

Which animal?

Probably something like a squid or an octopus.

Fossil-hunting is best after a storm. The whole landscape glistens wet seal-skin grey in its aftermath as these two bright aliens shuffle across their abandoned planet, plucking out scraps from the shore. I watch them from the sea. For today,
I am the tide.

What am I from?

I edge closer.

Me!

Sliding back and folding forward, *And Dada?*

Foam-fingered and persistent, *No, actually.*

Oh.

I catch splinters of their conversation as she tries to explain genes and DNA and the difference between biology and parenthood while their orange bags fill up and their scarves flap in the breeze and the daughter concentrates hard on the pebbles.

When we get home, the daughter says, eventually, *we should find a box for the very best ones.* I am pooling around their feet now, glazing the rocks with my salt. *So we don't lose them like we lose everything else.*

The mother smiles. *We'll do that,* she says. Wind kisses her gums.

(they won't)

After a while, they turn their backs to the sea and begin to make their way slowly
up the dunes; two colourful little blots against the charcoal shadow of the cliff.
Just before they're out of sight, she turns back, for a moment, and looks at me sadly, like she knows.

I will be
Very Near,
very here,
very yours,
always.

Click, goes my camera.

Preparations

The city is no place for a person to die. I'm so pleased we live here,
Anne had said to Lia on the week leading up to Peter's death.

The air is clean, it is quiet and peaceful – it's a good place to die.

Lia knew she was trying to make some sort of point. She was
unsure what, exactly, but the suggestion of it smeared through the
seconds, searching, a while, for definition, before drying up and
crusting into that familiar, unexplained quiet.

Yes.

> **We are grinning down the line, hoping she doesn't hear**
> **the sound of our lips turning.**

Lia did not want to find Anne's seriousness amusing.

Any free time Lia could carve out for herself in recent weeks had
been spent labouring over *Grandad Forgetmenot*, a minimal picture
book and the final project for her degree. It was about an old man
who had forgotten himself and everything he'd ever known, being
led around the new world by his granddaughter, who gradually
rewrote the place for the better. Forgetmenot's glasses were the
same as Father Peter's, but she never drew his eyes. Only the
smudged reflection of the glass world he was witnessing for the
very first time. *Dark, but charming*, the tutors had said. She had
loved every minute of it.

Time to come back now, Anne said, softly, as if the whole of Lia's life
so far had been a trial run. *You'll want to say your goodbyes.*

It had been hailing hard the night before Lia arrived, the parish
ground pummelled and churned upturned, the land exposing the
reverse of its palms just to prove nothing,

inside or out,
had changed.

That there was no more for her there now than there had ever been.

Who's that? her vanishing father asked, as she opened the door to
his bedroom.

The devil, Lia said, smiling, unbuttoning her coat and pulling up
a chair.

The father's face collapsed into an expression of
sincere hostage fear, searching the room, before
finding his daughter's face and
breaking into a thick wheezy laugh – *So bad.*
He chuckled on, licking dry lips, the *bad* word delicious on his
tongue.

He sank back into his pillow and was gone again,
his eyes knocking away at a closed door for a second
before passing through into a new, undiscovered room
inside himself.

Suddenly quite uncatchable.

> **Here is the thing about diseases of the brain:**
> **You are relatively free so long as nobody tries to drag**
> **you back to the person you once were.**

It wasn't as sad or as ugly as Lia expected it to be, and when they
weren't helping him to the toilet or washing or feeding him or
managing his short violent outbursts of confusion, she would sit
by Peter's bed while he slept, reading out fragments of *Grandad
Forgetmenot*, making final touches, leading them both through
the last of their days. When Peter woke, sometimes little truths
would glint out from their conversations like pale, iridescent shells,

glimpsing out from a bed of desert, and Lia would collect them up one by one, press her ears close, decipher the leak of a secret, the swell of a half-formed revelation, the sound of his old life crashing and fading like the memory of a tide passing through a beached pink corridor of time;

The woman said he would come.

She did?

Who did? Goddammit. That damn dog.

Madness suits you!

Did I ever tell you how my wife and I met?

No.

On a pilgrimage. You know — Earth is round so that a pilgrim's map never ends.

That's lovely. Let me write that down.

Shhh. Hear that? Is it knocking or sobbing?

You know, Dad, you are more passionate in your death than you were in your life.

I have my passions!

> *You think I haven't desired?*

> *Ha! We have a whole ship to feed!*

It's impossible not to join in.

> ***Let them in through the window!***

What was the song?

Prince. 1985. Raspberry Beret.

Roadsides

Sunburns!

Beautiful

Irregular

Shoeboxes

Lemons and turnips and blossom and cats

We knock about nonsense, tongues beating like bats.

It's the illness, Anne would say, heart breaking, always distressed, *makes him odd, aggressive.*

I know, Lia would nod.

While the father went on fading upstairs, Anne prepared the house for his passing as if preparing for a visitor. As if God Himself may arrive for tea before taking him away. Lia realized that this was, in many ways, the event their life had built towards. The final instruction. The sum of all their faith, charity and goodness. *I cannot imagine a certainty like that,* Lia would say, and Anne would half smile, simmering with something resembling smugness, collecting up the doorstep pies and daffodils and visitors; proud and strong and steely.

On the night of Peter's death, right on time, a distinctive knock went hammering through the house.

body is marble
cold and still at the top of the
stairs

Who's that?

Anne patted herself down, tucked her hair behind her ears.

That'll be Matthew.

It can't be

Did I tell you he was coming? I must have. Got hold of him last week. Funny. It was like he knew.

No, no, no

She strode to the front door and

no

swung it open like it was the easiest thing.

Lia dropped to the floor,
knocked back by the impact.

She clutched the banister, released it.

Slid down
        a step.

From his room, Peter groaned to invisible people about ferrets, aeroplanes, pear cider.

And there she was. Back again. And the shape of the moment felt an exact summation of what being an adult was; sitting at the top stair of your childhood trying to get a fresh look at the world beyond, with an elderly mother and an ageing lost lover like cork-stoppers, blocking the way.

Love and Cruelty

Love, like cruelty, does not withdraw from a life over time,
as some suggest.

Love, like cruelty, only learns to understand itself better.
It grows self-conscious. Becomes less eager to thrust its head
above the parapet, teaches itself to count and queue and make
lists so that one day it wakes up to find it has quietened. It has a
day job. It has bought a dog with the money made from its day
job. And just like that, it is civilized. It is bearable. The dog sleeps
easy. The love does not always.

Before the Rooster Crows

A dense quiet flooded the playground, before the last sacred essence
of Iris's childhood shattered and went

                    splintering off   into the distance.

It's true. She spotted him with someone on Tuesday, a voice whispered,
pointing at Burn Girl.

I heard it was a teenager. He was kissing a teenager.

I heard there's a photo.

No!

I didn't know her mum was actually dying.

My mum says she's an odd one.

Odd or mad or not, it's still sad.

Imagine that. Cheating on a dying woman.

Their sentences split off at their edges like
little red blood cells desperately trying to
regenerate themselves; poisonous rumours
feeding the horrid, hungry air.

What a monster.

Poor Iris. Poor Iris's dying mum.

Men! someone said very loudly, in a perfectly rehearsed
Nineties American Movie Twang. *Just typical, really!*

Three other girls rolled their eyes and tutted,
stuck their necks out long and flared their nostrils
like scorned women in nail salons.

The more fury Iris felt,

the quicker earth's particles undid themselves.

But he's not my dad.

She said it first very quietly, very bitterly. She had never said these
words aloud, never even really
thought them.

He's not my dad. Not really.

Spinning on the balls of their monstrous feet, the procession of
kids began to repeat in whispers;

He's not her dad! He's not her dad!

Did you hear that? He's not even her dad?

Everyone had turned to her now, eyebrows raised, expecting more. She looked at them all, smothered in the pressure of their attention, remembering the blistering applause of the audience as each dancer had taken to the stage; *It would be the best thing in the world, I think.* It was the worst. She wondered just how much of her life she had misunderstood.

No. He's not my real dad. And my mum isn't dying.

The afternoon bell went suddenly, blazing through the landscape like an alarm, a siren,
a flock of roosters, all crowing in delight. The congregation scattered. Solero Boy came and squeezed her sweaty palm.

Leave me alone, she said, *please,* her voice fighting against the bell, the air refusing to diffuse its pigments. Playground clotting away.

He leant in closer. *It's OK. It's OK,* he said. *Here. I have something for you.* He pressed a piece of paper into her hand. She held it tightly, hardly listening, eyes burning.

She isn't dying. She isn't.

Well. That's good, then.

He smiled weakly, his face anchoring her back to her body, back under her scalp into the streaming hot guilt of her arms and legs, her perfectly functioning organs.

She opened her fist, unfolded the paper. On it were the numbers

3 6 7 7 4 5

He's not my dad my mum isn't dying he's not my dad my mum isn't dying he's not my dad my mum isn't dying he's not my dad my mu

the code to the locker.

How did you find it?

It's the same as her phone password. I watched her type it in.

Iris looked blankly down at the numbers. It was too late, she thought. It was all too late.

Does it work?

Yes. He looked up at her, wiping his leaking nose, a glimmer of excitement brightening his eyes. *I thought you should be the one to do it.*

He was trying hard not to look too pleased with himself. Her expression remained unchanged.

I'm sorry, he added, putting the last of the light out, *if it feels a bit late, now.*

It doesn't, she said, as kindly as she could. She would do it tomorrow, she thought. During P.E. She would replace the box of secrets with the cigarette packet, so that Burn Girl knew it was her. She might even write a little note for her, some quippy one-liner like the sort of thing spoken after the kill in superhero movies. *Fighting for truth and justice.* But as she turned over gravel stones gently with the nib of her shoe and pocketed the code with the burn mark hand, she felt pathetic, and she could still hear the sound of her lies ringing with the knell of the afternoon bell, only now through her new monstrous body;

, not my dad my mum isn't dying he's not my dad my mum isn't dying he's not my mum isn't dying he's not my dad my mum isn't dying he's not my dad my mum isn't dying

ten

The Reunion

Two bodies stand facing one another in a shrunken vicarage kitchen.

We've rehearsed this reunion so many times.

The version where she shoots him square between the eyes and sets the whole house on fire and rides away on a palomino called Dawn. The version where he falls to his knees and sobs his sorrys quietly into her stomach before she shoots him square between the eyes, sets the whole house on fire and rides away on a palomino called Dawn. The version where she climbs up his body, sobs her sorrys into his neck, kisses him everywhere and takes off all his clothes before she shoots him square between the eyes, sets the whole house on fire and rides away on a palomino called Dawn.

Who knows which one she'll go for.

So here I am, waiting and watching from my Director's Chair, positioned perfectly in the space where the devil once sat between the sink and the window

thinking –

Yes.

This is good. Better, perhaps. The anticlimax. The tragedy of them just taking each other in, silently, eight years on, sitting and sipping breakfast tea, forgetting their lines, pretending they're both absolutely fine, while Anne fusses, takes his coat, cuts the toast, sends the explosives team and the palomino home.

It's so bleak even I couldn't think it.

It also allows me the option of some inventive intertitles:

BANG

Meet Cute

Lia, bored of the ceiling and her new flat, windless life, took off one early morning while Harry was on the loo. She slid on his distractingly ugly gardening shoes, crept quietly out the door and shuffled off into the waking ancient city.

Oooohhhh I do love a spontaneous outing.

Under the wide basin of blue open sky, Lia felt as if she could breathe again.

The world is our lobster!

She would take herself on a little tour, she thought. A final tour of her short life's great locations.

Where first? The hotel? The theatre? The flat in the East End above the butcher's shop? The parish? The beach? Hell, we could hop on a plane and go to –

She would begin with the allotment along the Thames bank, where she had first met Harry.

Urgh. fine.

It was windy by the riverbank. The breeze kissed along the water. Its skin goose-bumped and freckled, blushing in the early April sun. And though Lia could not move with any speed or certainty, she found she could lift her arms a little, twist her fingers around delicately, letting the cold ripple through them as she began to feel her way along another morning, many years old:

She is younger and fitter and healthier and dancing so wildly with her headphones on down this empty path, and it feels glorious to spin one's arms, to stretch and leap secure in the belief that absolutely no one is watching.

He had been in his mid-thirties, or thereabouts, bent over a tiny patch of land separated from the path by a flimsy fence.

His plot is not big or even particularly neat but it is flourishing, and he is laughing, uncynically, at us.

Once she had spotted him, she had stopped dancing immediately. He leant on his pitchfork and applauded, and she noticed that he had a lovely boyish face, an undeniable radiancy.

She performs a mock-bow for him.

I lean a little on her cortex.

Lia felt the morning crack.

I push a little heavier.

She swayed, sky caved, light bent.

I want to smash the day up. To have a little fun. I want to grab his pitchfork and do something inexplicably naughty like impale him with it, but she is taking her headphones off and walking right up to the fence, and as they begin to talk, I find I cannot touch them, cannot even hear them I

lean my whole weight

on the memory
swallow a skyscraper
chew some swans

                              nobody notices a thing

                    there is so much light enshrining them
                                                         it
                    becomes very clear   there is simply

                        no   space for me
                                                      here

Lia turned from the allotment to the river. Stared for a moment
at the still of its silver. Steadied herself. Very carefully, she began
to make her way down the watermen's stairs. On the bank, the
tide was low. The rocks chuckled and slid about beneath her as she
walked right to the water's edge, where she lowered herself and sat
amongst the silt and the pebbles, the bottle caps and orange peel,
letting the Thames spill over her numb, sockless feet, filling the toes
of Harry's shoes. Just ahead of her, two swans tangled their necks
together. An empty condom wrapper floated beside them. Quite
limp with exhaustion, she yawned, and then lay flat, the rough
edges of the rocks grinding happily up against the bones in her back.

The sky was mostly cloudless. There was no sound at all but the
gentle chug of a nearby road.

It was half an hour later when Harry and Connie found her, white
and still on the bank, looking like a washed-up sea creature the
incoming tide had just gutted out of its depths.

Lia! Lia! Oh God.

There she is.

Oh fuck.

Sit up now. Yes.

Let's get you home.

[363]

Exit Door

You must find some way of telling me, Lia said on her father's deathbed, *if it's all true.* He was pale and nearly there, there at the threshold of the passing over. *I'll need a clear strong sign. A glass smashing or a tree bursting into flames — something like that. You will, won't you? You must.*

She is trying far too hard to be clever and funny and sincere.

So bad, Peter said, half smiling, before turning to Matthew. Matthew. He had aged well, which was no surprise, but he had a new composure that she did not recognize. A startling alien calmness set deep into the cool of his eyes, eyes that had once gleamed and flashed and roared around a room. He must be thirty-five now, Lia thought, staring at the tiny silver hairs that frosted the sides of his face. She did not feel the same pulses of panic and excitement he had once sent through her body. Only the small press of her heart's quiet bruises.

Matthew stroked a thin grey hair from Peter's soaking forehead. Pressed his lips against the bridge of his nose. Kept them there a few elastic seconds. Something in Lia's gut squirmed.

There wasn't a person in the world he didn't try to seduce!

She stared at them both, their affection seeking itself out, recognizing itself, a little aged and changed, but very naked. Quite unashamed.

To be honest, they've probably fucked too.

Lia shut away the nasty thought. And then Peter opened his mouth and said *you*, very simply, without any surprise or recognition in his voice, as if it were merely an answer.

Her/you

her/you

I tap its little staccato rhythm

right through

Shadows of a departing life began to shift about in the room. As if the last of Peter had been ignited by Matthew's lips, the house inside him began to burn; the doors, the walls, the structure. All alight. Roaring his black-winged soul up and out. Matthew called for Anne. Anne rushed in, kissed her husband's hands, and Lia felt a swell of sincere affection for her. A last door, untouched by the flames. Peter inhaled thickly, twinkling, before passing through, and Lia found herself praying that his God was there, on the other side, praying hard that his welcome was everything he'd ever imagined it to be.

Recovering the Body from the Bank

You cannot call and just say you've 'lost her'. You cannot begin with a thing like that.

I'm sorry.

I thought you meant—

I know, I know. I'm sorry.

You look terrible.

Yes.

How many times has she done this?

A few. Sometimes I wake up and she is gone. Sometimes I am in the shower or having a shit and she is out the front door as if I have been holding her captive here, as if I am some terrible physician drugging her, making her mad.

She is not running from you. She is dying.

A tuneless cold fact.

I have been terrible.

You have been brilliant.

Silence.

How did you know she would be there?

I didn't. I guessed. It was where we first met.

Ah. Of course.

Silence.

You know, sometimes it's like drowning, Con, sometimes I forget and it is like we are all
nearly free.

Me too. Me too. And thank God, really.

Why?

Because that is love.

The Burial of a Father

The path up to the church was a long one. The day was eerily
quiet. Only the clicks and the little shuffles of Sunday best shoes,
mottling away at the stone. The congregation's overcast expressions.

we are trying desperately to hook ourselves up to their devastation

Matthew squeezed Lia's palm. His touch rolled cold right through
her, like a nut along a bolt.

Momentarily, her life felt wild, eventful, tragic. Not because he
was touching her, but because they were there together, right
where they had begun. Because they were older now, and she felt
as if she'd made it through the worst. Because death had its way of
sharpening life. Because even her mother had become briefly vivid
in her suffering.

He lived for his flock, they said during the service. *He lived through
the lives of us here today. He rarely strayed far from the parish, but
his kindness was vast, it knew no bounds. Never have I known such
selflessness.*

Matthew nodded and nodded. Anne wept. Lia felt as if she had
never known him.

My yoke is easy and my burden is light.

When it was over, a sky of exhausted, yawning angels in overcoats
congregated
to watch a flock's loving act of necrophoresis;
bent-backed and black
insects, carrying their king on exoskeletal shoulders,

hoping for trumpets, for at least
the creak of a golden hinge swinging,
for some sign that another good soul
was taking his rightful place.

The clouds chuckled. The rain came. The sandwiches were better
than expected.

A Family Meeting

Daughter has called a family meeting in the kitchen.

We slide down the stairs on our bum, a little weak from our
outing. Each step at a time, the friction of carpet against cotton,
muscles in our legs straining. She hopes the daughter never sees
that even stairs are becoming impossible.

On top of the radiator by the front door we spot a small
ammonite fossil and some more charcoal stone shards and try
desperately not to scream. Because he is here, we know he is,
playing one last little game, fingering through our possessions
at night. Leaving little clues for us around the place. It's only a
matter of time before he reveals himself.

In the kitchen, the daughter is so solemn. She tells us about the
secret reading.

It's been the worst day of my life, she says.

Somewhere deep within us, an avalanche starts. Catastrophic
mass of rubble and rumour and cheap little trauma, all heading
for the oblivious family, perched at the foot of the cliff. We stare
at the miserable lilac bags under the daughter's eyes. We watch
the avalanche nearing behind us in the flat-black-fear of the
husband's shrinking pupils.

It's not true, he says, his voice feigning strength, *you know that's not true, Iris, it's not true,* but she isn't listening.

I want to see my real dad, she says, conclusively. *I want to talk to him.* She looks hard in our direction. *Who will I have when you are gone?*

She is so matter of fact about her mother's *going* they are all quite startled.

(all but me who understands that children's minds are without a doubt better equipped to deal with matters of death and destruction)

The husband is shaking his head.

You will have me, Iris, you will always have me.

He is trying to keep it together, bless him, really trying not to cry or scream or shout, these large bulbous radishes are heaving out from his collar bones.

But you are not my blood.

The husband's bloodless body hollows and shudders.

Since when have you ever cared about blood?

They are both looking at us, for help, I presume. For anything.

Well. Since today.

The daughter looks as if she could rule a kingdom.

We feel her tyrannical fury slowly drain out the little energy we have left. But none of us around this table can argue with *since today,* because death also makes
the things that never seemed to matter

**begin to matter,
all in a matter
of seconds.**

Deliberations

It was the week between the second (Hockney) and third date (Goya) with the gardener, the man with the kind uncynical laugh, when Lia found out she was pregnant. They had not yet slept together.

> **Daughter is the size of a bottle cap. Buds breaking off into the beginning of hands and feet. Cellophane skin.
> Alien eyes, categorizing light. A speckle of ear. Tail tucked.**

I can understand, she practised telling Harry, *I can understand if you would rather us be friends. I could do with a friend. I could do with one of those, too.*

> **A pulse now, a real beating human heart.**

I am pregnant, she practised telling Matthew, *I am pregnant with this foetus-thing that is half yours. I can understand if you want nothing to do with it, with us. I would be fine with that, too.*

She would reach for her phone often, on the bus, in the park, at the front desk of the hotel, the mobile which now had both of their numbers crackling about inside it the way statues beat about inside stone.

She had never believed that she would have children. For a day or two or three she had been very certain that she wouldn't keep it. But what she had developed, over the week of knowing, was this pure and nagging curiosity. This overwhelming sense that there was nothing in her life more interesting than the prospect of what the cells growing inside her would turn out to be.

There was nothing quite so important.

And just like September in the farm came and went, just like tomorrow would tumble over into tomorrow, the little human life continued to develop, and Lia would often worry that she had never made one definitive decision all her life, that she had never made any solid plans or carved out a path for herself, only fallen aimlessly from one day to the next.

Because she is, first and foremost, a little spineless coward.

She would clutch her belly at night and hope very hard that this child would turn out to be bold and decisive and go looking for the life that they wanted.

Very occasionally she would let herself think: Perhaps simply adjusting to what life throws your way is enough. Perhaps, just perhaps, there is nobility in that too.

She only ever had one of the two conversations she had practised.

(Naughty thing)

Bildungsroman

The husband is counting pills into his palms he is saying, *You know it was just a drink. Nothing more. Nothing more.*

He looks so embarrassed, so appalled with himself.

He places them one by one between our dry lips, helps us with a sip of water.

It's OK, we are saying. *We know. We know.*

He is trying not to notice the glaze of pride edging into the new yellow whites of our eyes, trying not to notice the secret pleasure we have found in his restless act of daring.

Our dying wife truth is that we never believed him capable.

Our dying wife *worst* truth is now that we know he is – we love him more than ever.

It is nice to be reminded that love is as much a choice as it is a feeling. With the alchemy of this fact, it finds boundless ways to strengthen itself.

We go to watch the daughter in her yellow room cooking up old-as-time comprehension questions based on the themes of fatherhood, estrangement and identity.

Question 1: Who are you?

A) A Villain
B) A Good Guy
C) An Unlikely Hero

We are near-certain that Fossil is behind the window, waiting with his pen, ready to circle some answers. We try not to feel jealous that he is here for her, now, not for us.

After the questions, she writes him a letter addressed to Real Dad. Once she is asleep, we sneak in to snatch the papers away to read under the soft glow of corridor light.

She writes candidly of drama and pain, but mostly of mothers.

The fact that the best characters are without them.
The fact that the best stories begin with their departure.

The fact that she must learn to flourish not in spite of, but *because* of this absence.

And I just love this bit. (I have seen it many times.)

The bit where someone turns death into a device;
a plot-point, propelling a soul towards its ultimate goal,
setting it straight on the path of its Best Character Arc.

Although I do believe life is not a bildungsroman –
it is one of the many funny ways human nature goes on
protecting itself.

And, really, it cannot hurt. It cannot hurt at all.

We circle all three.

ABC.

Harry goes to put the kettle on.

Her Best Performance Yet

It happened the night of the funeral.

I knead myself through every inch of her organs
                          because I don't want to miss a second of it.

Anne had cooked veal and cabbage stew for the three of them, and
Lia thought of the fatted calf that was prepared upon the arrival of
the prodigal son as her fork parted her smile like a pink sea.

He was four years, five months, one week and two days sober. He
talked about the AA meetings he ran, how fulfilling it was to help
others out of those numb, horizonless plains, and when he casually

mentioned his recent conversion to Buddhism (though he took issue with the word *conversion*), Lia watched with delight as a small watery mouthful of stew fell from Anne's lips, followed by three green peas. She knew her mother well enough to know she would rather Matthew be an atheist than a Buddhist. She took a moment to bask in the flimsy glory of being one thing, at last, in Anne's eyes, that was marginally better than him.

**One gold
godless star
to us.**

I guess what I'm trying to say is that people change, he said, which Lia found odd because it was not what he had been saying at all. *Every minute. Every second. We change.* He looked intently at Lia, and Anne raised her eyebrows, dabbing her mouth with her napkin. Lia noticed how aged her hands had become, how mottled they were, swelling up around the ring welded to her wedding finger.

Yes, Anne said suddenly, the bewilderment in her face clearing to reveal a steadfast pride behind. *People are saved. They are forgiven. The circumstances of your life might change. Indeed, you might change them yourself. But take Peter* – her voice broke a little at the sound of his name – *I know it didn't seem like it, but Peter was Peter until the day he died, and he remains the same man now as he always was, up in heaven, beside the Lord. Because nature is nature. Character, character.*

Of course, Matthew said softly, embarrassed to have upset her.

Anne mumbled something very quietly to herself about mercy, and closed her eyes for a moment, her lips drawing upwards into what should have been a smile but was, instead, an unusual expression of absolute serenity. Her wrists flat on the table, she swayed backwards, ever so slightly, and seemed elevated, as if briefly possessed by the Spirit Himself. When she opened her eyes, her pupils contracted, collecting up the splinters of the room, and though Lia would never have expected to, she felt very moved by it all.

Matthew was still sipping on stew as if nothing of note had happened and perhaps it hadn't, Lia thought, as Anne stood.

I'm very tired, she said, wearily. *I hope you don't mind if I go to bed.*

On her way out of the room, as she passed Matthew, he turned and reached out and took her hand so smoothly, so easily, as if she'd intended him to, though Lia knew that she hadn't. *Thank you*, he said, so seriously. For dinner, perhaps. For everything. But his tone was more loaded, as if he were saying, I am sorry. As if he were asking for her forgiveness. Lia was certain she'd seen her mother's body recoil, ever so slightly. Fight the instinct to snap her hand away. But instead, she stared down at her coarse wrinkled flesh held tight in his, this rare expression of disbelief rippling into every crease of her face. And then she opened her mouth ever so slightly to speak, and though the words seemed to be right on the end of her tongue, just behind her teeth, poised on the edge of her lips, she sighed a simple quiet sigh, and let her hand fall away.

Anne turned to the cupboard where she kept her box of pills, took out a packet of Ambien, pushed her nail into the foil, placed two on her tongue, swallowed them dry, and went up to bed.

Silence collapsed in. Matthew went to the sink and filled a glass of water. He drunk without drawing breath. Lia watched beads of water escape down his chin, the mad sliding shape of his quick, urgent swallows. He looked remarkably like the Matthew she had once known, which pleased her.

He came up finally for air. *I'm sorry for the letter*, he said. *I know that would have upset you. I'm sorry for it all.*

It was ironic, Lia thought, that of all the things he could choose to apologize for, he would start with the apology.

I can't say that I forgive you, she said. *If that's what you're looking for.*

No. No, I don't expect that.

Upstairs, nothing about either of their rooms had changed, except in each of the doors, Anne had put a key.

Lia examined the key in its lock, wondering why the object struck her as a very funny, very depressing, very sinister thing indeed. Wondering whether her life would have looked very different had it been there from the start. *Have you seen?* she whispered quietly to Matthew, who had followed her up the stairs. He was suddenly the sort of close that once would have made her heart forget its rhythm.

Once?

The keys. And then he laughed and leant in and kissed her lips very lightly, like it was something she might be expecting of him, and perhaps it was.

Perhaps it is.

In the bedroom, he undressed her with such caution, as if he were still trying to resist, as if afraid he might descend
into that animal feasting roughness.
It's OK, she said. *It's me. You don't have to be gentle.* She unbuckled the belt of his trousers.

The single mattress springs plucked their raw melancholy tune beneath their bodies. His hands shook like instruments under strain, played too hard for too long, and she felt very sorry for him, very disgusted with herself.

the veal cabbage potato wine hydrochloric acid
mulch is folding and
knocking about her stomach lining

What's wrong? she whispered. *What is it?* His heavy breaths bubbled
hot along her neck.

she is purpling and swelling,
her walls clutching and clinging and coaxing
trying so hard to welcome him home

It was over quickly. Lia pretended to come.

It was so stark, she thought, so depressing and empty, this thrusting
up towards some unreachable thing they would never again
achieve. For she had been certain of nothing in her life except
the way their bodies responded to one another. The fact that her
instructions had been written into his bones before birth. And yet
here they were, and it wasn't how she remembered it at all.

Aha! Here we go! The real fun
begins.

He faltered, sunk deep, released.

Inside, millions of complex little instructions
shoot, spread and gleam, splitting off in groups
like flocks of birds
or schools of fish.

He pulled himself out of her and went to put the bedside light on.

Most don't make it through. Most
drop
like
flies
through clouds of nuclear poison.

Sorry, he said. *That was so short.* He slid his boxers back on.

That's OK.

> I think of the abandoned radioactive city
> > declared unsafe for 24,000 years.
> 1,200 buses carrying 49,000 people away from their Pripyat homes.

> They were told they'd be leaving for a couple of days,
> > enough time for a quick trip to the coast. Of course –
> > > they never returned.

He squeezed back next to her and she slotted herself under his armpit. It smelt just as it always had. Sweet sweating beach before a storm. She felt a little residue of his wet heat ooze from her.

> **We are told that they are bold,**
> **fierce swimmers. Heroes.**
> **Fighters. Warriors. Winners.**

We shouldn't have done that, Matthew said.

No.

No, I mean, I really shouldn't have. I'm on a programme.

Oh.

Of course, Lia thought. It made sense; it was obvious. So obvious she had nearly missed it. For a moment she felt ridiculous, selfish, naive for not understanding sooner the varying degrees of addiction that had blackened the lanes of his life. He had always been so wide open, he let so much of the world into him. He had never managed to quench the yearn alone.

> **These millions of silver halflings appear to me now much**
> **more like accidental travellers, guided by a great pull of**
> **gravity.**

I think I have a pretty unhealthy relationship with sex too, she said. *For what it's worth.* Now that it was out there in front of them, she wondered if it was a tautology.

Anyway I'm pleased you came, she added, *because I wanted to thank you.*

Thank me?

For leaving. I never would have. And look at us now.

The last phrase hung limp and sour in the air. She thought of that first year on the farm, the way she would lean back in their bed and say things like, *We are happy, aren't we?* knowing in her heart of hearts that too much of a blissful thing leads only towards a particular sort of hell.

I think, he said, eventually, *I think we were just very bad for each other.*

Lia felt a quiet chill of anger through her ribs;
the rustling of cypresses, unprepared for autumn.

It did not have to be this way,
she wanted to say.
You did not need to choose that. We did not need to be.

Instead, they listened a while to the clicks of a tired bed frame, as if God were tutting His tongue against the back of His teeth, looking down sadly at the two troubled souls who had made
    much of life quite unbearable for the other.

> **When the egg is activated by a sperm enzyme**
> **an explosion of zinc sparks**
> **erupt.**

I've met someone, he said very quietly, his fingers circling the mole on Lia's shoulder. *She's on the programme too.*

Lia was surprised not to feel much about this.

That's good, she said. *I think I want to do kids' books.*

He laughed. *That's good*, he said.

When she got up from the bed, she looked down to examine his body one last time, taking in his new skin which sagged and draped a little indifferently from bone to bone, the salt of his sweat glowing in the blue. He looked remarkably peaceful. Perhaps he is right, she thought. Perhaps people really do change.

You should go, she whispered, sliding a T-shirt over her shoulders. *You should go*. And though she hoped that he hadn't noticed, there had been a bitterness in her voice, and she had watched it dance out towards him, inscribing the dark with that ancient flare – fear of unrequited love.

> **And now, all around me, the sound of a feeble engine switching off. Detaching itself. Plummeting into the deep. Acrosin bores its hole in the zona pellucida the way chlorofluorocarbons make ruptures in the ozone. It is a common misconception that creation and discovery don't require**

rather a lot of destruction.

The next morning, Lia went out into the untended garden to look at the limestone ruins. In her memory, they were taller, more substantial, with this discreet magical air about them. Now they just looked like stubs of toddler's teeth. Moss rotting away at their roots.

She stepped over the threshold, stood in their centre. Wide shadows of storm clouds slid across the hills, blemishing the land in pewter and pearl and gunmetal greys. She regretted not apologizing to Matthew. She wished she'd said something profound, like – I was so desperate to be your answer, I'd hardly listened to the question.

Lia turned to observe his figure behind the glass, his silhouette standing in the kitchen, gathering his things to leave. It occurred to her that the God-shaped hole in their vicarage home had, for each of them, in their own very separate and peculiar ways, been filled with him. That he had kept the Lord's seat warm when the Lord had felt absent, that the Lord had done quite the same for him, and this relentless pattern of substitution, doubt and blind adoration meant that what Matthew had come to represent in their lives was not just a matter of the familial, the intimate or the sexual, but of the deeply theological. Rain began to hiss in the distance. Matthew stepped out of the frame, and Lia felt quite done with it all.

Lightning came next. She counted distance on her fingers.

Twelve. A great stain of thunder shook and parted the sky twelve miles away.

Things weren't so bad. There was work. There was Connie. There was the man she'd met on the allotments by the river only a few weeks ago now. She would ask him to dinner maybe, take him to an exhibition in town. She would open up her life to everything and everyone, she would nurture her body, feed it with light until it was as porous and as absorbent as she'd always hoped it would be. She would let good love in. Yes, she was done with it all, pleased, even, that it had happened, that it had been her life, but done with it.

Conception

It is ironic that a night so full of departure could be the night the daughter was made.

Wonderful that the little hatching is happening so perfectly, eighteen hours on.

The miraculous twitch of the embryo beginning to divide into two, then four, then sixteen, then thirty-two. The fact of the morula skimming through the tube into cavity, teeming into blastocyst, the sudden switching on of genes, the growing of the yolk, the building blocks of a life lined with intricate scaffolding systems; heave of respiratory, strokes of urogenital, a trace of tooth enamel here, the first sliver of spine there, and it's all happening, remarkably, without her having a clue.

I settle in the tiny cord connecting them. Marvel at the way her body accommodates this growth before she has even decided to.

Suspended between being and non-being I sing some terrible things quietly through the chambers, plant a few secret horrors in her hormones;

> *Your mother will die too soon, too young,*
> *and it will be your fault.*

And now, of course, in some sick and masterfully curated way – she will simply never be rid of him.

Threshold

The doctors had told them to stay far apart. Not to touch.

Lia's immune system would not handle even the slightest infection.

> The daughter's respiratory tract is a little swollen from flu, see, flu who has bound itself to the surface of her cells and is making its slow steady way through her bloodstream.

Lia and Iris were on either side of the bedroom door threshold.

Threshold is a word of uncertain origin.

We know this much; naughty first component *thresh* probably derives from Old English *þrescan* – to tread, trample, knock, beat, and strike.

See – even words are made up of little internal transgressions;
even language disobeys itself, because most living things carry the instructions for their own undoing everywhere they go.

The two of them were not speaking, only looking at each other; Lia cross-legged on the floor wrapped in blankets, picking at threads of tissue with her thin yellow claws behind her invisible boundary, Iris tucked up in bed, delicate wisps of wet hair stuck to her forehead. She looked like she had when she was born; flushed, spluttering, a little of that tumbling expression, thick wet coughs into the corner of her pillow.

Do you think he'd like me?

Iris said quietly, tucking her hand under her cheek.

Lia tried to maintain her composure.

Yes. Of course.

Iris wiped her nose and frowned. Perhaps, one day, she would go looking for him, she thought. Perhaps she'd have to get very famous first and go on one of those ancestry shows. It seemed a shame that someone with half of her DNA had no idea that she existed.

I wonder where he is.

Lia wondered what Iris would say if she told her everything, right now, as they sat on either side of the threshold. If she took her from the day that he arrived on the vicarage doorstop to the very last moment he walked out. The absolute unfiltered truth.

You know that she would hate you. You know that.

There had been days when she found she could spin elegant tales from the mess of it. Brief moments when she could cook up a clean coherent case for herself, to feast on it whenever the guilt had scraped her insides dry. She had saved herself. Saved even him, perhaps. For there had been something about the way he had looked at her that night – like he, too, wanted their part in each other's lives to be well and truly over. And then there was the worst, the weakest, most cowardly thought of them all –

He would have been a bad father.

She was ashamed to have ever lingered on it. But now, looking at his stubborn nose on Iris's face, letting her eyes slowly follow along the line of his jaw passing right through hers the way a pen might strain to trace the gradient of a great distant mountain, she knew it was really very simple. He'd taken up so much of her past, and she had not let him into their future. It was unforgivable, and she was running out of time.

Iris watched her mother balancing sideways against the world; robbed of all gravity.
She changed direction.

Mum?

Yes.

You know how you said you couldn't have another kid because the cancer would come back.

Yes.

Does that mean it arrived in the first place because of me?

Lia felt a shuddering through one of her systems.

Does that mean I have done this? That – really – it is my fault.

Skeletal. Muscular. Somewhere through the creases between.

No, she said, voice adamant, *do not think that for a second, not one second, you hear me?*

Iris nodded seriously and Lia wondered if this was what it would feel like
to be a ghost,
to continue on after death –
stuck on the wrong side of the door, always;
looking in without life or eyes or flesh, fearing the door may close, at any point –
that your knuckles would not make a sound.

Knock knock.

Nothing.

Only a vast, unending

nothing.

Lia wrenched herself from the floor,

Oh, don't do that

trampled through the threshold as quickly as she could –

you really shouldn't.

because she could – because she would until she couldn't;

stopstopstopstopstop

she clambered into Iris's bed as if they had been parted for many years by something other than herself, some force separate to her own slowing organs.

Mum, don't do that – you'll make it worse.

Under the duvet, Iris rubbed her feet gently against her mother's socks, their toes clutching at each other.

I think we need to try something else now, I think we need a miracle.

Lia looked down at her daughter's head against her chest, the familiar unchanging smell of her scalp, the sweat and grease and texture of her hair. She thought of her own mother, of the way that her scent – not her washing powder or her soap but that real, private scent of elbows and armpits – was always stowed away from her.

Can I ask – one more thing.

Go on.

I've been thinking. If you can't finish Lexical Spectacles, *maybe I could? We've done so many word-talks together. We've been practising them for most of my life. I'm not a bad drawer, either. It should be finished.*

Lia smiled. How beautiful, she thought. The books had always been Iris's after all. Growing with her. How fitting that the young woman growing out of the child would have the last word. And it would be done.

Yes?

Yes, she said, stroking her fingertips down her daughter's parting.
Yes. I would love that.

Perched on each row of her bookcase – a chorus audience sighs.

Very good, **they tut**, *she would, she would,*

applauding and dabbing and smudging very puffed-up teary eyes.

Iris nodded.

A furious quiet came, echoing from wall to wall.

I'm so angry, she said, eventually, her voice breathless.

I know. Me too.
                                                                    (Me too!)

(Me too!)
                                                        (Me too!)

(Me too!)
                                                                    (Me too!)

Lia opened her sore scabbing mouth to say she had always loved
Iris's anger. To say that she wanted everything; her arguments, her
stubbornness, her fury. All her most difficult days. She wanted,
more than anything in this world, to watch her daughter's life's
transgressions unfold. But everything tightened. Closed. Sealed.
Because nothing was good enough, nothing was good enough,
nothing was even the tiniest bit good enough.

Tomorrow, I will pray for a miracle, Lia thought, as the two of
them drifted off to sleep,
fastened tightly together.

It would be cruel to suggest that this was what did it.
The Final infection.
Devastating to imply that this was the last straw;

the match in the powder barrel; the final pulling of the floor out from under cold feet; their undoing instruction; my last gentle defeat.

So I will not.
I will not.

The Wrong Parent

From behind the threshold, Harry could hardly bear the sight of his two girls, locked together in the single bed as if their bodies were one, as if the small mattress were the only safe slice of world left. Nothing could touch them there; he was sure of it. Nothing would dare puncture such peace.

Two for the price of one, Lia had called them, peeling stickers off the pasta packets in the supermarket, pressing them to her jumper or the taut skin on her belly, parading around his flat humming *two for one, two for one*. It had only been a few months, but there had been no doubt in his mind what he had wanted. It was not that he felt up to any task or attracted by any particular challenge – only that he considered it a privilege she was there with her cutting, infinite eyes, ever-surprising mind, offering to share her days, her hours, her child, with him.

A romantic. A sentimental type, she called him. The truth was he did not think himself either of these things. He had simply wanted to know her, from the moment he first saw her, dancing madly along the Thames path.

Four years later, they had been married at the local registry office in the deep of winter. Iris, who had been cast as Part One Mary in the school nativity, wore her Virgin Mary costume and spent the whole day on Lia's hip, her tiny plump palms resting on her mother's cheek so that she could turn her face furiously back if ever her attention strayed.

Harry had watched her press her little lips to Lia's earlobes, the dip of her nose, the crease before her nostrils began, hissing and scowling at anyone who came near them. And then she had caught his eye. Her face had opened wide as sudden daylight. *Dada! Come*, she'd said, and she had beckoned him over, beaming, and the whole place had felt ablaze with beginnings.

But he had failed. Husband. Father. Human. He had failed.
He had found his life – he would lose half of it –
and to the other half, live on only as a constant and monstrous reminder that the wrong parent had died.

Harry took his body out into his beloved garden. He fell to his knees, and slowly began to pull at the soil, rip up the roots of each and every bulb he had ever planted, tearing at the interior connections they had made beneath. The more furious he became, the more alive the garden seemed, weeping along with him as he plunged through years of growth, hours of his work, love and labour.

With nothing more to destroy – he left the earth
heaving.

Half-dead beast, sinews bleeding out across a
country road.

Bulging cupboards. Broken food processor. Vodka bottle in its regular hiding place. Husband took a swig. Leak of ethanol stinging down his chin before dropping to the floor. Floor went on growling like an intestine while Harry made his slow way up to their empty bed, where the indent of her body remained, where the stain of her smell soaked their pillows, where the memories of all their peaceful nights perspired out from pulsing walls – it was as if she had already gone.

The First Reconciliation

It's past midnight. 1.29 a.m.
There are these
inhuman
eyes on us. The kind that
chisel away at the dark so fiercely –
even when they are gone
they are not.

We snap our eyes open, feeling the tug of those
live-wire-wake-chains;

stain of a concentrated stare by the window.

The daughter is fast asleep.

But outside – a throb of sound, coming from the garden.

Lia, Lia, Lia.

What is it? she asks, but of course
she knows what it is.

It's him. I relish the *him*, really linger on the mmm, letting
the word spread thick across the night,
richest lick of wet paint;
wicked suggestion;
It's him.

*The first of your three essential reconciliations, Lia. And he's here for
you, not her. He was always coming for you.*

Lia!

Why is it, she is thinking, pulling one of the daughter's baggy jumpers over her neck, heart in her throat, why is it after all these years I still feel electric, wild, urgent.

I tell her it's because she is not dead yet. Because he was always the great love of her life – she just settled, understandably, for something much safer. Nothing to be ashamed of.

She hates this so much.

He is hurling little stones at the windowpane; they tap, tap, tap away. Very John Hughes, I think; very *arise, fair sun*, very *jealous moon*, very *sick and pale with grief*, very Cusack-holding-boombox, very Romeo-come-Heathcliff.

The daughter stirs. Struggling free from another bad dream.

Down the stairs I tell her a recent New York survey states that 73 per cent of married people believe they did not end up with who they should have. She has no interest in statistics right now.

Lia!

His voice coils out, tugs at our stomach.

Where are you? she says, perched on the patio step far as the kitchen light reaches.

He emerges from the dark like bone from soil. The landscape recedes. And we are fifteen again. That reflection – swimming, fractured, hopeful – in his all-seeing, citrine eyes. Familiar fossil body.

Lia, he says, his loud, gravel-voice only half his.

Shhh, they are sleeping.

His body stiffens at *they*.

What do you want? she asks.

He blinks. *You tell me.*

We lead him down
to the back of the ripped-up garden. She is thinking –
Look at what he's done to my husband's plants! His savaged fruits
and flowers!

Shed opens. Brutal interior light. Funny how romance can
slide down so many notches in a moment; scene goes from two
quivering souls without context to two bright monsters huddled
in a cage,
lined with books.

It's not long now, he says, leaning slightly on our desk; each
syllable holds such weight. *I have seen inside.* He looks down at
our body.

(In the distance we hear meteors
pounding deep into Earth's surface,
flattening 73 per cent of New York.)

You have been haunting us, she says, in our best mother-voice,
and I think, You brave, strong thing, because all she wants to say
is, It's you! It's you! All she wants to do is climb up his back, ask
him where he has been, if his life continued to iron itself out.

He flashes a devilish smile, the structure of his face, the clean cut
of his jaw, still perfect. I try to bury myself inside him, but he is,
of course, as he always was to her – impenetrable.

I feel like a kid who cannot rip open their own gift at Christmas.

We watch him examining our office, our tiny square kingdom, the Lexical Spectacles littered across the desk. We nudge the Fossil page under Zephyr, hoping he hasn't seen it.

You built it, he says, eventually, *you got it. Your ruins. Your little ancient city in the back of the vicarage garden.*

He is quite right. How strange these connections are, the ones we never mean to make for ourselves. We smile widely and he is looking at our lips as if he could kiss them, as if they disgust him, somewhere in the murk between the two.

(The last of the meteor shower
gets the final 27 per cent.)

I've been thinking about you a lot, she says. I am trying to let her know it's embarrassing seeing her like this, stripped of all autonomy, but she knows.

He runs his finger along a row of books the same way he would devour her spine. Each book shudders and hardens.

Much easier to miss someone than it is to love them, Lia. Easier to regret than it is to act.

We have no response because we know he is, indeed, quite right.

I am digging around inside her lungs,
fingering through a store of gasps,
I flick through their lives' many intersections
and log this one as The Last.

I was selfish too, she says. *And jealous. I never got to say that to you. I was so desperate to be your answer I – I hardly listened to the question.*

He laughs. *It's less profound when you say it out loud.* And then his chipped fossil lips quiver and he says, *Does she ever remind you of me?* very sadly, and we think of him moving around the daughter's room. Watching her. Hurting her.

Yes. And no.

He waits for us to elaborate.

She is so serious, sometimes. Passionate. She has a temper.

Our eyes begin to sting and his brows are so stern above his sad, sunken eyes. There is a mourning silence. The kind of quietening the day performs before the bin trucks come.

We drop to our knees.

Not telling you is, without a doubt, the worst thing that I have ever done. I am sorry. So sorry.

He is next to us now, on the rug, nodding. Huddled close, but not touching, his tone is more soothing than it ever really was. *Leave it alone now, Lia. It is done.*

She is not done.

But if you meet, one day, will you be kind? If she finds you. Her voice, her eyes, her skin, they're all burning with an intensity that evades me, a little, to tell the truth, for these are pure-mother-fears, which though I understand, I will simply never share. *You won't punish her for my sins?*

He laughs softly and eventually shakes his head.

These are not questions for me. You know that. I belong only to your past.

She nods weakly and I tell her it is ridiculous how desperate she is for a romantic conclusion. For absolution.

I know it makes no sense, she says, quietly, *but sometimes I think it was this secret that made me ill.*

That is not the work of guilt, he says, pointing at our thin, decaying body. *This is.* He looks down at his own mottled stone skin, the angular ridges of his ribs, the great boulders of his feet.

Our breaths begin to come and go a little easier.

Outside the small shed window,
the husband's ruined garden itches.

Is there anything I can do for you? he says, voice drained of menace. *At the end of your life. Any last Dying Wife Wishes?*

Our body stiffens at *Wife.*

We look around at the mess he has already made. The petrification of our shed, his stone bleeding quick as watercolour into the rug, the sheets of plain paper piled up on our desk already hardened into ancient tablets under his accidental touch.

A light idea comes like a small curdle of pleasure.

Yes. There is —
one thing. It is tiny. But bad.

The *bad* word reacts to some mineral in his pigment, and he glistens. As we tell him about Burn Girl and the box full of secrets, his eyes gleam and flash and roar around the room and it is depressing, I think, how humans are captivated mostly by the things that disturb them.

When we finish speaking, he lifts from the floor, heaves his large fossil body across the space, opens the shed door, and stops.

We did, by the way, he says. *I can answer you that.*

We did what?

Love each other.

He smiles at us, and it's as if he has thrown open the shutters of his soul at last, weeping his very own unobstructed light. And then he walks out, just like that. Like leaving is the easiest act. Like he was sketched to serve. We doubt that he looks back.

But how fitting, we think, as the night inches into cobalt, that our last, hopeful image of him should bear such resemblance to our first. Moving through spring shadows, sliding his shape into a little girl's room, scouring for something in the dark.

How strange that at this end we find traces of his start.

The Great Escape

We crawl back through the house and into the daughter's bed. Her little arms clench tight around our torso and fasten, as if we never left.

The room feels smaller than ever.

I do not want to die.

It is past 5 a.m. We are un-attaching from the daughter's body again as if unplugging from life support. When her arms are gone from us, the world bucks and chokes then numbs altogether.

Remember shoes this time, we are going some way.

We get to the station in the centre of town. It is unusually empty. Great scooped-out ceiling. A lightless chamber, the dripping arcs of a left atrium built only for us. In every direction barriers are opening and shutting tight.

Look, look, the vicar's daughter is bleeding.

Our nerves release a current of noradrenaline, the thunk thunk of our bad heart's chug. All the valves begin to quicken.

Time to come back now. You'll be wanting to say your goodbyes.

The inside of our left cheek is burning while we wait on the platform.

We think about the day the daughter went missing in the airport. The way we felt her drain from the place as if she'd never been born. How we found her trying on sunglasses in Boots, talking to a lady with an eye patch.

Hello, Mummy, she said, as if we had only just walked through the front door. As if it hadn't been an hour of hell.

As we move through barriers I feel her begin to panic – *Where is she*, she asks suddenly, her arms out in front flailing and clutching for a daughter that isn't there because Time and all its tendrils are currently inside-out; remarkable, elastic, making it hard to know where we are or why we are here.

It's OK, I croon, *it is just us, she's not here, they are safe.*

A little slot-machine trickle of a lie. None of us are safe.

Her nerves soften and she nods the way her father would when being told what he needed was a soup spoon, not a toothbrush; a towel, not a teapot.

Peter was Peter until the day he died!

Train comes.

We walk through carriages, clutching the shoulders of seats to keep our body from collapse. In our bones – hundreds of little osteolytic lesions. Outside, a city crumbles.

I have seen death, she says. *I have seen it and it was easy and peaceful, he passed through practically smiling.*

What was his secret? she asks, but of course she knows the answer.

We sit and watch the sky bleed into the morning bleed into the countryside, thinking of faith. Of Hebrews 11: *The assurance of things hoped for and the conviction of things not seen*, and she prays, and the prayers hang around us; stamp-less and unaddressed, quite unsure of where, exactly, they are supposed to be heading.

Dear God,
I know we have not always seen
eye to eye

but I will do anything.

I have not come this far to end so soon.

I know something in my core is violent. Disobedient and superficial. I know I have lied, I have been ungrateful and greedy. I know I have landed on my feet too many times. I know I do not deserve them.

I laugh and laugh,
while the parish chews us closer.

Spleen. Speed. Scattered towns. Black rivers drain down the hunched red hill of a failing lung.

Stepping off the train it is nice to feel air on our cheeks,
as if a fire is being
extinguished.

She murmurs about a church, quite delirious.

We press on by foot.

She murmurs about fields and family, socks and miracles.

Does it happen in the first or third person?

I'm not ready, she says, over and over. *I'm not ready, I'm not ready.*

We are close, but very sore now, all over, especially the soles.

Silly thing! You forgot your shoes! I say.

Shit.

And then the world seizes; the fields and Mr Birch's tree and the
outline of the boxy vicarage and the church turret are all flung
upside-down in the back of her sockets, the electrics mad, nerves
flaying.

And I have the skills of a master puppeteer or an accomplished
concert pianist, my fingers dancing away on her keys.

Pills, I say.

Shit.

And shit, indeed, because

it's all   feeling a little like

                                   the end of the road.

(wolf sways across cornfields, come to blow the house down)

(keys descend into the relative minor)

(legs tremble on the end of their strings)

(switch-fumbling)

(earth-grumbling)

(toes-very-sliced)

But then –

(*Heavens open*)

a cut of white.

(*Spirit of God?*)

A mother's coo.

This cool, private scent rises and then scoops.
And we are flat on a plate of wing.
And she is closer than she has ever been; nipping and kissing
and pinching, and there are feathers in our mouth and we are
drowning in the intimacy.

There is no *for God's sake.*
No *why are you not wearing any shoes?*
Not even a *what are you trying to do?*

Only the *I've got you, I've got you*
of her silky bird-speak.
And it is heaven. And all around us –
flight.

Translation

When Lia came to, Anne was perching next to a bed that was
not her bed, in a room that was not her room. Her mother's large
planet-black eyes tapped shut every few seconds. She twitched
curiously the way birds do when studying their very first hatching,
their first glistening object of great and undivided interest.

Everything about her looked polished, precise.

All that restlessness had vanished.

It's OK, Anne said, *you're in the hospital.*

She had performed one of her intruding mind-tricks.

Lia tried to speak.

Shhh – the hush of soft feather against a forehead.

You had a bad seizure. The ambulance came.

Lia's eyes made their adjustments. The room trembled,
then cleared and she
marvelled at her mother's beautiful bird body.

Hello.

Hello.

For a moment, Lia wanted more than anything to laugh, but
before the signals had completed their journey, Anne was already
giggling, before Lia could even begin her **Look at us, look at how
ridiculous we must look, a bird and her dying yellow daughter**, the
two of them were laughing together for the very first time. The very
last time. Each of their laughs began to rest, lean, test the other's

weight, howl, tone and character – relishing the unlikely harmony of two such newly acquainted sounds.

There she is. There she always was, thought Anne – her little girl's gums, her little girl's grin, the naughty chill in her giggle – devilish glee swimming about in her bottomless eyes. Whatever had come before – this was theirs.

Lia watched her mother shaking with faint, stubborn radiancy in her new white feathers.

Well, Lia thought – there she is. There she always was.

> **Sometimes it takes a lifetime to receive the world in a language different to your own; to let the shape and taste and sense of a thing eclipse its own translation.**

A nurse with a particularly feline walk came and took Lia's blood pressure. Anne felt an acute intrusion.

You'll be good to go soon, the nurse said.

You're going home. Harry is just getting the car, Anne said quietly. *Iris is with him, too.*

She hasn't left your side all morning, the nurse added, grinning kindly as she peeled off the Velcro before sliding elegantly away.

Time flung forward. The bird tried to wrench it back. She moved closer to her daughter's bed, her shoes like claws making little clicks on the vinyl floors. She spoke so quietly, now, in less than a whisper – *She is the best of you both, you know*, her wings shut tight behind her back, her eyes like pools of slick bristling with the clearest meaning she did not need to expound – *Really*, she added, correcting herself, *she is the best of all three of you.*

Somebody opened the blinds. Grey, mid-afternoon light swept across the room. Beds lined up in rows like sardines, silver in their oil and machinery.

You have no idea, Anne said. *No idea how much you've taught me.*

I have been a bad daughter to you, Lia said, her voice strengthened by the laughter.

Anne shook her head.

You haven't.

She let her rehearsed confessions simmer certainly up her throat, for she was prepared. She was ready:

I have been cowardly,
I have been cold, coarse, controlling, inarticulate and selfish,
I have turned a blind eye to protect myself,
I have not, in truth, known how to love you.

But Lia looked at her mother and said, **Can I ask a question, first.**

Yes. Go on.

It's silly. But something I want to know. You whispered to Matthew. In the hospital, after the accident, something about losing one of us. You said – I would rather die than lose—

Her. It was her. Of course it was.

Me?

It has always. Always. Been you.

The Second Reconciliation

Dove bows her neck low. She is pressing the crown of her pearly head against our cheek. We feel a stroke of tender bird-breath against our sickly, ghost-stained face.

And then the bird turns to face the light, gazing up and out at something – we do not and will never know what. She begins to spread her wings so wide that we gasp a little in spite of ourself because it is, indeed, the saintliest thing we have ever seen. She throws a fierce but loving look back at us, lifts a little into the air, and smashes through the hospital windows as if it were the most ordinary way for a mother to exit a scene.

Great shards of glass shatter and skim across the hospital floor. We watch the interrupted reflection of the bird's silhouette. Large, outrageous, excellent; taking flight against a flat white sky.

And people are shouting. And we are beaming. And it is impossible, I believe, not to delight in the singular torture of reconciliation, in the glorious chaos of it all.

eleven

Battle of the Bedroom

In the car home we are spread flat out across the back seats like
a body the two of them have recently murdered. Thick blanket
beneath us, over us, we use our toes to play with the child lock.
The daughter used to do this a lot. He would tell her to stop, tell
her it was driving him *absolutely bat-shit crazy*, but sometimes it
was nicer than talking. Or singing. Or playing I-Spy, which only
ever consisted of words beginning with S or R or K for a Sky or a
Road or a Kar.

They are quiet in the front. Smell of their fear – suffocating.

The world outside is indistinguishable from our insides. With us,
it unravels and decays. With our guilt, our shame. Our body and
shadow. Out there, she thinks, there is no limit, no protection,
no child lock on the damage
nature can do.

Pa! Nature? I respond. *This is not nature, this is you, Lia. This is you.*

* * *

They say about three million children were left without parents
or homes after the Sichuan earthquake in China. Too many
numbers for a mind to hold so they just fall through the cracks.
There was a photograph in the newspaper. The kind that stays.
Woman crying into her daughter's crimson pillow. Bones of a

school. Abandoned city. As if God got halfway through, went
on His lunch break, never came back. That crimson pillow is the
only colour in miles and miles of rubble.

* * *

They help us out of the car. Our arms around each of their bodies,
we must look as if we are being pulled out from under a building.
Our street has been ripped up and flattened. Nothing but our
small house and pitiful little dug-up garden with the tiny shed in it
remains. *Who did this?* we ask them, as if it is a surprise. (It's not.)

* * *

Simone Weil suffered from terrible migraines her whole life. Three
days after her death the coroner pronounced it had been an act of
suicide. Cardiac failure from self-starvation. It is true she hardly
ate. When she did, she only consumed what those suffering in
German-occupied France would. 1943. She made her body one
with the state of the war-torn world. Opened herself up so wide.
All that pain and for what? she would ask herself, trying not to
understand. Trying not to let it excite her. But we have both
always had a profound respect for those bold characters in history
who have gone and ended it all themselves. Such defiance. Such a
severing. Such curiosity. *You know for what,* I say, *the question is
why not? Why not test all your edges? Abandon the body and fling
yourself right off?* She is still and quiet because she has no response.

* * *

I am rattling around the house like a violent draught, watching
the husband watching the daughter watching her mother

                                                    stairs.
                                        the
                            up
                    crawl

Everyone is here; past and present and future all imitating her slow incline, throbbing and groaning and clawing we have practised this heaving half-dead-zombie-tower vibe. *How could you leave me?* they all whisper, over and over, in menacing rasps of different pitches and volumes. The daughter is trying desperately not to cry at the sight of it. The husband is trying to speak. To comfort her. To shout them all away. Nothing. Not because of the sheer sadness of the scene but because his larynx has been replaced with this stonking great knob of ginger. Because he can barely call himself a man. *Perspective,* I whisper against his auditory nerve, *what you all need right now is some perspective.* (Goes nicely with lemon in tea.)

* * *

Flood in the kitchen. I am a beloved table, floating. Every drawing, every story, soaked. Blotted out and bloodless. Forty-three thousand children dead in Sumatra. One boy seven or eight or thereabouts clings to a stripped tree, his thighs clamped tight around its trunk. Another wave comes. The boy keeps his grip. The roots do not. (Swell beats him like a yolk against the side of a hotel.)

* * *

Upstairs – worse than downstairs. The husband is using a knife to make it through a bedroom door because obviously I have designed it so that he must perform a mastectomy in order to enter (hah!). He begins the elliptical incision. Followed by a little axillary lymph node dissection. Infected nodes shiver under armpits the way beasts wait under the bridges. He is characteristically careful. *You're being too delicate!* I say. *Just think of them as weeds.* So he begins to slice away madly. Adipose tissue. Lobules. Ducts. I help him pluck through a few ribbons of her pectoralis muscle. *Whoops.* They each make the sound of a harp string snapping. You only need a few notes to build a soundtrack.

E F E F. Remember *Jaws*. Remember Barthes: Each of us has his own rhythm of suffering.

* * *

The daughter watches her house come down. Her room is not her room any more. Even Fossil's toy statues are being ground down into pulp. Burn Girl is there with her beautiful knees, pulling plastic bags out of her throat. Daughter goes running through the slice in the parents' door, calling for Mum, for Dad. Real horror-show speed. But just like in her dream, her voice breaks against a soft, damp wall. Maternal noises. The heartbeat that once measured her days, familiar chug of blood flow, leak of fluid in lungs. *This is it*, she says. *She is dying and I am dying with her.* Wax skin. A cord plunging out of her belly. She tugs at her new, near-numb limb. The ugliest assault. With each heavy breath she is shrinking in the Womb Room, her organs are un-learning their patterns and judgement. Bones soften, skull cracks and parts into spongy plates. Milk teeth. Tiny thumbs. Knees buck into purple chest and she is locked back to this life support, feeding on her waste, her poison. All the while – the sac goes on tightening – and she can – hardly – breathe.

* * *

Please, please stop, she cannot breathe. Her eyes search for me, madly. Trying to get a hold of my many shifting parts. *First or third?* The room is very busy. *How could you leave us?* Busier than those Russian orgies we used to watch whilst spooning yoghurt into our wide pink mouth. *What is this,* she's sobbing now, *what are you?* And I am being fucked very hard at fifteen. Not quite sure how to stop it. Life of lightless basements. Hundreds of little fists, knocking. *I'll do anything,* she says, *anything. Just make it stop.*

* * *

Husband is being sucked into the floorboards with the tendrils of his garden and frankly it is hilarious. There are thick roots plunging their way down his throat so deep he looks like he's choking on cock. There are weeds rising from the roughest patches of his soil skin, shoots of new stems drooling resin, thistles bursting from his crevices, potato vines climbing his thigh, and I am a postgraduate squatting over him, kissing down his earthy body. *He loves me, he loves me not.* Just like the fresco but live-action. *Stop, stop, stop.* She lurches at me, but I am splintering off in hundreds of directions, dancing with the great raucous cast of her life. *How could you leave them?* we all sing with glee. *I'm not leaving*, she croaks. *I won't, I won't.*

* * *

(Though I am having fun, the end is not quite as satisfying as I hoped it would be.)

* * *

You know what to do, I say, with a director's conviction, and next I am conductor, choreographer, devil in tights *(take off the mask!)* spinning around their room. *Who are you?* I am singing in the rain but the rain is paper secrets, I am a fossil box of twenty, thirty, forty broken little hearts barely beating in formaldehyde, I am a red car crashing, glass shards lodged into arteries sticking out like bookmarks, I am him kissing one of the twins, I am poor little chess-piece-Enzo, just writhing in his skin, *You know, Lia, you know what to do!* I am maggots in the walls, getting dragged by my ankles across a hard farm floor, I am rape and murder and kids getting fiddled with in parks, I am back-of-hand-cigarette, palm-to-cheek burn marks. *DO IT (please) DO IT (do what?) DO IT!* I am deadly sins ripped up bins heavy lunch pelvis crunch house on fire her desire nerve itch little bitch truth is:

I am running out of parts to play.

I am running out of masks
patience
skin and
humour.

Please, just do it, I say.

I am begging her now.

She is weeping. Real weep. Worse than tears or sound.
The silence of life exhausting itself.

Just tell me, she says. *Tell me and I'll do it.*

The chorus around us has gone very still.

The daughter is at her beginning (her very last cells descending
in multiples of two). The husband is in the earth (his last soft,
grievous, spring breath glazes, then dews).

And though it is torture, I begin to collect myself
back from every terrible edge.

I begin to undo my monstrous many-skins, fears and faces,
my form
fastening into
its regular,
unseen outline.

(Tape of reverse eruption.)

(City slides back up its mountain.)

And I feel
like dust packing into a sharp, tight shadow
before the secret light tells.

* * *

Her eyes. My eyes. Everything
widens because – of course –

I am her.

She is me.

We are one and the same. We always have been.

She gasps, clutching her hands to her mouth.

You, she says simply.

Forgive me, I say. *Forgive me.*

The room is empty of all but her. She stares sadly at the yellow
in my iridescent skin. The hollow dips in my cheeks. Frail little
skeletal body. Faint heart still beating its *I'm still here*s to the
rhythm of this short, perhaps, but good life lived.

For what?

I grin a little. It is not the full works, but it'll do.

For dying.

She drinks the fading light from our eyes and nods.
She understands.

Yes.

You need to think it, not just say it. You need to promise.
Pinky promise. You need to feel the spread of it everywhere.
The letting go. You need to forgive me. You need to forgive yourself.

I do. I do. I

promise—

It's done.

spill spill

Spill

You

Forgiveness does not happen with the flick of a switch;
there is residue everywhere.

Fragments. Visitors. Fingers. The light but lasting voices of
old friends, kind strangers, dresses and devils and sharp edges
of memory, I feel them
all make their final, slow exits out of me.

Settle quietly around the room.

Perching on the edge of photo frames, they tap their
weary eyes. *We tried*, they hum. Simple, tuneful. *We tried*.

A life has its palette. Its key.

The house is back to its usual self, and Harry tidies quietly
around the bed.

He switches the vacuum onto its lowest setting. There is only
this vanishing grey noise and I am briefly pleased we went
for the slightly more expensive model five or six years ago or
thereabouts. *Robust and durable, requires little to no maintenance*,
the packaging said. When he is done, he comes over and kisses
my forehead. I do not feel set alight by his lips. I feel relieved by
them. This, I am sure, is better. *Hello you*, he says. He is no longer
beastly but there is still a little of the earth under his fingernails.

Flexible. Rechargeable. Cordless.

—

Connie has come. She smells how I always hoped I would smell at our age. Equivocal friend. Expensive, warm, efficient. Much life to go.

She says Iris will be back soon. Apparently I have been calling for her.

Hospital bed arrives. Top to toe they slide me onto it and I make a joke about a soldier that nobody hears. Our bed disappears. I do not know where to. I am finding this a lot. Things are swapped, arranged, repositioned. My few possessions seem to have improved themselves. I make a joke about a fat queen. Nobody hears.

—

Water.

In the bath I feel like a Martian mudstone being examined by scientists.

Body expansive. Not mine.

They can now prove there was once a lake on Mars. Lake of water. Not quite water. They know about the nature of the lake, its rhythms, shape, depth and pattern, by studying the minerals in these mudstones. Magnetite. Haematite. The other tites. I remember reading about the scientists submerging these stones in chemicals, waiting for the crucial reaction that would reveal some new and ancient truth about the cosmos. The whole operation cost about $2.5 billion dollars. I remember Harry slamming the newspaper down and saying *America* in that voice reserved only for one-word statements.

I want to tell them this. I want to share the small connections my mind can still make, I want to remind them I am still here, that this body they see now says nothing of my nature, nothing of my life's rhythm. I look at Harry, open my mouth. *Remember.* His eyebrows lift, ready to receive what it is I want to say, but the whole thing suddenly feels unclear, convoluted. And I am not sure what it is that I hope to mean by it.

Connie lights a match. The flame is so bright she cups it, leans it down to the wick of a candle, and a punchline springs up suddenly through me –

Calling all bunnies, I croak. It's frightening how small the sound is.

Yes, she says, smiling so wide, so thrilled, her lovely face crumpling *Yes!*

She composes herself quickly, because she has always been
so brave
and I cannot believe how lucky I've been to have her. There.
Always.

Connie takes the shower head, cups my skull with her velvet hand. Hot water in hair. First soak. Nothing like it. Such simple luxury.

They begin to knead away at me, up my thighs,
my sides, my arms, my chest, they drain me of my
waste.

How is it, she adds, *how is it that you manage to look so beautiful,
still?*

Doesn't she? She looks at Harry, pushing his thumbs up a ridge
of shin.

Yes. He means it. *Radiant.* They are both trying not to cry.

Liars.

I am smiling, I think. Spoilt undeserving child smile.

I have forgotten all about the mudstones.

—

Intimacy can be a tricky thing,
I am thinking,
as they dry me.

When Iris was four, she would cling to the old doctor and kiss each side of his hands, thanking him three times over after the appointment had ended.

Intimacy can be the easiest thing.

Like avoiding tears when you chop onions; you only have to run each side of the blade under a cold tap before, and your eyes stay dry from the beginning to end.

—

Door opens. Iris is back. Pigments of the place soften. She is up the stairs so quick. She is kissing my face and I am summoning all of my attention to each and every one. She is playing with the buttons on the new mechanical bed and it is unlikely that a person has ever been so happy to see another.

Look, she says. Streetlamp flickers. Throws its orange at the afternoon, not yet indigo.

She places a jewellery box on my bed. It is covered with shells. I look at her. *Burn Girl's?* She nods and lifts the lid.

Inside, a small collection of the most impressive fossils. I gasp.
I imagine him reaching into the box, the crackling sound of each
secret, turning to stone at his touch. For a moment, I forget
where and who and what I am. For a moment, she is watching
the forgetting taking place in my eyes so closely it is happening in
hers too; both of our pupils full of this naughty little miracle.

She lightly touches their mottled surfaces and I think of Matthew.
Of how committed to the romantic vision I have been for so
much of my life, as if the tragedy of a love like that could sustain
a person through temporary periods of joy. But of course, hunger
and grit and melancholy are not the only things that make poets
out of men. I hope he is fiercely happy somewhere. Perhaps if
I were wiser. Kinder. More enlightened. I may have excavated
something further, something golden from our years.

But then, of course, I have.

People are so nice to me, now they know you are dying, Iris says,
sitting at the foot of the bed, closing the box. *Everyone is nicer
to everyone.*

Sometimes it takes big things, I say, *to remind us we're so very small.*
I feel like Tom Hanks at the end of a movie. *Something very cruel
to remind us to be kind.* She agrees, and says,

Yes. Sometimes you have to let outcome weigh more than intention.

History applauds around us. I try to laugh my *you impress me so
much* laugh but instead my lungs rattle uselessly. She pretends she
hasn't noticed the fact that I have lost all control.

—

Husband puts a straw to my lips. Husband
puts his lips to a mattress. Blows.

[419]

Places it next to me on the floor.

He tells me meerkats can spot an eagle in flight more than a
thousand feet away. One of the group will keep its head craned
up to the sky for hours while the rest go on eating. Sleeping.
I keep trying to tell him I love him but he just shoots back
meerkat facts as if to say, I know, Lia, I know.

So much, I say. *So much*. He understands.

Later – the sound of the husband sobbing,
gently, into his pillow. His mattress sighs.
They go on
deflating together
through the night.

The truth is I have never been so afraid of sleep.

—

Very early morning. Favourite hour. Iris's finger travelling down
the bridge of my nose.

Startled. But lovely
to be alive.

What month is it? I ask.

April, she says.

In poetry, all time begins in April.

No school, she says. *No school today?* I realize this is a question.

I realize I am surprised she is even asking me. As if I am capable
of mothering.

Kind girl.

I imagine the school calling us in days to come with an
ultimatum: *I am sorry but either you hurry up and die or she has
to come in.*

Days to come.

No. No school.

—

While she crunches away at cereal, I entertain the idea of God.

A mother's near-smug certainty.

I have discovered there is a lot worse a person can do
than presuppose the divine.

I did not always think this.

But sometimes a passionate spirit can bind itself to a cause
too soon.
Must spend the rest of its life gnawing free.
Convention. Rebellion – all the
same.

Iris is eating from the chipped ceramic bowl she painted herself;
it is decorated with a dog in a yellow hat (looks like a Marmite
jar). Floating stick woman who she says is me leads it by a thin
blue line. I also wear a yellow hat. Looks like a halo.
If the scene was titled it would be called
Angel with Appetite for Marmite Hauls Jar Up to Heaven

Perhaps I have been fearful of faith finding its way into me
because I knew it was already there – slight, imperfect, elusive –

sparking up like a flint on the days the body grinds against the
soul. Snuffed out quickly by something cowardly, unoriginal, easy.
Like certainty. Bitterness. Cynicism.

(In the Bible, angels come in threes)

Never enough time
to excavate what we want.
Make sense of a life.

(The rebels hurl their pitchforks at the wrong city's walls)
(Sulk home, tails between their legs)
(For dinner – penance)

Milk from Iris's spoon drops and soaks the bedsheets she
picks at the spilt wet flakes quickly placing them
back in her mouth and I do not
know. I do not know.

—

Freezing feet. She is sitting on them. Harry
rummages around the house for hot water bottles.

She wants to say something but does not know
if she should. I can tell by
tumbling eyebrows. Twitching mouth.

What is it?

You are so yellow, Mum. Why are you so yellow?

I know I am frightening. I know she will never forget the image,
never be free of my frightening staleness.

So I tell her it is my love for her –

The strongest thing left in me. And it's
everywhere. It drenches me.

This isn't smart or helpful, I don't think. But I have run out of good ideas. She smiles the saddest smile. I know that she knows it's not that. I know that she knows it's to do with my liver and my failing insides, but we are quiet and respectful of the little fictions we must make together in order to get through.

—

Yellow Haiku

A trick of illness;
take the kid's favourite colour –
go – paint hell with it.

—

Harry has this technique with the toothpaste. Makes it really last.
He finds a way of squeezing so much out
even when it looks like there is nothing left.

I am trying to do this with my voice. I am all run out, all dried up, but when I start, I cannot stop.

He is so good, I say suddenly, as if Iris does not know.

(Squeeze tighter, slide thumbs up sides; tiny smudge of
white emerges then
vanishes)

He is good in ways I find hard to explain.

Yes. He is also tidy, she adds, as solemn as ever, and I find myself hoping somebody someday loves her mostly for how funny she is.

From the kitchen –
sweet flood of cello. Wisest instrument.

Layers of boiling water bottles
piled up at the foot of the bed like
sandbags in trenches.

I am watching her working away in a sketchbook.

I am also holding a pen, I do not know how long it's been there.
Another sketchbook, waiting, patient as paper (*Hello paper, lovely paper*) has always been,
on my lap.

I do not remember it ever being put there.

I am trying to do what I could not before trying to write her some
letters for future birthdays. Sixteen today. Eighteen. Twenty-one.

I try but it feels
so cheap, so unkind. Like theft.
As if I would, in some way,
be stealing the moment for my own.

The truth is I will not get her there.

Huge upside-down charcoal house
teetering on a cliff edge. Wild sea.
At the bottom of the page,
she begins a story I will never
read.

So instead, I push the last of my voice up into my
throat and ask her earnestly
if she will write to me.

A note, I say, *a story. Anything, once in a while, perhaps when something good or interesting or big happens,* and then I insist that she rip the note up or burn it because it's useful to get into the habit of creating and then destroying, making and breaking, doing and undoing.

She asks me why.

I tell her acts like these remind us that we never arrive – we never really know or possess or own a thing, but must recognize life and all its material only as a great gesture
forward. A perpetual hunt for
that unsurmountable
thing.

That's where the bliss is.

I say all this but not in these exact words.

She asks me if I have seen the Hannah Montana movie.

I tell her I have not.

We work quietly on our separate pages.

—

Curtains open, light
bleeds in like the flesh
under a scab after
a quick rip.

Upside-down charcoal family take a boat out to sea. I have managed only one line:

Wondering if I have spent a whole lifetime
hiding from its clutch. Its beams.

I am no expert on sin or the self, shadows or this
getting in the way of God,

but

perhaps the I is the source,
the great guiding obstruction; after all,
without it throwing its glow across a page
we are all but lost at this
cream, unending sea.

(*Mum? You still there? Show me yours.*)

I put a title on my I.

Lighthouse Sketch,

I call it.

Masterpiece, she says.

I think she will be a remarkable woman one day.

I tell her this but not in these exact words and she says, *Yes, well you'll see. I will write. I will let you know.*

I imagine all her prayers getting stamped and I am
jealous. So jealous.

—

(Death means losing a life but gaining someone to address)

—

Time distilled in
the nib of a dribbling
syringe, morphine sulphate
on a tongue (not mine, not
mine).

Either I've had thousands, or I've had none.

His hands. His lips. Hush of spring. Her hands. Her lips.

Soon now, he says, *soon now I think.*

Thousands, I try to say, *I think thousands.*

What's she saying?

Something about trousers.

—

The survivors; the planets;
the room

still as a gift; precise as a
blessing.

—

Nothing but the gloaming in my throat.

These little rattle-breaths, retiring up the stairs for the night.

—

The guests make their thanks. Tip their hats. Heels click into the
distance, their whispers filling an ambivalent city with
the rhythm of departure.

—

Another earth sharpens itself, piece by piece; each swollen cell,
each mottled bone, every dimming nerve cord, flex, duct, gland
and vessel makes its quivering bow towards them, *for* them –
gentle husband, brilliant daughter –
for they are everything.

(*It's OK, Mum. You can go.*)

But of course! A death does not happen
in the first or third person,
but in the second!

And there is
no knock, no hinge,
no threshold, fire or soul coursing up and out;

none of this life shimmering free of itself,

only – the space he made

(*you can go*)

all around us –

(*go!*)

the light she scattered,

(*go!*)

the agony, the peace, the happiness we have known,

(*that's it*)

only –

the quiet passing of the I

              into the vast and

                          boundless

                                    you.

The End of the Beginning

Lia's ashes weighed exactly one pound less than she had weighed when she was born.

Iris carried her through the days after like a newborn through its first weeks on earth.

It is fitting, she would think, clutching the box of remains to her own budding breasts, that our burden ends as it begins. She would whisper into Lia's new, cardboard container late at night, as if the sound of her voice might react with the splinters, might spark up some buried seed of her soul and help her grow back out of the ashes.

I won't forget a thing. I promise. Not even the smallest thing.

In the morning she would plunge her hand into the grey bone fragments.

She practised this until she was no longer scared or disgusted by the thought of her thumb grazing a chunk of molar or a chip of spine getting stuck between the webs of her fingers, until the cold material sensation of Lia just falling through her fingertips became the nearest thing she could feel to a closeness. Her mind went to dark, strange places often. She would consider spooning her like sugar into tea. Dusting her over dinner that day. Ingesting her all down in one go, as if she might find some comfort in their being one body, one flesh again.

Lia's absence clung tightly to every surface, every solid and tangible thing.

It released its grip one quiet June morning.

We should spread her as far as she will go, Iris had said quite suddenly, sitting at the kitchen table, working on a list of words beginning with L, the last Lexical Spectacle. The sky was heavy with a bright, unusual haze. Perhaps it was a sign, she thought. A sign that somewhere in the world, something was stirring. The travelling winds of a hurricane were scooping a little sand from the Sahara, or the ashes of a Canadian wildfire were scattering Earth's blue pigment out into space, leaving nothing but this gentle hue of orange, flushing the start of the day.

We should spread her out through the years, the earth, the ocean. Everywhere.

Harry's brilliant shadow slid across the kitchen wall.

We will, he said, *I promise. We will.*

And they would.

But for a minute or two, none of these physical details seemed to matter, because Harry had moved to open the kitchen doors as wide as they would go, and Iris had begun to feel overcome by a rare, precise chill. She would encounter it only a few times in her life. By the Thames bank, watching the shards of an unseen message blow quietly into the water, ink bleeding out from its wounds. On a pebble beach looking down at her own freckled knees, startled to find they had grown into Lia's. But for now, as she turned her face towards the early sun and watched Harry move out into his garden, there it was — the relief of a sudden nearness. And it was as if a gentle breeze were dispersing all of life's bleak, forgetful contents right out of its margins, leaving only the morning, the moment, a daughter — drenched — in her mother's lasting light.

Light

1. [Noun] A source that makes things visible.
2. [Verb] To provide illumination.
3. [Adjective] Bright. Not heavy. Gentle.
4. Never far. Comes at the end. Uncertain. Constant. Peace.

Acknowledgements

My thanks to my editor, Sophie Jonathan, whose patience, precision and remarkable instinct has made this novel infinitely better than what it was, and whose unwavering support makes me a braver, better writer.

To my agent, the brilliant Zoe Waldie, who has nurtured *Maps* from one hundred mad pages to here, and without whom I (and my readers) would be quite lost.

To all the team at Picador, for embracing both me and this book wholeheartedly; to Laura, Kate and Hope, to Claire, and to Lindsay for never saying 'no, we cannot turn that phrase into a firework', and for helping to make this book the visual experience I always hoped it would be. To Vi-An Nguyen and Jaya Miceli, for this bold, original cover, which I know Lia would love, too. Thanks to Valerie Steiker, for giving *Maps* a home in the US, to Sally Howe at Scribner, for asking the perfect questions at the perfect time, and to Rebekah Jett, for all the work that comes after. My gratitude to Sam and Tristan and the foreign rights team at RCW, who have taken Lia, Iris and Co. around the globe with such enthusiasm – and to my international publishers, who saw them, and understood.

None of this would have been possible without the guidance, warmth and wisdom of Gillian Stern; you did what she asked, and so much more.

My thanks to the class at Faber Academy, particularly Sarah May, whose early encouragement and insight got the thing going, and to my first reader, Paolo, who has held this book in his heart for nearly as long as I have; thank you for your ear, your time, your faith.

To Anna, Emma, Carolyn, Gaye, Eric, and the network of fierce friends that she made, too large to list here – thank you all for staying.

To the friends that I made, both new and old, who know who they are, but particularly to Lottie, Izzy, Alex, Fran, Emily, Sienna, Len, Saskia and, of course, Miles – my beloved Connie. If writing takes me away from life, it is all of you who bring me back.

To lovely Ben, for being good in ways I find hard to explain, and for being tidy.

I owe more to Kate and John than they will ever know; thank you for our modern family, for the second sisters I never knew I needed. May there be Christmases, walks, dinners and dances always.

Most of all, I thank my sister, Bella, and my dad, Marcus. Like all my writing that came before it and with any luck will come after – this book belongs to you both. You are my inspiration, my hope, my heart.

Permissions Acknowledgements

On page 63 I quote Simone Weil: 'The beautiful takes our desire captive and empties it of its object . . . forbidding it to fly off towards the future', which is taken from her book *Gravity and Grace* (first English edition published by Routledge & Kegan Paul, 1952).

On page 110, the quote 'if God is Male then Male is God' is taken from Mary Daly's book *Beyond God the Father: Toward a Philosophy of Women's Liberation* (Beacon Press, 1973).

On page 135, I quote an extract from W. H. Auden's poem 'Miss Gee', taken from his *Collected Shorter Poems, 1930–1944* (Faber, 1950).

On page 180, Thierry Noir is quoted talking about his painting on the Berlin Wall, which is taken from a *Guardian* article titled 'Graffiti in the death strip: the Berlin wall's first street artist tells his story' (3 April 2014).

On page 180, T. S. Eliot is quoted from his essay 'Tradition and the Individual Talent' in the book *The Sacred Wood* (Faber, 1920).

On pages 210–13, Anne reads from *Metastasis of Breast Cancer*, edited by Robert E. Mansel, Oystein Fodstad and Wen G. Jiang (Springer, 2007).

On pages 268–9, the lines 'We will forget him! / You and I, tonight! / You may forget the warmth he gave / I will forget the light' are quoted from Emily Dickinson's poem 'Heart, We Will Forget Him', taken from *The Complete Poems of Emily Dickinson* (Little Brown, 1924).

On page 272, Edward Hopper is quoted: 'Maybe I am not very human. What I wanted to do was paint sunlight on the side of a house'. Interview with Lloyd Goodrich, 20 April 1946; S. Wagstaff (ed.) *Edward Hopper* (Tate Publishing, 2004).

On page 277, Einstein's 1939 letter to President Roosevelt is quoted: 'Extremely powerful bombs of a new type may thus be constructed'.

On page 291, the quote 'The Self is the shadow which sin and error cast by stopping the light of God' is taken from *Gravity and Grace*.

On page 328, I quote Kierkegaard: '[. . .] to seek relief not through extensity, but intensity', a part of a sentence taken from his essay 'The Rotation of Crops: A Venture in a Theory of Social Prudence' (1852).

On page 331, Harry and his students read from Euripides' 'Alcestis', English translation by David Kovacs (Harvard University Press, 1994).

On page 343, I quote an abbreviated Francisco de Goya: 'But now? well now, now I have no fear of Witches, goblins, ghosts, thugs, Giants, ghouls, scallywags, etc, nor any sort of body, except human', an extract from a letter written to his friend Don Martín Zapater in February 1784.